THE DRAGON PRINCESS

Empire of the Dragon Gods Book 1

PARIS HANSCH

ORIGIN
·PUBLICATIONS·

To my parents,
because you asked
and also because you feed me, like a lot

CONTENTS

who rescued their people from certain death and brought peace to all for two thousand years.

Or so the legends say.

If you love strong female leads, intricate magic, complex fantasy plots and of course, dragons — join the journey and stay tuned for the Empire of the Dragon Gods Trilogy!

https://parishansch.com/jointhejourney

THE EMPIRE OF THE DRAGON GODS MAP

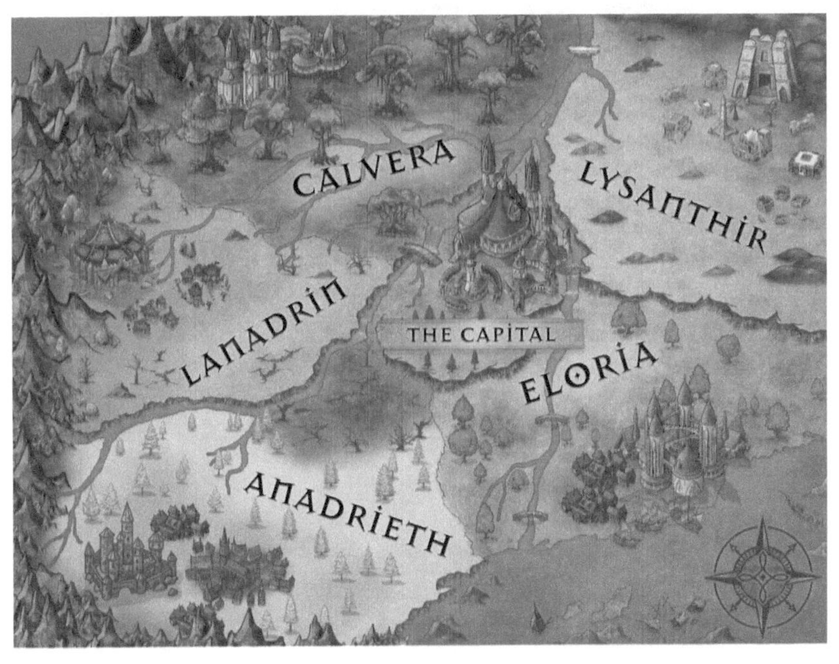

Empire of the Dragon Gods - Year 2161 of the Fey Dynasty

THE DRAGON PRINCESS

Empire of the Dragon Gods — Year 2150 of the Fey Dynasty

"It wasn't your fault, Ryuko," the princess said. He wasn't going to believe her, but someone needed to say it. She stood in the Imperial Chamber of Wishing Lyrecranes—a small but lavish room—the walls painted with flying birds, their beautiful white plumage a symbol of good luck. It was usually where imperial requests were received, but tonight, she had brought this man to her.

His cheeks were hollow, his dark hair plastered around his neck. It was obvious Ryuko hadn't taken care of himself over the last few months, though it was understandable. She had never met him before, but she was possibly the only person who knew the whole truth.

Ryuko knelt before her, pressing a blade against his own neck, his eyes impassive. His stiff leather gloves creaked as he tightened his grip.

"You're just a child. What would you know?" His voice was flat and lifeless.

The princess frowned for a moment, then glanced down at herself. Her limbs were skinny, and her frame was short—the body of a seven-year-old girl. She had almost forgotten, her new memories from the dawn of existence skewing her reality. With the death of her mother, the spirit of one of the three legendary dragon gods passed to her, irreversibly entwining with her own spirit.

"The empress is dead, and the emperor will follow soon," she said, a slight bite to her tone. Her father was left to a painful fate, as the imperial couple must rule and die together. No one but the imperial family knew why, and their people had simply accepted it as part of the legend.

"I'm no longer a child, but the sole heir to the throne," she said, flicking her long hair out of her eyes. At least, the sole blood heir. The other dragon spirit had chosen her partner, the future emperor, from the branch family. "And I'm giving you a full pardon."

Ryuko didn't move the blade away, replying without hesitation. "I don't want it."

The princess let out a breath. She had every right to execute him for his behavior, but she wanted him alive.

"So, you're going to take the easy way out and let *that* woman escape, after everything she's done?" The princess shook her head. "I expected more from you."

Ryuko's jaw stiffened, the knife moving slightly away from his skin.

The princess smirked, resting a hand on the two swords which hung at her waist. Although they were physically identical in every way, passed down from generation to generation, no pair of swords were truly alike.

"I'm gathering a group to hunt the Mistress down and destroy every thread of rebellion she's pulling across the empire. If you still decide this is the path you want to take, do it after you've gotten your revenge." She met his eyes. He was finally seeing her, so she pushed further. "Lucille would have wanted you to finish this." It was a cruel tactic, but Ryuko's muscles tensed. "Are you in?"

He lowered the knife, staring down at his gloved hands for a long moment.

"Fine."

She held out her hand. "Follow me."

Ryuko ignored it, pushing himself to his feet. He was almost double her height now, black attire covering every inch of his slim figure. The blade began to lose its shape, the metal twisting and melting into a liquid in his palm. It slid up his sleeve, out of sight. His bloodline possessed that unique, elemental affinity, and along with his background, Ryuko would certainly be one of the most skilled members of her group. He was simply switching his loyalties to her.

The princess sprinted out the door, glancing down every hallway as she left the palace, slipping into the night. There was no time to waste, but she didn't want to draw the attention of her palace guards. She didn't stop to make sure Ryuko followed behind her. Although it would take time to earn his true loyalty, he wanted the revenge she had promised. As they reached the end of the palace grounds, a figure stopped them in the shadows, the moonlight shining on his silver hair.

Kakeru drew his sword, his eyes fixed on Ryuko. Her mentor

was well into middle age, but his muscles were as defined as any younger man. Besides herself, he was probably the best swordsman in the empire, though he had a bit of a temper.

"*This* is the man you wanted? The traitor?" he hissed.

The princess ignored his tone as she usually did. This wasn't the time for arguments.

Ryuko clenched his jaw. "Don't call me that, old man."

Kakeru narrowed his eyes, not moving an inch. "He's on death row for treason."

"Not anymore. Put it away," the princess said.

"But we're tracking a group suspected of treason."

She sighed, glancing between them. It was true that Ryuko had committed treason, but that wasn't the whole truth. She'd already predicted it, but these two weren't going to get along.

"It's not up for discussion."

Kakeru sheathed his sword with emphasis. "I'll be watching your back, then. Come on, the others are waiting."

The princess nodded. He might have an attitude, but Kakeru would always respect her final decision.

They took off again, weaving through the streets of the capital. All of the rooftops were painted in a thin layer of gold and the walls in pure white, reflecting the imperial colors. It was beautiful, even at night, but there was no time to admire the scenery. Their steps were light, their movements quick. She had the best people in the empire gathered to track down *that* woman—Mistress Marionette, as they called her—the one who pulled the strings.

Perhaps the Mistress wasn't even a woman at all, as the mere whisper of her name was difficult enough to encounter. Trouble always seemed to point to her, and the princess had to take care of it. Not only had the Lady of Lanadrin been murdered, and a war began brewing between her empire's regions, but there were now thirty-six missing children. And those were only the ones of which she knew. If her empire was going to remain in one piece, they had to stop the Mistress.

The streets were quiet, the only sound the distant cry of a lyrecrane. But they wouldn't need luck with this mission. The princess leaped over a wall and scaled the next few buildings with more ease than normal, almost over-jumping in some places. She needed to learn to control her powers in this new body and fast. She weaved through the city, avoiding her own soldiers' patrols. It was imperative that they weren't aware of these activities, at least not under her name.

The other two members of her imperial guard were crouched on a rooftop, waiting at the rendezvous point.

Sara put a hand on her hip, checking a device around her wrist. "You're all late." She flicked her ponytail over one shoulder and pushed her glasses up her nose—another one of her father's Lysanthian inventions. He was so gifted that they had brought him and his daughter to the capital.

Kakeru pursed his lips. "By whose account? You're the only one with that weird time thing."

"Exactly. Father always says to use what you've got."

"That makes no sense if nobody else *has* what you've got."

The princess rolled her eyes, turning to Cynric. Although he was only just of age, his willowy figure was far taller than the rest of them, a characteristic Calveran trait. Some called the Calverans half-giants, though there was nothing in her memories to suggest truth in that rumor.

Cynric bowed, blonde locks sweeping over his face. "Will these do, Princess?" He handed her a black mask, molded into the shape of a dragon, a sliver of gold decorating the edges. She never demanded subservience from her imperial guard, as they were more her family than her parents ever were, but he was the only one who ever showed her customary respect. It was odd since he technically outranked the rest of her guard, though none of the others knew that.

The princess slipped the mask on. It covered the top half of her face, slightly restricting her peripheral vision. As long as no one recognized them, it would do. She nodded, and Cynric silently handed them out to the others.

Ryuko frowned, wiping the mask vigorously with a handkerchief, then inspecting it before touching it to his skin. "Must we wear these?" Minor disgust lingered in his tone.

"Yes," said Cynric.

"You want to be recognized, traitor?" said Kakeru, securing his mask.

"I want this over with."

Sara tucked her glasses into her satchel. "Father says impatience is the worst trait one can have."

Ryuko raised his eyebrows. "Excuse me?"

"You heard me." Sara blinked, adjusting the mask. "Oh, dragons, I can't see now."

The princess snapped her fingers. They stopped bickering, turning toward her. It was a risk to bring them all together like this, but she couldn't do everything on her own.

"Stop it, all of you. Report, now." She pointed at Kakeru.

Kakeru nodded. "The suspected rebel group has been gathering in the brewhouse across from us, twenty-two in total. Fifteen are armed but none of any considerable skill. It should be easy enough to handle them. We certainly didn't need the extra... help."

Sara nodded, jumping in before Ryuko could interject. "We should still be careful and ensure they're truly committing treason. The majority are commoners, but five of them are noblemen, three servant representatives of noble families and two powerful merchants."

The princess bit her lip, glancing at her body again. Their presence could cause problems. She wasn't technically old enough to ascend the throne until she turned sixteen. Until then, her imperial council and the nobility held a significant amount of power as a whole. The empire would be without an imperial couple for a long time; if she wanted to act, she needed to do it discretely. This group was her solution.

Ryuko folded his arms, tapping his finger. "I'm guessing these rebels are in the factions that support the young prince or his older brother."

The princess stiffened, her hands curled into fists. Ryuko had only mentioned him; he wasn't here.

Calm down.

Kakeru took a step forward, staring down at him. "You're the last person who should be questioning loyalty."

Ryuko raised an eyebrow. "That's amusing, coming from someone like you. I know more about you than you do about me."

"I doubt it," Kakeru said, his face reddening under his mask. "In fact, the emperor *ordered* me to protect his only daughter instead of himself, whilst you were dragged here from death row."

Ryuko stood his ground. "I'm after the Mistress and everything she's done. I've no reason to act otherwise. A man who's simply ordered around can claim loyalty, but all the while, his own motivations are hidden."

Kakeru's fist flew toward his opponent's face, but Ryuko caught it, a silvery substance hardening around his own hand. Kakeru's lips curled upwards.

"So, it *is* true. You can manipulate metal." He yanked his arm back, shaking it.

The princess' head throbbed, her hands curled into fists as unsteady breaths shook her chest. Her aura was slipping from her control, her presence flooding outward. Little colored lights dotted her vision as the spirits awaited her command.

Control it.

Everyone was looking at her now with wide eyes, like prey deciding whether or not to flee. She directed her gaze at the iron encasing Ryuko's hand, forcing it to alter its shape. The liquid metal slid back into his sleeve. Surprise flicked across his face, but he hid it immediately.

"Enough," she managed. The princess closed her eyes, taking a deep breath. "Cynric, Sara, cover the back exits. We'll take the front. Our aim is information, so prioritize capture, but don't hesitate to take them out if necessary. Understood?" The members of her guard put their arms across their chests, bowing their heads. "Move out."

They scattered, positioning themselves around the brew-house. The princess ducked beneath a window, peering inside. The flicker of candlelight cast shadows across the walls, and barrels of various sizes filled the warehouse, brimming with aging liquor.

The men inside gathered in the center, muttering amongst themselves and doling out mugs from an open barrel. One of the noblemen strode to the front, quieting the room and throwing out his arms in an extravagant gesture.

"Welcome, my friends, to the dawn of a new age. I won't

waste your valuable time." He spoke far too loud for a secretive meeting. They were clearly not a true threat, at least not now.

"With the imperial couple out of the picture, the Empire of the Dragon Gods is weak, and it'll be hardworking people like us who take the fall for their incompetence. We can't put our faith in the strength of the imperial family. Why should we be forced to wait for the princess to be of age for the throne? Neither the prince nor the princess can rule without the other—a ridiculous tradition, nothing more than an excuse to allow the imperial council to rule in their stead. It's a pity the prince isn't of true imperial blood." He paused, and the men nodded, muttering amongst themselves.

"We have nothing to fear. The ancient power of the dragon gods is a myth only fools believe in. Now is the time to act. With the combined might of the five regions, we can take back the fate of our people. I see an empire where we don't rely on the whims of the imperial couple, an empire where we are free to make our own decisions, an empire united in true peace!"

Several loud cheers broke out, but they were quickly hushed.

The princess glanced at Kakeru, who nodded. They had heard enough to confirm their guilt, but executing all of them would cause more trouble than it solved. It seemed that there were those who no longer supported the imperial rule entirely, as well as those who were divided over who should rule. Even if she took the throne, the problems would only be mended on the surface.

The princess moved toward the door, nudging it open with her foot. It cracked off the hinges with more force than she'd intended, flying across the room. She was still getting used to that, though it did get their undivided attention. The men leaped to their feet with hands on their weapons. She strode inside with Kakeru and Ryuko following her.

"Good evening, gentlemen." Her voice was eerily calm. "I regret to inform you this little gathering will be relocated to the dungeons, as you are all under arrest for treason against the empire."

The nobleman bristled, addressing her guard. "Who do you think you are?"

"We're..." The princess tilted her head thoughtfully. They only had one first impression. "The... Celestial Assassins, acting under the authority of the empire." Yes, that would do fine.

The nobleman smirked. "Some entrance for assassins. This isn't a child's game. You're far outnumbered, little miss." He pointed his sword at her. "Let's make an example of these dogs of the empire."

Some of the men advanced, hesitantly drawing their weapons, though most of them weren't even holding them correctly. It was a foolish move, and they would pay for it. As they charged, Kakeru and Ryuko responded without hesitation. Kakeru leaped forward, flourishing his blade with more skill than necessary. He kept glancing at Ryuko as though he were sizing up his skills.

The princess sighed. She really should have split those two up, but they were going to have to learn to work together at some point.

Ryuko held out his arm, and the metallic substance swept from his sleeve, forming a glaive. The blade on the end of the pole disarmed his opponents with ease. It moved like it possessed a mind of its own, snaking in different directions. To the rebels, he would be wielding an unknown, powerful force, but compared to her, his control was quite clumsy. He clearly had a comfortable limit he could use in combat, but perhaps she was being too harsh on an ordinary human.

As the men fell one after another, a few attempted to escape, though she knew exactly how that would turn out with the rest of her guard at the back door. The princess stared at the nobleman, who had taken a step back.

"I was planning on letting you all live, but you've left us no choice. Who do you answer to?"

He shook his sword at her, a slight tremble in his grip. "What are you on about? We don't want to answer to anyone."

The princess unhooked one of her swords from her side, leaving it sheathed. She connected with his wrist with a light tap, and his sword was flung across the room. His wrist snapped back at an awkward angle. Still too much force.

"Don't point that at me. I'll ask again, are you working for the Mistress?"

The nobleman's face scrunched, clutching his wrist. "Who?" he hissed through his teeth.

The princess studied his face. He wasn't lying, unfortunately. Perhaps they were just rebelling on their own. Or perhaps they didn't know that they were being manipulated by that woman. Her imperial guard regathered before her, with the remaining rebels on their knees in surrender. She glanced over them. Some of them were injured, but most of them were alive. No one she recognized.

"Question them," she ordered.

Their stories poured out readily, the mere wave of a weapon enough to make them talk. A disgruntled farmer, a cheated merchant, an insulted noble. The princess rubbed her forehead. These weren't people truly prepared for a revolt. They didn't know anything after all. Most of them could be let off after serving time, but the nobleman would have a more severe sentence. She waved her hand at her guard, and they stood down. No, it was better to let them go in order to track their movements. They might still lead her closer yet.

The princess finally approached the last man, who had his arms wrapped around his knees while making slight rocking motions. He had been like that since they captured them. Hopefully, waiting his turn would have made him more nervous, but something felt off.

The man looked up at her, breaking into a toothy grin. "You're asking about *her*, aren't you?"

Not quite the reaction she expected. She leaned forward. "Yes."

His grin widened, and he covered his mouth with a dirty hand like he was telling her a secret. "You're no match for her."

Ryuko was suddenly in front of him, gripping his shirt. "Tell me everything."

The man threw back his head in a high-pitched giggle.

The princess tapped Ryuko on the shoulder, and he flinched. Then, he exhaled, slowly loosening his grip and taking a step back.

"She's already moving... and you can't stop her, especially not a selfish princess like yourself," the man said, bits of saliva escaping his mouth. "And you're getting nothing more out of me!" He stuck out his tongue briefly, showing them a tiny, round seed, then bit down on it.

Ryuko lunged again, shaking him violently. It was of little

use, and in a few moments, the man's head lolled to the side. Ryuko threw his limp body to the ground, cursing. "We could have had her!"

The princess shook her head. "I don't think so. He wasn't her underling; he was a fanatic. That woman wouldn't keep an unstable person like that close to her."

Kakeru nodded. "Indeed, the Mistress is far too clever."

"Or this was deliberate. As if she's laughing at us," Ryuko shot back.

Cynric knelt beside the man, methodically checking him over. "His heart stopped."

Sara pursed her lips. "Only vythorn would cause a rapid death like that, and there are very few places you can find it in the empire. I'll talk to my father."

Ryuko glanced at the man in disgust. "Can't believe that woman would have admirers."

The princess pursed her lips. The poison was a message of either influence or resourcefulness. She looked at the man, and it was unlikely he had either. His clothes were ragged, and his hands told the story of a hard life's work. That woman could have given the poison to him, but it was too much of a gamble. She couldn't have known that he *wasn't* going to spill more details than intended or even take the poison in the first place.

Unless that woman is a...

The princess sucked in a breath. She looked at the body again, concentrating. It only took a moment; her spirit sight was as natural as breathing now. There it was—traces of a broken thread, the soft violet glow fading into nothingness.

She took off, sprinting out the door. The thread was long gone, but that woman had to be nearby. Her eyes darted around, searching for the Mistress' presence. Nothing. She dashed around the area, covering every nearby street. Again, nothing. Running aimlessly wasn't going to help. She leaped onto a roof, scanning the horizon. She concentrated on expanding her range, feeling the presence of those around her. Still nothing.

The princess restrained the urge to stomp her foot. How could she have been so foolish? If the Mistress was one of *those,* everything would make sense. It couldn't be true, though; there was only one of them left.

She sensed Ryuko behind her, but no one else she didn't recognize.

"Did you find anything?" he hissed.

The princess shook her head. "But come with me. There's one more person we need to recruit." Or rather, keep an eye on. She was doubtful that the remaining person was the Mistress, but it was best to make sure.

The rest of her guard caught up with them.

"We released them as you asked," said Sara. "Kakeru is taking the nobleman into custody. I suspect we'll have created quite the stir tomorrow."

The princess nodded. The town criers would have no voice left by the end of the day. At least this part was going according to plan. Order had to be restored, and right now, this was her only option.

In time, people would come to fear those who came in the night to silence the unworthy, to clean up the scum of the empire, and vanish, leaving behind only what they wanted people to see—the Celestial Assassins.

CHAPTER ONE

ALEXANDER

Present day — Year 2161 of the Fey Dynasty

LORD ALEXANDER WINTER slammed his fist onto the round table. The silverlight wood cracked in half, and translucent shards littered the ground, ever so slightly caked with frost. He leaned back against the wall as he slid to the floor, clutching a crumpled piece of parchment in his hand. His fist throbbed, but he didn't care. The negotiations had failed—if he could even have called them negotiations. Alexander stared at the words as they replayed over and over in his mind.

The region of Lanadrin officially declares a state of war against the region of Anadrieth.

It was signed and sealed by Lord Tamar. Alexander slumped against his knees, resting his head in his hands. Scarlet locks brushed against his shoulders, and his stubble pricked at his skin. He wondered what Mina would say. The news had awful timing; it was only a few days before the annual Celestial Dragon Festival for which every person in the empire was preparing. An ironic symbol of peace, equality and unity.

"What have we done wrong..." he murmured.

None of it made sense. Anadrieth's relationship with Lanadrin had been growing tense, but surely, there wasn't enough cause for war. They hadn't done anything to anger Lord Tamar that he knew of. It couldn't be their fault. He had always made sure that he had control of every little detail. His council's eyes and ears were all over his city. It had to be something else, though he had no idea what. Lord Tamar had refused to respond to any messengers or correspondence thus far. That man was entirely unreasonable.

There was no ignoring the fact that, against people as strong as the Lanadese, they would be annihilated. He had to save his people. Especially his siblings. Alexander exhaled, rubbing his temples. If he went to Lanadrin in person now, he would probably be killed. The entire empire might be falling apart, but Lord Tamar couldn't possibly get away with civil war right underneath the imperial council's nose.

That's it!

Alexander jumped to his feet, scrambling for a fresh sheet of parchment and ink. They still had a little time. Lanadrin would have to petition to the capital before war could be waged, and therefore, he could, too. He paused, a drop of ink falling onto the floor. But to whom could he petition? The imperial council held weight, but it was the prince who would become emperor. His Highness may have more sympathy than a council full of corrupt officials.

Alexander's hand swept across the page, carefully choosing

his most diplomatic words for the prince. As he gripped the quill, an almost invisible layer of ice spread along it. A few moments later, it snapped in half, and he sighed. This always seemed to happen when he was stressed. He made do with the broken quill.

He would have petitioned to Her Highness, as well, but the imperial princess had gone missing the very night when she had come of age. The whole situation was ridiculous. The empire had survived far too long without a proper imperial couple, simply waiting for Her Highness to ascend the throne. That extra two years had the five regions at each other's throats, and the council wouldn't lift a finger. They refused to give them an emperor without an empress, nor would they select anyone else—all because of some silly legend that was nothing more than a children's story.

Alexander carefully sealed the letter and approached the window. His messenger bird ruffled its feathers, shaking off the tiny flecks of snow that had accumulated. Giving his bird the letter, he sent it off, and it soared across his castle grounds and beyond the Celestine Forest. It would only take a day at most for it to reach the capital, but until then, he had to think of an alternate plan. Alexander rested his hand on the hilt of his sword, the weight comforting against his hip. He was never without his beloved sword, his Golden Dawn, not after *that* incident.

He shook his head, tucking Lanadrin's declaration into his pocket and throwing his formal cloak around his shoulders—Anadrieth's official colors of ash gray and white, with the emblem of a priestess temple embroidered onto the back. It was an odd image, as they didn't have a priestess temple. Only the capital had one, and it belonged to the last fools of the empire who believed in the legend of the dragon gods. He wanted to have it changed; perhaps the jagged peaks of the Jade Mountains behind them would be more fitting.

Lord Alexander strode out of his room and down the hallway, putting on his best smile. His people depended on him, and it wouldn't do to show them his true feelings. The smile came naturally as he nodded to his servants, the well-practiced mask never once failing him for over a decade.

Alexander hurried through his castle, absorbed in his thoughts. His little brother and sister would want to be involved, of course, but he didn't need to entangle them in this mess. He needed to inform his council of the situation at once and come up with an alternate plan, as there was every chance that the prince would deny his petition. More importantly, he needed to investigate why in dragon's name Lord Tamar was declaring war in the first place.

Alexander rounded a corner, running straight into a young maidservant, and the tray she was holding knocked into her. She yelped as a teapot spilled boiling liquid over her chest before crashing to the floor along with the cups and saucers.

"Mina!" he cried, snatching the tray from her hands and grabbing her by the shoulders. He was about to call out for cold water and their healer, but he paused. Her skin had a tinge of red, though it was fading fast, and she seemed completely unharmed.

Mina gazed up at him, and his breath caught in his throat. Ebony locks framed her face, and her matching eyes were as dark as the night. Whenever she looked at him, she always seemed to be looking deeper, like she was peering into his very spirit.

"I'm fine, Alexander," she said. Her voice was warm, and

the way she said his name slipped over his skin like silk, stirring another kind of warmth within him.

Alexander blinked, internally slapping himself. There was never a time when her beauty didn't catch him off guard.

"Please accept my deepest apologies," he said, stooping to pick up the pieces of the broken cups and saucers. Usually, Mina was the clumsy one, but this time, it was on him. Alexander frowned. The liquid was still quite hot, and steam rose from the puddle. The teacup shard in his hand even had a drop of blood on it. He was positive that the tea was boiling since Mina would have been taking it straight to his little sister. Strange.

Another servant girl rounded the corner, and Alexander snapped his fingers at her. The maid hurried to clean up the mess at once. He glanced Mina up and down once more. "Are you sure you're all right?" Even her expression was calm.

Mina brushed her damp dress with her fingertips. It was ripped in several places around the arms and hem. He could have sworn that he had ordered the head matron to replace it only a few days ago.

"I'm quite sure." Mina tilted her head. "On the contrary, you seem rather upset."

Every time, he thought. *How does she pick up on it every time?*

She was the only one who ever saw through his mask. Alexander cleared his throat, glancing around them. They were alone, but this still wasn't where he wanted to discuss something like this. He pulled the letter from his pocket, flashing the Lanadese seal. "Lord Tamar has... declared war. Come by later at the usual time, and we'll discuss it."

Mina nodded. "Then, I'll be taking my leave for now. I'll have to get more tea," she said with a wink.

Alexander watched her leave, his breath visible in the cold air. She had always been a beautiful mystery to him, and every time he thought that he was getting close, the more questions he seemed to have. But Mina was intelligent, observant and strong-willed; her body literally clung to life when he found her two years ago. If only she hadn't come to them with an unknown background, he would have asked for her hand already.

He turned over the shard in his palm. It seemed to be somewhat smaller, though the drop of blood was still there, as though it had eaten away at the ceramic. Alexander's fingertip brushed against the droplet. He immediately recoiled, dropping the shard and shaking his hand as a burning sensation shot through his arm. It disappeared so quickly that he thought that he'd imagined it. He flexed his fingers, pulling himself together. This wasn't the time to be stalling; he needed to speak with his head councilor.

Before he could make it down the hall, Alexander spied his little brother, skulking away through the corridor. Lord Anton Winter was six years his younger but was more serious than their father had ever been. He was walking with his head down, his shoulders stiff and his arms kept close to his body. He looked like he'd overheard them.

Alexander clapped him on the shoulder. Anton jumped but quickly composed himself.

"My lord," said Anton, bowing his head. His hair—the same shade of scarlet as his and their father's—was ragged and grown out to cover his face.

Alexander caught himself before he rolled his eyes. "Brother, again, there's no need to be so formal. Cheer up." His brother still didn't meet his eyes, keeping his face slightly turned. He was self-conscious of his scar, as usual. The thin pink line stretched from his forehead to his cheek across Anton's left eye, the deep shade of ocean blue slightly marred and cloudy.

Anton shook his head so that his hair fell over some of the scar. "Of course." He stuffed his hands in his pockets. "Have you heard from Lanadrin?"

Alexander hesitated. He didn't want to worry his little brother or force him to carry the burden of his duties. He'd been through enough. But at the same time, the whole region would find out sooner or later, and Anton shouldn't be the last to know.

"The outcome has been... unfavorable. But not to worry," he added quickly, "I'm about to meet Councilor Dallan, and we'll sort this situation out soon." Alexander patted him on the head.

Anton jerked away. "Let me come with you. I've—"

"No, I'll take care of this." It was for his own good; he wouldn't be able to handle the stress. His episodes had lessened over the years, but there was no telling when they'd return.

Hurt flashed across Anton's face. "You'll take care of this? I suppose that's why you're wasting your time with that temptress, then. You realize that servant girl has caused nothing short of natural disasters throughout the castle lately. What, with an avalanche of snow at the gates, all the fireplaces smothered, a mass of breakages in the pantries—"

"That's enough," said Alexander. "Accidents happen. There's no logical way that any normal person could have caused that, especially Mina." His little brother was always trying to pin things on her like a jealous child. Maybe if he had more time to spend with Anton, he'd be less bitter.

"That's because the girl's *not* normal." Anton straightened his back. "I've warned you about her from day one. There's something not right about that girl, and yet, you would divulge the secrets of Anadrieth because she bats her eyelashes before you would tell your own flesh and blood."

Alexander exhaled. When would he ever let this one go? It was only natural that his brother would be suspicious of strangers after their parents were assassinated, but Mina had been with them for two years. He patted Anton on the shoulder as he walked away. "I'll take it into consideration," he called out, heading straight for the head councilor's chambers.

If Alexander trusted her, that should be enough. There was no reason for his brother to be concerning himself with these matters. He had it under control, and it allowed his siblings to have their freedom. Anton wasn't under the scrutiny of Anadrieth's council. He was free to do as he pleased, he was free to go wherever he wanted, he was free to marry whomever he liked. And he treated the privilege like it was nothing. Alexander grimaced.

Alexander rapped at his councilor's door. A few moments later, Councilor Dallan appeared before him, his robes haphazardly thrown on.

"Forgive me, my lord. I didn't expect you this early." He straightened his collar, gesturing him inside. "I do hope this isn't about your intentions with that servant girl again."

Alexander ignored the comment and strode in without a word, handing him the letter. It wasn't the moment to bring up Mina, but he wasn't going to let it go. The councilor took it, stroking his graying beard. Dallan had been his father's head councilor, too, and he'd been his greatest confidant and mentor through his own transition to leadership.

Councilor Dallan frowned, and several lines creased his forehead. "This is most certainly terrible news to wake up to." He shook his head slightly. "In all my years, I've never seen a situation escalate this fast."

Alexander raised his hands. "What can I do? I've sent word to His Imperial Highness, but with the state of things, I'm not sure we can count on his support."

Councilor Dallan paced across the room, his arms crossed. "I believe you're right." He stopped and stared out the window.

Alexander joined him. The glass was frosted over, but he could still see the training grounds from here. He watched his soldiers starting their morning drills.

"If it comes to an all-out battle," said Councilor Dallan, "we will lose without question. And thousands of Anadese lives will be threatened. The Lanadese barbarians are said to be built like two men in one, and they have the power of blackscale on their side. Not only that, but their alliance with the northern region of Calvera with their stonewood makes things impossible."

Alexander nodded grimly. The Calverans were rumored to be half-giants, their statures towering over normal men; combined with the two strongest materials in the empire, they were a formidable force. The great Calveran stonewood trees made for an impregnable defense, and Lanadese blackscale was the only metal sturdy enough to break it.

Alexander fiddled with his sword hilt—ordinary steel, like all of their weapons. Their own natural resource, the silverlight trees of the Celestine Forest, were completely useless as weapons. The lightweight material could be sharpened enough to be deadly, but like his table, it was easily broken. Even against all odds, there was no way that they were getting out of this unharmed.

Councilor Dallan clasped his hands behind his back. "There might be one solution."

Alexander glanced up. "Anything."

"Eloria," said Councilor Dallan. "We could propose an alliance with Eloria."

Alexander rubbed his forehead. Their coastal neighbor to the east, Eloria was twice their size, and their special food was said to make one man fight like ten. Their presence and support would make Lanadrin think twice about an all-out war. "But we have nothing of value to offer them. Lord Reinhardt and I barely know each other."

Councilor Dallan had a glint in his eye. "Lord Reinhardt, like you, is an unmarried man. And Lady Adelia has become a young woman that any man would go to war for."

Alexander furrowed his brows. "My little sister?"

Councilor Dallan nodded. "You do realize that regardless of whether we surrender or fight, if the worst should happen, you and your brother will most certainly be killed. In the hands of someone like Lord Tamar, what do you think will happen to Lady Adelia?"

Alexander swallowed. After the untimely death of Lord Tamar's wife, the rumors were that he went slightly insane, kidnapping women all over the empire. He was not a man of reason by any means. His sister would definitely be at his mercy.

"If Lady Adelia is in Eloria, she'll not only be useful in preventing war, but she will be out of harm's way," said Councilor Dallan. He was now staring directly at him, his steely eyes boring into his skull. "When people find out about this, they need to know that there is hope, something to hold onto. Otherwise, who knows who might turn on you."

Alexander stared at his feet, slowly nodding his head. He made a good point. The last thing he wanted was for his sister to be in the hands of some barbarian warlord. What would Mina think of this?

A true Lord of Anadrieth should be willing to go to whatever end to protect his people.

His late father was right.

Councilor Dallan held out a quill. "Then, it would be best not to waste time."

Alexander took it. His head councilor always had excellent judgment; Adelia would be safe in Eloria and have the life she deserved. This was their best chance—for all of them.

And it might be their only one.

2

CHAPTER TWO

ANTON

L ORD A NTON STARED INCREDULOUSLY at his brother's back as he waltzed off without another word. Anton's jaw twitched, and he turned on his heel, heading for the western quarters. War was practically on their doorstep, and Alexander was busy messing about with that servant girl. What in dragon's name was he thinking? No doubt that temptress knew exactly what she was doing. She didn't deserve to be called by name.

Amnesia? Utter nonsense.

Anton shook his head, his pace increasing. If everyone used that flimsy excuse, they'd be overrun with beggars and assassins alike. His brother confided in that girl more than he confided in him. In fact, it seemed like Alexander confided in *everyone* more than him, whether it be about the fate of their homeland or what was on next week's supper list. Everyone apart from their sister, of course. He couldn't remember a time when Alexander gave a dragon's claw about what the two of them thought. Or their people, for that matter. When was the last time Alexander had met with a commoner? He'd only heard the cries of his people through the filtered words of his council.

At least there was one place he could go where someone would listen to him. Anton paused in his tracks as a loud crash echoed through the halls. He clenched his fists. It could only be that temptress. Unfortunately, the quickest way to his destination was through the servants' quarters. He stood in the doorway, watching the servant girl practically drown in broken crockery.

There was no one else around, so it was definitely her fault, but of course, no one was here to see it, as usual. The girl seemed like she expected every disaster, unlike most of their maids, who would be panicking as though their lives depended on it. In a way, it did; these things cost gold, and Anadrieth's extensive treasury had taken a huge blow in their pre-emptive efforts to prepare for battle.

"I made sure her grave was well tended to, Anton."

Anton opened his mouth. The girl hadn't even turned around to look at him. She was still cleaning up the mess on the floor. She didn't address him properly, and she acted like she didn't even need to. Come to think of it, he had never heard her use an honorary title before.

Wait, did she say "grave"?

Anadrieth's official graveyard was on the other side of the castle. The girl couldn't possibly have known where he was headed. He blinked. Barely anyone even knew that it was there in the first place.

"What do you mean?" It wasn't exactly what he wanted to say.

The girl stood and gazed at him. Like endless pools of

pure ink, her eyes pulled him into their depths, ensnaring him. Though the room was already cold, what little warmth there was seemed to evaporate.

"The only grave that's there," she said, a hint of confusion in her voice. "The one you visit every day."

Anton swallowed, but his throat was dry. No one ever paid attention to what he did—not the second son, the *spare*. She was dangerous. The girl returned to her task, preparing yet another tea tray. Her movements were graceful, elegant, and she reminded him of a lyrecrane. Far too graceful, in fact, for someone whose very presence seemed to cause one accident after another. How dare that girl intrude on his sanctuary? What if she had somehow ruined that, too? His scar stung, and he shook his head.

"I don't care what you were doing. Don't ever return there again." His words held the appropriate amount of bite this time, and he didn't wait for her response. She had certainly stolen enough time from him today as it was.

Anton stormed through the servants' quarters. It was deserted at this hour of the morning as the staff scattered about the castle, seeing to their duties. He slipped out of the castle, pulling his cloak tighter around his shoulders. The nerve of that girl. Who did she think she was? Just because his siblings took a liking to her didn't mean that she had any real leverage. Even most of the servants gossiped about the girl, as well. Dragons, the whole castle did, and they had every right to. A mildly attractive girl showing up out of the blue, rescued from the brink of death, apparently remembering nothing but a name, then immediately given the position of his sister's handmaiden—it was ridiculous. They should never have patrolled the border that day.

His boots squelched in the snow as he left a trail of foot-prints behind him. The little trek never felt like an inconvenience; it was more like a gift. The air out here was crisper and cleaner. The noise of the castle faded away, along with the judgment, the contempt, and was replaced by a wonderful silence—out here, he was truly at home.

Anton made his way into the little clearing where the only sounds present were the trickling stream and occasional bird calls. Faint blue lights danced in the stream, fading into different colors across the snow and trees. They always danced just out of reach, as though they were willing to be seen but not touched. They tended to appear everywhere, though the lights mostly showed up here, where he was at his calmest. In the center of the clearing, under a single tree, a small stone was nestled, misshapen and unlike the other stones chosen for proper graves. It didn't matter, though; it was perfect.

Anton frowned as he approached. There was a small bunch of winter lilies lying in front of the stone. The brambles that had been endlessly creeping back into the area, even just yesterday, had withered away, their thorns no longer threatening to ensnare his sanctuary. He was constantly chipping away at them, but they had always proven to grow too fast. He shivered, though it wasn't because of the cold.

That girl.

She couldn't have done this. She must have had help—or some kind of ulterior motive. It was unlikely that anyone would help with a useless job like this, though. He most definitely didn't like that the girl had been here. Anton sat beside the stone, shaking off the feeling. He could deal with it later, but for now, he was here. He laid a gentle hand on the stone, brushing his fingers over the crude engraving.

Here lies Lady Doll the Kind-hearted. Year 2150.

His brother had done this for him eleven years ago, an ode to the name Anton had called her. Of course, Doll hadn't been a true lady of Anadrieth; his nursemaid was nothing more than the Winter family's servant, and neither was her body actually lying beneath the stone. There wasn't a body left to find, after all. Anton felt the corners of his mouth turn up, the slight movement the only form of a smile he had left.

"Mama, it's me." He closed his eyes. *It's me, Anton the Brave,* he thought, her comforting voice echoing in his head. "It's winter lily season again. They're growing in the middle of the forest. I've always wanted to plant some for you—I know they're your favorite—but they don't take to the earth here." They were beautiful, just like her.

Anton laid back, his hands clasped behind his head. "But at least the bearions are in hibernation, so we don't have to worry about that..." He continued on for several minutes, filling her in on yesterday's events. She was always a good listener. He could feel her arms wrap around him, the warmth of her lips pressing against his cheek. After a pause, Anton sat up.

"Mama, war is coming. I might not be able to come as often anymore. I hope you'll understand." Doll always understood. He grimaced. "But my brother doesn't trust me to handle anything, as usual. No one does. Do you think I should keep trying to talk to him?"

Anton could see her smile and nod, the pretty dimple showing on her right side. "You're right, as always. I don't know if he'll listen, though. He hasn't even let me go on a real patrol yet, let alone something as terrifying as…" He rubbed his arms, shivering a little. The empire had been peaceful for over two thousand years. Was war really terrifying? Everyone seemed to be afraid of it, though no one had experienced it.

It was strange. Every region had its own army, developed weapons and strategies and spent their time training for combat. Sure, there were minor skirmishes here and there; even his brother had fought in a few of them. But it was like they had been preparing for a war that would never come. It was too convenient that now would suddenly be the time when war was upon them; humans couldn't possibly have gotten along happily for this long. Anton shook his head. He wasn't a history fanatic like his sister, but it was still something that even he had noticed.

Anton squinted in the distance as he spied a figure jogging toward him. He grimaced, recognizing the man's easy gait.

Of all the people to bother me now…

Ban approached him with a broad smile, not even slightly out of breath. He stood with a hand on his hip, his collar unbuttoned. The rigid uniform, which produced crisp edges on every soldier, seemed to slip easily over his shoulders and follow the natural curves of his physique. He looked every bit his father's son but acted nothing like the general.

"Fancy running into you here," said Ban, winking.

Anton rolled his eyes. "Hardly. You clearly ran *to* me. Whatever it is you want, speak quickly."

Ban gestured at the ground as though he didn't catch that Anton wanted to be left alone. "May I sit?"

"No," Anton snapped. As Ban's face fell, he sighed. "Do as you please."

Ban made himself comfortable, propping one knee up. He

gazed at the stone for a moment, bowing his head. He brushed the lilies with his fingers.

"Pretty. You venture out into the Celestine Forest by yourself?"

Anton shook his head. "It wasn't me. Did you have business with me or not? I'm not in the mood for your antics."

Ban threw back his head with a laugh, a move that made all of the maidens swoon. "Hah! When are you ever, I wonder..." He let out a breath, a warm fog escaping his lips. "I just wanted to check up on my friend. And pay my respects." He patted the gravestone.

Anton resisted the urge to grab the stone from him and settled for swatting his hand away instead. "If that's all, then you may leave."

"Though, I recall you saying I could do as I please."

Anton flexed his fingers. "Fine, just not near me. I don't need you constantly checking up on me out of some bizarre obligation you've got in that thick head of yours. I've already got a brother who does that."

Ban raised his eyebrows. "You think this is obligation?"

"Well, speaking of obligations, don't you have some? For, you know, the impending war?"

Ban's expression hardened, his forehead showing lines that he was far too young to have. "Is that confirmed?"

Anton recognized his tone and lowered his voice. "By my brother, just this morning."

"Dragons, I hoped it wouldn't have come to this." Ban leaned back against the tree, laying a hand over his eyes. "My father is already running the men ragged. We don't stand a chance against the Lanadese, not even at peak strength. What can I do?"

Anton shrugged. "Be your usual, cheerful self. People like to cling onto something normal." Annoying as he was, Ban had a way with people that Anton would never achieve himself, just like his brother.

Ban nodded slowly. "Good idea. You were always observant in that way." He stood, dusting himself off, a grin creeping back onto his face. "How about a sparring match, for old times' sake?"

"Not on your life," Anton muttered. He didn't need to land on his ass in front of a few hundred men.

Ban leaned into his face. "Scared of losing again?" He held out a hand.

"No." Anton shuffled to face away, crossing his arms. No way was he going anywhere with him.

"Ban!" A figure yelled across the grounds. They weren't happy.

Ban stood up straight. "That's my cue. Wouldn't want to keep Father waiting. Don't worry, one day we'll fight together again, just you and me." He jogged off, waving a hand.

Anton pulled his knees to his chest with a sigh. General Barrett hated it when his son spent time with him instead of Alexander.

"The more *useful* one, he says. Don't waste your time with the *spare*." Anton pursed his lips. The general was right; no one should waste their time on him. Ban must simply feel sorry for him. There was no other reason why he would continuously bother him so. He was always the one with plenty of other friends. Anton gave Doll's grave a lingering gaze.

"I'll be back as soon as I can, Mama."

He got up, trudging back toward the castle. There was

nothing for him to attend to, no duties to uphold. The first-born had the bearion's share of the inheritance and the responsibilities. At least if he had been born a woman, it wouldn't seem odd to devote his time to other things, like his sister. Traditionally, he should have been given a position of relative importance, such as the general or a councilor over-seeing some area of Anadrieth. But Alexander refused to burden him with anything of the sort. And so, he wandered around the castle like a lonely spirit, not skilled at anything in particular but not a complete dunce, either.

The maids steered clear of him as though they could feel his irritation, and Anton found himself in front of a familiar door. Pure white Calveran stonewood, intricately carved with golden symbols. His sister had gotten it commissioned ages ago, her obsession with the empire rendering her room a cacophony of random artifacts. Or so he remembered; it'd been a long time since he had been in her room. Or since they'd really spoken.

You don't need her.

Anton shivered as cold fingers wrapped around his neck, the woman's voice whispering in his ear.

You have me.

She ran her fingertips down the length of his scar.

I know you best.

Anton closed his hand over hers, but he could only feel his face. The woman wasn't there, of course—just a shadow in his mind. Like a leech, waiting to prey on his innermost thoughts. It had been a little while since she had appeared.

I never left.

Anton shivered, rubbing his arms. Laughter echoed from inside the room, and he took a step back from his sister's door. That servant girl must be in there now. He shook his head, turning on his heel and stalking in the opposite direction.

Even if it were possible, there was no point in reconciling with his sister, not after eleven years. She wouldn't know who he was. He didn't even know anymore. The woman gripped his hand.

But I do... Anton the Brave.

3

CHAPTER THREE

ADELIA

LADY ADELIA PULLED the Lanadese deerabit blanket around her shoulders with one hand while the other furiously scrawled across the parchment with her quill. Candle wax had long since hardened in small puddles on her table, and pieces of parchment covered every spare surface, including the floor, with strange symbols repeatedly written and crossed out. Mountains of books were piled around her in a small fortress, containing everything from children's stories and romantic tales to military tactics and the history of the empire.

As she copied the symbols over and over, her understanding of dragon script grew more muddled by the minute. Comprehending the words was one thing, but understanding the sentence structure was proving impossible. It was a dead language spoken only by the dragon gods, after all. Adelia scrunched up the parchment and threw it across the room.

"Dragons," she cursed. "This is impossible."

A proper lady must not be prone to outbursts.

She blinked, rubbing her face as the morning sun reflected in her eyes, casting a rainbow of colors through the Lysanthian stained glass windows. Was it already morning? She hadn't slept at all. She didn't have time.

Adelia suppressed a yawn and gently brushed the pages of a leather-bound book, admiring the faint crest of a single dragon clutching a book pressed into the strap—a mark she had only seen in reference to the capital's dragon temple and the only mark bearing one dragon, not two. It was always somewhat comforting to touch, as though she could feel a familiar presence emanating from the pages, and this particular page could greatly assist in their battle efforts, should it come to that.

Adelia jumped at the sudden knock at her door and quickly shut the book. When Mina entered, she let her shoulders relax.

Mina took one look at her and tilted her head in an almost motherly gesture, even though she was younger than Adelia. At least, so they assumed.

"You were up all night again." Mina's tone reprimanded her, but her eyes held a spark of humor.

Adelia fiddled with her golden hair, glancing up at the ceiling. "Maybe."

Mina stepped through the only bare spots on the floor amongst the parchment and began pouring her tea.

"And you're not dressed, are you?" She nodded her head at Adelia's blanket.

"You're one to talk," said Adelia. Mina's uniform was practically falling to shreds around her; if it had been anyone else, she would have been absolutely mortified to be found in this state.

A proper lady must always be presentable.

"Come now, we can't have that." Adelia stood, taking a sip of the tea. It was completely ice-cold somehow, but she drank it anyway. She ushered her handmaiden over to her closet, rifling through a sea of Elorian gowns as they chatted for several minutes, bursting out in laughter when Mina recounted the earlier tea incident. The look on her brother's face would have been something indeed. Adelia basked in the warmth of their conversation. Her best friend was always willing to talk to her.

A sudden pang of regret filled her, but it didn't belong to her. It was like a dark cloud passing through her body, there and gone as quickly as it had arrived. These strange feelings seemed to be getting stronger by the day.

"Adelia?"

Adelia shook herself from the moment.

A proper lady must always be focused.

"Right. As I was saying, I've been terribly stuck on this one particular passage," said Adelia as she did up the clasp on Mina's dress. "The gist is about the legend of the dragon gods, but there's something off about it." It would be interesting to translate, but the real reason she wanted to understand it was because it was next to a page marked *forbidden*. At least, that's what she thought it said.

"What legend?"

Adelia frowned, gesturing to the massive tapestry covering her entire back wall. The hanging was intricately weaved in Lysanthian spidion silk, the edges decorated with Elorian oyfish pearls. "What do you mean, what legend? You must know of it. Everyone does."

They turned toward the tapestry. It depicted the three

great dragon gods—Chaos, Destruction and Rebirth—controlling the balance of nature, the four elemental guardians of Earth, Air, Fire and Water. The spirit guardians manifested into the Golem, Pegasus, Phoenix and Sea Serpent, opposing each other from each corner. It was a magnificent centerpiece, the pride and joy of all of her treasures. Although it was only an artist's interpretation, Adelia kept it dust-free at all times.

A proper lady must always be surrounded by elegant things.

Mina shrugged. "I thought it was just art. If I knew of such a legend, I don't remember."

Adelia bit her tongue. *Just art.* That piece was worth more than a year's wages in gold, not to mention it depicted their very gods themselves. She let out a breath. Of course, Mina probably wouldn't remember—it was lucky they even found her alive. How insensitive of her. Every child was taught the legend, though it seemed to be more out of obligation nowadays rather than reverence. A pity.

A proper lady must always know her history, but only voice it when necessary.

As they helped each other dress, Adelia began with the most dramatic storytelling tone she could muster.

"Two thousand years ago, at the dawn of time, our lands were filled with nothing but endless war and death, almost wiping out humanity." She paused for effect, but Mina didn't react. "Two of the three dragon gods took pity on our plight: Destruction and Rebirth—the two lovers who could never be apart. They crossed from the spirit realm to take on human forms, becoming the progenitors of the Fey family and forging the Empire of the Dragon Gods as we know it today."

Adelia pointed at the tapestry to the two dragons intertwined, just like they were on the imperial crest. She pulled a brush through Mina's hair, working out the knots and picking out the bits of straw. "Their divine presence granted the legendary power of the spirit arts to their people in order to protect that newfound peace. The Dragon Goddess of Chaos remained behind to oversee the elemental guardians and guide fallen humans safely across realms. We've lived in peace ever since."

There was a long silence.

"That's it?" asked Mina, wincing as Adelia yanked out a particularly tough knot. "I'm no scholar, but it seems rather... short?"

"Well, of course, there are more details. I was just giving you the quick version," Adelia huffed.

"Like?"

Adelia finished pinning a lock of her own hair back with a jeweled hairpin and readjusted her lyrecrane pendant—a moonstone carving of the bird in flight—her precious gift from Mina.

A proper lady must always be as beautiful and delicate as a winter lily.

Adelia opened her mouth, then paused. She had scoured every book there was on their gods, but there wasn't much more information besides that. The wording hadn't even changed much over time, as if the same person had written every book.

"I'm... not sure." It was just their legend, as it always had been.

Mina met her eyes, a look of almost pity crossing her face. "What is written isn't always the truth." She glanced at Adelia's desk. "May I see this book?"

Adelia picked up the book and held it close to her chest. It was heavy, and the worn cover wrapped protectively around its treasure, the front drooping over the rough edges of torn-out pages. She'd searched everywhere for the missing pages but hadn't had any luck in finding them. After a moment of hesitation, she handed it to Mina, hovering over her shoulder as her friend brushed her thumb over the strap.

"Four hundred years old... I cannot open it," Mina murmured.

"What do you mean? The strap is quite flimsy. I'm more worried about it falling apart than anything."

Mina shook her head, handing it back. "It's not mine to open."

Adelia furrowed her brows. Mina had always been both straightforward and cryptic at times, but this didn't even make sense.

"You seem more on edge than usual," said Mina.

Adelia stiffened.

A proper lady must never show her true emotions.

But Mina can always tell, Adelia retorted inwardly. Truthfully, she didn't know what was wrong. Perhaps she was just surrounded by everyone else's stress. But she had to tell Mina something or else she'd never let it go. "I guess I've just been worried about my brothers. Alexander's grown even more distant, and Anton... well, you know."

Mina gave her a gentle smile. "I'm not the one you should be telling that to."

Adelia clutched the book, glancing at the floor. "I can't."

Mina retrieved the tea tray, placing a hand on her arm. "You'll find a way; you always do." Her hand slipped away. "The festival is right around the corner, after all. That should cheer you up. I'd better return to the rest of my duties now. I'll come by later."

"Oh, all right."

Adelia's gaze lingered at the door as Mina left, the violet finery of her dress flowing away. She'd never liked the color for herself, but the dress perfectly followed the curves of her friend's figure, and the color brought out her eyes. Though, on second thought, it probably wasn't the most appropriate thing for a servant to wear. Adelia smiled. It suited her far more than a servant's rags did, anyway. Mina wouldn't mind, and if anyone complained, they could answer to her.

Adelia flopped onto her bed, practically engulfed by the mound of soft blankets. What would she do now? The silence in her room was suffocating. She wasn't tired, and she couldn't bear to look at one more symbol of dragon script. And now, there was no one to talk to.

A proper lady shouldn't consort with servants.

She threw her pillow against the wall. "Shut up!"

A proper lady shouldn't raise her voice.

Adelia clenched her fists. She shouldn't give a dragon's claw about what the late Lady Adalynn—*her mother*—had thought. But she wasn't wrong, either. Adelia wiped her face and straightened her clothes. It would do no one any good if they saw their lady in such a state. She needed to clear her head.

As she opened her door, she came face to face with another maid, her hand raised to knock. It was just Jane, who covered her momentary shock well. A perfectly presentable maid, several years younger than herself, and never so much as a word out of place.

"Pardon me, Lady Adelia. I was just coming to see if you needed anything."

Adelia pursed her lips thoughtfully. "Converse with me."

Her face fell. "It... wouldn't be my place, milady."

Adelia tapped her finger on the doorframe. "Forget about place. Just ask me how my day was."

Jane fiddled with her apron, balling it in her palms. "How was your day... milady?"

"Awful. I've been reading the same sentence over and over, and I can't understand it at all. But I believe the information could help my brother, if he'll ever listen to me. Do you want to come and take a look?" She gestured inside.

Jane visibly paled, swallowing. "Me?" she squeaked.

Adelia fought not to sigh. She could sense that this wasn't going to go anywhere. Every maid's reaction was the same. No one would dare talk to her, and even if they tried, they were too ignorant to manage a decent conversation.

"Never mind. Come with me." She grabbed Jane's arm, almost dragging her through the castle. If she couldn't talk, she could at least be good company. Several servants stared at them but quickly looked away, pretending to be busy. They crossed the center courtyard and under the stone archway, coming to a set of tall, double doors.

Adelia pushed one open, taking a deep breath of the musty air. Tall shelves filled the room as far as the eye could see, with precious books lining every possible inch. She let go of Jane as she wandered down the rows, the narrow windows around the room illuminating the dust in the air. No one was ever in here except for her, and though she appreciated the silence, it was just another place she faced alone.

Adelia headed straight for the back row, sliding the ladder

over and plucking two books from the tenth shelf. The books weren't organized in any logical order, but she knew exactly where to find anything she wanted.

"Milady?"

Adelia climbed down the ladder. "Yes?" She could almost feel Jane's discomfort, like a prickling sensation on the back of her neck.

Jane glanced around the room. "What can I do for you now, milady?"

Adelia pushed one of the books into her hands and settled herself into a chair. "Read with me."

Jane awkwardly clutched the book, turning it over.

Adelia waved a hand. "Go on, it's all right. That's one of my favorites. The knight in that one braves the terrors of the sea to rescue his princess." Someone had once said that her eyes looked like the sea, just like Anton's. Maybe she could see the ocean someday, too. It was supposedly like an endless river, both beautiful and dangerous. Eloria was the only region with direct access to the Sea of Dunite, though not a single person had managed to cross the sea. If only she were allowed to leave, perhaps she could board one of the great ships and sail off to a new land.

Adelia curled her legs up, diving into her own book. As she sped through the pages, she couldn't help but let her mind wander. What about her own story? Was this the part where a handsome young knight came to whisk her away to a new adventure? The stories never talked about what the lady did while she waited—only that she must have a handkerchief to give her knight, and perhaps bestow a kiss on his cheek. Her fingertips brushed against the handkerchief that she kept in her pocket at all times, just in case.

Jane was still standing there, eyes wide, like a foxen who had just realized that it had been spotted. She seemed to be stuck on the first page.

Adelia closed her eyes for a moment. How foolish of her. The poor girl probably couldn't read, though 'education was at an all-time high,' according to Anadrieth's councilors. Unfortunately, her brother took their word for it as law. Footsteps echoed down the hall, and Adelia stiffened.

Speak of the bastard, and they appear.

Councilor Dallan strode toward them, his shoulders pulled back in a way that made his chest puff out. He was so obnoxiously arrogant; she couldn't understand why her brother kept him by her side, though at times, they acted exactly the same.

"My lady," he drawled, holding out his hand.

She didn't want to, but she couldn't refuse. Adelia stood, slowly giving him her hand. She struggled not to flinch as his bristles tickled her skin, and he lingered for just a moment too long.

"I thought I would find you here," Councilor Dallan said.

When he didn't let go of her, Adelia tugged her hand out of his grasp, subtly wiping it on the back of her dress.

"Did you require something of me, Councilor?"

He smiled, sticking the tip of his tongue out to wet his lips. "Not in particular. I was just passing by. I don't have much longer to enjoy our little chats, after all." His gaze noticeably traveled across her figure.

Adelia narrowed her eyes. "A pity. Please do explain."

Councilor Dallan chuckled. "I'm afraid I cannot, my dear. Some things aren't mine to tell."

She let the book slide through her hand, allowing the paper to slice through the skin of her finger.

"Oh," she feigned, glancing at the drop of blood. "We should see Elaine right away. I'm afraid we'll be taking our leave, Councilor." Adelia nodded at Jane and walked past him without a second glance.

Councilor Dallan caught up in a few strides, easily hooking his arm through hers.

"Allow me to escort you, then, my lady."

Adelia just pasted a smile on her face. Her teeth ground against each other, but at the very least, he didn't say anything more. It was like a game to him to make her squirm, but she wasn't planning on playing. Underneath all of his pride, she sensed uncertainty, as though he was unsure of himself—a man at a crossroads. But she didn't wish to engage any more than she already had. As foul as he made her feel, Councilor Dallan was still a man of Anadrieth, and to pry into his business would be ill-mannered. Luckily, he released her at the infirmary with nothing more than a sly smile and a brief bow.

Adelia entered, with Jane tagging along behind her, breathing a small sigh of relief to be rid of him. Activity wasn't stagnant in this wing of the castle—there was always someone to be spoon-fed, bedspreads to be cleaned or techniques to be learned. However, the air grew even more stifling inside than it had been in the library.

Adelia stood with her back pressed against the wall. Through a gap in the curtain, she spotted several figures strapped to their beds in the farthest corner, unintelligible sounds escaping their lips—the undesirables, as their people called them—permanent residents of the ward.

They had each contracted an incurable illness that seemed to pick and choose their victims at random during adulthood.

It quickly stole their sanity, rendering them nothing more than frothing lunatics for the remainder of their lives. Their skin became flaky and ashen, their eyes fading to a milky gray. These undesirables, in particular, were from noble families, though she almost thought it would be kinder to let them *disappear,* like the fate of every commoner who fell prey to the illness.

A quiet breeze drifted through the room, but it did little to alleviate the heavy atmosphere. Adelia's chest tightened, and her mouth hung open slightly in an attempt to breathe in relative comfort. The undesirables were making a racket now, reaching out in her direction and making horrible, screeching yowls.

Several nurses went to quiet them down, but Adelia noticed that their empty eyes locked directly on her. More than once, the nurses had commented that the undesirables were livelier when she visited. She always felt an unending sense of despair coming from their direction. It was almost overwhelming today, but she pushed through. There was only one reason to come here.

Elaine shuffled into the room, her back curved as if she was constantly carrying a stack of bricks. Her wrinkled hand flew left and right as her rough voice barked orders. Even at over seventy years old, she was still the only one who could run the place. Her nurses were skilled, but Elaine was one of a kind. She motioned for Adelia to wait. After she handed out her tasks, she hobbled over, taking Adelia's hands in hers. At the sound of another gargled scream, they turned toward the undesirables.

Elaine shook her head. "If I could help them, I would. What brings you in here, lass?"

Adelia wiggled her cut finger, squeezing it slightly to push another drop of blood to the surface.

"I was careless with my books."

Elaine snorted. "You, careless? Dragon dung. Not with your own young'uns." She gestured to her bench, overflowing with unorganized bandages. Every time Adelia had attempted to rearrange them for her, she was scolded. "Help yourself. You don't have to injure yourself every time you want to visit me, you know."

Adelia stuck out her lip. "Can't you use your powers?" She had to see them again, just once more. She was sure that it was a key part of decoding the dragon script in her book—the last remaining evidence of the legendary spirit arts.

The old woman's eyebrow arched, pushing the wrinkles up along with it. "I ain't your personal circus."

Adelia gripped her hands. "Please?"

"Not a chance."

The door banged open. Two soldiers rushed through, carrying a third between them. Elaine immediately shuffled into action, pointing them to an empty bed.

"How serious?"

"We were training, and—"

"Didn't ask for your exposition, lad. I asked where he's wounded." Elaine ushered the men to the side and snapped her fingers toward Jane. "You, there, lass. Don't just stand there; get me clean water."

Adelia blinked as Jane managed to squeak her affirmative before rushing off. She had forgotten that Jane was still here; she was so quiet, she blended into the background. But this was the perfect opportunity. Adelia sidled closer to the wounded man, poking her head around the two soldiers.

There was an arrow embedded in his left foot. Elaine directed the soldiers to break off the shaft and take his boot off as the man gripped the side of the bed, whimpering. Jane lugged back a pail of water, the liquid sloshing over the floor as she heaved it onto the bedside table. Elaine shooed the soldiers away.

"This is gonna hurt, lad." She drew a small blade from her belt, opening the wound as the man let out a yelp through his teeth, beads of sweat running down his temples. Elaine slowly pulled out the metal arrowhead and dropped it straight into Jane's hands, who suddenly looked as though she'd been handed a burning piece of coal.

Adelia edged forward, leaning over the bed. She was going to do it, for sure; she wouldn't have asked for the water otherwise. Elaine cupped the water in her hands, letting it drip onto the man's foot. She placed her palms over the wound, closing her eyes.

Adelia crouched, grasping the bedframe. Her face was less than a foot away. All for research, of course—she had to get a closer look. On the surface, Elaine's withered hands were covering the wound so that there wasn't anything to see. But Adelia could sense the woman's intense concentration, and she could almost feel the flesh knitting together under her own fingertips. Water—the neutral elemental spirit that could both heal and destroy.

Just like the ocean, Adelia thought.

As Elaine finally pulled her hands away, the soldier's wound was nothing more than a pink scar, and she collapsed back onto the bed behind her, panting heavily.

Adelia was by Elaine's side at once, wiping her brow with a cool cloth. She appeared weaker, as though the act had taken a few years from her. The room had gone strangely silent as the nurses stared at Elaine. Even Jane felt more nervous than usual. When Adelia glared back at them, they quickly returned to work, but the feeling of disdain still hung in the air. Adelia shook her head. She could understand jealousy, but to hate, to be afraid of something as beautiful as this didn't make sense.

Elaine didn't seem to pay them any attention as she wagged a finger at the two soldiers. "Tell your general... to stop running everyone ragged. Piling up more *accidents* for me ain't helping no one."

Adelia studied the men. On closer inspection, they did look exhausted. Malnourished, even. They just shook their heads, and she could feel their resignation. She pitied them. Of course, they couldn't talk back to their superior. After they thanked her and left, Elaine sat up.

Adelia glanced between her and Jane, then at the soldier on the bed. When they were all next to each other, it was strange. The man felt completely ordinary, like his aura was neutral. But Elaine and Jane felt similar. She couldn't put her finger on it, but it was like there was an *energy* emanating from them was almost identical, even though they were two distinct people. It was calm and cool, like water. Adelia shook her head. What a silly thought. Still, she was dying to ask questions.

"Were you—"

"Don't pester me now, lass." Elaine rested her hand on her forehead. The undesirables were still making a racket, and her nurses were clearly failing to calm them down. "You should probably go." Elaine nodded at Jane. "Not you. I need an extra pair of hands."

Adelia's heart sank. "Just one question?"

Elaine rolled her eyes, giving her an expectant look.

Adelia thought for a moment. "Were you born with, you know..." she lowered her voice to a whisper, though she didn't know why, "...*the spirit arts?*"

"Nay."

"Then how—"

"One question."

Adelia pursed her lips. "You didn't answer properly."

Elaine sighed. "Don't know how it works. One day, I couldn't. The next day, I met someone, and then suddenly, I could. Like it was awakened or something." She stood, checking over the man's scar. "That's all you get, so you better be satisfied."

A grin spread across Adelia's face. "All I needed!" she said, sprinting from the infirmary as fast as she could, heading straight back for her room. Elaine would never have used a word like 'awaken' unless it meant something, and to Adelia, it did. *Awyviene* must be dragon tongue for 'awaken.' It fit.

Adelia raced into her room, papers flying everywhere. She flipped back to the page on which she was stuck all night, and there it was. *Awyviene syra artse.* Awaken the spirit arts. Adelia couldn't stop smiling. She finally had a lead.

But if the spirit arts were awakened, who was the someone that did the awakening?

❅ 4 ❅

CHAPTER FOUR

ALEXANDER

LORD ALEXANDER SAT across from Councilor Raoul—the man he entrusted with Anadrieth's treasury and trading routes—as he droned through his report. Councilor Raoul's enormous figure bulged from the sides of the chair. Rumor had it, his unfortunate seamstresses struggled to keep up with his ever-expanding girth. Alexander fidgeted uncomfortably. In a meeting room this small, Councilor Raoul occupied most of the space.

"Allocating most of our gold to prepare for war has effectively drained our most abundant resource," said Raoul, rubbing a meaty finger along his face. "Our miners stationed in the Jade Mountains can't sustain this rate of consumption, even with sole access. Nor will it be any easier to trade between regions moving forward. Lysanthir prefers to keep to themselves, considering the current tension between them and Calvera. And Calvera, of course, has closed their trade to us entirely following their alliance with Lanadrin."

As he leaned back, the chair groaned. "Which means our weaponry and resources will remain inferior, though I'll defer to the good general, if he should so happen to arrive in a timely manner. In other news, our education is at peak standard since my son—"

The door burst open, and General Barrett entered. Although he appeared somewhat frazzled, his hair still sat neatly tied at the back of his collar, and the state of his uniform was impeccable—the only wrinkles present were around his eyes, and they weren't from laughter. General Barrett gave a swift bow.

"My deepest apologies, my lord. I was held up by my foolish son, who always seems to disappear at the most inopportune times." He lowered himself into his seat like he had a rod in his spine. "However, my report remains the same as it has been. My men are training day and night, including the crowcodile trainers, but there's a limit to their improvement. We've increased patrols throughout the city to counter rising crime, but it's had little effect. If we don't bring back the noose, I don't think people will get the message."

Alexander frowned. It had taken him years to convince them to move away from his grandfather's methods, but they had never quite let go of the past. "I don't believe that's—"

"An excellent idea!" exclaimed Councilor Raoul. "It would deter those commoners and help us manage the number of mouths to feed, killing two crowcodiles with one arrow. We don't want a repeat of what happened with *her*."

General Barrett paled slightly. "Don't speak of it," he hissed. "It's a bad omen." In all the years that Alexander had known him, *she* was the only subject of which he seemed to be fearful. Perhaps he felt responsible for their losses, or perhaps he was simply afraid of the unknown influence that the Mistress seemed to hold.

"Calm yourself, my good man." Councilor Raoul slapped a heavy hand on the general's shoulder. To his credit, Barrett didn't flinch under the weight. "The Mistress hasn't been heard of for over a decade. Surely, those Celestial Assassins would have long disposed of filth like that."

Alexander nodded. Councilor Raoul had a good point, as usual, though one could never be too sure. But she was hardly their priority now.

General Barrett cleared his throat, ignoring Raoul. "Where's Councilor Dallan? He's been unusually absent these last few months, and he's definitely not on a diplomacy trip this time."

Alexander waved a hand. "I spoke with him just this morning, and he's taken leave on an important errand. Regarding the death penalty, we don't have time for that to take effect." He laid Lord Tamar's war declaration on the table with a grim smile. "And I'd rather not lose any more of my citizens to needless violence."

Councilor Raoul took one glance at it and turned up his nose, his untrimmed hairs in full view.

"Ah, just as I predicted it would turn out all along. Unfortunate."

General Barrett narrowed his eyes, but the rest of his face didn't move. "Weren't you saying you were certain you could placate Lord Tamar with a generous trade agreement?"

"That was merely a front to appease the whole council. I suspect a traitor in our midst."

"Yet, the only one always saying two different things is you."

Councilor Raoul bristled, and Alexander interjected. "Councilor Dallan has provided a solution, however. One which is already in progress." He quickly detailed the proposal that he'd sent to the Lord of Eloria.

"Wonderful. I was about to suggest the very same myself," said Raoul, nodding.

"Of course, you were," muttered General Barrett, turning away from the councilor. "And I hope that servant girl will be accompanying your sister."

Alexander steeled himself. Their council was always valuable, but he had to draw the line somewhere.

"About that—"

"For once, I agree with the general." Councilor Raoul scratched the folds of his neck, pulling the tight cloth away from his skin. "Have I introduced you to my cousin's daughter? She's a pretty little thing. Adores you, too."

Alexander didn't object. It wasn't the time to cause another dispute, and certainly not within his council. As they continued their meeting, the feeling in the pit of his stomach grew, and it wasn't from his lunch. If he let his sister go, Mina wouldn't have much of a reason to stay in Anadrieth. He could certainly order her to remain, though it was clear that the other servants were as fond of her as his councilors were. On the other hand, he couldn't afford to be looking over his shoulder to protect her while fighting off the Lanadese at the same time. She would be safer in Eloria with his sister.

"This is all the capital's fault," exclaimed Councilor Raoul. "If they would just crown Prince Yukiya already, he would have the authority to make decisions and set the empire straight." He rolled his eyes. "It's like we're the only council in the empire actually doing something."

"Don't scoff about the importance of tradition." General Barrett straightened his back. "The empire is nothing without it. However, I do agree. If the imperial bloodline had done its job, the princess wouldn't be the only blood heir left."

"Or they could just accept that she's dead and move on," said Councilor Raoul. "The only heir goes missing right before she's able to ascend the throne for two whole years? It's clearly foul play."

General Barrett wagged a finger at him. "No, she's alive. You forget, there cannot be one without another. His Imperial Highness passed only a few months after our empress, may their spirits rest in peace."

"Coincidence," spat Councilor Raoul.

"Check your history books. It's happened every time."

Alexander sighed. They were bound to keep going for a while. Even though he spent a great deal of his time sitting down, the hours upon hours of meetings took their toll. He had no interest in the affairs of the capital unless they directly affected Anadrieth. There was too much to worry about without wasting his energy on the empire's problems, as well.

After the councilors had finished, the nobles had arrived to take it in turn to eloquently describe to him all of their woes and petty complaints. Then, he had to settle several disputes between high-ranking merchants regarding land and their gold—a volatile combination. Next, the guards had arrived with a few arrested citizens in tow for his final decision on their punishments. Afterward, the matron had come to him with a list of problems regarding the festival preparations. And *then,* he had almost tripped over a chandelier—an actual chandelier, properly secured in the ceiling, which had mysteriously decided that today was the day it would collapse.

What a day.

He could feel his eyes shutting already, and he still had several things to do, as no one else seemed capable enough to do them. Perhaps he could get a few minutes of sleep first. Alexander trudged back to his room, but before he could open the door, heavy footsteps echoed down his hall. He turned to see his little sister bounding up to him, her cheeks flushed.

"Alexander," she said, waving an open book in his face. "I've got an idea. Allow me to go to the capital and—"

Alexander put a hand on her shoulder. "You shouldn't run through the halls like that." He couldn't count the number of times she'd tripped on the uneven stones, and it certainly wasn't ladylike behavior.

Adelia shook her head. "Sorry, but you have to see this—" She thrust the book in his face, and he peered at it.

"Not this again." He was too tired to even try to understand the pages in front of him; they weren't even written in proper words. It could very well be children's scribbles she'd found and convinced herself were some made-up ancient language, and he didn't have the energy to entertain her. When his sister's face fell, he patted her on the head. "Another time. I promise."

He moved toward his room, but Adelia stepped in front of him. "Why won't you ever listen to me?"

Alexander ran his fingers through his hair. "All right, all right."

Her demeanor shifted, and she happily chattered on for a while, pulling out pieces of parchment from dragon knows where and speaking in complicated riddles. Something about art and the Plains of Scoria. He just nodded his head. At times, he admired his little sister's creativity, cleverness and devotion to her studies, but today was not a good day. He could practically feel the minutes slipping through his fingers.

"So, what do you think?" She looked at him, her eyes wide and hopeful.

Alexander blinked as the setting sun flashed in his face. It was too late to steal a few moments of rest now.

"I appreciate your hard work, and I'll take it into consideration. If you'll excuse me." He gave her a warm smile and walked off. With the amount of time she spent talking about the rest of the empire, he was sure that she would be happy in Eloria. There was no doubt about it. Alexander scratched his stubble. She certainly didn't seem happy here, not after their parents were killed, at least. It had undeniably changed all three of them.

Alexander went through the rest of his duties in a slight daze, like he was doing training drills again. Throughout it all, he rested a hand on his sword. Despite his schedule, he needed to make time for practice. After all, if it truly came to an all-out war, his people would be looking to him to lead.

He shuddered. Would he be able to do that? To stand in the face of certain death and knowingly lead his people along with him? He was sure that the fights he had been in were nothing compared to a real war. Alexander gripped his sword, heading straight for the training grounds. It didn't matter if he could or couldn't do it; he had no choice.

His soldiers were done for the night, and the grounds were quiet, a large, open expanse littered with various wooden structures and targets. Alexander let out a breath, the fog swirling in the air. In one swift movement, he lopped off the head of one of the structures, then hit the body of it again and again.

His Golden Dawn struck true each time, simply named from the many early mornings that he had spent alone with his sword. A new dawn to protect his people, his siblings, his family. Sweat rolled over his lip as he dashed around the grounds, practicing his movements. Without a doubt, he was one of the best swordsmen in Anadrieth. He could do this. He had this situation under control—his siblings would be fine, and his people would be safe.

"You'd fare better with a partner."

Alexander whirled around. It was Mina. He quickly wiped the sweat from his face and fixed his hair.

"How long have you been there?"

She tilted her head. "A while."

Alexander dusted off his shirt and sheathed his sword. He must have been so focused that he didn't realize that she was standing right behind him. She stood there with her arms crossed, evidently having been dressed by his sister again. It suited her far better than the servant's uniform, almost like she was meant to wear finery like that, but it wasn't exactly practical. Her leg was exposed, her bare skin at the mercy of the frosty breeze. Alexander swallowed, unhooking his cloak and holding it out to her. He was staring again.

"Let's go inside. You must be freezing."

"I'm not cold."

Alexander paused awkwardly, his cloak still in his hand. He was rarely cold himself, but he was well accustomed to Anadrieth's perpetual wintery state. As far as he knew, their home had always been like that. It was probably where his ancestors had gotten their family name from, as unimaginative as it was.

"What are you going to do about the war?" Mina prompted.

He had almost forgotten that he'd told her. "Oh, right. Councilor Dallan came up with a plan." Alexander gave her a confident nod.

Mina raised her brows. "And?"

"And..." Alexander walked past her. "And there's nothing to worry about. We'll have an alliance with Eloria in no time." He bit his lip. For some reason, he didn't want to tell her about marrying his little sister off. Talking to his councilors, it had felt like a good idea—the only option to save his people—but with Mina, he felt uneasy about it all. He knew that she would give him that disapproving look of hers.

"An alliance with Eloria..." Mina mused. She didn't seem too convinced, as though she was waiting for him to say more. It was hardly fair. As clever as she was, Mina didn't know what it was like to have this kind of responsibility.

"What would you do about it, then?" Alexander half-snapped, but he instantly regretted it. He shouldn't take it out on her.

"Find the cause."

Alexander frowned. "The cause of what?"

She waved her hand. "The war, of course. You told me before, you had no idea why Lord Tamar was hostile toward you." Mina nudged a small, thorny growth poking through the snow with her foot. "All weeds are killed by pulling them from the roots, not by plucking a few leaves off or breaking the stem."

"I have investigated, but that man refuses to speak at all.

Councilor Dallan has returned on many unsuccessful diplomacy trips."

"Then maybe you weren't looking in the right direction."

"There's not enough time," Alexander rubbed the back of his neck. "I don't know when the Lanadese will be on our doorstep, and I can't afford to run around looking for whatever thorn he's got in his foot." He kicked the weed, sending chunks of snow flying, but the plant stayed firmly in the ground. "Even if we find it, there might be nothing I can do about it, and there's nothing to say that there *is* a reason in the first place. He could just be a greedy man who wants more land or wants to be violent for the sake of being violent."

Mina was quiet for a moment. "Have you met with him?"

Alexander stared at her. "Surely, you're joking. He would have me killed the instant I stepped foot in Lanadrin."

Mina shook her head, meeting his gaze. "All I'm saying is that an alliance is a temporary solution. Even if it does deter them from war initially, there's nothing stopping them from bringing Calvera into this, as well. You're involving half of the empire in your problems."

Alexander slapped his forehead. "I'm just one man, for dragon's sake!" It wasn't *his* fault that Lord Tamar had turned into a lunatic. He turned away from her. Why she was suddenly pinning all of this on him, he couldn't fathom. He was doing the best he could, but there were very few moves left on the board, and sacrifices had to be made for the good of everyone.

"Exactly," said Mina. She whirled away from him, throwing her last words over her shoulder. "And that's your biggest problem."

Alexander stood there in stunned silence. He always

seemed to make the mistake of thinking that she'd agree with his decisions, or at least pretend to. But no, she always caught him off guard, and he could never read her. He exhaled, shrugging his cloak back on. As frustrating as she was, Mina usually had a point—of course, if he could have gotten to the bottom of this earlier, they might not be in this situation, but there was very little information on Lord Tamar in general, almost suspiciously so. There was no use in worrying about it now; he just needed to wait for Eloria's response.

Alexander couldn't help but let out a chuckle. No other woman would have the courage to speak as freely as Mina, and even if they did, he hadn't met anyone who thought the way she did. He trudged back to the castle. She was mystery itself. Each time he thought that he had unraveled a thread, he would only become further entangled. Just like when they had first met two years ago—what a strange day that had been.

Two years ago — Year 2159 of the Fey Dynasty

ALEXANDER SPURRED his horse through the forest of silverlight trees, their glass-like branches creating a myriad of illusions. He closed his eyes and inhaled deeply as the crisp air caressed his cheeks, breathing life into his weary body. Hooves hit the snow, the wind almost immediately covering their tracks. Veer left to dodge the hidden root. Curve at the forked tree to avoid the cliff. Alexander grinned, racing forward at top speed.

The Celestine Forest encompassed the majority of his territory, creating a protective shroud around his city. Even his own men weren't game enough to ride here at more than a trot, as the white landscape tricked the eye and sent many a horse flying, their riders soaring with them. But he had to make sure that he could navigate blind. Heavy galloping came from behind him, and the rider was clearly struggling in the terrain. Alexander sighed, slowing his mare. Unfortunately, he was never alone for long.

"Brother, you must learn to communicate with your horse, or you'll always be left behind."

Anton pulled on his reins a little too sharply, causing his horse to toss its head back and shake its feathery mane. "I can't." He clutched his chest, gasping for air. "This has to be the hairiest horse in all of Anadricth. My nose won't stop running, and my throat is on fire." He pulled out a handkerchief and blew his nose.

Alexander frowned as the ugly sound interrupted his serene environment. "Go home and consult Elaine. The Calveran nettlefern might have arrived, and she can make a poultice."

"Don't be—" Anton sneezed violently several times," — ridiculous. I'm not letting you run off by yourself. I can't believe you'd just leave at a time like this."

"Have faith, little brother. Times are tense, but there hasn't been a war since the empire was forged. I'm certain Lanadrin will back off soon." Lanadrin had come out of nowhere, threatening Anadrieth with war. Lord Tamar refused to speak with him or any of his representatives, but he was sure that diplomacy would come through in the end.

"I don't think—" Anton's hand went for his sword as a rustling came from their right. "A bearion?" he hissed.

Alexander motioned for silence. A moment later, a small, four-legged creature emerged from the bushes, its fur almost translucent, with two curled horns and a bushy tail. "Just a foxen," he said. "Don't be so jumpy."

"Oh, right. Bearions should still be hibernating," said Anton, wiping his watery eyes. "Everything always blends in..." he muttered, snapping a twig from the frostberry bush and watching as it melted into his palm.

Alexander kept moving. He wanted to at least make it to the river. They rode in relative silence, apart from his brother's incessant sniffling and occasional bouts of sneezing. Soon, they came to a halt as the water stretched forward like a sea, partially frozen against the edges of the bank. The Moonstone River was a central feature in the empire, passing through every region and serving as the main border between Anadrieth and Lanadrin. The barbarians would have to take the long way around to reach them on foot since no one could cross the treacherous river.

Alexander peered along the bank. The pristine landscape was marred by a small black shape. Scanning his surroundings, he spurred his horse toward the figure, drawing his sword. He could hear his brother shouting behind him, but he didn't wait for him to catch up.

As Alexander approached the shape, he realized that it was a young woman, collapsed face-down on the riverbank, her slender fingers locked in a claw-like pose. Deep gashes exposed the earth beneath the snow, as though a bearion had made its mark. Sleek ebony locks draped themselves around the length of her body, still glistening from the river, and dark blood trickled from the back of her head, partially dried and matting her silky hair.

Alexander sheathed his sword at once, diving toward her. Her smooth skin was slightly colored compared to his pale complexion, a standard characteristic of the northern regions. Pressing his thumb to her wrist, his eyes widened at her strong pulse—she was still alive.

A horse whinnied behind him, and his brother dismounted, though less gracefully than Alexander had. He pointed his sword at the woman.

"Get away from her!" Anton shouted, raising the blade above her head.

Alexander whirled around to catch his arm. "Stop it! She's alive," he said. "I'm not about to kill a defenseless girl."

Anton pursed his lips. "It's probably a trap. You know how these woods are."

"This is nothing like that," Alexander muttered as he carefully turned her over. He sucked in a breath. She was beautiful. Her long lashes closed over her eyes, and her hair fell across her forehead. A petite nose sat above her full and inviting lips, tinged blue from the cold. His thumb brushed the flecks of snow from her face.

Anton coughed. "If you're going to insist on rescuing some damsel in distress, you might want to stop gawking and start putting pressure on the massive, gaping hole in her chest." His brother threw a bundled cloak at him.

Alexander blinked as the material hit his face, then fell into action.

"Right. Yes, that's what I was about to do if you hadn't

interrupted." He hooked his arms under hers, pulling the rest of her body from the river. Upon closer inspection, the wound wasn't large but was far from clean, as if a jagged blade had been thrust into her chest, creating a messy exterior as it was pulled out. He immediately pressed the cloak against the wound, turning his face away to calm his stomach.

Who was this woman? She wore what appeared to be a nightgown. No Anadese woman would be wearing anything this thin. It was obviously expensive—a noble's cloth. No identifiable marks, jewelry or insignias. She was far too short to be Calveran, her skin too unmarked to be Lanadese. Her figure was slender but well-fed. There was evidence of muscle, as well as callouses on her hands, suggesting a life of hard work that could only come from a commoner.

Perhaps she had been kidnapped. Or worse. He suddenly wanted to hold her in his arms. Whoever she was, she must have been through a terrifying ordeal. Alexander removed his cloak and wrapped it around her, glancing at his brother, who stood to the side with his arms folded.

"Aren't you going to help?"

Anton turned his head, bringing the scar over his left eye briefly into view. "Only if you command me, my lord. Nothing good comes from things like this. I hope you're planning on leaving her at the nearest infirmary."

He shook his head. "I'll be personally ensuring the culprit is brought to justice. No one gets away with this in my region."

Anton sputtered but quickly turned it into a cough. "You can't be serious. Surely, you haven't forgotten."

Alexander lifted her, signaling his horse to lie down. "I haven't." He cradled her in his arms as the horse stood. It would be a miracle if she were still alive by the time they made it home.

"Move out," he called to Anton, leaving him to grumble a series of curses at his retreating brother.

They hurried back to the castle, causing quite a stir amongst the servants as they rushed toward the infirmary. His little sister was there, as usual, chattering to Elaine. Alexander pushed past her, setting the young woman onto a bed.

Elaine's sharp eyes were on her immediately. "What happened?"

"We found her unconscious at the river, a fatal wound to the head and stomach," said Alexander. Anton trudged in afterward, lingering by the door.

Elaine waved them off as she turned away. "Talk to the gravedigger, then."

Adelia shook her head rapidly, pulling her back. "No, she's still alive."

Alexander glanced at his sister, but there wasn't time to question it. "She's got a pulse."

"You said fatal," grumbled Elaine as she examined her. "Now, the lass is in a pretty bad state. I sense there's something off in her blood, probably some kind of poison or disease. Are you sure—"

Alexander hit his fist on the bed frame. "Yes. Do everything you can."

Elaine raised an eyebrow. "She important or something?"

"No," muttered Anton. Alexander cleared his throat.

"I'm sure she's no one special. But I don't like unnecessary loss of life, especially in my region. I'll track down the culprit, so make note of anything you find."

Elaine began pouring water over the young woman's

wounds. She usually saved her abilities for serious injuries, but he was more concerned about whether the woman would make it.

"That's it. Get out, all of you," said Elaine. "You," she glared at Adelia, "are getting your hair in the wound, and you," she elbowed Alexander in the chest, "are breathing down my neck. And your brother is just making the room miserable."

His brother threw up his hands, storming out.

Adelia jolted backward, gathering her hair. "But—"

Alexander straightened himself. "I should really supervise—"

"Out!"

"I'll let you handle it." Alexander made it to the door in a few strides, but not before he heard Elaine mutter, "Damn kids." Of all of the people in his castle, sometimes, she was the scariest.

It was a few days later when the young woman had awoken. The moment Alexander heard word of it, he marched straight to the infirmary. His brother had insisted on coming, too, though it probably wasn't for the same reasons. The door was ajar, and the infirmary was strangely quiet as they approached. He slowly pushed on the door, his hand on his sword. A chill drifted through the air, and he spotted a broken window barely hanging onto its remaining shards.

Elaine was sprawled out on the floor, resembling an insect that had been flipped onto its back. The other nurses seemed to be collapsed, as well. Crouching in the corner was the girl, her posture like a wounded foxen willing to escape by any means necessary. She clutched a large glass shard in her hand, a trickle of blood running through her fingers. Her hair partially covered her face in a dark shroud disturbed only by the breeze.

"I told you she'd be nothing but trouble," Anton hissed.

Alexander ignored him and entered the room with his palms showing. "We don't mean you any harm. My name is Alexander, and I am the Lord of Anadrieth. You're safe here." He took a step forward, and she bunched her muscles at his movement.

Anton pulled on his sword, making a slight metallic rasping sound.

The girl immediately shifted her weight toward Anton, and Alexander put his hand out to stop him. Her eyes, an unnatural violet, darted left and right, her pupils narrowed into slits.

Their sister barreled into the room, almost running into them. "I heard she was awake—"

"Leave at once," Alexander hissed at her. She was always around at the most inconvenient times, as if she had nothing else to do.

Adelia completely ignored him, walking up to the crouched girl and holding out her hand.

As the woman reached out, Alexander felt a strange sensation wash through him. He hadn't realized how thick and dominating the atmosphere was until something calm began cutting through the noise. For a moment, there was an extraordinary presence in the room, terrifyingly vast and all-encompassing, yet somehow familiar and warm. Then, it was gone.

The girl dropped the shard, and Adelia gathered her into an embrace. Alexander crept over, subtly kicking the glass out of arm's reach as he knelt down. The girl's eyes focused on him, the violet fading to an inky black.

"What's your name?" he murmured.

She blinked, frowning. "I don't remember... I think it's Mina."

CHAPTER FIVE

ANTON

Present day — Year 2161 of the Fey Dynasty

ANTON TWIDDLED his thumbs as he sat between two councilors on one side of a long table. Of course, the left- and right-hand seat beside his brother's empty seat was reserved for Councilor Dallan and General Barrett—another subtle hint of his lack of importance. Anton suppressed a yawn. It'd been two days since his brother had received the war declaration, and apparently, now was the appropriate time to tell the rest of the council and their people. What had he been waiting for?

He glanced along the table of high-ranking army members, merchants and noblemen. There were several faces he recognized as the heads of noble families, their crest banners lined up in all of their glory on the wall. It was meant to be a display of power, a unified front, but it felt more like a display of idiots. The only real power they had was the power that Alexander gave them, and they did nothing useful with it.

Alexander finally arrived, fully clothed in his most formal robes. White and ash gray, just like everything else in this castle. Whoever chose Anadrieth's colors must have been color-blind. He rubbed his left eye. Not that he cared, but it was incredibly bland compared to the vibrant reds and blues of the other regions.

His brother sat in a large, ornate chair at the head of the table, which was unnecessarily decorated with jewels. The great hall was meant to be the finest reception room in the castle, but it just seemed like they were trying too hard to be formal; the stiff elegance wasn't welcoming at all. But he noticed that one of the chandeliers was missing. Probably compliments of that servant girl.

Anton's eyes widened. *Speak of her, and she appears.* Accompanied by his sister, the two of them walked into the great hall together and stood by the table. The girl was dressed up, but he didn't want to pay her any heed. Instead, he leaned forward to get a better look at his little sister. She had grown into a beautiful young woman, but he could still see the girl she had once been in her face. He could almost feel her tugging on his sleeve and dragging him out to play. He shook his head. It wasn't like he *hadn't* seen her around the castle; it was just that she avoided him. As in, ran-in-the-opposite-direction avoided him.

And rightly so.

The men at the table had various expressions plastered on their faces at the women's sudden appearance, and none of them were particularly pleased. They stared at them and muttered amongst themselves.

"What are they doing here?"

"Don't they know this is an important meeting?"

His sister had assumed the placid face of a lady, but he could tell that she was clearly uncomfortable with all of the attention. The councilor beside him turned his nose up at the girls.

"Is there something you need?" he said, flecks of spit flying from his lips.

Alexander gave him a stern look. "They were invited." Then, he swept out his hands, projecting his voice across the room. "Welcome, my friends and honored councilmen. I've called this meeting to discuss the future of Anadrieth, in full detail. My councilors and I have been working hard behind the scenes in order to brighten the unfortunate news I must bring you today." He showed them the declaration. "Lanadrin has declared war."

The table immediately went into an uproar.

"We don't stand a chance against those barbarians."

"Their allies are even worse. I've heard Calverans are half-giants."

"There's no such thing—"

"Can we offer them our gold and jewels?"

"My wife just had a baby—"

Anton shrank back as the noise continued to escalate. Every meeting always went this way, like the men were too self-absorbed to listen to their lord. He glanced at his sister, who was looking off into the distance. He could practically hear the wheels whirring in her head, as her mind was probably scanning every book she'd ever read for ideas. The servant girl, however, was impassive. Of course, she was; his brother had already told her everything.

"We cannot simply surrender!" one cried, banging his fist on the table.

"This is the empire's fault. The prince should be keeping them under control."

"We haven't had a true imperial couple for over a decade. It's not his fault he's not of imperial blood."

"Then, it's the missing princess' fault."

"We have to appeal to him!"

"Dragons, help us—"

Alexander stood, and the room slowly quieted. "Don't be alarmed. I would never give up on my people, which is why I have been working on a solution. Although Councilor Dallan could not be here with us today, his brilliant idea has borne fruit." He held up a document bearing the Elorian seal, a mighty sea serpent. "The esteemed Lord Reinhardt of Eloria has agreed to forge an alliance with us," he held his hand out toward Adelia, "for my little sister's hand in marriage."

What? Anton immediately searched his sister's face. Her composure broke, then, and her mouth hung open. Even the girl actually seemed surprised. They didn't know. He gritted his teeth, and his heart pounded louder in his chest. She didn't *know.* Alexander never asked her. Of course, he didn't. Of course, he would make that kind of decision without telling anyone who cared—anyone who mattered. Hadn't he seen what that kind of marriage did to their parents? What it did to Adelia? Of course, he didn't. Alexander never saw anything like that. He clenched his fists, willing his blood to stop boiling. It wasn't his business anymore. Adelia wouldn't want it to be his business.

Several men cheered, and the suggestion of ale circulated the room as they all congratulated each other.

"Our alliance would make them think twice about waging war upon us."

"Perhaps this calls for an early celebration!"

"I knew our lord wouldn't be without a plan."

"Cheers!"

"Eloria is a powerful ally, indeed."

They were so quick to change their attitude. Adelia was glaring at Alexander, fiddling with her left hand. She was about to cry. Anton shook his head. His brother was nodding and looking pleased with himself, an unfortunate side effect of his ignorant arrogance. He didn't even look at their sister; he was too busy evaluating the men's reactions. Adelia took a few steps backward and ran off, rubbing her face with a sleeve. Anton gripped the chair, forcing himself to stay seated. She wouldn't want him to come. There was nothing he could say, anyway.

Suddenly, the room died down. An overwhelming sensation filled his chest, almost like someone else was taking up residence there—a chilling presence. Everyone was staring where his sister had been, but all that remained was that girl, still standing there. Her eyes were like arrows, locked onto their targets without mercy, like a hunter stalking its prey. If he didn't know any better, he would have been scared. The girl turned her gaze toward Alexander.

"Why didn't you say anything?" she said in a low voice. "You should have asked her."

Alexander hesitated. He seemed like he didn't know what was going on.

General Barrett stood up, walking around to stand directly in front of her. "Servants should be seen and not heard." Although he towered over the girl and spoke in a threatening tone, he was, strangely, not as menacing as she was. Anton shook himself. What in dragon's name was he thinking? That girl was trouble and probably a threat, but she wasn't terrifying. He put his hands on his slightly trembling knees. He wasn't going to give her the credit, at least.

The girl didn't back down. "Or perhaps everyone has the right to speak."

Alexander quickly inserted himself between them. "This isn't the time."

"I believe it is," said General Barrett. "With all due respect, my lord, this isn't the first time she's been too outspoken, and now she's questioning your decisions in public." He turned to the council. "For the sake of maintaining our lord's focus during these trying times, I insist that this servant girl accompany Lady Adelia to Eloria." Even Anton found himself nodding at that. As the men murmured their agreement, General Barrett turned back to Alexander.

His brother's face was blank, and he almost felt sorry for him. Not that he cared about the girl, but the pressure his brother was facing right now must be intense. Alexander gave the slightest nod. He was giving into them again.

General Barrett smiled. "Run along, then, after your mistress."

The girl gave Alexander one last look of disappointment before turning on her heel. When she reached the door, she began sprinting, presumably after his sister. The general and his brother sat down again, and the meeting continued as planned. Anton sunk back into his chair. The air had relaxed, and he could just about breathe through the remaining tension. He tried to pay attention to all of the meticulous planning details—apparently, they would still hold the festival tomorrow, regardless of the impending war—but his mind continued to drift.

The girls would leave at once after the festival to Eloria, and his sister would be gone. Perhaps they would see each other again at certain social occasions, but it was unlikely. The regions rarely visited each other, made evident by the presence of border patrols in an empire that was supposed to be at peace. He wouldn't have a reason to see her, either. Not that she would want to. At the very least, that girl would be gone, and soon, she would be Eloria's problem.

Anton sighed. The girl wasn't wrong, though. His brother should have asked their sister, or at least warned her in advance. Out of the three of them, Adelia was the clever one. She could have come up with a multitude of solutions, perhaps even talked Lord Tamar out of war altogether.

Their places should have been reversed. She would have been far more useful here, and Anton should have been cast off to Eloria, instead. He wasn't tactically minded, diplomatic or even a great soldier. There was nothing he could offer his brother, even if Alexander let him. Unfortunately, it would be rather impossible to switch places.

As the council convened, the men lingered around to talk amongst themselves. Anton sat up. Was it over already? Perhaps he could get a word in with his brother now. He waited through several conversations, until Alexander was finally free, before he approached him. His brother was visibly exhausted, and there were dark circles under his eyes, but he still managed to give him a big grin and a pat on the shoulder.

"Ah, Brother, what can I do for you?"

Anton shifted out from under his hand. Now that he actually had his brother's attention, he wasn't sure what to say. He couldn't debate the tax issue on flour or discuss the best techniques against a larger opponent. He didn't even know how to pretend to talk like everyone else did when they wanted to act social for the sake of it. Perhaps he should just say what was on his mind.

"Why did you do it?"

Alexander was taken aback, and Anton internally grimaced. It wasn't the worst thing to come out of his mouth, but it certainly wasn't the best, either.

His brother's smile dampened. "You, too?" Alexander ran a hand through his hair. "I don't understand. This is the best solution for Anadrieth."

Anton didn't meet his eyes. "What, sacrificing our little sister?"

Alexander frowned. "It's better than her getting caught in a war, or worse, captured by the Lanadese. You speak like she's sentenced to die, but she's certain to love Eloria and, perhaps one day, Lord Reinhardt."

"You don't know that at all," snapped Anton, struggling to keep his voice calm. "Our parents were forced together, and you know it. Adelia got the worst of it, while you were the golden child. You haven't even met Lord Reinhardt—what if he's just as bad as Lord Tamar?"

"That's enough," Alexander hissed.

General Barrett appeared beside Alexander, scowling at Anton. "My lord, I believe it would be best for you to have some well-deserved rest. We can handle things for now."

Alexander nodded. "Indeed, I'll be taking my leave now." He glanced back at Anton. "We'll talk later."

As soon as his brother was out of earshot, General Barrett

turned on him. "You'll do well not to disgrace Lord Alexander in public like that uncouth servant girl. You may be the second son, but if he falls, we won't be looking to you to lead us." He stalked away without another word.

Anton clenched his fists, exiting the great hall as fast as he could without running. He kept his head down as he weaved through the castle. He knew the way blindfolded. Barrett was right. He should have picked a more appropriate time, or even had the sense to keep his mouth shut.

He couldn't deny that a marriage alliance was a smart move—probably their only one. Anton shoved his hands in his pockets. But he couldn't help himself. Better still, he should have grown up to be more like Alexander, the leader everyone looked to for guidance and strength. He was just the impulsive, useless little brother.

He could hear Ban calling out to him in the distance, but Anton ignored him, jogging outside through the snow. If he were more like Alexander, he would have been one half of a powerful team instead of an embarrassment. If he were more like Alexander, he would have been respected. If he were more like Alexander, he would have been able to put aside his feelings and make tough choices in order to protect them all.

Anton all but collapsed in the little clearing. He wrapped his arms around the tombstone, pressing his face against the ice-cold rock.

"Mama... I wish you were here," he whispered.

She didn't skip a beat, her arms wrapping around his shoulders.

I am, my darling.

※ 6 ※

CHAPTER SIX

ADELIA

ADELIA SPRINTED FROM THE CASTLE, ignoring that her hair was getting tangled into knots and her dress was dragging in the snow. She panted with each heavy step she took. She couldn't believe what her brother had just done. Even worse, he was just listening to that idiotic councilor. Alexander had every opportunity to ask her, to talk to her, to tell her what was going on. She could feel his hand patting her on the head and talking to her like she was still a child.

I'll take it into consideration.

Adelia let out a frustrated cry. A proper lady shouldn't get angry, but she didn't care. How could her own brother trade her away to a man he'd never met to save people he'd never met in order to stop a war declared by another man he'd never met? It was ridiculous. She wasn't exactly allowed to leave Anadrieth, but Alexander had no excuse. The regions remained entirely separate entities from each other, even though they all belonged to one empire. But forget the customs. He should have said dragons to the social rules and just gone to Lord Tamar to solve the problems in person.

The soldiers were training in the grounds, as usual, and Adelia gritted her teeth as she ran the long way to the castle wall. She needed some air, to get away from the castle for once, dragons to whoever wanted to stop her. At the very least, it felt good to run, even though her lungs were bursting. Proper ladies never ran, but dragons to being a proper lady.

And *then,* there was the fact that her brother knew full well what it was like when two people were forced together. Dragons, it was the whole reason that he was pushing his council so hard for the right to court Mina.

Adelia leaned against the wall as the world spun around her. Her stomach heaved, but she clamped her mouth shut, willing the bile back down. Perhaps Alexander hadn't paid attention to their parent's marriage, even back then. Knowing him now, it wouldn't be a surprise.

"Are you all right, Milady?" asked a patrolling guard. "Would you like me to escort you back?"

Adelia waved a hand, shaking her head. "I'm fine. I'm going out, just return to your duties." It wasn't his fault, but it would be nice if they didn't treat her like she was about to break. She had two working arms and legs like everyone else. She was just a bit out of breath, was all. As the guard walked off, she stared up at the castle, and her heartbeat began to slow. The structure was like an ominous gray shadow, the design functional but not appealing in the slightest. If anything, it resembled a prison.

A figure sprinted out from the way she came in a blur of purple, dashing straight through the training grounds toward her. She squinted, but even at that speed, she could recognize her friend. The men dove left and right to avoid Mina as she expertly weaved and ducked her way through the crowd, tucking her shoulder to roll beneath the dueling blades. Wood splintered, and arrows seemed to haphazardly fly off course, as though a gust of wind was knocking everything over. Adelia couldn't help but smile, despite the turmoil. Mina sure knew how to make an entrance.

The soldiers seemed frozen, with their heads turned to the general's son, who was helping another man to his feet. Adelia didn't blame them; a ruckus like that would have General Barrett sending them all on a ten-lap warmup around the grounds. She often watched them train from her window, pitying their misfortune.

Ban rotated in a slow circle, taking in the chaos, and his head tilted back, spilling laughter across the grounds. The men dusted themselves off, their posture relaxing and their growing chuckles joining a chorus of mirth. Mina looked behind her, scratching her head. She shrugged.

Ban jogged over to them, still grinning. "Never a dull day with you here," he said, nodding at Mina.

Mina bit her lip. "Sorry, I was just passing through," she said, twirling a finger through her hair. Bits of snow glistened in her locks, forming a delicate film, before melting away.

"I can certainly see that." Ban's dimples were full of child-like energy, though he was no longer a child. "What had you both in such a hurry?"

Adelia glanced at the ground, and Mina piped up.

"Alexander's—or should I say Councilor Dallan's—solution is to marry Adelia off to Lord Reinhardt to form an alliance. Of course, we were only just told."

"An alliance, huh?" Ban stroked his chin. "Eloria has an

army twice as good as ours, and their food is said to give one man the strength of ten." He paced back and forth. "But even so, a marriage is a one-time thing. Sooner or later, they'd be draining far more from us in order to continue their support. It would only be a matter of time before..."

Mina nodded. "I told him it was unsustainable."

Adelia frowned. "You knew?" She knew that they talked but not about things like this.

"Only that he sought an alliance. He never said how."

Adelia shook her head. Her brother would talk about something as important as that to Mina, but wouldn't even pay attention to the information that she had to offer. She had to stop being surprised by his behavior. It only made her disappointment feel worse.

Ban shrugged. "I suppose all we can really do is trust that our lord knows what he's doing. I truly hope you'll be able to make the best of the situation, my lady. They do say Eloria is a beautiful region, and you deserve to be happy." He kicked the snow with his boot. "I'd do anything to get out of this cold weather." Ban glanced between the two of them. "How is Anton taking everything?"

Adelia gave him a blank stare. "The fact that you have to ask *us* is truly a testimony to your dying friendship." It wasn't like Anton ever talked to her. If she wanted to know something about her brother, she would have asked Ban.

"Worth a shot," said Ban, smiling sheepishly. "He won't talk to me, but I figure one day, I can crack him again. It only takes one person to be a friend, after all."

"I wouldn't bother..." Adelia murmured. Her brother was gone. He had been for a long time. She sighed, tapping Mina on the arm. "You weren't coming to bring me back, were you?"

Mina shook her head. "Where would you like to go?"

"Anywhere but here."

They left the castle grounds together, walking down the main road. Like the castle, the city of Anadrieth was built with the same dreary stone. The morning sun reflected specks of light through the thin layers of ice encasing the windows and slanted rooftops.

Despite the gloomy appearance, the city was bustling at this hour, erupting in a cacophony of sound. Merchants proclaimed their wares, some engaged in heated arguments as they haggled over price, others sang praises of their goods. Wagons rolled over the cobblestones, the horses snorting and rubbing their faces in feed bags. Lively violin music wafted through the streets, and street dancers twirled and waved silk ribbons around them in mesmerizing patterns as they attracted a small crowd of onlookers, throwing copper coins into a basket.

Adelia tried to enjoy the city life around her, to absorb the infectious energy of their people, but her mind kept circling back to the impending marriage. Now that she had calmed down, logic took over. Her brother was in a difficult situation, but his decision hadn't been wrong. Even if it was only a temporary solution, it would buy them time to look for a permanent one.

She glanced around at their people. Children giggled and squealed, throwing snow at each other, while passers-by scolded them as they ran haphazardly through the streets. Young ladies drew water from the well, water sloshing about as they gossiped about their festival outfits. People greeted each other in the streets with warm smiles. For a city that had feared war for the past two years, they did a good job of remaining cheerful.

Adelia smiled faintly. If she had to leave to protect them, so be it. Perhaps she was looking at things in the wrong way. She found that whenever she hit a wall in her work, it always helped to turn the whole thing upside down, sometimes literally—some of the dragon script packed in the margins had actually been written from another angle.

Eloria *was* said to be beautiful. She would get to see the great Sea of Dunite, maybe even sail its waters. And there had to be a whole other world of books over there that she could get her hands on, which could even hold missing pieces of information.

Mina nudged her. "If you're hungry, I know where the best bakery in the city is. Alexander even has them baking for the festival."

Adelia grinned. "I'm starving."

As they weaved through the streets, the aroma of freshly baked bread drifted past, and Adelia's stomach growled in response. There was a house with a little shopfront attached, complete with a large open counter where you could watch the bread being baked. A plump man was busily rolling out dough, his apron already covered in flour, while a woman—presumably his wife—was checking the pastries in the oven. Unlike the man who had his arms exposed, she wore a long-sleeved, high-necked dress.

Mina leaned over the counter. "Morning, Henry, Marianne!"

Henry turned, and his cheeks puffed up into a smile. "Morning, lass. And who's this you've brought with you?"

Adelia cut in. "Just a friend."

He seemed to pause, his eyes running over their attire, and Mina piped up again. "I see you're in a good mood today. How's business?"

Henry sighed. "Not booming. Thieves have been running rampant in the city lately. With all this talk of war, folks are scared, and soldiers don't have time to deal with petty theft." He leaned forward, speaking under his breath. "Between you and me, people ain't so confident that Lord Alexander can protect us from them barbarians. The empire needs its leaders back, or this'll turn into a bloodbath sooner or later."

Marianne nudged his side, placing a tray of pastries on the counter, their shapes twisted into miniature dragons. Her dull blonde hair was pulled into a messy bun, and her face held the remnants of a woman who was clearly beautiful in her youth.

"Don't be such a downer. Our lord is truly doing his very best." Marianne handed both of them a pastry. "We've even got the honor of making these for the festival." There was a reddish birthmark creeping onto the left side of her cheek that looked slightly scarred. Marianne seemed to be self-conscious of it, wearing especially long clothes to conceal it. She averted her eyes when she noticed Adelia staring.

Adelia focused on the dragon-shaped pastry instead. It had a bright red frostberry for an eye, and the glaze stuck to her fingers. She took a small nibble, then ate the rest in a single bite. "Those are amazing."

Mina nodded at Henry. "But I'm afraid their speculation is correct. War is upon us."

Henry grimaced, slipping his arm around his wife. "Thought as much," he said, wiping the sweat from his brow. "Suppose there's not much we can do, except what we've always done."

Marianne squeezed his hand to her chest. "We'll be all right." Then, her eyes widened, and she glanced back at Mina. "Haven't told you the best news yet! The orphanage is letting us adopt some kids again, two of them, in fact. One young'un and an older one. Must be a couple of troublemakers since they seemed insistent we take both... what were their names again?"

Henry thought for a moment, then clicked his fingers. "Scarlet and Penelope. Too bad they're too old to name after us. Would have liked a Henrietta or a Marie."

Marianne frowned. "Be truly thankful you'll have a daughter at all, especially after our last apprentice disappeared, and our adopted son..."

Adelia paused as she licked her fingers. It was only faint, but for a moment, there was a sense of sadness. It shouldn't have been odd, given the subject, but there was a strange flavor about the sadness. Almost as if it was false, but at the same time, it wasn't. She wiped her hand. Maybe the frostberry was just off.

Marianne seemed to pull herself together. "Anyway, the neighbors might scoff at breaking the family naming tradition, but they were all blessed with several children each." She shook her head, pulling out a little wooden doll with blonde hair and a blue dress. Hand-carved, its appearance was almost lifelike. "This one's for the young'un. I hope they like it." Marianne locked eyes with Adelia. "Family is important to take care of, after all, even if you don't know them." She held out another pastry.

Adelia hesitated, then took it. Perhaps Marianne did know who she was, and her issues with her brothers were written that plainly across her face. By now, the rumors of their strained relationship had probably trickled down to the commoners.

Mina peered at the doll. "I'm telling you, you should sell these. They're lovely."

"I could never—"

"Talented, ain't she?" Henry kissed her on the cheek. "Got lucky with this one. Never thought I'd find another wife, as old as I was."

Marianne rolled her eyes but smiled at him all the same. A clang caught their attention as the oven's iron door fell from its hinges, black smoke billowing from the opening.

"Not again," muttered Henry, rushing for his gloves. Marianne bid them a good day and ran to help him, fanning the smoke with her skirts.

Adelia watched them for a moment before leaving. They were a kind couple, especially to be taking in children at a time like this. Was it really such an inconvenience for her to leave? It wasn't like she was needed here, and at least she would have Mina.

They wandered down the streets in relative silence, while the citizens dashed about with decorations and armfuls of white and gold cloth, hanging lanterns and preparing for the festival. If these were to be her last days in Anadrieth, she was going to enjoy them. Her translations could wait.

One of the town squares was particularly alight with activity, and an air of tense curiosity hung over the area. They edged through the dense crowd, weaving their way toward the front. People looked annoyed as they pushed through, then backed off as they glanced at their dresses. They probably wouldn't recognize her as Lady Adelia, but they would definitely recognize them as nobles of some sort. A town crier stood on the central podium, waving a piece of parchment.

"Attention, all citizens! Lanadrin has officially declared war. An alliance with Eloria is underway. Stand by for further orders!" As he repeated his message, the crowd began to shout, pointing fingers and waving their arms.

"We're all going to die!"

"What can we do?"

"I knew it!"

"—they're not gonna protect us."

Decorations abandoned, the crowd jostled and shoved each other forward and back, some attempting to get closer to the crier, while others made their hasty retreat. Adelia was pushed in several different directions at once. She struggled to keep her footing as she reached out for Mina, but she was pushed in the opposite direction. She silently cursed Alexander. He shouldn't have kept them completely in the dark. It was one thing not to worry people, but this kind of announcement would cause riots.

Suddenly, the crowd quieted, and everyone's heads turned in waves toward the middle of the square. They collectively began to edge away, leaving Adelia with a little more room to breathe. She turned toward the podium to see a young man staggering back and forth, shouting unintelligible words in the town crier's face as one arm flailed while the other hung limply at his side. Skin flaked off in large pieces, and a charcoal tinge stained his body. His neck was rubbery, unable to support his head. Some of the adults covered their children's eyes, and murmurs rippled through the crowd.

"Wasn't that the new blacksmith's apprentice?"

"What's that thing doing here?"

"It's not fit to be in society."

"Third one this week—"

"—an undesirable."

Adelia shuddered. The undesirable had a stagnant aura, the kind that made one want to turn away. He was the same as the ones kept in the castle, only this one wasn't tied down. The young man paused, and his eyes rolled in their sockets, staring directly at her. He clambered down from the podium and sprinted toward her with outstretched arms.

"Ne... nee... need!" he cried.

The crowd parted in a hurry, as though his disease was contagious. Adelia couldn't help but stumble back. She knew it couldn't spread like that, but it was terrifying all the same. Mina pushed her aside, and Adelia hit the floor. The undesirable half-collapsed on top of Mina, clawing his fingers across her skin as she pressed her hands into his face.

Adelia gasped for air, the hard stone winding her. Through the cacophony of the crowd, she heard a shout.

"Anchiore!"

Despite the commotion, there was a moment of complete clarity, as though everything had aligned in perfect harmony, and she could breathe once again. As the crowd dissipated, Adelia clambered to her feet. Mina had her hands on the young man's head, but she seemed confused. The man, however, was different. He had stopped babbling, and his ragged breathing had slowed. Adelia bent down to peer at him. His pupils contracted, and a slight blush returned to his cheeks as his skin slowly regained its color. She could almost feel the sickness, his aura of rot, disappearing.

The young man suddenly rolled off of Mina, rubbing his arms and shaking his head. He cleared his throat a few times.

"Th... thank you," he wheezed. "I don't know—I don't know what..." He stopped, giving Mina his hand and pulling her up. He stared at his palms in wonder. "My strength is back."

Adelia rubbed her eyes. An undesirable was incurable—it was a fact. And yet, this young man stood before her, moving and speaking as normal. She grabbed his shoulders, looking him over. His skin had all but lost its grayish sheen, and his eyes had returned to a bright blue.

"What happened?" she demanded.

The man's eyes widened, and he put his hands up. "Don't know, Ma'am. I was working one minute, and the next... I was here. Haven't been feeling too good over the past two weeks, but I didn't think nothing of it."

Adelia's mind raced. She couldn't let him go. Not that it was her priority, but he could be a key factor in curing the rest of the undesirables. "You need to come with me to see Elaine. What's your name?"

"James," he said. "But Ma'am, I really have to get back to work. He's gonna kill me for how long—"

"James, my name is Lady Adelia, and I need you to come back with me."

His eyes widened even more, and he bowed deeply. "A-apologies, Milady, I didn't know."

Adelia patted his shoulder. "It doesn't matter. Just come. Oh, Mina." She had almost forgotten that she was here. "You can have the rest of the day off if you need to do anything. Come by my room later." She steered James toward the main road, waving to the nearest carriage. As they rode back to the castle, Adelia bombarded him with questions.

"How old are you?"

"Just turned sixteen, Milady."

"Do you have any siblings?"

"My younger sister, Jane. She just started working at the castle."

"Parents?"

"Mama died a long time ago, and Papa works in the mines."

"And your Papa didn't... experience what you just did?"

"No, Milady."

Adelia rested her chin in her hand, tapping her face. Whatever this was, it didn't seem to affect children, and it wasn't passed on by blood, as far as they knew. The feeling she had felt from him was gone, replaced by something different, something strong and sturdy, yet malleable and ever-changing. She shook her head. It didn't make sense.

"Can you describe what it was like?"

James gripped the long apron hanging over his knees. "Freezing. Like everything was wrong with the world. Could hear people screaming at me, see them running, but when I tried to call for help, my body just wouldn't respond. Felt like time had stopped, it did, like I was wandering in the darkness between worlds, neither here nor there. I know it sounds crazy." He shook his head, and Adelia nodded for him to continue. "Then, I saw a light, but it wasn't really a light. I just knew it was the way back home, so I reached out for it. Next thing I knew, I was on the ground in the square."

Adelia placed her hand on his. "Did it hurt?"

"Sorta. I could feel my body rotting on the outside, but it was like it wasn't mine. The real pain was this..." James pushed his tongue into his cheek as he searched for the word.

"Loneliness. Like I'd be the only one there for the rest of time." He shuddered.

Adelia couldn't help but pull him into an embrace, stroking his hair. Poor thing. He must have been terrified. If he was semi-conscious through the whole thing, the others must be, too.

She didn't quite understand what he had described, but it was just as convoluted as dragon script. Adelia snapped her fingers. She'd heard something back there. *Anchiore.* Anchor? She knew the meaning, but there were no ships in Anadrieth, and an anchor was hardly relevant to undesirables.

Anchor, anchor, anchor...

They made their way back to the castle, and Adelia dragged him straight to Elaine, who glanced at him once before putting her hands on her hips.

"What's a healthy one doing here? Out, child, I'm busy."

Adelia explained the situation, and Elaine frowned. After looking him over, he was given the all-clear, and they drilled him with more questions, but James didn't have anything else to say. Elaine eventually sent him back home, instructing him to return if any symptoms returned.

Adelia wandered back to her room and sifted through her desk. If an anchor wasn't a *thing*, perhaps it was an *action*. But anchor to what? She buried herself in her books, searching for hours. Before she knew it, she woke up with her face on the desk. It was just past sundown, and the sky was dark. Mina should have come to wake her. Adelia shrugged on a cloak and made her way down to the servant's quarters, but no one had seen her. She wasn't in her room, either. It wasn't like Mina not to come home.

Adelia quickened her step. It was dangerous for her to be

out there alone in the dark. Something might have already happened to her. She hurried through the corridors. The only other person who would care was one with whom she didn't want to speak, but she didn't have a choice. If she went out alone, it would only complicate the situation.

Adelia banged on Alexander's door, her heart thumping with each resonating sound.

✤ 7 ✤

CHAPTER SEVEN

ALEXANDER

ALEXANDER TOSSED and turned in his bed, pulling a pillow over his ear. It took him forever to find a comfortable position in which to fall asleep, and now, there was an incessant rapping at his door. He was certain that he had made it clear that no one should bother him. Alexander sighed into his pillow. Whoever it was, they clearly weren't going to leave. He rolled out of bed, tightening his sword on his belt, and opened the door. It was just his sister.

"Adelia, I don't—"

"Mina is missing."

Alexander frowned. "What?"

His sister's face was flushed as though she was out of breath. "We parted ways in the markets today, and she still hasn't come home."

Alexander glanced out of the window, then jogged back to the bed to pull on his boots. It was already dark, and it was dangerous on the streets, especially now with the threat of war looming over them. Thankfully, his little sister had gotten to the point faster than normal. But there wasn't time to gather a search party, and certainly, none of the councilors would help. They would probably think that it was a good thing that she had disappeared.

"I'll come help you," said Adelia.

Alexander grabbed his cloak and moved past her. "I'll find her, don't worry. You stay here in case she comes back." He really just wanted her to stay within the perimeter of the castle. She definitely wouldn't be safe out there.

He sprinted from the castle toward the stables. Mina might be clever, but no amount of witty remarks or plucky courage was going to save her from bandits, or worse, the Lanadese. She had been wearing Adelia's dress, too, so she would be a prime target. What if their soldiers had already infiltrated and had mistaken her for his sister?

Alexander groaned as he scanned along the rows of horses. Of course, they would all be unsaddled by now. But there wasn't enough time to saddle them again. He went straight for his horse, and she let him mount without a problem. It would be more difficult than normal, but luckily, they had practiced riding without a saddle before.

With one squeeze of his thighs, they took off toward the city. Maybe Mina was doing this on purpose; maybe she was still mad. Maybe she was even trying to find another solution by herself. It wouldn't surprise him. He shouldn't have avoided mentioning the marriage. She and his sister had the right to know—he just hadn't had the courage to face them.

The city was silent. The deserted streets were filled only with the pounding of his heart, falling into sync with the horse's hooves. They dashed up and down the streets, scanning every alleyway and square. Alexander gripped his horse's feathery mane between his fingers. The stable boy had already removed her decorations—the silver droplets woven amongst her feathers to indicate his lordly status—but their absence had little effect on his grip.

He could see Mina's smile in his head, the spark of joy in her eyes as she ran.

Alexander, you forgot this!

The way she never missed a detail.

Alexander, your cloak is crooked. Let me fix it.

The way she could always see right through him.

Alexander, I know there's something wrong.

He shook his head vigorously. He would never forgive himself if he let her get hurt again. He'd never even found the vermin who hurt her in the first place.

Alexander spurred his mare, concentrating so hard on his surroundings that he almost didn't see the woman hobbling across the street in front of him. He dove to the left, and the woman's eyes widened as both she and her basket of bread tumbled backward to the ground. Alexander pulled his horse to a stop and leaped off, offering the woman his hand.

"My deepest apologies, madam," he said. The skin on her hand was unusually rough and reddened, as though it had never properly healed from some kind of burn injury. "Are you all right?"

The woman dusted herself off, her skirts covered in dirt and soot. "I'm quite all right," she said, her gaze sweeping him up and down. She seemed to stare straight through him for a moment.

Alexander quickly broke her gaze and knelt to gather the escaped bread rolls, placing them back into the basket. Food was expensive in Anadrieth, and that wouldn't change anytime soon.

"Please, allow me to escort you home. It's not safe at this time, and I'm sure you've heard the news."

The woman shook her head, taking the basket from him. "No need. I was just delivering these to a neighbor." She smiled, the warmth reaching her rounded cheeks. "Take care, *nephraile*," she murmured.

"What?" said Alexander, scrunching his nose, but she was already walking away. He guessed that she would be all right, but he couldn't shake the vaguely familiar feeling that he felt from her. She must have come to petition to him at some stage, and he had simply remembered her face, though it had been a while since he'd held the last open hall for complaints.

Alexander took a deep breath, running his fingers through his hair. He wasn't going to get anywhere by galloping around, making a scene and alerting everyone to his presence. It might be better on foot for now. He led his mare around the area for several minutes. The light was all but gone in the sky now, with only the occasional glow of a lantern to light his way, with many left unlit to conserve oil for the festival. Even oil was about to become scarce.

He paused. There was a muffled commotion in the next alleyway. He left his horse, drew his sword and crept forward until he could make out words.

"Well, well, what a find we have here. Think the Mistress will want this one? She's a pretty lass."

Alexander stopped dead in his tracks, willing his heart to stop thudding in his chest. They couldn't be talking about *that* woman. She was dead—she had to be. He stole a glance around the corner. There were at least four men standing around a girl.

"Are you sure we should—"

"We need the gold."

Alexander's knuckles whitened, and he stared at his boots, straining his ears to listen. There was clearly someone in trouble, but he had to hear more. For these bandits to be speaking of the Mistress was bad news. Perhaps it was a false alarm, and they were simply hiding behind the name. Or perhaps, after nearly a decade, she had begun to move again. If she truly wasn't dead, the whole empire would suffer, just like last time. His heart thumped in his chest. He couldn't handle that. Not again—not now.

A snapping sound echoed in the alley, followed by a high-pitched yelp.

"My arm!"

Alexander readied his sword. He couldn't wait any longer, and he stepped out, brandishing his Golden Dawn. His words faltered in his throat as the woman's face came into view.

Mina!

A burly man was cradling his wrist, and a taller one had his arm wrapped around Mina's neck. The other men turned toward him, stalking closer. Alexander matched their stride. His sword arm was shaking slightly, but his fingers held the hilt with an iron grip. He had to get ahold of himself.

"Release her," he called out, "and I'll consider lightening your sentence." The men looked at each other, and he could almost see the math solving itself in their thick heads—four to one. They grinned at him.

"Sure. You and what army?"

"Better scram, or you won't see another day," said the skinny one, drawing his short sword.

Alexander frowned, glancing down at his clothes. He forgot that he had changed out of his formal robes. They must not recognize him. Three of them rushed him at once, while the fourth backed away, with Mina in tow.

Alexander deflected their blows with ease, closing the distance to slam his fist into the short one's temple, making the man fall. Their movements were sluggish, their swings unpracticed. It was clear that their primary skills were intimidation and brute strength, not sword fighting finesse.

He dodged a fist, spinning to disarm the burly one. Out of the corner of his eye, a shape crashed with a sickening thud. Mina stood over him, rubbing her neck, and Alexander did a double-take. The tall bandit seemed to be knocked out cold.

Desperate footsteps pulled his attention back to the remaining bandit, who had set off at a run. Something whizzed past his ear, planting itself firmly in the back of the bandit's thigh. The bandit howled, tripping and landing face-first.

Mina's voice echoed over his shoulder. "Don't take your eyes off your opponent."

Alexander blinked. He looked at her, then the bandit, then back at her. What had just happened? More footsteps rounded the corner as the night patrol arrived on the scene, their swords already drawn.

"Stop right there!"

Alexander sheathed his sword, drawing his shoulders back. His soldiers rounded on them, some grabbing the bandits.

"Milord... is that you? Are you all right?" asked the captain of the patrol, his quick gestures signaling the men to sheathe their weapons and bow. Alexander frowned. General Barrett may be an excellent fighter, but he was apparently not capable of training the soldiers or scheduling patrols. Had he not have arrived on time, Mina would have surely been kidnapped, or worse.

Alexander waved a hand. "I'm fine. Arrest these men at once. I'll join you in the dungeons." The soldiers' arms slapped across their chests in unison before they hauled the bandits away. He turned his attention back to Mina. "Are you hurt?"

Mina raised an eyebrow. "No. Are you?"

Alexander paused. "No." He brushed his hair out of his eyes. "Why didn't you return?"

She gestured at the scene. "I was a little preoccupied, as you probably saw. Why did you come?"

"I—Adelia was worried."

Mina folded her arms. "I don't recall your concern for her earlier. You could have just sent your men."

Alexander gritted his teeth. "I needed to make sure you were okay—"

"Why?"

"Because!" He turned his face, exhaling. He could feel the heat rising in his cheeks. "I'm getting the horse." He stomped away, placing his fingers between his lips to whistle. A conversation with her never went how he expected. It was like stepping onto an icy lake with the intention of making it across, only to find that you never had a solid footing in the first place. He should have guessed that she would still be mad at him.

Alexander sighed, nudging his horse to its feet. He turned and almost jumped. Mina was standing right behind him, and he hadn't even heard her approach. Shaking off his surprise, he knelt with his fingers intertwined to give her a boost onto the horse.

"Here," he said, motioning with his hands. When nothing happened, he glanced around. Mina was already on the horse, adjusting her dress and stroking its neck.

"Were you planning on walking back?" Mina asked. "It's a nice night for it." She grasped the horse's feathers as though she knew what she was doing.

Alexander placed his hand on the horse, which flicked its tail at him, leading them toward the castle. He didn't understand. Mina acted more like she was going for a pleasant evening stroll rather than someone who had just survived a kidnapping.

"What are you doing? Get on," she said.

He opened his mouth, and she stared at him. Deciding it would be faster than walking back, he swung his leg over, mounting behind her. She was warm against his chest, and he tried to concentrate on his boots while he rearranged his clothes. It didn't help that he had to lean forward more than usual to grasp the mane. His arms pressed into her sides.

Any respectable maiden would be appropriately mortified, but Mina had leaned forward, her legs locked around the horse's sides rather than being in a graceful side-saddle. Practical yet entirely unladylike. They didn't speak the entire way home.

Had Mina actually taken down two of them by herself?

No.

If he admitted that she was trained to fight, it would mean that his brother was right about her. He couldn't entertain that possibility. Alexander shook the thought from his mind. This was the strangest night he'd had in a while.

After returning the somewhat irritated horse to the stables, a messenger ran up to him. "The prisoners are in the dungeons now, Milord."

Alexander nodded. He didn't bother asking Mina to return upstairs to appease his sister. It seemed like she was coming with him whether he liked it or not, anyway. They descended the stairwell, the dungeon walls even colder than the rest of the castle. Torches were lit at the farthest intervals possible, sending shadows creeping around the walls and hiding large patches of the ground. He made a mental note to fix that; tripping was the last thing that anyone needed when handling a prisoner.

Alexander stood in front of the bars, running his eyes across the captives. The four men were in a holding cell, the skinny one with a crude, bloody bandage wrapped around his thigh and the burly one with a splint on his wrist. Common thugs. They probably wouldn't know much, but even the smallest details fell to the bottom of the ladder.

"If you answer my questions, I'll spare you from the noose," he said. They didn't look him in the eye. "What were you planning on doing with this woman?" Alexander gestured to Mina.

"Nothing," said the tall one, his chin tilted up. "Nothing you nobles would give a dragon's claw about, anyway."

"So, this is the great Lord Alexander? That barbarian lord might be a better leader for us, after all."

The short one chuckled. "Bet you think there's some grand plot for this lass of yours. Well, don't get too disappointed. We're just doing what we can to survive."

Alexander frowned. He knew that jobs were scarce, but no one should be starving. "What do you mean, survive? I've done the calculations. There's enough to go—"

"How would you know? You don't see," said the burly one. "You just sit up here in this cozy castle, doing dragon knows what."

"Had to leave my kid in one of the homes."

"The noose ain't a threat. Death's a mercy for people like us."

Alexander gripped the bars, his knuckles whitening. They were lying, obviously; they had to be. Councilor Raoul calculated the reports himself. There were certainly enough resources distributed to everyone, even if it was tight. They were bandits because they chose to be bandits, and there was nothing that he could do about that. He decided to press on.

"Then, what about the Mistress?"

The men fell silent, glancing at each other. The burly one shrugged. "Couldn't say."

"What about her?"

Alexander's lips curved. They must know something. The tall one spoke before he could.

"Bribes or threats won't work. We don't know nothing. She ain't more than a terrifying rumor."

"Then, how—"

"You don't find her. She finds you."

"And eats you whole," added the short one. Everyone stared at him. "Well, that's what I heard," he mumbled.

"Don't lie," said Alexander. "I heard you talking about her, and it didn't sound like trivial speculation."

"Sorry, mister," drawled the burly one. "You're gonna have to use some easier words, us being lowly bandits and all."

Alexander gritted his teeth. "You mentioned her like you knew her."

The tall one rolled his eyes. "We already told you. Rumor has it that the Mistress is on the move again. Just a rumor, is all. But everyone knows she deals in people. No one else would pay."

"We got to eat somehow."

Alexander was about to retort when a gentle hand fell on his arm.

"You're not going to get anything more from them like that," said Mina. She turned to head up the stairs, finished with the conversation.

Perhaps he *had* expected too much from the men. He was getting too riled up regardless. Leaving his captain in charge, Alexander followed her back to the hallway.

"We're not done," he said, his voice echoing against the walls.

Mina cocked her head. "My apologies. I thought you'd already gleaned the necessary information with that masterful interrogation."

Alexander's hand went to his hip. "I can't let any lead concerning the Mistress slip through my hands. Not sure if you *remember*, but she kidnapped dozens of our children across the empire, started rebellions and dragons knows what else."

She sighed. "Even so, you can't get angry at them for trying to survive. Whether they're thieves or nobles, soldiers or servants, they're still your people, and they've entrusted their lives to you."

Alexander rubbed his temples. "I am working day and night to keep this region alive. If they know about something that could endanger my people, I need to know. I have to focus on what's best for Anadrieth."

Mina's face softened, and she gave him that look, the one that said that she was disappointed in him. "But you're listening to all the wrong people. When's the last time you were actually in the city? When's the last time you talked to one of your people?"

He clenched and unclenched his fists. She never held back, and it was something that he found both refreshing and infuriating. Right now, it was the latter. "Fine. Tell me what you think I'm missing."

Mina shook her head. "I'm not one of the people you need to hear it from." She paused at the top of the steps, the breeze blowing through her hair. "I'll be taking my leave now. Wouldn't want to worry Adelia too much."

Alexander managed a curt nod, then headed back for his chambers. He couldn't please everyone—that was the burden of being a ruler. He had no choice but to try to do what was best for the most people, not just some of them.

A wave of exhaustion hit him, and his mind was a fog. He could think about tonight's events later. He collapsed into bed, barely managing to kick his boots off. Tomorrow would be a long day.

The next day was as busy as Alexander had expected. Every year, the Celestial Dragon Festival, an auspicious celebration for the entire empire, was held to honor the dragon gods and the imperial family. It seemed somewhat ridiculous to hold a grand celebration in light of recent events, but the impending war only made the Festival all the more necessary.

By the time evening had arrived, the celebrations were in full swing, though the atmosphere was still tense. The city had been preparing for weeks, but with war around the corner, the people didn't seem to know how to react. Today of all days, Alexander had to be seen amongst his people without the slightest bit of worry showing in his face. This year, it wasn't a celebration—it was a salve for a fresh wound.

Alexander gazed at the decorations lining the streets, which coated his city in imperial white and gold. The commoners bowed on either side of the main street as he passed by with his entourage, waving at his people. Some were smiling at him, but others held the same disappointed look that Mina had.

Alexander tightened the sash around his waist; his entire outfit hung in the balance of this single knot. The chilly air drifted across his skin, with his toes sticking out of the sandals. If the need arose, it would be impossible to fight in this ridiculous design—it offered no protection from a sword or the elements—but it would be a grave insult if he were to be the only one who refused to wear the capital's traditional clothing. If there were one thing he hated about the festival, it was the outfit.

The procession ended in the main square, where thousands of folded paper lanterns had been stacked along the streets, ready for the ceremony. Quill in hand, Alexander read his message aloud for his people, asking the dragon gods for protection in the coming weeks. He didn't mention the final words that he'd written on the lantern—the opportunity to speak to Mina. Tonight would probably be his last chance to do so before he saw her off with his sister.

He held up the lantern, the flickering light illuminating his letters. A cheer erupted from the crowd as it sailed into the sky, and then his people scrambled to write their own messages. Alexander glanced to his left, spotting one of his maids struggling, her crude handwriting spelling out *happy, luck* and *nice fortunes*. She must not have studied hard enough when she was a child. He moved to offer his assistance but stopped as she lit her lantern. She seemed happy enough with her efforts.

Soon, all of the lanterns were let go as the people sent their messages toward the spirit realm like tiny beacons of hope. Thousands upon thousands of lights rose across the empire at once in a beautiful display.

Alexander was still staring upward when the music started. His people began dancing around him, and he knew that the celebrations wouldn't cease until dawn. A gaggle of young women approached him, nudging each other forward, and he suppressed a sigh. It was already starting. Alexander pasted on a smile, greeting them one by one and briefly pressing his lips against their outstretched hands.

Councilor Dallan nodded approvingly in his direction. It was no secret that his council wanted an heir, and his lack of betrothal at twenty-seven years of age was concerning.

Alexander twirled the women around, his feet moving automatically. He could feel their desperation to get close to him, and he felt crowded. His household was scattered amongst the commoners, nobles with the poor, soldiers with the servants. His smile was reflected in the nobles' faces, their displeasure thinly masked by duty and tradition. Tonight was the one occasion in which it was acceptable to approach anyone, no matter their status, and it wasn't a surprise that people took advantage of that.

Someone bumped into him, and he stumbled forward, causing his current dance partner to shoot a nasty glare behind him. A woman spun away, her figure a thick barrel of golden fabric, layered to resemble dragon scales, the tail sweeping into people's legs. Her hands gripped Anton's, and his brother was visibly sweating as he mouthed *help me*. Alexander shrugged, smirking at him. This was something his brother could handle alone. Besides, he had his own situation to deal with.

His partner blushed slightly, gazing up at him. "Perhaps my lord wishes to go somewhere we won't be disturbed?" she asked, her finger twirling a lock of her hair. It was so practiced, it made him feel physically ill. The song ended, and he gave her a tight-lipped smile, his eyes darting across the crowd.

"Thank you for the dance," he said, but there was only one person with whom he wanted to dance. He finally caught a glimpse of her, slipping away from the square, and he excused himself, weaving through the throng of people and following her onto a little alcove.

Mina leaned over the wall, looking out at the horizon and the lanterns lining the streets below, creating a warm glow around the city. Her hair was pinned back in a way that only his sister could do, with a single winter lily tucked behind her ear. Her robes hugged her body in a far more natural fit than his own. Even the air around her was different from the other women.

Alexander leaned on his elbow next to her, making sure that his sash was tight enough. He could do this.

Her eyes didn't leave the city as she spoke. "There's a fire."

He jerked his head, scanning the horizon. One of his people in the streets below them yelped, dropping a lantern and shaking their hands rapidly as the paper caught alight. He relaxed his shoulders. Not that kind of fire, though it was certainly foolish of them; one should know better than to play with an open flame. Alexander shook his head.

The corner of Mina's lips turned up as she faced him. "I take it you're not enjoying the festival." She could always see right through him.

Alexander wiped his brow. "It wouldn't be the first time." The music picked up once more, and he let out a breath. His palms were suddenly sweaty. "You're... the one woman who hasn't asked me to dance yet."

Mina raised an eyebrow. "Is that your way of asking?"

Alexander swallowed, offering his hand. "Yes."

She placed her hand in his, the other resting on his shoulder, and his settled around her waist. It was actually happening. Alexander led her a few steps away from the wall as the soft melody echoed in the background.

Mina glanced toward the square. "I know this tune."

He gently twirled her around. "The Aria of the Gods? Everyone knows that one." It was nostalgic, the kind of lullaby that sang life into his very spirit, building up to a magnificent crescendo—but he was too nervous to enjoy it.

"When the light meets the darkness, all will hold their breath," she murmured, her voice following the music. "As the world regains composure, and the end results in death."

"Those would be interesting lyrics," Alexander remarked.

It was strange that no one had ever tried to put lyrics to it before.

She looked up at him, and his breath caught in his throat, his pulse quickening. He had always dodged the subject before, unable to bring it up. But it was now or never.

"Mina... I wanted to ask you something."

"Yes?"

One of his lieutenants rounded the corner, his head scanning left to right. He scrambled toward them at once, bowing his head before speaking low into Alexander's ear. "Milord, report from the eastern sector. There's been an attack." His eyes darted out toward the horizon.

Alexander pursed his lips. Couldn't Anadrieth survive without him for one minute? He reluctantly pulled his hands from Mina's, following his lieutenant's gaze. Black smoke was drifting steadily across the sky. Alexander opened his mouth. That was not there before.

"Go," said Mina, giving him a little push.

Alexander nodded, sprinting out into the streets after the lieutenant. There was no time to change clothes, and a horse was already waiting for him. He set off immediately with a handful of soldiers, while the lieutenant gathered backup. If this were a Lanadese attack, they would be in trouble. He spurred his horse forward.

As they neared the outskirts of the city, the smoke was thick, and bits of ash and debris rained down upon them. Alexander pulled his cloak up to cover his mouth. The houses here seemed to get smaller and smaller as they neared the source of the smoke, their structures far less sturdy than those in the center.

Citizens crowded the scene, a wall of bodies surrounding

the remnants of a single house, though it could hardly be called that anymore. It was nothing more than a pile of smoldering wood. Some people were still hurling buckets of water at the shack, catching the embers as they strayed from the area.

Alexander dismounted, approaching the remains. He ordered his men to scout the area and question the witnesses. He could tell immediately that this was no ordinary fire. The houses on either side, though made of wood, were singed but otherwise completely intact. It clearly wasn't a small fire, either, given the speed at which it had destroyed a single house. There must have been a short-lived but intense, concentrated heat source.

Like an explosion.

Alexander scratched his head. That kind of explosive power was difficult to come by—way out of league for a few bandits. It must have been an attack of some kind, surely, but there was no advantage to this location; it wasn't a wealthy area, it didn't provide tactical benefits, nor did it cause him a significant loss. If anything, this seemed like a test, as though the culprit were rehearsing an attack before the real thing.

Somehow, it didn't feel like Lanadrin was responsible. Lord Tamar was impulsive, not calculating. There was no way he'd risk alerting his position like that, unless it was a distraction. Alexander shuddered. It could have been the Mistress.

Alexander immediately grabbed one of his men to ride back and put his army on high alert.

"But be discreet," he said. "If this is a false alarm, I don't want to frighten the rest of the people."

Another soldier ran up to him, bowing with his arm across his chest. There were a few people in tow.

"Reporting, Milord! The perimeter is clear. As of yet, no causalities have been accounted for. We haven't been able to locate those who lived here, but these were the first witnesses on scene."

Alexander nodded. "I see. Gather my council for an urgent meeting when I return." He turned his attention to the witnesses, a young couple and an old man. "Please explain what you saw."

The old man bowed his head. "I was walking by when I heard some raised voices and a scream. Figured it was those two fighting again, so didn't think much of it. Not long later, flames burst out of the windows," he said, rubbing his arms. "Was burning up just being near it."

The woman clutched her husband. "Milord, we were coming home early from the festival. Had to put our kid to bed. We ran over when we heard the ruckus since we live two houses down. I was real frightened." She pointed to the burnt house. "That couple who live there don't talk much to the rest of us. They keep to themselves, they do, but we hear them fighting all the time."

Her husband nodded. "We couldn't do nothing. The fire was too big. I was about to grab our things and run when it suddenly died down. Then, everyone came to help put out the rest. The whole thing was over in a few minutes, believe it or not."

Alexander stroked his chin. "I see. Was there anything else unusual? Anyone leaving the scene?"

The three of them glanced at each other.

"Don't think you'll believe us, but there was something."

"A figure on fire."

"An evil spirit, I tell you," said the old man, shaking his head.

Alexander questioned them further, but they just kept repeating the same things. Their stories confirmed his suspicions—it certainly wasn't an evil spirit, but there was definitely someone responsible. The heat was already beginning to dissipate, and the smoke was clearing.

He walked through the ashes, scanning the ground. There was one particularly burnt area that stood out—a blackened spot about as wide as two people if he stood in the middle. Presumably, this was where the explosion had been set off. He knelt, picking up a dull white shard from the floor. It felt like bone, though human or animal, it was difficult to tell. He couldn't do anything else here for now. Alexander wiped his hands on his robes, mounting his horse. Hopefully, his council would be able to give him advice.

When he returned to the castle, they were already assembled in the war room, sharing drinks around the table. His presence caused the merriment in the room to quieten, and his councilors attempted to set down their cups. They couldn't seem to sit still with their glassy eyes and red faces. It may or may not have been a Lanadese attack, but the timing was too perfect to be coincidental. This couldn't wait until morning.

"A single house in the eastern sector was attacked tonight," Alexander began. As he finished explaining the details, his men erupted, shouting at each other.

"This won't be the last time—"

"It was Lanadrin!" shouted Councilor Raoul.

"They wouldn't get this far without *my* knowledge," snapped General Barrett, taking a long swig of his ale.

"—about time we did something!"

"It could be *that* woman."

"Silence!" Councilor Dallan slammed his fist on the table. "Sober up, all of you. This is serious business."

Alexander gave him a thankful nod. It was a good thing that his head councilor had returned when he did.

"My lord," Councilor Dallan said. "No matter who is responsible, the sooner our alliance is solidified, the safer we'll be. The preparations are already made for your departure, but it's best if you make haste when dawn comes."

General Barrett raised his cup. "I agree. My men have already been scouting the city and haven't seen any signs of the Lanadese or any other fires." He hiccupped. "I'm confident we will be able to hold the fort until you return."

The other councilors nodded along with Alexander. Prolonging the alliance wasn't going to do them any good, and the sooner he left, the sooner he could return. It wouldn't be a good idea to give the Lanadese any more time to prepare.

"Then, we leave at dawn."

❧ 8 ❧

CHAPTER EIGHT

ANTON

ANTON SNEEZED, rubbing his nose on his sleeve and attempting to breathe through his mouth, but to no avail. His horse trudged forward in their procession through the snow, shaking its thick feathers in a taunting manner.

Damn horse.

It wasn't really the horse's fault, but he was certain that they had given him the hairiest one on purpose. Its feathers tickled his nose, and its coat was thick enough to grab a fistful of hair. But he couldn't hold his breath the whole way.

Two carriages rolled along beside him—one carrying Adelia, the servant girl and supplies, the other filled to the brim with expensive gifts and whatnot. They were already giving Eloria his little sister; what more could they want? The gifts were just as unnecessary as the number of people accompanying the wedding convoy, including himself. An extra two dozen men were far too conspicuous. It was like they were begging to be found by the Lanadese.

There was no logical reason as to why he was being dragged along, either. His brother couldn't see the dangers of all three of them leaving Anadrieth at once, and the councilors obviously didn't want to be trapped under the leadership of the spare. He wasn't even summoned for the incident last night; he'd only heard of it through the soldier's conversations this morning.

Anton nudged his horse forward to come up alongside his brother. Maybe he could bring the problem up now while it was just the two of them.

"Alexa—" He sneezed violently several times, and his eyes began to water.

Alexander patted him on the back. "Did you bring that poultice Elaine made for you?"

Anton pulled a small bottle from his bag, uncorking it and positioning it over his tongue. A single drop fell out before the bottle was empty.

His brother shook his head. "It's only been a day."

Anton shoved the bottle back in his bag. "You'd be downing it, too, if you couldn't breathe. I can't help that horses and I don't mix well." An awkward silence passed between them as Alexander chuckled, then returned to his thoughts. Anton gathered his courage. "I... Don't you think it's strange that all three of us are leaving Anadrieth at the same time?"

Alexander gave him one of his comforting smiles, which meant that he wasn't really paying attention. "Don't worry, Brother. The return journey will be quicker, and Anadrieth is in good hands. Councilor Dallan and General Barrett are in charge."

"That's what I'm concerned about," Anton muttered.

Even away from his councilors, his brother was still ensnared by them. It was almost as bad as his obsession with the servant girl. He blew his nose into a white handkerchief, a monogrammed 'A' in one corner. Adelia had only ever made three of them when she had first learned how to sew—one for him, his brother and her future husband.

They're more special that way. And if you love it, think of how my knight in shining armor will react!

Anton bit back a smile, tucking the handkerchief away in his pocket. She'd always been so obsessed with the prospect of falling in love, just like the heroines in all of the storybooks she had read. This probably wasn't the happy ending she'd hoped for, but at least he was coming along to make sure that this Lord Reinhardt character was a decent man. Not that he cared; it would just be inconvenient if she were unhappy. The only good thing about this whole trip was that he'd never have to see that servant girl again.

The Celestine Forest soon gave way to a small clearing, the silverlight trees and snow forming a visible borderline of white. On the other side, lush green meadows blanketed the landscape, the tiny flowers dotting the Elorian ground with color. Anton couldn't help but stare, and he wasn't the only one. He'd never been to this side of their border, and it was certainly something to see. The Moonstone River separated Anadrieth and Lanadrin, so the bordering region wasn't as visible, but here, there was nothing but an open field—it was almost as if someone had drawn a line between the two regions, and nature itself had listened.

He dismounted and stood with one foot in Anadrieth and the other in Eloria. He'd never seen so much green. It was such a strange color, and he could almost feel the life radiating from it. Anton kicked some of the snow across, and it melted almost instantly. It was even a little warmer on the other side.

An unladylike shout echoed from behind him. His little sister was leaning as far out of the carriage window as she could manage, getting tangled in the curtains but not seeming to care. Her momentary excitement sent a pulse of warmth through his chest.

Brother, can we stay out here?

You mean run away? We can't leave Alexander.

We'll go get him, and then the three of us can go explore the world!

Anton shook his head. They weren't kids anymore. Even if he could rewind time, it was an impossible dream.

Something whizzed past his ear, striking his horse's flank and pulling him from his thoughts. He turned as she whinnied, just in time for her to rear up and kick him in the stomach. He hit the ground hard, unable to draw breath. Through his watery vision, he saw that a flaming arrow had pierced his horse, and more arrows were flying through the sky.

Ambush!

Anton tried to shout, but he couldn't. There was frantic movement all around him as swords were drawn and shields were raised. Toward the tree line, large figures poured from the north, pulling off white cloaks that had camouflaged their skin. Shouts echoed across the clearing, and the Anadese huddled together defensively.

"Get in formation!" Alexander cried.

"It's the Lanadese!"

"Barbarians!"

Several arrows struck the carriage, and as the curtains caught fire, his sister screamed. A dozen Lanadese were suddenly upon them. Anton clawed at the ground to pull himself up and drew his sword just in time to block the axe aimed at his head. His arm shook under the strain, and his breath came in short gasps. His eye was playing up again, and his nose was still running.

The huge man before him grinned. The unmistakable Lanadese crest was displayed prominently on his chest amongst the many inked designs. The barbarian swept his leg, knocking Anton off balance and flinging his sword from his grasp.

Anton crashed to the ground face-first once more, tasting blood and dirt. His vision blurred, and his thoughts were muddled. He rolled out of the way just as an axe struck the ground beside him, and his fingers scrambled for his sword. The man lunged for him, and Anton rolled again, swinging his sword blindly. To his surprise, the blade connected with the barbarian's arm, but it didn't faze the beast. Anton leaped to his feet and readjusted his wavering grip, his heart pounding in his ears.

Out of the corner of his eye, he could see his brother fighting off two barbarians at once on horseback. Bodies fell in every direction, shields flew across the snow in pieces and their screams filled his ears. The Lanadese were utterly slaughtering them, though some of their men were holding their own.

The barbarian stalked toward him once more with a grin, and everything seemed to move in slow motion. He could see his parents' bodies before him, warm and wet on the floor, their limbs twisted like marionette dolls. He felt the cold steel against his face, and the presence of the woman caressed his shoulder. Her long fingers wrapped around his neck as she whispered in his ear. Her voice was the only thing he could hear.

You're so brave.

Anton's feet moved without hesitation, and he launched himself at his opponent. He dodged the axe, feinting with his fist and bringing his sword upward to slice the barbarian's thigh. All the while, the woman's hand was on his, a gentle guide.

The barbarian grimaced as he advanced, but Anton sidestepped his attack, using the opening to thrust the blade into his chest. The barbarian struggled for a moment, then slumped forward, landing on top of Anton.

You're so brave.

They hit the floor together, and the woman's fingers let go of his throat, her presence fading. Anton lay there, his jaw slack and his hands shaking. The man's mouth was open, and his breath foul.

He was dead. Anton had killed him. His stomach heaved, and he pushed the body off in a burst of effort. He had ended someone's life—with his own two hands. He sat up in a daze, trembling.

"Anton!" Alexander dashed through the field of bodies, grabbing his hand and pulling him to his feet. "Are you all right?"

Anton couldn't respond. A flash of imperial white and gold caught his eye as it disappeared through the trees. It looked like a scout, but as a high-pitched scream in the other direction drew their attention, he didn't have time to think about it.

The last barbarian was advancing on his sister, and Anton was sprinting before he realized it. The barbarian drew a short sword from his belt. Anton's lungs were bursting. He had to get there. But he wasn't going to make it.

A blur knocked Adelia to the ground and rolled toward the barbarian in one swift motion—the servant girl—yanking his sword arm down with one hand and landing a strike on his temple with the other. He staggered, but she twisted his wrist back, slamming her hand into his elbow, producing an audible pop. The barbarian cried out, and she wrenched the short sword from his limp grip, slicing clean through his throat.

Anton stopped a few paces away from her, his mouth hanging open. It couldn't be. The servant girl let the barbarian fall back into the snow, and an eerie silence fell over the clearing. Impossible.

The woman's shadow was back, and she rested on his shoulder. She pressed her cold lips against his cheek, her fingers running across the scar on his face.

Anton stepped toward the servant girl, slowly raising his sword. His vision was hazy. He blinked several times, but the servant girl's appearance kept shifting. Tawny brown hair, taller than average, a soft smile from the most beautiful girl in the world—the face of the woman who had murdered his parents. Anton squeezed his eyes shut for a moment.

Not her, he whispered in his mind. *It's not her.*

The servant girl lowered the barbarian's sword, giving him a quizzical look. "Are you all right?"

Anton's head throbbed. The girl's face shifted back and forth. Back and forth. The only women trained to fight were assassins.

"I knew it," he said. The woman's arm wrapped around his waist, her kindness a comforting blanket. His cheeks were burning.

Not her.

The servant girl cocked her head at him. "What do you know?"

"Brother, what are you doing?"

Anton felt Alexander come up, panting beside him, though it was like he was a mile away. The woman's hand reached out to cup his, tightening his grip on the sword. Cold steel left a searing trail against his face, dragging over his eye. She wanted him to kill the servant girl, but her face kept morphing into one he couldn't bear to see.

Anyone but her.

The woman murmured in his ear that he should start by carving his name into the servant girl's flesh. That way, she would always remember whose blade it was from—*Anton the Brave.*

"Anton!"

A warm hand knocked the sword from his grasp. The woman's presence left him. Adelia was shaking him by the shoulders, her eyes frantically searching his. Anton blinked. He could breathe again. The air felt crisper, cleaner. He met his sister's gaze, and his feet seemed more grounded than they had been a moment ago.

Adelia slowly let go of him, then took a big step back, her eyes suddenly fixed on the floor. "Pull yourself together," she said under her breath.

Alexander was rubbing his forehead, one hand clenching and unclenching his sword. "It's all my fault... it's all my fault..."

"My lord!" One of his brother's lieutenants ran up, limping with his left leg. "Are you all right?"

"I'm fine," said Alexander. "Search for survivors. Everyone

else, gather anything essential. We need to move out now. It's too dangerous to linger here. We'll have to backtrack to the eastern outpost we passed around noon and figure out what to do from there."

Anton was finally able to look around. The pristine snow was marred by a crimson stain. Bodies from both sides lay everywhere, and it didn't seem like anyone else made it out alive, except for Alexander's horse, which was sniffing the body of another. The wagons were destroyed, and pieces of half-burnt wood littered the area. It was a narrow win but a devastating loss, all the same. If the Lanadese had sent even one or two more men, they might not have made it at all.

They all trudged through the carnage. Anton was acutely aware of every sound, and he couldn't help but flinch when Adelia flung open the carriage door. The lieutenant was checking over every barbarian to make sure that they were dead, but there were no more Anadese survivors. Anton almost lost his stomach when he came across one of their men's heads. Almost their entire squad was taken out by a dozen Lanadese. If they had done this to strike fear into their people's hearts, it was going to work.

He picked up one of their axes, almost dropping it from the weight, before peering at the blackscale. It had a wide blade on one side and a narrow blade on the other. The metal was impossibly black, with thin, iridescent threads running through the blades. He gave it a few experimental swings before swinging it straight down onto a stray wooden shield, splitting it in half as if it hadn't met any resistance at all. It was as close to a clean break as it could get. Anton shook his head. No wonder they had lost so badly.

He kept the axe, heading back to the others. It was a pity

that they wouldn't be able to carry the rest of them, but it was heavy enough to take just one. Adelia was tucking the book she always carried in a pouch around her waist, and the servant girl had an axe over one shoulder and the short sword of her opponent in her other hand. He was not going to walk in front of her, that was for sure.

Alexander handed his horse's reins to the lieutenant. "Ride ahead to the outpost and have them meet us, then send word to the castle to get us back home."

"At once, my lord."

As the lieutenant disappeared into the forest, Alexander turned to the three of them. "We'll have to go on foot and quickly. It's probably a few hours trek back. There's every chance there are more Lanadese out there, and it's almost dusk. "

They set out immediately, leaving the wreckage behind. Anton rubbed his arm as he walked. His episodes were returning and in full force. It had taken years for the shadows to leave him, but he guessed that they would never truly leave —like a disease that clung to his mind, a fungus that lay dormant, just waiting for the opportunity to consume him. Although, *him* didn't quite exist anymore. Perhaps this was what it was like to turn into an undesirable. He tripped over a hidden glass-like root but caught himself before he fell. If he was fated to lose his mind in the end, there wasn't really much to lose.

Anton could hear the panting behind him as his sister stumbled her way through the snow with her silly book. She refused to look at him, concentrating, instead, on the ground. Her face was flushed, and she was clearly exhausted, but she was keeping up. He would certainly struggle in a dress, but his little sister was one of the most tenacious people he knew.

Alexander was maintaining a steady pace just behind her, scanning their rear every so often. The servant girl was just ahead of them, scouting the forest. As she flitted between the trees, the weapons she held seemed as light as air.

Anton gripped the heavy axe. His brother was blind not to execute her on the spot; even he could recognize a skilled assassin. He had seen her face when she did it—expressionless. That was the face of someone completing an errand, and it clearly wasn't her first time killing another person. No wonder she was an awful servant; it'd clearly never been her day job. She was just like *her.* Maybe that's why his episodes were returning—it was yet another reason to despise her.

The outpost came into view as the last of the light disappeared behind the silverlight trees, casting threatening shadows along the ground. In the near-dark, the slightest movement startled him. Their men ran to meet them, helping them inside the tiny outpost.

It wasn't long before Anton sank into the bath, the steam clearing his mind. Now that he could relax for a moment, exhaustion hit him all at once. He massaged his jaw and inspected his body. Thankfully, the horse hadn't broken anything, and the barbarian hadn't managed to do any real damage. Besides a few dark bruises, he was all in one piece.

"Mama... what do I do?" he whispered.

The face of the man he had killed lingered when he shut his eyes, and the smell of his breath was still under his nose. He had never been out on more than a mundane patrol or done more than spar with the other men. Now, he was a killer. He didn't seem to have much of a right to complain about the servant girl now. Alexander would, of course, assure him that it would mean nothing in due time, that it was either kill or be killed.

Anton scrubbed the flecks of blood from his skin, rubbing it raw. He brushed away the little blue lights, which were more of an annoyance than a comfort right now. Perhaps those were just his imagination, too—the effects of his mind falling further into instability. Maybe his brother was right to keep him away from all of this and shelter their city from the horrors of battle. He had to admit that he hadn't been able to pull himself together as well as his brother had.

The door opened at the same time as he heard the knock. Alexander let himself in, grabbing a chair and sitting down beside the bath. Anton scrambled to pull his knees to his chest, the water sloshing around. He was having a bad enough day as it was, but now his brother probably wanted to lecture him, or worse, make small talk.

"May I not have one moment of peace?" he growled.

Alexander shook his head. "We need to talk. Are you okay, Brother?"

Clearly, small talk it was. Anton turned his face to the wall so that Alexander wouldn't see his eyes roll. He might not have been able to handle himself, but he didn't need to be reminded of the fact. "I'm fine. If you came for a brotherly chat, I'd appreciate my time alone."

"I don't believe you're fine."

"I'm currently in the bath. Leave me alone."

Alexander ignored him, leaning forward with his elbow on his knee. "I'm sorry. I should have listened to you."

Anton's ears pricked up. He couldn't have heard that correctly.

"If I had just told you to stay in Anadrieth with everyone else, you wouldn't have had to go through that," Alexander continued.

Anton almost slapped his forehead. "That's not what I said at all."

"I'm just trying to protect you." Alexander clasped his hands together. "And these... episodes still seem to affect you."

"If you didn't keep pushing me aside, maybe I wouldn't have reacted like that. Maybe I'd *actually* be able to fight by your side. Maybe I'd—"

Alexander was suddenly in his face. "You almost died! It's a miracle you were able to survive when the rest of my men are dead. I have to tell their families that I let their husbands and fathers die on my watch, but I would have had to *live* with your death."

Anton shook his head. "Sorry my death would cause you so much of a problem."

His brother clenched his teeth, letting out a breath. He sat back down in a deliberate motion, closing his eyes for a moment. "I can't see you get hurt again."

"And yet, you keep that servant girl in our midst."

"She's not—"

Anton hit the water with his hand. "You saw her," he hissed. "You can't possibly tell me she's not a danger to us."

"I *will* take care of it."

"There was even an imperial scout at the scene, and dragons knows how they're involved in all of this. You don't have everything under control, and that's exactly why you should have let us help."

Alexander stood, his expression dark. "Your only job is to stay alive and safe. Can you manage that?"

Anton stared at him in disbelief, almost letting out a laugh. "You're not Mama," he muttered. "So, don't you dare try and act like her."

His brother opened his mouth but stormed out, instead, slamming the door behind him.

Anton huddled in the bath for all but a few moments before launching himself out to get dressed. He didn't bother drying himself properly, and his clothes stuck to his slick skin. He gripped his head. This was ridiculous. He was sure that if his brother had it his way, he and his sister would be locked in a cage. Anton took a few deep breaths before walking down the hall. It wouldn't look good if anyone else saw him lose his composure.

Raised voices echoed from the main room, and he crept closer. It sounded like his siblings. The door flung open, barely missing his face. Adelia burst out, shooting a glare behind her, then at him.

"I don't know who either of you are anymore, but you're not my brothers."

Anton's eyes widened, and Alexander emerged from the room, stalking off in the other direction. Adelia rarely lost her temper, unlike their brother, but Anton shook it off, heading straight for bed. He didn't even know what he'd done this time. Maybe he shouldn't have gotten out of the bath. He collapsed into the pillows, exhaustion sending him into a restless sleep.

The next morning, several horses were waiting for them, and they returned to the castle in a much quicker fashion than they had left. Thankfully, it was a less-than-eventful journey, though none of them spoke to each other, except for a few curt exchanges. The servant girl was silent, too, almost annoyingly so, and she handled a horse as well as she handled a blade. She reminded Anton of a hunter watching their prey, waiting for the right moment to strike. He wasn't about to lose sight of her, though—he yawned—or at least, he would do his best not to lose sight of her. Sleep had come easy, but it hadn't stayed that way.

By the time they had finally arrived back at the castle in the late afternoon, their reception was nothing short of unexpected. Not only was his brother's council waiting in the courtyard, but so was their entire household and a group of well-armed soldiers. Some of their people pressed their faces up against the glass, while others poked their heads out behind pillars, as though they expected something to happen. Anton frowned. Whatever it was, it wasn't going to be good.

Alexander dismounted, approaching his councilors. "What is the meaning of all this?" He gestured to the onlookers.

Councilor Dallan stepped forward, bowing curtly. "My apologies, my lord. We simply wanted a moment of your time, but the news seems to have spread like wildfire. We tried to keep it quiet, but they appear to have heard, regardless."

General Barrett gestured at the injured lieutenant who they had sent back before them. "He informed us of the terrible tragedy which befell you, which we will address... but I had to see it with my own eyes." Barrett pointed directly at the servant girl. "A squad of my most well-trained soldiers, armed and prepared, fall to an ambush, yet out of the few survivors, this girl is one of them. There should have been no chance that she would survive," he tilted his nose up at her, "unless she was the one who led the barbarians to you in the first place."

All eyes fell on the servant, including Anton's. The general wasn't wrong, but he wasn't exactly right, either. It was clear that she had killed the barbarian with her own strength, and though it may have been a complicated ruse, if she *had* been luring them into a trap, she would surely have let his sister die.

"We wish to arrest her on suspicion of treason," said General Barrett triumphantly.

Anton wanted her gone as much as the general; they could at least agree on that. But he couldn't quite squash the nagging feeling of indebtedness toward her, as much as he tried. If she were found guilty of treason, it would mean the death penalty. Anton glanced at his brother, who kept a blank face.

"Denied."

"My lord—"

"Denied."

The servant girl stepped forward, staring down the general without a word. She grabbed her right sleeve, tearing away a strip of cloth and dropping it at the general's feet. The air around her was still, as though everyone held their breath.

Anton narrowed his eyes. Surely, she wasn't about to do that.

The girl spoke to the general in a clear voice that was loud enough for all to hear.

"I challenge you to a duel."

CHAPTER NINE

ADELIA

ADELIA ALMOST TRIPPED as she dismounted the horse and ran over to Mina. A duel? She did not just say that. No one beat the general. Adelia dug her fingernails into Mina's arm, but Mina's gaze was locked onto the general's. There was no way that she was going to let her best friend go to her death.

Alexander interjected. "Absolutely not—"

Mina gestured at the cloth. "Anadrieth's standard practice for disputes of honor is currently a duel, Alexander. If that isn't how you want things to be done, you should change them." She pointed to the general. "If you win, you may do whatever you like." Her voice was strangely calm. "If I win, you'll admit my innocence."

General Barrett stroked his chin, and a smile formed on his face. "Standard practice it is, then. Of course, I will not back down from a challenge. And as the challenged, I decide the weapon..." he mused. "I admire your courage, girl, but it will be your undoing."

Adelia let go of Mina's arm. They were right. Everyone has the right to challenge an accusation, but it had never been done by a servant. Even most of their soldiers wouldn't dare challenge their general. But it was their law, and neither she nor her brother could do anything about it now.

She'd already pointed out how unjust it was, but her brother had been more concerned about the fact that his people enjoyed the sport. But the general never lost a battle; the accused were given a chance, but they were simply thrown into the dungeons, anyway.

Adelia sighed. This was different. General Barrett despised Mina and would surely ask for her death. Alexander wouldn't have the right to intercede like he would if she were simply arrested. This was just a quicker route to her execution. Adelia's shoulders drooped. It seemed like no matter what happened, she would never truly have a say in the matter. If Papa were here, he would know what to do about it.

The crowd began to shift, and people began pushing and shoving each other as they headed toward the arena. Mina and the general followed them, but Adelia and her brothers lingered. Alexander seemed to be at a loss, staring blankly after the crowd, while Anton was rubbing his arms. There was an odd feeling coming from him, like he wasn't happy about the situation, even though it was clear that Anton had never liked Mina.

Adelia shook her head, shooting a glare at her brothers, before hurrying after Mina. They weren't her concern right now. Mina had saved her life—in more ways than one. She had always been able to count on her to be there every morning, to never judge her for what she did or said, to be by her side. Her steps fell quicker. Perhaps there was nothing she could do to stop this, but she would never let Mina face her fate alone.

Adelia caught up with her in the armory beside the arena, pulling out clothes from several chests and sizing them up. Mina leaned over the chest for a moment, and her eyes squeezed shut, her breath coming out in pants. Adelia gently put a hand on her shoulder.

...A desolate wasteland. Sky blue eyes. Beautiful scales, like ice...

Adelia recoiled as images flashed through her mind. Mina's skin was burning.

...White hair. A loving embrace. A great lake, dancing...

Adelia rubbed her head, taking a step back. What was going on?

Mina took a deep breath, giving her a smile, and the stifling atmosphere ebbed away. "How are you feeling?"

"Me?" asked Adelia.

"You've been really quiet since we left the outpost."

"I'm... fine," Adelia said. It wasn't entirely true, but although the last day hadn't exactly been pleasant, she wasn't about to break down as her brother had. There were times when a proper lady must hold herself together, and this was most certainly one of them.

Mina went back to rifling through the clothes, which were a mix of spare uniforms and pieces of leather armor. "Can you see if you can find something more suitable?" She gestured at her dress. "Everything is far too big."

"Right," said Adelia. She pried open another chest in the corner, which appeared to be full of leftover costumes from the festival. Something white caught her eye. It was a dancer's costume, the elegant flowing fabric designed to look like a lyrecrane in flight. Like the pendant Mina had given her, it was a symbol of good fortune.

"That'll do. As long as it has pants." Mina took it from her, ducking behind a folding screen to change.

Adelia fiddled with her hands. "Why?" The word slipped from her lips; she couldn't stay quiet any longer.

"Because I'll need the movement."

Adelia held back a frustrated sigh. "No, why are you doing this? I know you're not a Lanadese spy, and we could have proven it another way." There was no response, just the rustling of clothing. "Do you even know what you're doing?" She couldn't help the rise in her voice. If Mina lost, she would die. If she won through skill, it would only appear to prove the general's point in front of everyone. Adelia waited for another moment, but Mina didn't answer. She shoved the screen to the side. "Are you listening to me?"

Mina fell straight into her, knocking them both to the floor. Her touch seemed to connect their very minds together.

...Searing agony. New flesh, tearing bone. Freedom...

Adelia opened her mouth to scream, but nothing came out. Everything was burning, the vivid scenes overwhelming her mind.

...Mountainous form. Clay scent. Shaking ground...

The room was gone, and her senses flooded with rapid, broken images. Or were they memories?

...Ethereal wings. Sudden gale. Delicate wisps...

She had never seen anything like it, but at the same time, it was familiar.

...Shrieking call. Burning plume. Falling ashes...

Energy coursed through her body from the tips of her fingers to her toes.

...Slippery scales. Monstrous surge. Dripping fangs...

Then, everything was silent, and a strange calm fell over her. Adelia blinked.

Mina was on her feet, adjusting the belt to her waist, though it was normally worn higher to accentuate the bust. Her face told the story of complete normality, but there was an overwhelming feeling of confused exhaustion surrounding her. Adelia tentatively pushed against the stone ground to get up. It was solid and real, thankfully. There had been no mistake about it; what she'd seen wasn't of this realm, and it wasn't a vision or a dream—it felt like memories.

"Mina," she said slowly. "Who are you?"

Mina met her gaze. Her eyes were clouded and distant, as though she weren't really there at all.

"I'm not sure."

"You're not... human, are you?" pressed Adelia. The silence was unnerving.

"I am... mortal."

There was a knock at the door before it creaked open slightly.

"Are you ready in there?" called a voice.

Mina nodded at Adelia and headed out. "Everything will be fine."

Adelia clutched the pendant around her neck and shivered. What she had seen—no, what she had *experienced*—was nothing short of terrifying. Her near-death experience earlier didn't even come close. Whatever was going on was far greater than her, perhaps determining the balance of the entire world. The only thing she knew for sure was that the legends about which she'd read in her books—the spirit realm, the dragon gods, the four elemental guardians—were no mere myths.

Adelia entered the arena after composing herself, squinting as she stepped out into the bright sunlight. The stands were packed to the brim with people, and there was an air of unbridled excitement as the spectators jostled in their seats, vying for the best vantage point. It seemed like no one wanted to be left out, and she didn't blame them; this unprecedented act would be the talk of Anadrieth for months. A woman against a man, a servant against a general. It would certainly be a one-of-a-kind show, and their people weren't shy about voicing their opinions.

"Put her in her place!"

"That general's taking it a bit far—"

"Last bets!"

"Traitor!"

"—liar."

Adelia peered around, searching for a friendly face, as she tried to shut out their comments. Whatever rumor had gone around had clearly spun out of control, and it showed just how easily people could be influenced by a few words. Of course, no one wanted to believe that Mina had saved her life without believing that she was some sort of Lanadese assassin. They probably thought that today's main event would be a hanging. Somehow, Adelia wasn't as worried about Mina as she'd been before.

She ended up at the front of the arena next to Elaine and spied Anton not far from her, who was keeping a watchful eye on Mina as she stood in the middle of the arena. Alexander, on the other hand, was pacing along the sidelines, clearly distressed. The other councilors were gathered in the seats behind him, whispering to each other. She couldn't quite see their faces, but she could imagine their collective disdain. Finally, General Barrett emerged from the other side of the armory, brandishing two heavy swords with blades that looked almost as wide as her palm.

"Dirty bastard," spat Elaine. "Full of himself, he is. Those are two-handed swords, lass. Don't know who he's trying to impress."

Adelia glanced around. His men certainly weren't taking to his display; they were calling out in disgust and shaking their heads. The general was obviously trying to put Mina at a humiliating disadvantage, but it only made him look like a conceited fool. Adelia turned back to Elaine.

"I didn't think you'd be here."

"Can't a woman leave her work for a minute?"

"Well, yes, but—"

Elaine narrowed her eyes. "Didn't think I'd be interested, did you?" She pointed a stubby finger at Mina. "That lass is something else, and you should pay close attention to this fight."

Adelia stared at her. Elaine was never anything but practical, and she always had a reason for the things she did, even if those reasons weren't always clear.

"What do you know?"

"Don't know nothing. That's why I'm here. Just a feeling I have."

It wasn't entirely convincing, but when Elaine didn't want to speak about something, her jaws shut tighter than a bearion claiming its prey. Adelia gripped the wooden barricade, leaning into the arena as General Barrett reached the center, with one sword thrust out toward Mina. Their difference in height was painfully obvious.

Barrett turned his nose up, flicking his hair across his back. "White suits you," he said. "Though it won't stay white for long. Would you prefer the sword or the rope?"

Mina grabbed the hilt. "Neither. My fate is already determined."

Barrett raised an eyebrow. "Oh? Enlighten me."

Mina ignored him, tucking a strand of hair behind her ear and glancing up and down at the sword. "An interesting choice of weapon. You want to show off your prowess with a difficult sword and disadvantage me at the same time. How honorable."

General Barrett cracked his knuckles. "I don't care what you think. I'm here to show everyone we have no mercy for traitors, and your sentence is long overdue."

Mina smirked. "Not today, Barrett."

They retreated ten paces, as was custom, waiting for the signal to begin. Mina let her sword trail along the ground, still sheathed. Barrett, however, tossed his sheath to the ground in a grandiose gesture, swinging the great sword around with flair. Some of the crowd whooped, others jeered.

Adelia's eyes were glued to the scene. She knew Barrett well and had seen him train many times before. He was right-handed, which often resulted in unprotected areas on his left side, especially since he'd cracked his left rib last month, and an old injury had left him slightly deaf in his right ear. He was overconfident to a fault and would often taunt his opponents into making a mistake before finishing them off with a frightful combination of speed and strength—the skills that earned him his title.

He wouldn't even consider the possibility of losing to a woman who apparently couldn't even fully pick up her heavy weapon. But Mina was gripping her sword with the familiarity of an old friend. She stood tall, without a hint of nervousness. Although Adelia had had her eyes closed during the ambush, she was sure that Mina was capable of more than she seemed. Adelia shook her head.

"Even if she can fight, it's still been two years..." she muttered. Even the best fighter wouldn't be at their peak if they hadn't been practicing.

Elaine scoffed. "Ain't got nothing to do with training. Use your eyes, lass." She tapped her temple.

Adelia frowned. "I am."

"Not those eyes." Elaine pulled her down by the back of her head.

Adelia stared hard at the arena, but all she could see was Alexander exchanging frantic words with his councilors. When he trudged toward his seat in the middle of the arena, she knew that he had failed to convince them to stop the duel. The crowd began to quieten down, and all eyes were on their lord. He was meant to begin a duel by acknowledging the two opponents' merits or transgressions, but he was silent. Alexander simply raised his hand.

"Begin."

The two opponents faced each other. Neither of them moved. General Barrett spread his arms out, as though he were doing her a great service by giving her the first opportunity, but Mina hadn't even drawn her blade, the sheath still in place as the tip of her sword rested on the gravel. He shrugged and began to close the gap, circling her. Still, she didn't move.

General Barrett kicked off from the ground, rushing toward her. He swung with a confident stroke that would cleave any man in half. But Mina was gone. Barrett spun around to see her standing behind him, clutching her sword as it dug into the ground.

Adelia blinked. Had she missed the dodge? As General Barret swung over and over to meet only air, Adelia smiled. His irritation was rippling off of him, and she savored every moment.

Barrett's face was twisted into a scowl, his eye twitching. He paused, scanning the ground. Adelia strained her eyes, as well. The only patterns on the gravel seemed to be his, as though Mina hadn't even moved. She was beginning to think that Elaine was right; maybe there was something more going on.

"Running away won't win you this battle... you've underestimated my stamina," Barrett growled, coming at her with a series of heavy attacks. Mina moved effortlessly, just out of reach each time.

Adelia squinted. There was a gentle hum radiating from her, like something was simmering just below the surface. She was definitely moving, that was for sure. But no human could move that fast.

"I'm not running," said Mina.

General Barrett grunted, sweat beginning to roll from his brow. "Then, draw your sword."

Mina tilted her head. "I only draw my weapon when I intend to kill."

Adelia involuntarily shivered. It wasn't the words that struck her—it was the feeling that was emanating from her. She wanted to fall to her knees and flee at the same time, but her hands were firmly stuck on the barricade. An ethereal violet glow appeared to flow from Mina's body, the shimmering outline not quite human, commanding attention —obedience.

General Barrett's mouth hung open, but he didn't have time to retort. Mina raced toward him, and the very air itself seemed to part for her, offering no resistance. Barrett swung his sword, though somehow it was far slower than it had been, as though it was much harder for him to cut through the air. Earth connected with Mina's feet, and her last step launched her into the air, the energy propelling her into a graceful flip. For a split second, she landed neatly on his sword, mid-swing. Her own weapon followed close behind, crashing down into his shoulder. The impact reverberated, forcing the general's grip to loosen and the sword to fly from his hand.

He stumbled, spinning on his heel to retrieve it. Mina rushed after him as Barrett aimed for her throat. She ducked with perfect timing, and his sword arced clear over her head. She slammed her hilt into his ribs with the momentum of her charge, and there was an audible crack as Barrett clutched his left side, faltering back. He spat blood on the ground, wiping it away with the back of his hand. With a roar, he ran at her again.

The arena was in absolute silence, the only sound being the blunt whack of metal hitting leather. Mina wielded the heavy sword with ease, never once unsheathing the blade. She struck his sword over and over at what seemed to be the same spot on the blade. It was a relentless onslaught, like the force of a great sea crashing into land or the insatiable frenzy of a fire consuming the earth. She had an otherworldly strength that was both beautiful and terrifying.

Adelia's mouth was dry, and her knees were shaking. The undeniable presence of *something* was growing stronger as the violet hue spilled from Mina in waves. It was the same presence that she had felt from her during the ambush, only far more potent this time. She stole a glance at the people around her, but all she could feel was their awe. Elaine was scratching her chin and nodding her head. Alexander seemed as confused as ever. Anton, however, was frozen to the spot, clutching his forearms like he did when he was having an episode.

Mina's sword slammed into the general's, and the metal gave way. Barrett's eyes widened as shards of steel flew past his face, hitting the gravel. He stared at the broken sword before collapsing to his knees. The enchantment that the duel had cast on the crowd shattered, and the crowd erupted into cheers.

But Adelia couldn't breathe. The aura had spread across the arena, blanketing them in a suffocating presence. She leaned against the barricade. Their cheers were muffled, and the air was hazy. A fainting spell? No, this wasn't physical. She tugged on Elaine's sleeve.

"Can't you feel it?" she managed.

Elaine peered at her in silence. Her gray eyes seemed older than they'd ever been, weighed down by life.

"Barely." Elaine pulled her arm away. "Then again, I ain't one of you." Her voice had almost dropped to an inaudible level.

"One of... me?" Adelia frowned. The aura over the arena shifted, becoming sharper, and a deep rumbling echoed through the air. She whipped her head back up.

"Now, that, I can hear," said Elaine.

The medics dashed over to General Barrett, but it was

Mina who was doubled over, clutching her head. The rumbling was getting louder, and people were starting to look around. Mina threw her head back, letting out a roar—a sound that would have been impossible for a human to make. General Barrett was kicking the gravel to scramble back, and the trees surrounding the arena bent backward, their branches snapping and groaning in distress.

Adelia shoved her fingers in her ears, though the noise was still shaking her to her core. She wanted nothing more than to hide in the safety of her bed, but another part of her desperately wanted to go to Mina. There was a sense of great sadness surrounding her friend, like a confused, wounded animal, desperate to return home—a wandering spirit separated from its body.

The roar gradually subsided and took with it the suffocating aura. Mina let go of her sword and bolted, disappearing into the Celestine Forest a few moments later. Adelia let out a breath, and her feet finally felt the solid ground again. Something told her not to go after her.

Their people seemed mostly in shock, not knowing whether to stay or leave. Anton's face was pale as he glanced around wildly, tripping over himself. She couldn't see Alexander in the confusion, but he wasn't in his seat.

Nothing made sense, and Adelia wanted answers. She grabbed Elaine's hand, dragging her out of the arena, and she was somewhat surprised that Elaine didn't resist. That old woman had a grip like a bearion, too. They made their way toward her bedroom, away from the growing cacophony of voices. She was sure that Alexander would sort out their people, just as he always did.

Adelia locked the door behind them, her fingers lingering

on the handle. Her mind was a whirlwind, her thoughts crashing against each other in a jumbled mess. An ambush. A potential betrayal. The impending war. Her best friend wasn't a human. Was Adelia herself even human? The marriage seemed like such a trivial problem now.

She turned to Elaine, who had taken a seat on her bed. She had to know something. Adelia sat next to her, unsure of where to start.

"Been around since your parents were little, I have," said Elaine. "Seen a lot in my time. I know you've got questions, but I can't answer them."

"But why?"

Elaine hiked up Adelia's skirt in one swift motion, revealing the jagged, circular scar that marred the smooth skin of her leg. Adelia pulled her hem back down in an instant, gritting her teeth.

"No one knows about that except for the people who were there." Elaine clicked her tongue. "You're not the only Winter who has begged me to keep secrets, you know. If it's not your story to tell, don't tell it, I always say."

Adelia gripped her dress. It was true. A proper lady always kept her body pristine and pure.

Young ladies should not have battle scars. Only your husband will know of it, on your wedding night.

Besides her family, no one else would ever know. It was a shameful, childish mistake.

Elaine's face softened; somehow, it seemed like even more wrinkles appeared. "But maybe it's time to tell you mine."

Adelia perked up. Elaine had never been particularly secretive about her past. She had always had a heart for helping others, and when the castle realized that she had talent, she was placed under the service of Adelia's grandfather. That was all there was to it.

Elaine lifted her palms. "Healers hands, they called it. Remnants of the ancient spirit arts. A long-lost gift." She balled her hands into fists. "I despise it. Always have."

Adelia's eyes widened. She never would have thought that.

"It's unnatural, it is. It stole me away from my family. Not because it was a gift, but because it was something to keep a watch on. The empire has a strange opinion on the spirit arts. Folks like you are curious, interested. But others, including me, believe it's like dirt, a stain on the inside. You've seen how the other nurses look at me, you have."

Adelia slowly nodded. She did seem to be the only one who was truly interested in the subject; even her brothers tended to avoid it. "But you've saved so many lives."

"And it has aged me, drained me faster than it should've." Elaine sighed. "And it's gotten people killed."

Adelia shook her head. "Some people can't be saved. That's not your fault."

"Lass, this one is. I was just a little girl myself at the time. I don't remember when it started, but I began feeling weaker and weaker. Losing my mind, like my feet weren't firm on the ground, and I was neither here nor there."

Elaine closed her eyes for a moment. "I remember a woman, hair as golden as the sun, with two little girls. She found me in the forest one day, wandering without purpose. And suddenly, everything was better. The world was sharper, clearer, as if I was connected to everything, like a tree digging its roots into the soil. She took me in, told me everything would be all right."

Elaine turned away. "I didn't thank her. I ran. I started

seeing these little blue lights. She'd done something to me, something unnatural, and I was scared. I told the guards and brought them to her house." Elaine paused. "It was just the woman, then, like she knew I was bringing trouble. The girls were gone. There was evidence of the spirit arts—books and whatnot. And they killed her right in front of me. Beat her till there was nothing left. Shared my opinion, the guards did, that the unnatural should be put down."

Adelia was silent. It was wrong, but she couldn't condemn her. Elaine was like a mother to her, and this didn't change that fact.

Elaine shrugged. "My opinion hasn't changed, but... there's a part of me that regrets it. She showed me nothing but kindness." Elaine pulled a small flask from her medic's pouch, pouring water into her hand. "Wasn't long after that when I discovered that she'd made me into one of them." The water shifted into a sphere, then circled around her hand, breaking off into tiny streams that danced in the air.

Adelia's mouth opened. She reached out a hand to touch it, but the water shied away, sliding back into Elaine's flask.

"Healing ain't the only thing I can do, lass. Not really my forte, but water is designed for many things." Elaine put the stopper back in. "And so, I'd become what I despised. Different. My parents despised me, too, and if it wasn't for your grandfather, I might have been on the streets. No one could deny my talents, but I've learned that we are afraid of things we cannot understand, and no one could understand me, not even myself. But I was useful, far more so than regular medicine. The soldiers, in particular, took a liking to me," said Elaine with a little chuckle. "It wasn't until you three were born that I came face to face with one of the woman's daughters."

"What happened?" asked Adelia after a long pause.

"That's someone else's story to tell. And I'm afraid they've taken it to their grave."

Adelia bit her tongue. Of course. There was no point in pressing her for the rest of the story if she'd made a promise. But that didn't mean that she couldn't ask her way around it. "So, you're saying I'm one of *them?* Aren't you one, too?"

"Don't know for sure. I don't study them old books like you do. You'd know more than me. I only know what I've figured out myself. But you're different, too. You're more like those kids' mother than me."

Adelia had a suspicion, but she wasn't sure. People like Elaine seemed to be able to sense and use water, like she did for healing. But people like the mother in the forest had a different purpose. The pieces were starting to come together.

Elaine stood, her motion stiff. "Only reason I'm telling you is because I want you to know I don't despise you." She smoothed her sleeves down. "Fear my decision had a bigger effect than I could have imagined, though." She gave her a grim smile. "And I think you're about to have your hands full with that servant girl."

Adelia was on her feet. She had completely forgotten. "I have to go look for her."

"Nay, I don't think you should. Even I felt it, and I'm not like you. That lass is dangerous."

"I can't stand around and do nothing."

Elaine stared at her. "Sometimes, nothing is the best thing you can do." She unlocked the door with a click. "I need to return to the infirmary. Promise me you won't do anything stupid." Elaine didn't wait for a response, and the door shut behind her.

Adelia buried her face in the pillows.

She might be right.

She'd never seen Mina like that before, but there wasn't much that she could do about it. Besides, the last time she'd run off into the forest by herself, it hadn't ended well. She shuddered, brushing the jagged circular scar on her leg. The marriage wasn't such a big deal, after all, considering everything else. Adelia fingered her lyrecrane pendant, gazing at the brilliant shine of its wings.

Mina's smile flashed in her mind. Not long after, she felt the suffocating aura again. Adelia unlatched the window, leaning out into the night. It was faint, but it could only be Mina.

I hope she's okay.

CHAPTER TEN

ALEXANDER

ALEXANDER CLAPPED his hands over his ears, bracing himself against his seat. An awful sound was coming from Mina, a roar that pierced his spirit, the vibrations threatening to burst his eardrums. And yet... the sound was reminiscent of a lost child, wandering the streets in despair.

Then, it stopped.

The scene hung in the air, as though frozen in time. His people cowered in the stands, and no one moved a muscle. His general scrambled backward, trying to find his feet as he limped away, tripping over himself. Mina bolted toward the forest.

As if something had snapped, everyone ran for the exits. Alexander was pushed back against a sea of people, soldiers and servants alike clambering to get as far away as they could from the terrifying display. An arm hit him in the chest, a heavy foot crashed down on top of his, an elbow struck him in the shoulder. People seemed to look past him, their desperation akin to beasts about to be slaughtered.

Alexander gritted his teeth, weaving his way through the crowd, shielding his face but taking care not to hurt anyone. When he emerged on the other side of the arena, opposite the exits, he let out a long breath.

What am I doing?

He was just as perplexed as everyone else, but if there was ever a time his people needed a leader, it was now. Yet, he found himself staring at her footprints at the edge of the Celestine Forest, hesitant to follow. Now was not the time to lose his head.

Alexander planted his feet, taking a few deep breaths. If he went straight to his people before finding Mina, they would surely cause a riot against her—the servant girl who displayed otherworldly powers. His soldiers were part of the frightened crowd, and he wasn't sure that he could control their fear alone. This was a far cry from anything they had dealt with before. His people tolerated Elaine because she was the best healer in the land, but Mina had instilled a primal terror within them. His father's voice echoed in his mind.

The unknown is often the greatest source of fear.

His father was right. If he could understand her, if they could all understand everything that had happened, they may no longer need to be afraid. Alexander rubbed his knees, urging them to stop trembling. He had two choices. He could stay, give in to the fear of the unknown, bury his head in the sand and rally his people behind what they thought they knew; that would be the route that most leaders would choose. Or he could pursue the truth, no matter the cost.

Alexander turned toward the forest. He could already see

Mina's gentle smile, the way she gave every aspect of a situation careful thought.

All weeds are killed by pulling them from the roots, not by plucking a few leaves off or breaking the stem.

He took one step, then another. To stay would only be applying a bandage to a wound. He had to find answers, and there was only one person who had them. He broke into a run. Perhaps she even held the key to stopping the war. Alexander controlled his breathing, ducking under branches and leaping over almost invisible roots. His hazy reflection danced across the silverlight trees as the last rays of sunlight disappeared behind them.

The snow grew thick as he trudged deeper into the forest, but her footprints seemed to be getting farther and farther apart. He slowed to a jog, his senses more alert. Soon, he seemed to hit the end of the trail entirely. He spun in circles, catching his breath, careful to note where his own footprints lay. This was definitely the end of her trail. In these conditions, there shouldn't have been anything to cover her tracks. It was as if she had disappeared entirely.

Alexander examined his surroundings, mentally calculating his whereabouts. He recognized the two silverlight trees partially intertwined. The ravine would be a dozen yards to the west. He was around halfway to their northern border, a long way for anyone to run. He put his ear up to the tree and closed his eyes, the glasslike wood cold on his ear. There was a faint vibration, and it didn't sound like the Moonstone River. Slowly, the vibration turned into a low rumble.

Alexander ducked behind a large shrub. He regretted not taking his cloak with him, as the pattern was built to blend in with the snow and cover his red hair. He could hear the rumble loud and clear now. The distinct sound of heavy footsteps—a lot of them. His border scouts should have alerted him, but maybe the Lanadese had already gotten to them. He drew his sword, laying close to the floor and stealing a glance. Faint lights in the distance reflected through the trees as the lanterns bobbed through the forest, illuminating the soldiers' path as dusk gave way to night.

There had to be about fifty of them, all completely armored and armed, a standard party for *unfriendly* negotiations. Not large enough to be an army, but obviously not your average scouting party. Alexander narrowed his eyes. They were wearing white and gold—the imperial colors, not Lanadese. He let out a sigh of relief. Prince Yukiya had received his message after all and was sending reinforcements.

Still, it was a bit strange that no one had come to inform him of their arrival. Perhaps in all of the confusion, the message had just slipped through the ranks. Alexander sheathed his sword, brushing off the snow as he stood. Maybe they could even help him look for Mina. He put his arm across his chest, then raised it in the air—the standard greeting for non-hostile parties.

"Greetings," he called.

The men came to a halt a few yards away, though his salute wasn't returned. The man on the horse acknowledged him with a small nod. His horse's mane and tail held decorations woven between the feathers, similar to his flashy uniform; he was clearly a high-ranking official. The man's head was smooth, except for the long, sleek ponytail that rose from the top, matching the two whiskers hanging limply above his lips.

"Greetings, Lord Alexander of Anadrieth." He didn't

dismount, but rather just stared down at him. "I am Commander Ido."

Alexander lowered his head in respect. He'd heard of the name, and though the imperial commander technically ranked just below him, he wasn't foolish enough to offend a powerful man. The commander had actually recognized him, too, which was surprising.

"I apologize for the lack of reception. I'm afraid I wasn't informed of your prompt arrival."

Commander Ido's face hardened, but his whiskers didn't move an inch. "Cut the formalities. Where is Mina?"

Alexander blinked. "I beg your pardon?"

"We have irrefutable intelligence that you've been concealing her this whole time."

Alexander's mind was racing. Was she a wanted criminal? A weapon? Someone of significance? He froze, his chest pounding. She couldn't be. But it would make so much sense.

Some of the imperial foot soldiers slowly approached him as Commander Ido unfurled a scroll.

"By order of Supreme Commander Yuno, Lord Alexander of Anadrieth is to be arrested for high treason against the Empire of the Dragon Gods on the charges of kidnapping, concealment and enslavement of Princess Mina, rightful heir to the throne, and of deliberately sabotaging the coronation, the wellbeing of the imperial family and the fate of the empire as whole." He enunciated each word, clearly enjoying every second. "Full authorization to execute without trial." Commander Ido tucked the scroll back into his belt. "Seize him."

Several men launched themselves at him before he could react, disarming him in an instant and shoving him to his knees. His arms were jerked behind him, his wrist bound in thick rope. Alexander kicked backward at a man's shin, but they piled on top of him, forcing his face into the ground.

"There's been a mistake," he cried. Someone was setting him up.

Commander Ido clicked his tongue. "I'll give you one chance to tell me where you're hiding her."

They pulled his head up by his hair. Alexander's mind reeled. *Mina* was the princess? "I don't know where—"

Ido snapped his fingers, and the man closest to Alexander whirled around to punch him in the jaw. The others quickly joined in.

Alexander bit down on his lip, a low grunt escaping him as he received a swift kick to the stomach. He shouldn't have gone off alone. This was a mistake. He had no idea. Alexander tasted blood, and his head was ringing. They ripped the back of his shirt open, gripping his chin to wave an open lantern in front of him.

"Last chance," said Commander Ido.

Alexander couldn't respond. He didn't know. They wouldn't believe him.

Ido shrugged and waved a hand. The burning oil dripped onto his back, forcing him to cry out in pain. The smell of his burnt and blistered flesh made him throw up. He coughed, heaving for air. Two men held him in place, turning him around to face his final moment. The third man held a blade high above his head.

Alexander gritted his teeth. It was already over, and he wouldn't give them the satisfaction of begging for his life. Anton would be forced to step up, but his councilmen would surely assist him. Adelia may not understand, but his arrangements for her future were for the best. Unless all of them were being dragged under the same charge. The bonds around his wrists grew unbearably cold as ice pricked around his hands, but there was nothing he could do to escape.

A white blur rushed toward them out of the corner of his eye—Mina. She leaped, pulling steel from thin air with a flash of light. Two swords materialized in her hands, and she swept her arms outward with sickening impact, landing in a crouch in front of him.

The head of his executioner rolled onto the ground, the snow eagerly lapping up its new crimson coat. The imperial soldiers let go of Alexander, scrambling for their weapons. They were too slow, and she skewered them both, with only a few drops of blood decorating her clothes.

Alexander couldn't look away.

"Mina," he whispered. She stood beside him, her powerful presence radiated around her. Alexander swallowed. Her swords had appeared out of nowhere, identical in every way, with a simple white hilt and cross guards and elegant gold spiraling around the grips. On the blades, a line of strange symbols glowed a soft white, and the imperial crest was engraved at the base.

Mina stood, facing Ido, a slow smile forming at the corner of her lips. "So, he's sent you on a suicide mission, has he? What did you do?" she purred. "Get too close to the councilor's daughter again?"

Commander Ido bristled. His horse reversed into the others, and his men looked as shaken as the animal. Ido yanked on the reins to steady his mount, then grinned.

"Quite the contrary. Supreme Commander Yuno, with the

seal of Prince Yukiya, has entrusted me on this esteemed mission to bring you back to the capital."

Mina laughed, though it was nothing like he'd heard before. "How... gullible." She twirled her sword in her hands. "They're always leaving me to do the dirty work," she muttered. "Come now, do you think he sent you with a small army of delinquents to take care of him?" She pointed at Alexander.

"You were always an arrogant brat," Ido spluttered. "Seize her!"

The men hesitated, as though they were waiting for each other to make the first advance.

"We are under orders to do *whatever* it takes," shouted Commander Ido, spurring them into action.

Alexander struggled with his bonds, blood slowly dripping over his eye from the cut on his forehead. The stabbing pain in his chest as he shifted declared itself as a few broken ribs, but he didn't have a choice. He had to help her.

"Quick, cut the rope," he called to her.

Mina strode forward, not sparing him a glance. As the first soldiers approached her, his struggles grew more urgent. He couldn't watch her get hurt.

The air seemed to grow still around them, and then it moved as she became a whirlwind of snow, spinning to block the first attack with one sword while thrusting the other through the first soldier's stomach. Using him as a shield, she struck again, and another fell. Soldier after soldier—none of them stood a chance.

Alexander's vision blurred as he doubled over, but the constant clang of metal rang in his ears. Commander Ido signaled to his rearguard, and a volley of arrows flew toward them. One of the soldiers weaved around her attacks, charging straight for Alexander. Mina whirled around, giving another soldier the opening to attack her from behind.

"Look out!" shouted Alexander.

Mina sprinted back toward him, hurling one sword at his attacker. She deflected an arrow mid-flight, leaving it to plunge into the soldier's side. He collapsed, writhing in pain. She turned to finish off the ones behind her, dodging and blocking the arrows with ease. She leaped over a dead soldier to retrieve her second sword, dropping into a roll under the last arrow.

Alexander could barely stay conscious. His wrists were cold as he felt the ice encase his bonds, though he didn't understand why it was happening now. He had never imagined Mina like this; a sense of bloodlust practically dripped from her. She was lost in the dance with her swords, a beautiful, deadly woman that was completely unknown to him. Or perhaps, that side of her had always been there—he had just never acknowledged it.

Mina paused amongst the carnage. "Enough of this nonsense," she muttered, her voice taking on a silky quality.

She stalked toward the middle of the clearing, dragging the tips of her swords through the snow. An intense rumbling came from below. The very earth cracked open along the path of her swords, which she flicked into the air, sending the widening fissures straight toward the remaining soldiers.

His men scrambled for their footing, but there was none. They climbed over each other, clawing and screaming as the chasms swallowed them into the abyss. Those clambering on the edges were ripped from what little hold they had left by an unnatural gust of wind. Not a single soldier remained, leaving Ido alone.

Almost as quickly as it had begun, Mina lowered her swords, and the ground began to seal itself, the sounds of their screams muffled by their earthly entombment. The landscape shifted to hide the evidence, and the forest regained its silence once more.

Alexander swallowed, but his mouth was dry. Surely, he was hallucinating from the pain—this was the stuff of legends and fairy tales. But he couldn't deny what he'd seen.

Her aura was the same as before, yet this time, it was much more dangerous. Alexander blinked several times. Mina was *shimmering*, for lack of a better description. She bent over, her knees buckling, leaning her weight on her swords, which were now pushed into the ground. It could only be the legendary power of the dragon gods.

Commander Ido roared, spurring his horse forward and drawing his sword as he charged toward her.

Mina readjusted her grip. His horse was upon her, and he swung at her still form, but hit only air. She dropped into a low crouch, pulling her swords free and slashing through the leather strap of his saddle. Ido slid sideways as the saddle slipped off. His horse reared as he yanked on the reins, but his attempts were useless, and he was dumped unceremoniously to the ground.

Rolling onto his feet, he lunged at her wildly. Mina dodged his attack and sliced through the flesh of his knee, drawing first blood. Ido spun to go on the offensive, and their swords met again and again.

Alexander's mind settled in a moment of clarity, and he glanced around him. There was a sword pierced through a nearby fallen soldier. He wriggled closer. He could cut the rope if only he could get there.

Mina and Ido paused in their duel, breathing heavily. Several lines of deep red seeped through Commander Ido's clothes, permanently staining his attire, while Mina remained unscathed. But she looked exhausted, her movements far less graceful than before.

Commander Ido sneered. "I can't understand why anyone wants you back. His Highness was doing just fine on his own." No sooner had the words left his mouth did her sword slash toward him. He barely dodged the stab, but the side of her blade made a deep slice through his cheek. He flicked his ponytail over his shoulder. "He does miss you, though."

Commander Ido blocked her swords, their blades close to his neck. Her frenzied attacks were landing more and more haphazardly, and Ido was forced on the defensive to shield himself.

Alexander tore his eyes away from the battle and heaved himself against the edge of the sword, attempting to saw away at his bonds. He winced. His wrists were stiff, and his chest was burning. He didn't feel like he was making much progress. Craning his neck, he saw that the shards of ice had begun to crystalize through the rope, freezing onto his skin. He frowned. He couldn't control it, though he didn't know if he even was controlling it.

Commander Ido roared, shoving Mina back in a burst of effort. Ido's eyes met Alexander's, and he sprinted toward the bound man. Mina caught herself mid-stumble, launching off of the balls of her feet after him.

Alexander lost his balance, falling on his side. He couldn't get up, and Ido's sword was seconds from him. He squeezed his eyes shut, bracing himself. Then, steel met flesh, the sickening sound amplified in his ears. He opened his eyes to see Mina grunting, her grip loosening on her sword as it fell into the snow.

Alexander's eyes widened. His bonds cracked, and then the ice shattered, freeing his hands.

No!

Commander Ido had his blade triumphantly twisted through Mina's right shoulder, the bloodied tip mere inches from Alexander's face. Rivulets of fresh blood trickled down her arm, enveloping her hand in a sticky glove. Mina stepped forward, easing her body farther down the blade. Ido frowned, then his expression shifted to panic. Mina grasped his wrist, digging her nails into his flesh and raising her other sword. Ido frantically attempted to escape her grip. Moments later, a scream echoed through the forest.

Mina pried his severed hand off of the hilt, letting it fall with a muffled thud. Commander Ido clutched the stump of his arm, writhing in pain.

Alexander squeezed his eyes shut for a moment, willing his stomach to settle as the bile rose.

With a final burst of effort, Ido lunged at her, but he was met only with a swift kick to the stomach. As he fell, Mina leaped on top of him, followed quickly by the wrath of her sword as she returned the favor, pinning him to the ground through his shoulder. She paused, and the forest's silence was disturbed only by their ragged breathing.

"Tell me now," Mina said, her hand wandering down Ido's waist, grabbing a small dagger from his belt. "What were *his* exact words?"

Alexander strained his ears, but the only noise Ido made were faint gurgles.

"You will die, Ido. It's merely your choice when and in how many pieces you end up." He didn't speak. Mina shrugged, hovering the dagger over his eye. "I hereby find you unequivocally guilty of high treason. I am your trial, judge and executioner."

Ido screamed again, and Alexander looked away. He couldn't watch.

Mina flicked his eye away from them, the glistening sphere covered in blood. "And repeat." He screamed again.

Commander Ido was blubbering incoherently in broken phrases.

"Alliance... his blood..."

And then, there was silence.

Mina stood over his unmoving body, visibly panting, before she made her way over toward Alexander, drawing another dagger from a fallen soldier and grabbing the open lantern. Resting the clean blade inside, her hand reignited the wick. Fire danced at her command, and the metal burned white-hot. She ripped off a piece of her sleeve and bunched it in her mouth, grasping the hilt of the sword still in her shoulder. Agonizingly slowly, the steel separated from her flesh.

Mina gasped, clutching her arms. He couldn't do anything to help her. His head was still spinning. They were too far from the castle, too far from Elaine. But she didn't need to do it like this. She closed her eyes, lifting the molten knife to her wound.

The smell of burning tissue filled his nostrils, and he gagged.

She collapsed into the snow.

Alexander tried to crawl to her, but his limbs were stiff, and he could barely keep his eyes open. The adrenaline was leaving his body, and the pain was more intense than he had realized. Black spots danced along his vision, and he finally let go, collapsing beside her.

CHAPTER ELEVEN

ANTON

ANTON STOOD IN A WASTELAND. His hands were still clasped over his ears, and the arena still stood before him, but there was complete silence. He shivered, spinning in circles. A moment ago, he was surrounded by their people, while that girl acted like some sort of insane beast. Then, everyone disappeared.

"Hello?" he shouted. His voice echoed louder than it should have. He could still see the forest in the distance, but everything was shrouded in shades of brown and gray. Everything was unnervingly still, without even the slightest breeze. And he felt... hollow. An overwhelming sense of loneliness began to set in, as though something was begging him to stay —to keep it company. It had been alone for so long.

Anton reached out a hand to it, but whatever it was, it wasn't a person. His hand glowed purple, and he jumped back, checking himself. *He* was purple. And see-through. Like he wasn't even there. What in the name of dragons was going on?

He stumbled, falling back onto the ground.

The crowd was suddenly back, rushing past him and tripping over him. Anton covered his head instinctively, curling up into a ball to protect himself from the stampede. The roaring had stopped, and the last of the people had run past him. He shuddered, putting his hands on the ground. It was solid—he was solid. Had he been hallucinating again? He got up, dusting himself off. It had felt too real. Then again, they all did.

Anton glanced around. He was mostly alone in the arena again, but he was definitely in Anadrieth. Everyone had run off in fear of that girl. He followed the direction in which everyone had left. It was a complete mess—the councilors were frazzled, General Barrett was injured and even the soldiers seemed frightened. Where was Alexander? He should be controlling this situation.

The longer he looked around the castle, the more suspicious he became. No one had seen their leader after the girl had run off into the forest. His stupid brother must have gone after her instead of helping the rest of them. Someone grabbed his shoulder, and he whirled around.

"Have you seen Lord Alexander?" asked Ban. He seemed just as frazzled as the rest of them.

"He's probably trying to find the girl," said Anton. "I'm sure he'll be back with some sort of excuse."

Ban grabbed his arm and pulled him along. "Come on, we have to look for him."

"He can take care of himself."

"With the Lanadese about? If there any spies amongst us who saw him go off alone, it would be the perfect opportunity."

He wasn't taking no for an answer.

"Did you find him?" called Councilor Dallan.

"We've got a lead," said Ban.

Anton let himself be dragged along with them as they gathered a few soldiers on their way to the stables. With a sigh, he mounted one of the horses and held his breath. The small group rode into the forest, following Alexander's trail. Ban wasn't wrong to be worried, but the likelihood of his brother being defeated was slim. They would probably end up going through all of this effort, only to return to see him contentedly having supper. But Anton figured that he'd better make sure that that was the case.

It was dark by the time they reached the end of the trail and were forced to slow down. No one had thought to bring any lanterns with them, and the forest was even more dangerous at night.

"There!" Councilor Dallan pointed in the distance.

There were dark shapes littered across the clearing—bodies. Anton's heart picked up. Maybe Ban had been right. He threw himself off of his horse, scanning the ground. There was blood everywhere, far more than there should have been with this number of bodies. He touched the puddles with his fingers, just to make sure that it wasn't the shadows playing tricks on him. It wasn't. There was evidence of a small army, yet there were only a dozen or so bodies. He took a closer look at one of them. A cleanly slaughtered man, wearing imperial white and gold.

Oh, no.

This wasn't a battle of the Lanadese. This was treason against the empire itself.

"I found them! They're still breathing," called Ban.

Anton jogged over with the rest of them, but a silver glint in the snow caught his eye. He crouched, peering at the sword. It pulsated with a slight violet glow, the same glow that he'd seen throughout his body earlier. He realized that there were two swords—one stuck in a body, the other laying by his feet. He narrowed his eyes. They each had that script on them. The same scribbles his little sister was always going on about. And the imperial crest.

She must have stolen them; these swords were clearly property of the imperial family. That's why the empire had come. And his brother had gotten caught in the crossfire. He shook his head. The girl must have been hiding them in Anadrieth this entire time. Coward. But that would mean that the empire believed that they had been concealing a thief. Anton swallowed. Depending on how important these artifacts were, the entire region could be condemned for high treason.

He was about to get up when the sword glowed a little bit brighter. It had that same presence about it, the same as he had felt when the girl was in the arena, the same as his hallucination. Anton reached out a hand, and his palm connected with the blade.

A scream tore at his throat, but no sound came out. Searing pain coursed through his arm. He couldn't pull back, couldn't pull away. His vision blurred, his senses both muted and incredibly sharp.

A foreign land, yet intimately familiar. Titanic creatures soared above, tails as large as rivers. A silent song tugged on his spirit.

Anton felt his face hit the snow. There was an overwhelming presence commanding his attention, his sacrifice—the circle of three.

Mysoviere, mysoviere.
Then, nothing.

ANTON SHOT UP, his fingers gripping blankets. He swung his head around wildly, blinking through the darkness. Had he had another episode? He took a few deep breaths to calm his heart. No, this was different. It was far from his usual episode but no less confusing.

There was a bandage wrapped around his left hand. He attempted to unravel it, but he was unable to get past the last layer where his raw flesh stuck to the cloth. He grimaced, squeezing his eyes shut. Better not touch it.

His eyes adjusted to the darkness, and he saw his brother and the girl lying in the infirmary next to him, still passed out. He could hear Elaine snoring in her room next door. She must not have had enough energy left to heal his wound.

Anton's feet hit the cold floor, and he leaned close to see the gentle rise and fall of his brother's chest. He looked worse for wear, but at least it seemed like he'd make it through the night. He wandered over to the girl, gritting his teeth. That stupid servant girl. He should end her now while she was weak. It would save everyone else the trouble. He'd been right all along, but she was more dangerous than he'd ever imagined. Anton looked around for a weapon.

He felt a hand creep over his shoulder as the woman laid her head against him and muttered in his ear, detailing the many ways he could go about it. There were plenty of weapons right in front of him; he just had to get creative. Then, there were the twin swords laying on the bedside table, suffocating in layers of cloth. Alexander might hate him for it, but he would get over it eventually. This was the moment.

A sudden pang hit him in the chest, and he sunk to his knees. He couldn't do it. He couldn't kill someone. Not again. The woman's presence left him with a bad taste in his mouth. Besides, there was also no way he was going near those swords again.

Anton banged his head against the bed. Something was wrong with him. His mind drifted, the smell of the barbarian's foul breath wafting across the room. He squeezed his eyes shut.

Go away.

It wasn't real—the weight of the dead body crushing his own, threatening to take him down.

It's not real.

There was an awful feeling in the pit of his stomach. None of it was ever real. Was he fated to slowly lose his mind? Anton punched the stone floor, then bit his tongue, cradling his wrist. Wrong hand.

The room suddenly became brighter, and he leaped up with a start. His brother and the girl were glowing, an ethereal violet surrounding their entire bodies, concentrated at their hearts. Her light was unbearably bright. The swords were glowing, too. They both held an indescribable warmth, a fluttering innocence.

Anton rubbed his eyes, blinking furiously. Tiny colored lights danced through the air, everywhere he looked, and he backed away, bumping into the wall. This was far more intense than it had ever been. When he looked up again, everything was back to normal. It wasn't just his eye acting up this time—it was his whole mind. A laugh escaped his throat.

He was truly going insane. Maybe it was time he just embraced it.

Anton ran down the hall toward his room, a little bubble of air under each step. He jumped into his bed, grinning into his pillow. Perhaps there was peace in being insane. That would be nice.

TWO DAYS HAD PASSED since the *incident,* and the whole of Anadrieth was gossiping about who this servant girl really was. Anton stalked down the hall with dark circles under his eyes. Yet another night without sleep.

He'd heard nothing but talk of that girl and whether his brother was going to be fit enough to lead them into war. Alexander this, Alexander that. No one really cared about his brother's wellbeing; they were just interested in self-preservation. And gossip; can't forget how fascinating the gossip was. Neither Alexander nor the girl had woken up yet, and the rumors were growing out of control, becoming more outlandish every day.

Anton shook his head, willing the little lights to go away. He'd seen Elaine about his eye, but the lights didn't seem to have anything to do with his vision, and she'd avoided his questions. Maybe he could tire himself out in the training grounds instead by hitting some things. That seemed like a manly thing to do, and though it wasn't the ideal nighttime activity, it might send him to sleep at last.

As he neared the training grounds, he paused, spying one shape hiding behind a pillar and another lurking on the grounds. Anton stuck to the shadows. Was it an intruder? Maybe he should call the guards.

Moonlight illuminated the area briefly as the dark cloud drifted away. The figure behind the pillar was his brother, watching the figure on the grounds—the girl.

Anton frowned. He hadn't been informed that they were conscious. What in dragon's name were they doing?

The girl swung her swords around with frantic grace, her bandages discarded in a heap. Her chest heaved, and her exhaustion was evident. Droplets of rain started to fall, and Anton edged back as far into the shadows as he could. Slowly, the rain grew heavier.

Blood seeped through the girl's shoulder, the water enlarging the stain. She faltered, clutching her wound. It seemed to spur her on, and her strikes grew more fervent. Although she fought only air, she swung with a force that looked like it could smash iron walls. It was nothing like her duel. This was carnal.

The girl let out a roar, and Anton held his breath, gripping his arms around himself. He couldn't help but shudder.

Alexander ran out to her, and suddenly her blade was at his throat.

Anton's hand went for his sword, but it wasn't there. Of course, it wasn't; he didn't sleep with it, unlike his brother. It was stupid of him to wander the grounds without it, though.

After a moment, his brother drew his sword, and she came at him with incredible speed. Anton watched with his mouth agape. Now they were fighting? His brother was the best fighter he knew, but he was barely surviving on the defensive. Alexander was quickly disarmed, and his sword flung several paces away. It wasn't surprising, considering her show against

General Barrett. Not only was she some sort of terrifying beast, but she was also a trained fighter, just like he'd always said.

The girl fell to her knees, grasping her arms.

"Two years... two years!" she cried.

Anton hugged the wall as she pounded her fist into the ground, sending out a minor shock wave with each blow. That same aura surrounded her, but it was not nearly as intense. She'd better not do what she did in the arena, or they'd all be in trouble.

His brother didn't seem frightened as he knelt in front of her.

"And this! I've never made a mistake like this," the girl exclaimed, gesturing at her wound. "Two years out of practice."

Alexander pulled her into an embrace, and they stared at each other. Then, he pressed his lips against hers.

Anton retched silently. That had to be the worst method of courting he'd ever seen. Thank dragons no one else was here to see that.

"Are you serious?" Anton blurted out.

Alexander turned toward him in shock, grabbing his sword. Anton emerged from behind the wall, and his brother sighed.

Alexander stood, helping the girl to her feet and reaching for her swords.

"Don't," she said, retrieving them herself.

Anton narrowed his eyes. She was holding them with her bare hands, but she wouldn't let Alexander touch them. That temptress must have enchanted them somehow; that's why they glowed. He had just found out the hard way. He clenched his bandaged fist. It still hurt.

They walked past him without a word. His brother didn't even look at him.

Anton pursed his lips, spinning in the opposite direction and stomping back to his room. He could have lived his entire life without having witnessed that.

Utterly disgusting.

So much for training himself to sleep. It seemed like it was going to be yet another sleepless night. Anton threw himself into bed, crossing his arms. His gaze was drawn to the window, where the subsiding rain was a glowing shower of deep blue. As strange as everything in his life was, the rain had never looked more beautiful.

FOR THE THIRD time in just over a week, Lord Alexander's council was assembled in the great hall. Anton fidgeted in his seat. The air was stifling, and no one spoke. They were meeting as early as possible, but the anticipation was killing him. Alexander clearly had nothing against the girl, and he looked forward to seeing how he would talk his way out of this one.

General Barrett had his eyes firmly fixed on the table in front of him. His wounded pride made him even more irritable and dangerous than normal.

His brother entered with Adelia and the girl in tow. The girl was dressed in finery, her swords hanging on a belt around her waist. They hadn't had sheaths before, but they certainly did now. They were decorated too, all imperial-like with golden designs on the white sheaths. Where was she getting all of this stuff? Anton's eyes darted around the room; the other men looked just as perplexed, but this time, they didn't object to the presence of the two women.

Alexander didn't sit in his chair; instead, he stood to the right of it.

"Gentlemen, I understand that recent events have been nothing short of confusing and frightening, and the rumors have gotten out of hand. I can't apologize enough that I wasn't as present as I should have been. However, I hope this meeting will clear up any questions you might have." He bowed his head, one arm across his chest. "It is my honor to present to you Her Imperial Highness, Princess Mina, the long-missing heiress to the empire."

Anton gaped. There was a long moment of silence throughout the room before he'd finally had enough.

"What?" His brother was not usually one for practical jokes, and this was certainly not the time to start. Nervous laughter broke out amongst the table, the men's disbelief echoing throughout the room.

"Nonsense."

"That clumsy servant troublemaker? Impossible."

"She's manipulating you."

"A pretty dress doesn't make her our princess."

"Ridiculous."

Anton shut his mouth immediately. He could feel it again, strong and controlled. The girl's presence radiated across the room, and her left hand raised in a claw-like pose. A violet, ethereal shape extended from her arm, forming a transparent dragon claw. It looked exactly like her glowing form, only this time, everyone else seemed to be able to see it, too.

The silence only lasted for an instant before a deafening crack echoed in the hall. In one smooth motion, she brought her great claw through the table, her talons shredding the mahogany with the ease of cutting through butter. Giant splinters flew across the room, and the men threw themselves to the floor in panic.

Anton fell backward on his chair, landing in a heap.

The claw gradually receded, and her arm was once again normal. The girl leisurely drew one of her swords, holding it in front of her face, the imperial crest clearly visible. She took slow steps through the wreckage. The men scrambled to press their foreheads to the floor.

Anton averted his eyes as she passed. Whether she was truly the missing princess or not, she was dangerous; that, he could admit.

Her voice cut through the room's tangible fear.

"Long ago, my ancestors desperately desired power to forge this empire and put an end to war, once and for all. The power of the dragon gods came at a price—a curse that could not be broken by death. After a certain incident, this power passed into legend over the last four hundred years." She dragged the tip of her sword across the ground. "But I assure you, that absolute authority has always been present. No one would blink if I were to execute all of you for your display of treasonous behavior."

Her sword rested on the back of Councilor Dallan's neck, his body visibly trembling.

"So fragile." A drop of blood rolled down his skin as the sword pierced him. "However, I am not without mercy."

She walked back to the head of the table, placing herself in his brother's chair and leaning against one armrest, one leg crossed over the other. Some of the men began to offer apologies, but she waved her hand.

A messenger barged into the room, throwing himself at their feet. He looked unsure of who to turn to as he held a letter above his head.

"Urgent news from Lanadrin!"

The girl took the envelope, breaking the seal. Her expression didn't change, as though she expected what was written there.

"I called this meeting to discuss the future of Anadrieth," she said. "Currently, the reigning power in the capital believes that Lord Alexander has kidnapped me, which resulted in the aftermath you found us in. I will attempt to rectify this, but the situation has its... delicacies, which will take time to unravel."

The girl shrugged. "In regards to the war, negotiations on my behalf won't help. At the present time, Lanadrin and Calvera back my cousin, Prince Yukiya." She spat his name, holding up the letter from the messenger.

The words *last chance* were scrawled across the page in large handwriting—presumably Lord Tamar's—and it was marked with the Lanadese and Calveran seals. Beside them lay the imperial seal. Anton sucked in a breath, while those around him murmured their shock. There could be no clearer declaration of support. They had no chance now. It was over.

The girl continued as though nothing were amiss. "For now, we need to bolster the strength of the Anadese army, which is severely lacking. We're going to need to move quickly. Barrett, I want your men ready in precisely one hour."

General Barrett pursed his lips but bowed his head all the same.

Anton raised his eyebrows. Not even the general was going to challenge her anymore. His fingers touched a piece of the table. Well, it wasn't particularly surprising. Even the most stubborn of men would grovel under an unknown power. Anton was going to have to be more careful, but it would take more than a broken table to convince him that she should be followed. She might be the princess, but he didn't have to like it.

"Prepare five rooms," she said. "I have no doubt that some guests will be arriving shortly, given the news." She pointed to Alexander, Adelia and, finally, Anton. "Come with me. The rest of you are dismissed."

Anton hesitated. He had no reason to go with her. He felt her gaze upon him—on second thought, he wasn't doing anything else. He got up immediately, following her out.

The aura surrounding her now was completely different. She was no longer the clumsy servant girl who broke everything in sight. He wasn't sure what to think, but he was definitely going to keep an eye on her.

The four of them entered the war room, the door clicking shut behind them.

She gestured for them to have a seat, beaming.

"I'd like to thank you all for taking care of me, as you had every reason not to. In hindsight, it may have been a good idea to visit so that you would have actually recognized me, but in the end, things happen how they should. Speak freely, for I consider all of you my friends."

Anton frowned. That was clearly a lie. He had only ever treated her with well-deserved contempt and cynicism. She just wanted him to put his foot in his mouth; then, she would trip him up. He remained silent. His sister, however, did not.

"I knew there was something about you," said Adelia, almost bouncing in her seat. Her excitement didn't surprise him; this was the equivalent of meeting her childhood hero.

His brother nodded. "Will you please explain... what's going on?"

She leaned back in her chair, then glanced at Anton. He looked past her at a spot on the wall. This should be good.

"I'll start from the beginning, then. It was the very last night I spent as a child."

12

CHAPTER TWELVE

MINA

Eleven years ago — Year 2150 of the Fey Dynasty

MINA SWUNG HER OPEN PALM, sending an onslaught of water in her cousin's face. "Take that!" she cried.

Yukiya grinned, returning the favor. His striking white hair was plastered against his cheeks and down his back, his sky-blue eyes glistening in the moonlight. They stood knee-deep in the great lake, poised to attack. His older brother, Yuno, stood with his arms folded on the banks.

"Princess, you shouldn't be playing around in the lake!"

Mina stuck her tongue out at him. He always acted so high and mighty.

Her father, Emperor Masaru, came up behind him, putting a hand on his shoulder, and Yuno turned with a start. She looked at them together. He wasn't Yuno's father, but they looked shockingly similar.

"Your Highness—"

"Let them be young, lord." Her father smiled, patting his head. "What have you done to your hair?"

Yuno scrunched his face, looking away. His locks, once long like his brother's and every male descendant before him, were now jagged and short, sticking close to his head.

"Cut it."

"Why?"

"Because."

Mina flicked water at them both, giggling as Yuno flinched. "I said it didn't suit him like it does Yukiya. His face is too stern. But it looks better now, doesn't it, Papa?"

Her father frowned, leaning toward him. "The men of the imperial Fey family have always kept their hair long. You should take more pride in your family inheritance."

Yuno glanced at Mina, his eyes lingering for a moment too long. "I do."

"Now, go play while you can." Her father gave him a little push into the water as he left. Yuno grimaced, peeling off his now wet slippers and tossing them away.

Mina rolled her eyes, tightening the belt of her soaked robes.

"Afraid of a little water?"

He tilted his chin upward and strode into the water, stopping in front of her.

"No."

She splashed him. "Then, you're it!"

The three of them chased each other around in circles, laughing until they ran out of breath. Then, the two boys held out their hands to her as she leaned, panting, against her knees.

"That's quite enough. Come, I'll walk you to your room," said Yuno.

Yukiya shook his head. "But the stars are out now. Come dance with me."

Mina glanced between the two of them. They couldn't be any more different from each other. Yuno, the arrogant first-born, and Yukiya, the gentle second. But the only reason they associated with each other was because of her—and her status. She didn't want to cause a rift between them, yet she was the only reason they stayed together.

Mina peered into the water, adjusting her golden circlet, the intricate details dangling through her hair. Although she was only young, this was the first truth she had been taught. As the last heir of the original bloodline, she must marry one of the males from the branch family that would inherit her father's dragon spirit. She was lucky that it was only the two of them; her ancestors had had dozens of potential suitors. Not that she had any choice in the matter. The dragon would choose.

"I'm not ready to sleep yet," she said, putting her hand in Yukiya's. She was led through the water before his brother could protest, and Yukiya settled his arm around her waist. He spun her in the shallows with ease, and her leg swept a graceful arc of water through the air. The stars reflected on the surface, the pinpricks of light creating a beautiful stage.

"Can you hear it?" whispered Yukiya, gazing at her. There was no music, but the rhythm was engraved in their spirits.

The Aria of the Gods.

Mina smiled. "Yes."

Then, a distant scream caught their attention, followed quickly by another, this time much closer. Yukiya pulled her close. Attendants ran toward the sound, sending the imperial gardens into an immediate uproar.

Mina was knocked off her feet, the sudden impact stealing her breath, and Yukiya hit the water beside her. She clawed at her chest as the pain burned its way through. Her mouth opened, but the water muffled her scream as the surface drifted farther away.

Darkness.

Mina clutched her head as another wave of pain racked her body. She was suddenly in her mother's body, driving a blade through her stomach and dragging it upward. The weight of the golden bracelets encircling her wrists grew unbearably heavy. Her chest was tight, despair suffocating her being. Through her blurry vision, she saw her husband run through the imperial gardens, unable to reach her before he, too, collapsed. Spirits tore at them, the searing heat severing the bonds. Then, freedom at last.

Then, she saw herself as her grandmother, staring at the blood that pooled in her hands from the arrow in her chest. Acceptance flooded through her as she died. Then, she was her mother before that. And before that. And so on.

The scenes flickered further and further back, imbedding themselves into her young mind. The memories of all of those before her, bound together by blood and spirit.

A great war, the massacre. A deep satisfaction. Eyes that burned through her, searching for what was no longer hers to give. A jealous, twisted desire that had been festering since the dawn of time. A silvery tongue, echoing three words over and over.

Is it you?

Then, silence. Everything fell into place. Her mind was

still, her spirit in slumber at the beginning of time. Awakened. Her tail wrapped against another, and she rose her massive head with her teeth bared. The ritual couldn't be stopped, but she ran alongside him. A desperate roar. Heartbeats synced, eternally joined.

Dawn had broken.

Mina was dragged onto dry land, and she coughed violently. The world refocused around her. It was the same as she had left it but, somehow, entirely different. There was so much *more*.

Yuno caught his breath beside her, his arm on hers. His lips moved, but she didn't hear him. Her eyes were drawn to the figure on the other side of him. Yukiya sat up as she did, his mouth slightly agape.

She moved to a crouch, her muscles bunched. A sudden rage simmered to the surface, almost clouding her vision.

End this now.

Ethereal talons extended from Mina's hands, and she lunged for Yukiya. She didn't want to. But she had to.

She was thrown sideways as a heavy form barreled into her, but her talons still met flesh. Blood blossomed above her, dripping onto her cheek. She blinked, and the pounding in her ears subsided after a few moments.

"Kakeru?"

Her mentor grimaced, still pinning her to the ground. She pushed against him, and Kakeru was tossed across the garden like a ragdoll. Mina stared at her hands.

Yuno stood between her and his brother, shaking him by the collar. "What did you do? Get out of here already!"

Kakeru rolled to his feet, cradling his stomach. "That's no way to talk to your new prince."

Yuno pointed at his brother. "Prince? Him? Don't be ridiculous. I'm—"

"He was chosen, not you."

Yuno didn't respond as the attendants rushed to the scene. They attempted to usher Yukiya away, but he brushed them away, kneeling beside Kakeru and placing his hands over the wound. A surge of light pulsed from his palm, and the skin closed over almost instantly, leaving behind only a few faint scars.

Yukiya smiled. "I'm afraid this is the only thing I can fix for you, old friend."

As Yukiya was led away, Mina could only stare at their retreating figures. Everything fell into sharp focus. The scratch in the wooden roofing beam, the soft sound of a petal falling to the ground, the metallic smell of blood. Spirit lights glowed all around her, the mark of the living— and those that weren't quite alive. The rough earth between her fingertips, the cool air caressing her skin, the fire dancing in the torches, the still water behind her—she was home.

A voice pulled her attention back to the people around her. "My lord—"

"I told you, I'm fine," said Yuno, his voice eerily calm. His young servant, Lyra, had her head bowed before him. He pushed her out of the way and pulled Mina to her feet.

"What's going on?" he asked.

Mina drew her shoulders back, yanking her hand from his. The force pulled him face-first into the ground, and Lyra was quickly by his side. Ignoring him, Mina neared her mentor, who was tenderly touching his newly formed scars.

"I'm sorry."

Kakeru shook his head. "It's not your fault. Are you..." He pitied her; she could see it plastered across his face.

Mina turned away. "Yes. It's still me."

"You... should go see your father," he said. "Tell him why—"

"No." Her voice held a resounding finality. Her father still had traces of *his* presence still lingering within him. The one she was forced to despise.

Kakeru followed, stopping in front of her. "You know he'll only last a few months at most, now that... the successors are chosen."

"I know."

It was just like every other time. The death of one was the death of the other. And now, her life was bound in the same way—to Yukiya.

"I don't want you to lose them both," said Kakeru.

Mina moved around him. "That was my mother's decision." She had been weak, unable to wait to pass on the curse until her only daughter could grow up. Selfish enough to choose freedom for herself through death, condemning those who she claimed to love to *this*. A life of shackles.

"And a poor decision, that, but you could at least—"

She whirled around. "What's done cannot be undone. If anyone should see him, it should be you."

Kakeru's footsteps halted as he stopped following her. The servants knelt as she passed, her presence bringing them to their knees. The wooden flooring cracked behind her.

No one approached her. Not now.

The cycle began again, but she would make sure that this was the end.

As the months passed, Emperor Masaru locked himself in his room, unable to leave his bed. Mina didn't visit, but she knew that her father's sky-blue eyes would soon fade to a milky gray, sunken in their sockets. His hair would recede, the brittle white strands giving him the appearance of age well beyond his actual years. His human spirit would leave him soon, just as the dragon's had—she could feel it.

It was probably the last opportunity she would have with him, if only she could stomach his presence. Even though only faint whispers of the dragon spirit remained, he felt too much like the prince. Mina shuddered as she wandered by his room, waving away the guards and leaning against the heavy door. There was someone with him.

Kakeru's low voice echoed, their conversation inaudible to anyone but her. "Why have you summoned me now, after so many years?" It was strained.

"My daughter won't see me... but she trusts you," her father replied, the words crawling out of his throat with great effort.

"Do *you* trust me, Your Highness?"

"I wouldn't have summoned you otherwise."

A dull thump. "What did I do wrong? You said you valued our friendship. I thought..."

There was a long pause. "My Minako wasn't strong enough. I always knew she would choose to... I didn't want to put you in the same position."

"Let me get this straight. Knowing you'd die at any time, you thought to put me under the princess' care to somehow save me the pain?"

"Yes."

Kakeru's volume rose. "You're such a fool Masaru! I'd rather have my closest friend for a week than endure years of silence. I could have been beside you all this time."

"I thought... you would have moved on."

"Moved on? What on earth are you talking about?"

"I hoped you'd forget me."

Kakeru let out a long exhale. "How could I *possibly* forget someone as stubborn and ridiculous as you? I mean, what was with that decision last month to allow that pompous sculptor to put a statue of you, in your underclothes, dancing with a tree, in the middle of the town square?"

Mina raised her eyebrows. It had been an odd thing to do, and she considered having it removed when she took power.

Laughter filled the room, her father's turning into a wheezing cough. "All right, it wasn't my most informed decision." He paused. "I'm sorry. I thought it was right to push you away... then again, I haven't been able to make good decisions lately."

"I just wish you hadn't insisted on being alone." A few minutes of silence passed before Kakeru spoke again. "I've noticed something. It's taken them no effort at all to summon their spirit swords."

"I know. Their bonds are seamless. The children are nothing short of perfect vessels this time, as though they were the original dragons themselves."

"I fear she will lose herself."

"Watch over her. Don't... fail her as I have." Her father's voice grew weaker. "Say, Kakeru, did you ever confess to that girl?"

"Don't be absurd," Kakeru snapped. "I told you, it's not like that."

Her father chuckled lightly.

Mina turned her eyes toward the room. Her father's light was almost out, the ethereal violet of his spirit fading. And because of *her*, there was nowhere for them to go. Would their spirits disappear? Or would they forever wander the earth in search of a home? She didn't know.

"Minako, my love... I finally come to join you." Her father's words were barely a whisper as he took his final breath.

She closed her eyes, her fist balling against the door. There was only one heartbeat in the room now.

"Be at peace, my friend," whispered Kakeru.

Mina slipped away before he left the room. A few drops rolled down her cheek, but there was no point in mourning. It had only been a matter of time, after all.

NINE YEARS HAD PASSED without a reigning imperial couple, and the empire slowly descended into turmoil. Neither the prince nor the princess could overturn the ancient law. Bound together, they must rule together. As Mina's coming of age neared—her sixteenth birthday—their people breathed a collective sigh of relief. The last remaining blood heir could finally take the throne as empress, and they would once more have an imperial couple.

Mina rested against the low pavilion railing in the vast palace gardens. The roar of the waterfall beside her drowned out her unnecessary thoughts. She traced the ornate carvings on the smooth wood with her thumb. Every aspect of the palace had been crafted down to the tiniest detail.

She would be forced to face him again, and soon, for their coronation. They hadn't seen each other in person for the last nine years. Only *that* woman—Mistress Marionette—had forced their cooperation, by correspondence of course, during that incident in Anadrieth. Worse, still, were the certain expectations that came with their wedding night.

"Not in the mood for celebrations?" Lord Yuno approached her, a cup in each hand. He'd decided to keep his hair short, a look that suited his muscular form. He leaned against the railing, offering her a drink.

Mina took it, and it was gone in a single swallow. "There's nothing to celebrate." She held out the cup for him to take. "Although, I suppose congratulations are in order, supreme commander."

It was a consolation prize for the failed firstborn, both an insult and a blessing, but it was a smart move on Prince Yukiya's suggestion. It would somewhat placate their people, who would understand why Lord Yuno was not becoming emperor, and it would keep him close to the palace. Still, he deserved the position, more or less.

Yuno gave her a tight smile. "Thank you." He snapped his fingers.

Lyra trotted over to refill their cups, but Mina shook her head. The servant girl's eyes lingered on her for a moment too long.

"How is the situation between Calvera and Lysanthir?" Mina asked.

"A culprit was arrested, but Calvera won't release the dam.

The Lysanthians don't have more than a few years of water stored up."

Mina sighed. "And we can't overrule a region's decision unless it's by imperial decree."

Yuno smirked. "Don't worry, my brother will be back soon. He's not going to miss the most important night of his life for a little regional spat."

She rolled her eyes. "Don't remind me."

He slid closer, pressing his lips to her forehead. She frowned.

"I want nothing more than to free you from this obligation." Yuno wrapped an arm around her, and she stiffened.

"I don't think you understand the reality of this curse."

He smiled. "My dear, I'm quite certain I can handle it one way or another."

Mina bristled. "Your... overconfidence is a breath of fresh air." She blinked, and dots began to cloud her vision. Had she been getting enough sleep?

"Would you rather spend the night with him?" Yuno's hand glided down her back, speaking low into her ear. "Are you willing to let him do this?"

She shoved him back, only managing human force as the weighty fatigue settled in. "Don't be... crude." Her tongue was slow, her speech beginning to slur. "I'm not in... the mood... for your games."

Her eyelids were struggling to stay open, and her legs collapsed beneath her, falling into his grip. She'd caught on, but she was too late to stop it. Her blood would neutralize whatever he had put in her cup, but it would take time.

"There, there, it will be over soon," he murmured, rubbing his thumb across her cheek.

Mina jerked to the side as Yuno thrust a well-concealed dagger into her chest, narrowly missing her heart. She staggered back, grabbing onto the rail. He was such a fool. The curse couldn't be broken this way; he didn't understand how it worked. Her body was convulsing, her strength failing her. Vythorn. It had to be vythorn in that cup—the deadliest poison in the empire.

Yuno knew how she fought, how she moved, her reaction time. She wouldn't be able to dodge him in this state. As Mina coughed, a trickle of blood escaped her lips. She didn't have the energy to summon her swords.

"You're even stronger than I expected." He drew his sickle and chain, not wasting a moment. "But soon, you'll be free."

The weighted end of his chain struck her head with fatal accuracy.

Then, she was falling over the edge of the railing. The impact was freezing. Why was she in the water? Was it even water?

It didn't matter. It was warm. Her mind began to slip away as her body was carried through the rapids. Air and water encased her in a protective shroud, with no exertion on her part. There was no reason to wake.

For just a moment in her long life, she could be at peace.

CHAPTER THIRTEEN

ADELIA

ADELIA STARED INTENTLY AT MINA. It felt like they were witnessing one of her fairy-tales in action—a beautiful princess stolen away from her husband-to-be by his jealous older brother for the throne. And now, there was a chance for a happy ending. There was always some element of danger before the hero prevailed, after all.

Mina seemed to be telling the truth; Adelia couldn't sense any hint of dishonesty. Elaine had been right, though—she was certainly something else. A princess blessed with the spirit of a dragon god. If there was any doubt before, Adelia was sure that everything she'd read about the dragon gods was true now. By nature, the gods were here to protect them.

But everything was going to change now. No, it had always been this way; she was just never aware of it.

Adelia dropped her gaze to the floor. She felt stupid. Of all the tragedies in Mina's story, she was most upset about losing her only friend. It wouldn't be like that on the surface—a princess could easily be seen around a Lady of Anadrieth—but the reality was that Mina had an empire to run, and she couldn't afford to show favor.

She would be alone again.

Alexander rubbed his face. "I'm such a fool." He paused. "I don't know how to make everything up to you, Your Highness. It's my fault."

Mina shook her head. "I've kept a low profile for a reason. You wouldn't have recognized me. It's more than enough that you gave me a place to stay and didn't kill me or let me die on sight."

"Why didn't you die, then?" Anton blurted out. "If you're human, you shouldn't have survived. If you're a god, then—"

"Anton," snapped Alexander.

Mina held up a hand. "It's fine. I expect you will all have questions." She drew one of her swords, placing it gently on the table, and Anton immediately shrank back. "They are called *Syravia,* dragon tongue for 'spirit reaper.' These swords are pieces of my spirit, the dragon of which I am one and the same, yet entirely separate." She ran her fingertips over the edges of the dragon script. Adelia leaned forward to peer at them.

The beginning and the end.

She frowned. That didn't make much sense. Perhaps she'd translated it wrong. There was a curious symbol on the hilt, too, like a compass with no directions—something you'd only find on a map.

"The dragon's spirits are strong. It's true, he and I share many of their qualities, but we aren't infallible to steel or other means," said Mina. "The ancient priestesses bound a piece of our entwined spirits into three swords to take some of the burden, but still, many, like my mother, have been unable to bear it."

Alexander shook his head. "The official report was that the empress died from the imperial illness, like your father."

"Of course, it was. A pattern of suicides and assassinations wouldn't inspire much confidence, but few people understand the truth." Mina shrugged. "The dragon's memories span across all of time. When one vessel dies, they are all transferred to the next, along with the dragon's spirit. A mortal mind cannot handle the sheer extent of hundreds of lifetimes worth of my ancestor's memories. With all the pressure, my mother couldn't wait to end her turn, thereby starting the next cycle early." Mina turned to her and Anton. "I believe you two have experienced some of these memories."

Adelia blinked. *How did she know?*

Anton curled the fingers of his bandaged hand. For a moment, he looked so vulnerable. Adelia suddenly wanted to embrace him like old times, but she averted her eyes. Now wasn't the time to feel sorry for him, not after everything he'd done.

"How can you tell?" Anton mumbled.

"It's my spirit, Anton. Very few people have come in direct contact with it without dying."

Alexander nodded, slightly furrowing his brow, an expression that signaled that he didn't really understand what was going on. He obviously didn't read enough history to grasp the situation, but that was to be expected. He cleared his throat.

"If you remember everything, all the way back to when the dragon gods rescued humanity, does that mean you're really, you know..."

Mina narrowed her eyes. "Are you calling me old?"

"No," said Alexander, a little too loudly. "No. I just meant that you've lived for a really long time." There was a moment of silence as Alexander glanced back and forth between Mina and his siblings, but Adelia certainly wasn't going to cover for him, and Anton turned up his nose.

Mina cleared her throat. "I can *access* the memories of those before me, akin to choosing books off a shelf and flipping through the pages, but my personal memories are separate. So, while I am the age that I am, you could *technically* say I'm over two thousand years old."

Adelia fiddled with a loose thread on her sleeve. Her age was far from the thing that bothered her. "It's true, then, that one dragon can't live without the other? If so, then Lord Yuno's act would have been..."

"Attempted assassination of the last imperial couple, yes." Mina shook her head. "I'm not sure where he's getting his ideas from. Maybe he thinks he'll inherit the dragon spirits, but that's just not how it works." She clenched her fists, staring at each of them in turn. The tension in the room rose, the underlying presence of the dragon spirit like a subtle threat. "Everything has to end this time, do you understand? You have to help me end this and restore balance to the world. All of you."

"Why?" Adelia whispered. Wasn't this a good thing, more or less? She and the prince could use their powers to restore balance to the empire, and everything would go back to normal. Mina didn't need their help when she had the power of the gods on her side.

"I don't... remember." For a moment, Mina looked pained. Despair rolled off of her in waves, a sadness that was etched deep into her spirit. It was as though the feeling had grown and festered for far longer than Mina had lived, even taking the dragon's age into account. Adelia reached out a hand. There was something else going on underneath all of this—something far greater than she could imagine. If she could just understand a little more, maybe she'd be able to help.

Mina pulled back, recomposing herself. "Anyway, we need to focus on the situation at hand."

Alexander sighed. "All right. Well... we've got Lord Yuno wanting you dead, the empire wanting me dead, Lanadrin and Calvera wanting my people dead, an unfulfilled alliance, an unprepared region and the princess herself sitting with us instead of on the throne. If I'm not missing anything, what *can* we do?"

No one spoke for a few moments.

Adelia fiddled with her thumbs. "I'll go to Eloria and finish what we started." She took a deep breath as everyone turned to her. "You two can stay here to prepare our troops for the worst, and then Mina can go to the capital and talk to Prince—"

"No." Mina's tone was soft, but her presence was suddenly suffocating. She leaned forward over the table as she pushed her chair back, making an awful screech against the floor. "Let me make this perfectly clear," she enunciated. *"He* is the curse upon this world. One I will end."

Adelia shrank back in her chair. She didn't understand. It was one thing to have an arranged marriage with someone she'd never met, but he and Mina were childhood friends. What could have happened that was so terrible they couldn't talk anymore? Adelia's eyes caught Anton's. Perhaps that situation was more plausible than she thought.

Mina relaxed her stance, and the tension evaporated in an instant. "I need to talk to Lord Reinhardt myself, but I won't be returning to the capital. I'll remain here until my reinforcements arrive." She stood. "Time to go. We've got work to do." She flung the door open and walked out.

"Reinforcements?" Alexander looked hopeful.

"I wouldn't expect much," said Anton. "You heard her before. She's lost her influence in the capital. The army clearly belongs to the Prince Yukiya and Lord Yuno."

"Maybe she's not talking about an army." Adelia gritted her teeth. "She's helping us, which is more than you've ever done and more than we deserve. The evidence is right there in your face, yet you're still refusing to acknowledge her. The least you can do is shut up."

"Perhaps we've seen *different* evidence," Anton snapped back. "Can't you feel—"

"All right, stop, stop." Alexander stood between them. "This isn't the time."

Adelia's lip twitched as she turned on him. "And when is?"

"Yeah, I can't remember the last time we were in a room together for this long," muttered Anton.

"You are a Lord and Lady of Anadrieth," said Alexander, his expression hardening. "If you can't contain your own problems for a later time, this region will fall faster than you can blink." He pushed past them, following Mina.

"Dragons," said Adelia under her breath. "That's the problem, Alexander. You *never* want to deal with it."

"Tell me about it." Anton shook his head. "He's as stuck up as ever."

"No kidding. You remember that time he wouldn't let us

play in the snow, even under supervision, because you got hurt that once?"

Anton rolled his eyes. "It wasn't even our fault. I don't think we ever got to throw a snowball again."

Their eyes met, and there was an awkward silence. Anton glanced away and quickly walked out of the room without another word.

Adelia took a few deep breaths. She'd felt something from him for a moment, something other than his usual blank and empty feeling. Was it hope? Or was it sadness? She shook her head, hurrying after them. It wasn't worth worrying about. There was no way that she could rekindle anything by herself, and she was tired of trying.

She made her way out to the front of the castle, where their soldiers stood in motionless rows, like statues in the snow. They seemed uncertain, though that wasn't surprising. Mina stood before them with regal confidence, her shoulders back and her eyes holding a calm authority. It suddenly occurred to Adelia that she had always carried herself that way, and she always spoke with intelligence and fairness. She had gone from servant to princess, but she hadn't changed at all. Adelia shook her head. What a difference a simple title made.

Mina tapped her foot on the ground as she surveyed the men. "I thought I told you to have everyone ready," she frowned at General Barrett.

The general's hair was more frazzled than normal, bandages stuck out from underneath his crinkled uniform and the heavy bags under his eyes were dark. He deserved every bit of the humiliation Mina served to him, but Adelia couldn't help but pity him. There was such conflict in his heart. He couldn't deny that Mina was well and truly his superior, but his hatred for her seeped out from his aura.

He frowned, the bow in his hand as stiff as a crowcodile's jaw.

"Your Highness, I assure you all of my men are present and ready for instruction." The words dripped from his teeth, but she could tell that he was trying his hardest to remain polite. General Barrett was a traditional man, after all, and it was a sign that he acknowledged her rank, which was more than Barrett did for herself and Anton.

Mina sighed, rubbing her temples. "When I said everyone, I meant *everyone.*" She turned to the assembly. "Soldiers of Anadrieth, you know me as Mina, the servant. However, I have proven my imperial bloodline." She rested a hand on her swords. "I cannot stop the march against Anadrieth if it is ordered by the capital. And as Anadrieth is by far the weakest of my regions, if defeated, it will indicate you were never strong enough to stand on your own. If you don't want to be annihilated, you'll follow what I say." Mina snapped her fingers at the general. "Assemble the entire household. Now."

General Barrett's face was turning red, but to his credit, he left with a curt nod.

There was a commotion at the gates, and a fine carriage rolled into the castle grounds. The soldiers backed out of the way as it barreled straight toward them, halting in front of Mina.

Councilor Raoul squeezed out of the doors, waddling toward her. He bowed with his chin touching his stomach, audible wheezing escaping his lips.

"My princess," he announced after catching his breath. "If it pleases you, I've gathered some of the finest silks, dresses and jewels as my gift to you for all the trouble we have caused. I'm sure you miss the splendor of the capital, and I will endeavor to cater to your every whim." He gestured extravagantly to his carriage, where his servants were displaying his treasures.

Mina raised an eyebrow. "Your sudden... generosity is enlightening, as is your attempt to buy yourself into my good graces."

Adelia stifled a smirk as Councilor Raoul opened and closed his mouth, a bead of sweat rolling down his chin. Serves him right.

"Your Highness—"

"However, it would please me if you passed on this message." She pulled out a piece of folded parchment, holding it with the tips of her fingers. When Mina had time to write that, Adelia didn't know. "And stop spending Anadrieth's treasury. If you want to hold onto your position, you should know better. Give it all back."

Councilor Raoul almost deflated. His shoulders drooped as he took the message. "Right away, Your Highness," he muttered.

After a few minutes, General Barrett rounded the corner with the household servants in tow, and they filed beside the soldiers, though they were quite a bit less orderly. He came to stand at the front with all of them, but Mina clapped her hand on his shoulder, turning him around.

"All ranks amongst you are hereby dissolved. Until I say so, you are neither general nor lieutenant, servant nor soldier. You're simply people trying to help each other survive this mess."

General Barrett stumbled forward with his mouth hanging

open. Adelia sucked in a breath. Things were getting more interesting by the minute, and she loved every second of it. She stole a glance at Alexander. Now, he would *have* to listen to them.

Mina gestured to Ban, who stood awkwardly next to his demoted father, and Jane, who was hiding behind the matron.

"Partner up, everyone. You're going to teach each other everything you know."

Adelia pressed her hands into the snow, her fingers raw and blistered. The cold didn't help to soothe the ache. A bow rested against her leg, and her arrows littered the ground, not a single one close to its target. General Barrett had already walked away from her, claiming to need a few minutes to breathe. He was practically projecting his frustration, but it wasn't his fault that she was terrible. Of course, somehow, out of everyone here, Mina paired her up with him.

Her hands were soft, and her arms were too weak to draw back far enough to make a decent shot. Useless, as always. General Barrett had thrown her into archery because she was too weak to swing a sword, while the other servants, their lives ingrained with manual labor, were having no problem with it—at least, no problem with holding the weapons. Adelia jumped up, gritted her teeth and lined up her last arrow. This time, she would get it for sure. Her arms shook under the strain, and the target suddenly seemed a league away.

She couldn't do it.

Adelia cursed, throwing her arms up, flinging the arrow from her grasp. A nearby yelp made her turn, and she found Anton glaring at her as he rubbed the back of his head. He ushered his partner, Vivian, a few obvious steps away, out of touching distance.

Adelia huffed. It wasn't *her* fault that he was standing too close. Vivian seemed to be having an easier time of the whole exercise, the matron's life of hard work paying off in a rather unexpected way. Adelia tilted her head back, blinking away hot tears. She was utterly useless, despite Barrett's attempt to teach her. What would she even be able to offer the general in return?

General Barrett returned and cleared his throat. "Milady, try this one." He pushed another bow into her hands. It was considerably smaller and lighter, the bowstring less taut.

Adelia glanced at him. "Adelia. Just Adelia is fine." She felt his crumbling arrogance, a flicker of shame.

"Adelia, yes." The awkwardness was palpable. "It's for training children. I realize you probably should have started with this one." Barrett held out the new arrows. "It wasn't fair of me to put you at a disadvantage because I was... never mind." He went through the motions again with her, read-justing her grip and stance.

Adelia exhaled, letting the arrow fly, but her hand slipped, knocking it off course. It narrowly flew past Anton's face, and he stumbled to the side, tripping over his feet and landing unceremoniously on his behind.

"Are you trying to kill me?" Her brother picked himself up, this time steering a clear distance from her range.

Adelia couldn't help but giggle, though it soon subsided. She couldn't get close to her target, even with a child's toy.

Barrett nodded with his arms folded, seeming more pleased than she was. "Better, considering your lack of natural skill. Not quite the intended target, but you were more confident this time."

She fought back a smile despite his demeanor. He was slightly less brittle than before, and it was probably the only encouragement that he could manage. She flexed her fingers —time to try again.

It was another long hour before General Barrett told her to take a break for the day. Adelia nodded, grabbing handfuls of snow to ease the pain in her fingers. She wandered the grounds until she found Mina walking amongst her army, constantly pausing to give instructions.

Adelia stopped dead in her tracks. There was a strong sense of menace coming from the gates, an uncontrollable anger that flooded her senses. A blur crossed the grounds, expertly weaving their way toward Mina. There was a glint of silver in the figure's grip. Adelia shouted, but her voice was lost in the crowd.

Mina immediately spun on her heel, unhooking her sword from her belt. She blocked the strike, her blade still sheathed, and pushed the intruder back. Some of the soldiers, including Alexander, ran over, springing into action and surrounding them. But Mina held up a hand.

"No one is to interfere."

Adelia cocked her head. That girl was never worried about anything. She turned her gaze to the intruder, a cloaked figure with a black dragon mask, definitely male. His posture was aggressive, but she couldn't sense any real ill intent. She narrowed her eyes. This was no Lanadese assassin or enraged imperial commander. There was a warmth about him that she couldn't describe.

"I see you haven't entirely lost your touch." His voice was deep, the accent foreign. "Though that shoulder wound clearly demonstrates your incompetence."

"How dare you speak to her like that," said Alexander, drawing his sword.

Mina kept her eyes trained on the intruder, merely waving a hand to halt his approach. She matched her opponent's steps as they circled each other. "My deepest apologies, old man, but I doubt you could best me, even with one sword and an injury."

"Arrogant as always."

Mina smirked. "Not when it's the truth."

"Let's test that, then."

They lunged simultaneously.

Adelia watched on, her eyes following their every move. She was no expert, but she knew that neither was holding back, their strikes calculated and precise. The intruder held his own, unlike the general. He moved as effortlessly as his opponent, his sleeveless shirt highlighting his muscular arms. The man's anger had simmered down to frustration, though his movements reflected nothing but an exceedingly calm demeanor.

Without warning, the pair were locked in a stalemate. Each a sword's length away, their weapons were against each other's throats. No one moved, but Adelia smiled. She could feel it now that he was closer. Their familiarity with each other was obvious. Peculiar greeting for friends, though.

They lowered their swords, bowing to each other. Mina

launched herself at him, wrapping her arms around his neck, and Adelia's smile faded. He removed his mask, returning the embrace.

"Don't you ever scare me like that again," he said. His hair was ashen gray, the short spikes angled to the side. He was handsome, with a strong chin, though his age began to show in the wrinkles across his forehead and in the corners of his eyes.

Mina grinned. "I missed you, too."

A commotion echoed from the castle gates, and a tall woman waltzed across the grounds to join them, ignoring the threats and weapons of half a dozen guards. She dressed in strange clothing; the curves of her waist and hips were accentuated with leather, and her legs were exposed. Her skin was bronzed, and her dark hair was pulled back from her face. Metallic frames encasing two pieces of glass sat over her nose, and a circular blade hung at her waist. Adelia gaped. Lysanthian inventions, just like in her books.

The woman stood with a hand on her hip. "How touching. You were meant to wait for me."

Mina's face lit up, and she ran to embrace the woman.

Adelia frowned. It's not like she didn't expect Mina to know people from before, but they should be keeping their distance since they obviously knew her as their princess. It was only proper; *this* was not.

The woman shook Mina by the shoulders. "He's been constantly grumbling about all the punishments he's conjured up. Two years I've had to listen to that, and now, here he is, getting all emotional."

The man straightened up all of sudden, like he'd remembered something. "That's right, don't think you're getting off easy. And I'm not emotional," he snapped at the woman.

Mina cocked her head. "Like you haven't been slacking in my absence. Where were you?"

The woman slapped her forehead. "Here we go again."

The two strangers began to quarrel, though Adelia didn't sense any malice—rather, the indescribable warmth of close friends. Adelia fiddled with her dress, rubbing the cloth between her fingers. She couldn't remember if she and Mina had ever felt that warm. Had they ever joked around like that?

Eventually, Mina silenced them and turned to address the curious onlookers. "I apologize for that display. Let me introduce two of my imperial guards." She gestured to the man, "Kakeru, from the capital," then to the woman, "and Sara, from Lysanthir."

So, Adelia was right about the woman. But she didn't look all that special, even if she was Lysanthian, nor did she seem to be fit for the role of the princess' guard. Adelia leveled her gaze. It was irritating, the way Sara stood there like the rest of them were beneath her.

Her brother held out a stiff hand. "I am Lord Alexander. This is my brother Anton and my sister Adelia." He gestured to them.

Kakeru took his hand, but their eyes never left each other, their grip lingering for a moment too long.

"I know who you are, Lord Alexander, and I do hope you've been taking *good care* of our princess."

Adelia narrowed her eyes. Taking good care of Mina? If it weren't for Adelia, Mina wouldn't have had it as good as she did, under the circumstances. It was by *her* request that Mina was made her maidservant instead of being thrown somewhere in the bottom ranks. It was *she* who gave her everything she needed to be more than comfortable. It was *she* who defended her against people's suspicions. They should be asking *her*, not her brother. *She* knew Mina best.

But she just stood there, her jaw clenched.

Alexander hesitated. "Well—"

Mina took a step between them. "I'm fine, really. Like you said, the wound was my fault, and you know they didn't know who I was."

Adelia almost wanted to stop her. Mina didn't have to defend her brother.

Kakeru nodded after a pause. "True. We heard about Commander Ido. Good thing you finally caused a commotion, though, or we wouldn't have found you."

"Even when you're not hiding, you're difficult to find," remarked Sara. "And then, we got caught up trying to fulfill our mission without you." She patted Mina's shoulder. "Aren't the healers any good here? Cynric will be here soon, I'm sure, and we can get that fixed up in no time."

Adelia bit her tongue. Elaine did the best she could; she always did. It was a nasty wound to begin with, and even with the power of the spirit arts, it could take many sessions for things to heal.

Who did this woman think she was? She couldn't just waltz in and insult their only healer.

Mina put up a hand. "It's fine, both of you. Let's talk somewhere."

Adelia watched her walk off with the strangers, laughing and joking with each other. It wasn't fair. Some imperial guards they were, anyway, having disappeared for two years. They hadn't been with her when she was dying on the riverbank, and they'd left her alone this whole time. But now, all of a sudden, they felt like they had the right to come here and act like nothing had changed? Mina hadn't even scolded them.

Adelia stormed off, retrieving her bow. Though her hands ached and the general had told her to stop for today, she nocked an arrow. Well, she could be useful, too. No, not just useful—she was going to be even more useful than *they* were. She wasn't about to lose to them without a fight.

She moved away from everyone, closer to the outer walls. She just wanted some space. Adelia took aim at an ice pear tree, the giant trunk an easy target. Before she could release the arrow, the hairs of the back of her arms stood up, and she shivered. There was someone here. Not just any someone, either. Adelia whirled around, but there was no one. It was a strange feeling. Like Mina, but not; like her brothers, but not.

The ice pears jostled. Adelia let the arrow fly into the thick leaves. There was a stifled yelp, and a little girl tumbled out of the branches. She landed in a heap on the ground. Adelia edged closer, another arrow at the ready. She might be a child, but there was no mistaking that her aura was like an inferno, simmering under the surface—dangerous, yet comfortingly familiar.

The child quickly brushed herself off, her hood falling back. She was small and clearly malnourished; she appeared as though she'd never had a proper meal in her life. Her hair was a brilliant scarlet, and her eyes were like Eloria's fields. She took a dazed look at Adelia.

"Mama?"

CHAPTER FORTEEN

SCARLET

SCARLET SLIPPED THROUGH THE STREETS, avoiding the more populated areas. Lively music was everywhere, and the Celestial Dragon Festival drew people toward Anadrieth's main city. She rolled her eyes as she headed in the opposite direction, pushing open an unlocked door with her finger.

Fools.

It was the easiest day of the year to steal, and these villagers couldn't even remember to bar their doors. She waltzed right inside, slipping anything of value into her pockets as she passed. The other orphans scrounged around for scraps every day and begged on the streets, but Scarlet didn't bother. If they were smarter, they'd simply take advantage of the right times.

The door flung open, and she quickly dived into the next room.

Dragons, they shouldn't have come home this early.

Voices exploded through the house as Scarlet eyed the size of the window—too small. Under the bed—too visible. Her heart pounded. She was stuck in the room. Maybe they would leave.

"Look what you've done!" shouted the man.

"I didn't—"

"You useless, good for nothing—"

A scream, a shattering smash. Then, a dull thud.

Scarlet whirled toward the noise, her eyes widening. A slender arm lay on the floor, and Scarlet clapped a hand over her mouth. The man kicked the woman, his feet crunching on whatever had broken.

"Get up!" He kicked her harder, and her face rolled into view. "Lazy," he barked. A crimson stream trickled over her cheek under her glassy eyes.

Scarlet's forehead was hot. Her chest was burning.

He just killed her.

She was walking toward him before she even realized it, and he glanced up with a brief look of shock that soon twisted into a scowl. He lunged toward her.

"Get out of here, you little brat—"

She snapped her fingers on instinct, and her fingertips sparked, her palms bursting into flames. Her body grew hotter, uncomfortably so, but didn't burn. She never burned.

The man stumbled back, grasping wildly behind him, and found a vase, but it wouldn't help him. The flame grew, concentrating into white-hot balls of energy. He deserved it. Scarlet breathed out. The entire house exploded in flames. His flesh melted in a mere instant, his very bones disintegrating.

The heat was unbearable. It burned through her,

consuming every inch of her. But she reveled in it. It was like she was meant to do this. Through the flames, she saw a face, the same face she always saw—a beautiful woman with golden locks. The woman was surrounded by fire, but still, she smiled.

Freezing water was suddenly thrown into her face, and Scarlet jolted upright, gasping for air. Laughter filled the room as two of the boys stood over her, one holding the now empty bucket.

"Get up, Red. The matron's been calling for you," one said, tugging on a strand of her hair. She glared at them as they ran off. *Stupid boys.*

Scarlet wiped her face with her threadbare blanket, wringing the water from her hair. Maybe she should just cut it all off and be done with it. It would be easier to take care of, at least. Her hands were trembling, and she clutched her shoulders, hugging herself as she gritted her teeth.

She'd dreamed of that night ever since it happened, unable to forget. The strange, indescribable feeling that'd overcome her had happened before, but though she tried, she couldn't replicate the fire that had burst forth from her body. Not that she really wanted to. The memory of that man's melting face was ingrained in her mind every time she closed her eyes. It was a good thing that she'd gotten out of there before the guards came.

Her hand closed around her locket, the small piece of silver calming her heart once more. It was the only thing she had left from her mother. Scarlet flicked it open, gazing at the lock of short hair inside. Fiery red—exactly like hers.

"Red!" a voice called, the shrill tone not to be ignored.

Scarlet sighed. Only two people had ever called her by

name, but they were both long gone, and she had been too young to leave with them. They'd never returned for her as they'd promised. She dragged herself from the straw mattress, brushing off the dirt that clung to her baggy pants before heading downstairs. The other orphan girls wore dresses, but she refused. There was little point in trying to seem like a lady when she would never be one.

The matron pursed her lips, tapping her foot. One of the younger girls, Penelope, stood next to her, all prettied up with her pale blue pinafore and blonde pigtails.

Scarlet internally rolled her eyes.

The matron stuck out her finger. "Get cleaned up right now. Your new parents will be arriving shortly to collect both of you." She nudged Penelope forward. "Help her."

Scarlet raised an eyebrow. This wasn't what she'd expected. No one wanted to adopt an eleven-year-old with a troublesome reputation. Pretty little Penelope, however, hadn't been here long.

"Parents?" Scarlet asked.

The matron rubbed her temples. "Hurry up, or I'll never be rid of you."

"What about breakfast?"

"You get none since you can't be bothered to care about your personal appearance." The matron grabbed Scarlet's arm, throwing open the door to the bath and shoving both girls inside before locking it behind them. If that wretched woman gave them more than a measly spoonful of gruel, maybe she would have an appearance to care about.

Penelope turned up her nose, moving as far away from the bath as possible. "You can wash yourself. Don't think that just because we're being taken together that I'll ever call someone like you my sister."

Scarlet stripped off her rags and began scrubbing her body in the cold water. This was so unnecessary. "Likewise," she said. "I didn't ask to end up with a brat like you, either."

"So says the murderer."

Scarlet's hand froze. She couldn't possibly know about that. She turned, her voice slow and deliberate.

"Say that again."

Penelope folded her arms. "Everyone knows you're cursed, Red. There's no way an infant could have survived a fire like that, unless she started it. Bet that's where you got your red hair from. Face it, you killed your own—"

She shrieked as Scarlet lunged from the bath, tackling her to the ground. Wisps of steam rose from her body.

"Say that again!"

The door was flung open, and Scarlet was dragged to her feet by the matron's iron grip around her arm.

"Can't leave you two alone for one minute, can I?"

Penelope got up, looking at the dirt on her clothes. "Look what she did to my dress!"

"You'll be fine," the matron snapped, sending her out of the room. "Not much longer..." she muttered. "The more gone before the war, the better."

After a rather aggressive scrubbing, Scarlet stood in the waiting room, rubbing her bare arms. Her skin was still slightly red, and she wore a dress that matched the ridiculousness of the brat next to her. The matron had even put a little red bow in her hair.

Gross.

The matron paced in front of the door. She needn't be so nervous. Even if the matron had roped a poor couple into taking a troublemaker like her, sweet little Penelope would be enough to make sure that they showed. Sweet little Penelope, with a tongue as nasty as a crowcodile. Luckily, the stupid brat didn't seem to know about the festival—just the age-old rumor that had clung to her ever since she had arrived. Scarlet shook her head. With what happened with that man, she was sure that it wasn't just a rumor. She must have killed her beautiful, smiling mother as an infant—with the same fire that consumed the man.

Scarlet fiddled with her locket, closing her eyes for a moment. The matron was still pacing back and forth. Maybe these so-called new parents just wanted her to do back-breaking labor for them. There was no other reason why they'd want someone as old as she was. If that were the case, she'd be out of there in an instant. It didn't matter where she went, as long as she was out. She could take care of herself.

When the knock came at last, the matron straightened her dress and puffed out her chest before opening the door.

"Welcome back to the Last Chance Orphanage. Please come in."

Scarlet almost snorted. No one could say that absurd name with a straight face, let alone that cheerfully. The couple who walked in were nothing like she'd expected. A stout man with a kind face and a thin blonde woman in a high-necked dress—ordinary. And bakers, apparently. The woman glanced over at her and smiled, sending shivers down her spine.

Scarlet looked elsewhere, but she could feel the woman's eyes burning a hole through her. The matron eagerly counted out the small sack of gold coins the man handed her, and the two of them were ushered into their new lives.

The man, Henry, talked non-stop as they sat in the carriage; his wife, Marianne, didn't say much at all. Penelope took to them quickly, answering all his questions with an appropriate balance of child-like naivety and enthusiasm.

"I think we're going to get along quite nicely," said Henry, giving Penelope a nod.

Penelope shot her a smug look, and Scarlet turned to the window. Penelope was going to have them wrapped around her finger soon, if she didn't already. It didn't really bother her; they would either like her or not. Her bet was that they wouldn't. No one wanted a cursed child. Her stomach turned. She wasn't sure if it was from the nerves or the fact that Marianne had been staring at her the whole time. There was something familiar about her that she couldn't quite put her finger on.

Their cottage, attached to the bakery, was unexpectedly quaint. Marianne pulled out two dolls, one for each of them. While Penelope squealed, Scarlet held hers at a distance. It bore a remarkable resemblance to its new owner, with long scarlet hair, emerald eyes and a pointed nose—right down to the birthmark under its left ear. Beautiful, but creepy. Marianne couldn't have known what she looked like beforehand, not to this level of detail. She stole a glance at Penelope's doll, which, while blonde, looked nothing like her.

"Do you like it?" asked Marianne, bending down so that her face was level with hers. There was a reddish mark on her neck, and another mark on her hand, as though it had crept over her body like a disease, hiding under her clothing.

"Yes," said Scarlet after a pause. Better not to offend her.

Marianne cocked her head. "What's that around your neck?"

Scarlet's hand flung to her locket, a little warmer than normal. "Just something I was left with."

"May I see?"

Scarlet inched back, shaking her head and tucking it under her clothes. Over her dead body.

Marianne smiled and stood, heading for the room at the end of the hall, locking the door behind her.

She breathed a sigh of relief.

"Don't mind her. She don't like to be disturbed when she works," said Henry.

Penelope piped up with more chatter, and the attention was once again pulled away from Scarlet. They spent the rest of the day being shown around the bakery and what their roles would be. It wasn't backbreaking work and Henry seemed like a nice man, but the uneasiness remained. By the time they all sat down to supper, her stomach was in knots.

Henry looked at both of them with the most serious expression she'd seen from him so far. "I'll say it now. With a war coming and all that, it might seem silly to take on a couple of young'uns. But my wife and I have wanted children for a long time, and I hope you'll be able to feel at home here." Henry paused, looking at Marianne and giving her hand a squeeze. Then he clapped his hands together, his face springing back into his comforting smile.

Conversation was awkward at best, though Penelope filled in for her while she remained silent, not really paying attention to their chatter. Maybe it wouldn't be so bad here. There was food, at least. And if things went south, there was enough to steal and run. Scarlet wolfed down everything on her plate. It was far better than the gruel to which she'd become accustomed.

"—the missing princess was found. They say she destroyed an entire army," said Henry. "And defeated a general."

Scarlet's ears pricked up. Royalty meant valuables.

Marianne nodded. "Can't believe it was our little Mina, taken in as a mere servant."

Scarlet's face fell. She should have known a rumor like that would get out of control.

"You think she'll remember us?"

"Unlikely. We won't matter anymore."

The more she listened, the surer she was. There was no way a princess would get her hads dirty. Scarlet excused herself early, walking to their room. The door at the end of the hall was ajar, and a sliver of light peeked through the gap. It was the room into which Marianne had disappeared for hours earlier. She must have been up to something. Glancing over her shoulder, she slipped inside.

The room was filled to the brim with dolls of all sizes, just like the ones Marianne had given them. Wooden and porcelain faces stared back at her, their blank eyes and frozen smiles displayed in every direction. She was sure that their pretty, frilled dresses and expertly carved faces would make them quite popular. It would be better than slaving away in a hot bakery, in any case. But instead, they sat here, meticulously clean and untouched. This was less of a pastime and more of an obsession.

Scarlet shivered, and her eye was suddenly caught on a silver glint peeking out of a closet on the back wall. It felt like it was almost humming. Narrowing her eyes, she approached it, opening the door farther. She stifled a yelp as a hand fell from the closet and onto her arm. When it landed on the floor beside her, she let out a breath. It was just a doll's arm, wooden and unmoving.

She stuffed it back into the closet with a shudder and reached for the silver glint. It was a long, thin, almost glass-like rod, but somehow, it was more beautiful than the dolls. Footsteps sounded behind her, and Scarlet jerked her hand back, turning to the exit. She almost ran straight into Marianne, who caught her with one arm.

"I see you've found my workshop," she said. Her voice was smoother than before, more refined.

Scarlet swallowed as Marianne patted her head.

"It's all right. I was going to show you later, anyway. Run along now and get some sleep." She released her with a smile, and Scarlet nodded, gripping her skirts in an effort to prevent herself from bolting. When the bedroom door was safely closed, she dived under the warm blanket. She couldn't even appreciate the fact that she was in a real bed. There was abso- lutely no way she was staying here.

What was all that about? That woman wasn't normal; she didn't feel normal. And that silver rod was no ordinary piece of metal—it resembled something like a giant needle. It was all just too creepy.

Scarlet lay there until the early hours of the morning, her heart still pounding. Before the sun began to creep over the horizon, she changed into her old clothes, threw on a cloak and slipped out of the house. Thankfully, no one seemed to follow her. She walked aimlessly until the city began to wake up once more.

Scarlet slumped against a wall. She couldn't go back to the orphanage. Maybe she could search for her friends, instead. She scrunched her face as she struggled to recall their faces. If

Blue and Ivory couldn't return for her, she could go to them. She sighed. It would be a long shot. They were probably long gone, and she had no way of knowing where they'd be. Maybe she was making a mistake; maybe she was overreacting. There was nothing wrong with being a craftswoman, and Marianne had probably gone to extra lengths to make her feel at home. It *was* a workshop for sewing, after all. Maybe that's what the needle was for.

A town crier passed her, making his morning rounds. "Missing princess discovered in Anadrieth! All business at the castle temporarily closed!"

Scarlet tapped her finger on her knee. That's right; the princess was supposedly here. If she could just steal one measly trinket, she would have enough gold to get by on her own, to leave this place, to find her friends. But if she got caught, it would be a death sentence. She could deal with that; it wasn't like anyone needed her around. And if she got too close for comfort, she could always go back to the bakery, fill her belly and try again another day. Scarlet shivered. She would at least take the blanket next time.

With a new goal in mind, she made her way toward the castle, hitching a ride onto the backs of various carriages. The castle was much larger up close, with stone walls and a guarded iron gate encircling the menacing gray structure. It was intimidating, to say the least. Scarlet scouted around the perimeter, searching for a way in. A tall ice pear tree overhung the side of the wall. She scaled it, concealing herself within its leafy branches.

Once safely hidden away in the tree, she realized that she was overlooking what appeared to be the training grounds, filled with soldiers evidently preparing for war. It wasn't the best point of entrance with so many men around, but she could wait until nightfall. Scarlet plucked an ice pear from the tree, sinking her teeth into the velvety pink skin. It wasn't quite ripe, but a few of them began to satisfy her growling stomach.

Hours later, she readjusted her position to appease her sore behind. Not surprisingly, the princess was nowhere to be seen. There was no entourage, no fancy carriages, no royal gowns. She groaned. It was possible that the princess herself was nothing but a village rumor. There was absolutely no one important-looking around, not even a distinguished army general or a decorated imperial servant. What a life these rich people must lead. It didn't look organized in the least. Even the servants seemed to be mixed in with the soldiers.

Scarlet squinted, edging forward on her branch. They were definitely taking up arms. Strange. How hadn't she noticed it before? There were women on the training grounds, too. She leaned closer, poking her face through a bigger gap in the leaves. There she was. Or rather, there was a woman who looked important enough to be the princess. She was holding a bow in her hands, pointing it at the tree. Scarlet gasped as an arrow whizzed right into the foliage, and she lost her grip.

There was a brief moment of panic before she hit the ground hard, getting a face full of dirt and snow. Her vision filled with black spots, and she clutched her head. This was bad. She had to get out of here. That warm bed was starting to sound so much nicer, even if it did come with a creepy doll lady.

Scarlet staggered to her feet, and her eyes met the young woman's. Her mouth fell open. It was her. That same beautiful face she had always seen in her dreams.

"Mama?"

The young woman was pointing her bow at her, but she didn't look very threatening. The arrows weren't even tipped with metal. She seemed unsure of herself and unsteady on her feet.

"Who are you?"

Scarlet held her hands up anyway. "Uh, Scarlet." No one else had seemed to notice them. She stole a glance behind her. She could easily outrun the woman and try to scale the wall. Climbing had always been her forte.

"I'm Lady Adelia," the woman said.

Scarlet's heart sank. She couldn't help it. People had mentioned that her mother was a drunk, an unmarried woman who got herself pregnant and lived off of the money the father sent her to keep quiet. It was a far cry from the Lady of Anadrieth, who was now standing before her.

"What were you doing?" prompted Adelia.

"I was just leaving," mumbled Scarlet. It was just an unfortunate coincidence. Dragons, even Marianne looked somewhat like her mother. She couldn't just go around calling every blonde woman her mother. Besides, she was long dead.

Scarlet backed away, glancing up at the tree. It was too high from here, but the cracks in the wall should give her enough of a foothold.

"Wait." Adelia grabbed her by the shoulder. "This might sound strange, but you feel familiar somehow."

Scarlet took a closer look at her, noting the differences in her face. It definitely wasn't her. But there was no way that they had ever met before.

"Doubt it."

Adelia thought for a moment. "Will you come meet

someone before you run off?" She didn't wait for a response as she pulled Scarlet along.

Scarlet frowned but cautiously allowed herself to be dragged across the grounds. She could always bolt, should it come to that. They walked away from the castle toward a few individuals standing in a circle—a man and two women. The shorter woman turned toward her, and a look of shock crossed her face. Scarlet blinked as they stared at each other.

She couldn't look away. For a moment, they were no longer quite there in the castle grounds. The woman before her was glowing with a violet aura, an ethereal, commanding presence. It warmed her, filled her down to the very core, and every fiber of her being sang with joy.

Mysoviere, mysoviere.

She felt like she was home. She sank to the ground, dropping her head to her chest. It was like everything that she never knew she needed hit her at once. She had known this woman for a very long time, and yet she had no idea who she was. Her eyes were wet, but she wasn't sad. The woman approached her.

Mysoviere, mysoviere.

The chanting echoed in her mind as her spirit sang out the words.

"Mina," Adelia's sharp voice cut through the fog, "this girl fell out of the tree, and she's... I can't explain it, but there's something strange going on. Do you know her?"

The woman—Mina—knelt, embracing Scarlet's trembling body.

"Welcome back, my *phaenyx*," she whispered. Her hand softly stroked her hair, and Scarlet relaxed into her arms. And suddenly, she understood. Her memory was fleeting, but she would never truly forget this woman. It had been thousands of years since they had last met.

Mysoviere.

The one she served above all else.

My sovereign, we are reunited at last.

Scarlet smiled. She was the Spirit Guardian of Fire, servant to the three great dragon gods and, most of all, Mina.

❧ 15 ❧

CHAPTER FIFTEEN

YUKIYA

PRINCE YUKIYA LEANED over the balcony, searching the capital's streets. Sky-blue eyes honed in on the people far below, flickering across their faces.

Not her, not her.

He couldn't use his dragon's sight for long. After a few minutes, he dipped his head, closing his eyes as his white hair draped around his shoulders. Mina wasn't coming back after all. Ever since they'd sent out the retrieval party, he'd been on the balcony, waiting for her to come home. It shouldn't have been a surprise, but he'd hoped that she'd changed her mind. At least they knew where she was now.

It was all his fault that she'd run away two years ago, but he respected her need for space. Yukiya sighed. Did it have to be an empire's worth of space? Even to hear her voice would have been enough. He thought that he'd heard her once, almost eleven years ago, though it was only fleeting. Everyone thought that she'd been kidnapped, but he knew the truth.

She would never draw close to him again, not after that day—the day that every emperor before him loathed. It was part of their curse. To love, but never be loved in return. Only he was different; he had loved her before they were cursed.

Footsteps echoed behind him, one pair that was slightly heavier on the right foot and another that was almost silent—his older brother and his servant girl.

"Your Highness, may I have a word?"

Yukiya turned, the folds of his imperial robes following his slight movements across the dark wooden floor.

Lord Yuno bowed, his crisp uniform creasing as he shifted his body. While he was allowed to wear the imperial colors, the uniform was indicative of his lower rank as supreme commander; only the imperial couple was allowed to don the robes. It was an unprecedented situation that required gentle handling.

Appointing him as the supreme commander had been a strategic move to keep him close whilst pleasing the elders, who disapproved of the second-born ascending the throne. Even being addressed as lord, the same rank as their region's leaders, was a subtle insult. Every move they made was a game of dragon chess against each other.

"Of course, dear brother." Prince Yukiya brushed his hair behind his ear, the golden dragon earrings making a slight tinkling sound and the matching imperial signet ring clearly visible. The little reminder would annoy him. They exchanged smiles, their practiced pleasantries second nature, though no one important was present to watch.

Yuno's hand drifted to his belt, his thumb brushing over the handle of his sickle and chain—the counter to his own show of dominance. At first glance, the small, simple weapon was disproportionate to his body size, but those who underestimated his mastery with it didn't live long enough to tell anyone.

"I believe we've waited long enough for her to come home," said Yuno. "You should give the order to march on Anadrieth. The sooner we mobilize, the sooner the princess will be in your arms, and the sooner we'll be able to condemn them with high treason for concealing her."

Yukiya shook his head. "It's not that simple."

"Commander Ido was merely a pawn to determine if the rumors were true, as you're aware. I'll coordinate our forces. You won't have to concern yourself with any unfortunate mishaps this time."

He was always the confident one—sometimes overly so. "And your proposal this time?"

Lord Yuno snapped his fingers, and Lyra handed him a bundle of letters. Her lip was red where it had split, and there were several bruises around her wrists. Poor girl. Yuno snatched them from her, presenting the parchment to his brother.

"Correspondence to Lord Tamar of Lanadrin and Lord Cypress of Calvera to coordinate our marches."

Yukiya unfolded them, scanning his brother's neat handwriting. From a military standpoint, Anadrieth was weak—far too weak to warrant this. "You wish to use our troops in addition to theirs? Even if Eloria supports them, this is excessive."

"It's just for show. And Eloria won't join the battle." He handed him the third letter.

Yukiya raised an eyebrow. "That's..."

"An excellent use of your relationship with Lord Reinhardt, my liege."

Yuno held out his hand, and Lyra gave him a small, rectangular box. "It may be excessive, but the important part is forcing her to act. You won't get your opportunity if we don't force them into a corner."

He didn't have to look into the box to know that it contained the imperial heirlooms. Two golden dragon bracelets lay on a silk interior, a silent hum radiating from them—an extra precaution to placate her spirit, forged by some of the most powerful priestesses in existence.

"And finally, you are the key to bringing her home," said Yuno, with a triumphant smile.

Yukiya kept his expression neutral. His brother knew more than he let on—or maybe he was just very good at making educated guesses. He possessed a negligible level of spirit arts, so there was little opportunity for first-hand information. But perhaps his brother was getting it from someone else. This whole situation was a risk to Mina, even if all of the pieces aligned. He had to admit, it was a decent plan. But she would figure out exactly what they were up to, and that alone could have her standing on the sidelines and retreating into hiding once again.

"This hinges entirely on whether she cares enough about them to step in," Yukiya said.

"I have it on good authority that she does. And if we're wrong, we will simply march for real." Yuno edged the box closer. "Every princess before her has worn them before they ascended the throne. She will be safe."

"She'll despise me."

Yuno tilted his head. "Your Highness, I have been your liaison since the empress passed, may her spirit rest in peace. With all due respect, I believe it's safe to say, the princess cannot despise you any more than she already does. But if you were able to actually talk to her, she might have a change of heart."

Yukiya took the box, the sunlight glinting off of the gold. So, he didn't know everything, especially not how the curse worked. Although, his brother did have a point, even though his ulterior motives were obvious. The empire couldn't last much longer without a true imperial couple. Perhaps an excessive strategy was needed to stop an all-out war from breaking out.

"Make the preparations to march," he said.

Lyra moved to light a candle, then poured the melted wax in a small circle over each letter. Yukiya pressed his signet in, sealing the empire's fate.

Yuno waved a hand at his servant. "Deliver these at once."

As she gathered the letters, her hand slipped, knocking over the candle and leaving a trail of red wax running over the table. Yuno backhanded her, and she collapsed to the floor, clutching the side of her face. He immediately pulled her to her feet, rubbing his thumb over her jaw.

"Clumsy girl, look what you made me do," he murmured. "Hurry up and go."

Lyra bowed her head and scrambled away.

Yukiya frowned. "That was unnecessary."

Yuno shrugged, running his hand through his hair. "She's pretty but expendable."

"Yet, you trust her with matters of imperial importance."

"She's extremely loyal."

Yukiya refrained from shaking his head. That young woman had always been by Yuno's side, but everybody had their breaking point, and not everyone could keep their loyalty out of fear.

His brother bowed. "If you'll excuse me, then. We have much to prepare."

Yukiya nodded, and his brother left. Clutching the box, Yukiya slipped out of his room and into the hallway, sweeping toward the imperial chambers. The servants knelt with their foreheads touching the floor as he passed. Intended for newlyweds, he had avoided this part of the castle until now. Four guardsmen pulled one side of the stonewood doors open upon his arrival, the gap exactly wide enough for him to pass through.

As it closed behind him, he took in his surroundings for the first time, at least by his own experience. It was a massive room that could have housed a small army, the stonewood trees that grew inside branching out to create extraordinarily high ceilings, clearly made with dragon proportions in mind. He chuckled. Human imaginations had their limits, after all.

There was a small stone garden at the other end of the room, featuring a large indoor hot spring, complete with a miniature waterfall. It was truly a grand room befitting the imperial couple, though the architects had been a bit excessive with the decorations. Every piece of furniture, even the walls and floor, had elaborate depictions of dragons painted onto them. While there was a certain degree of vanity involved, it was rather distasteful to find images of himself everywhere he looked, though none of them were quite accurate. It was as though each of the artists had drawn a slightly different design in the hopes that one would actually be right.

Yukiya placed the box on the bedside table, next to a vase with a single red camellia—the symbol of eternal love. It drooped, and its petals were beginning to fall. He gently ran his fingers along the stem, and it stood tall again. Better. He glanced up. Carefully perched on the wall above the bed was his spirit sword. The blade was long with a teardrop-shaped hole parting the metal near the base, flowing seamlessly into the white hilt. It had been a long time since he'd summoned it to his side.

A figure dropped onto the balcony in complete silence. Sensing the new spirit, Yukiya walked over to draw back the curtain. Lucan always seemed to know exactly where he was. Then again, that was his job.

"Any news?" the prince asked.

Lucan kneeled before him, pulling the cloth from his face. While his princess tended to collect people around her, he was content with just one loyal servant.

"The princess remains in Anadrieth, with her imperial guard soon to follow, including my... previous commander." His jaw twitched. "I believe they intend to make a stand."

Yukiya's chest throbbed. The confirmation hurt. She was truly refusing to come home.

"As I feared."

Lucan scratched the back of his head, his scruffy copper hair peeking out from his hood. He hadn't been taking care of his facial hair, either, and he appeared older than he was. He'd been like that since he'd personally met Lucan, but the previous dragon's memories spoke otherwise. He didn't blame him. What happened between Lucan and Ryuko was a tragedy.

"That lord is getting close to her," said Lucan, disrupting his thoughts.

Yukiya stilled. His blood ran cold, and his breathing and heart rate slowed. "Lord Alexander, was it?"

"Affirmative."

He put his hand on the side of the doorframe. "Explain."

"He follows her around, sometimes too closely."

"And?"

Lucan swallowed. "He also kissed her... in the rain."

Yukiya took a deep breath, forcing his body to relax. "Leave."

Lucan was gone in an instant, propelling himself onto the roof.

Yukiya clenched his fist, and the stonewood doorframe buckled instantly. How dare that man even consider thinking about putting his hands on her. There would be no mercy for him, this Lord Alexander of Anadrieth, who had forced his betrothed to grovel as a mere servant. He would extract his judgment, piece by piece, until he was nothing more than a shred of meat.

And then, he would do it again.

Yukiya composed himself before exiting the imperial chambers, his servants leaping out of the way as he stormed through the palace. He needed information—history, fighting style, even his habits. He descended several flights of stairs in a few strides. At the lowest point in the palace, there was a single room, and he waved the guards away, slotting his key into the lock. Only those authorized by the imperial family had access to this room, where the very secrets of the empire were recorded. Securing the door behind him, he breathed in the scent of musty paper, allowing it to fill his lungs.

Calm down.

There was no use in getting worked up about it now. The

room of records was small, filled to the brim with information on everyone of relative importance since the dawn of the empire. Mina was rarely in here, as she herself had gathered the recent majority of the room's information.

His fingertips swept along the rows as he located the records on Anadrieth's ruling family. Lord Alexander, fathered by Lord Alastair and his wife, Lady Adalynn. Two younger siblings, illegitimate. He skimmed the page. He took over Anadrieth at the age of sixteen, after his parent's murder, subject to close investigation under the suspicion of the involvement of *that* woman, Mistress Marionette. He closed his eyes.

Those were the days when Mina had his brother delivering him almost daily correspondence. Perhaps he should thank Lord Alexander for that. He had almost wished the incidents would never cease so that they could have continued to work together, but her trail quickly went cold.

Apparently, the lord had a fear of heights, favored his right hand and was a virgin. Strange for a man of twenty-seven, though it explained his infatuation with his betrothed. A line of faded handwriting had been penned in at the bottom of the page. The barely legible scrawl was unmistakable; it belonged to Kakeru.

Confident, overprotective and dismissive of others. But he means well.

Yukiya sighed. The deceased emperor's memories were still fresh. It wasn't his job to maintain a prior vessel's friendships with those still living, but there was a twinge in his heart all the same. He returned the parchment, shaking his head. There was nothing particularly useful after all—the march would take care of Anadrieth for now—but gathering information on Lord Alexander wasn't the only reason he'd come here.

He moved toward the back shelf, pushing aside a few books. A small bag sat in the corner, and he pulled out two wrapped sweets, slipping them into his robes. Beside the bag was a small indent for his signet ring.

Pressing his seal into the indent with one hand and resting the other against the wall, he pushed his spirit through. The two barriers, present at all times, meant that he was the only one who had ever entered through here. A door slid open, revealing a passageway. There were only a few steps visible before he was engulfed in the darkness, descending far beneath the palace. But he didn't need light to see.

The air was damp and cool as the passageway opened out into a huge cavern. As far as he knew, not even Mina was aware of the network of caves and tunnels under the empire. Every exit was monitored by the cave's single inhabitant.

The cavern itself was dimly lit, the walls, pillars and large pools of still water illuminated by tiny creatures emitting a blueish glow. There were empty sconces to hold torches on the walls, but the natural lighting was rather beautiful. It seemed wrong to introduce the harsh light of fire.

Yukiya placed himself on a crate, arranging his robes as he sat. The piles of supplies stored in various locations were enough to last a lifetime, but he shouldn't need to wait long. While time was easily lost underground, they were able to keep to a regular schedule.

Sure enough, a young Lanadese boy scurried into the cavern a few moments later, raising a cloud of dust as he ran. Demetri barreled into him, smothering his robes with his grimy face and hands.

Yukiya ruffled his hair. He smelled like clay and earth. "Careful, my boy."

Demetri grinned, bouncing up and down. His brown eyes were wide with excitement.

"Are we going to play a game? Do you have any presents?"

Yukiya smiled, pointing at his soiled robes. "Is this how you greet me now?"

Demetri stopped bouncing and scrunched his small nose, puffing his cheeks. He let out a gentle breath, and the dirt lifted from the cloth, the prince's white robes pristine once more. His control was improving.

"Sorry, Papa."

Yukiya pulled the sweets from the pocket in his robes. "Now, of course, I have something for you."

Demetri stuffed the sweet into his mouth, then wiped his hand on his shirt. He didn't need elaborate clothes here, but he wasn't raised to be an animal, either. He was growing up quickly, however; it would be a good excuse to get him a new set of clothing.

Yukiya ate the other sweet, letting it melt on his tongue. "Perhaps I should hire some Elorian chefs for the palace."

"Then, we can eat sweets every day!" Demetri glanced at the ground, his mood swinging rapidly. "What's Eloria like?"

"It's a place full of wonderful food and great big ships that sail the sea."

The boy frowned. "Like what you see with your eyes?"

Yukiya shook his head, pointing toward the pools of water. "Like those, only as far as you can see."

"Will you take me, Papa?"

He couldn't. It wasn't safe, not if the right people found him. Especially *her*.

"One day."

The boy's face fell. It wasn't fair on him to keep him in the caves, but neither would it be to give him a glimpse of the outside world, only to confine him once more. With rumors of *the four* appearing, he had to keep Demetri's existence a secret.

Yukiya took his hand. "Have you been practicing?"

"You said if I practice, you'll take me on an adventure."

"Show me."

He crossed his arms, sticking out his lip. "Not till you tell me a story."

Yukiya chuckled. "All right, all right. Once upon a time, there was a beautiful maiden who was madly in love with a handsome prince. One day, an evil, jealous witch cursed the maiden with eternal hatred for the prince. The prince was very sad because he loved her with all his heart. He vowed to get his revenge on the witch and free his beloved from the curse. However, he couldn't do it alone—"

Demetri tugged on his arm. "I've *heard* this one before. You're talking about Miss Mina." He rolled his eyes. "Can't you just get a new wife?"

Yukiya raised his eyebrows. "Love doesn't work like that." He pinched his cheek. "If you were gone, I couldn't simply get a new you, could I?"

Demetri shrugged.

"Well, I couldn't. Now, about your practice?"

"But I didn't get to hear a story!"

"You didn't say it had to be a new one."

Demetri pouted but raised his hands anyway. The earth beneath them shook, and Yukiya managed a smile. Demetri had to be ready, whether he liked it or not.

CHAPTER SIXTEEN
ANTON

ANTON YELPED as the hot iron nipped his finger. He let it crash to the floor, narrowly missing his foot. This was ridiculous. Running around like a servant all day had been exhausting. Even with the other soldiers subjected to the same fate, it seemed like the work only continued to pile up, despite their best efforts. He hadn't realized just how much went into keeping the castle running.

Vivian clicked her tongue at him. "Come now, Milord. It's going to go cold before you've done a single pair." He suspected that she secretly enjoyed the power that she had over him as his teacher.

Anton sighed, picking up the iron again. Of all the things, too, she'd had him ironing women's undergarments, frills and all. No one was ever going to see them; why should it matter whether there were wrinkles or not?

"Isn't there something more useful we could be doing?"

In just two days, that girl had turned the entire castle

upside down, halting their war preparations and forcing them to work together. There were several more intruders in the castle now, as well, and he had no doubt that the girl's friends were going to be just as much trouble as she was.

"Just going on the princess' orders, Milord. Don't you want your sister to have nicely pressed delicates?"

Anton gagged, taking a step back. No wonder they were adorned with little bows. A servant wouldn't keep things like this. Beside them, Ban laughed, his dimples in full view.

"It's not that bad."

Anton shot him a glare. Ban had ended up following them around the entire day, all because that other servant girl, Jane, was too meek to be away from Vivian, the head matron. How someone as passive as her had survived under Vivian's hand, he couldn't fathom.

"That's because you're not ironing...this." He gestured in front of him, unable to make the words come out of his mouth.

Ban winked, and his smirk remained plastered to his face. He'd always been easygoing like that, nothing ever bothered him.

"Want to switch?" Ban asked, nodding to the shirt in his hands.

Anton made a show of turning his back, finishing the job as quickly as possible; there was no way that he would let Ban get his hands on anything of his sister's. Not that he cared if he touched anything of hers, but the idiot would likely never shut up about it.

"It—it goes like this," said Jane, adjusting the cloth.

Ban patted her hand, tucking his hair behind one ear. "Don't worry, darling. I've got this."

Anton put the iron down. That was it. "Don't you ever take anything seriously?"

Ban moved to the side, showing him his neatly folded stack of ironed clothes. "Well, while you've been whining, I've been working."

Anton bristled, forcing himself not to glance at his own meager pile of one garment.

"I'm only complaining because this entire thing is a ridiculous waste of time. The Lanadese are probably sharpening their axes, getting ready to murder us all, and here we are, folding silk delicates and scrubbing the floors." That stupid girl just wanted to punish them; he was sure of it. "She doesn't give a dragon's claw whether we live or die, and she evidently knows nothing of war."

No matter what memories the girl claimed to have, she was still the same bumbling idiot, just in better clothes. Even his brother was being unusually subservient. If *his* castle had been turned upside down like this, he wouldn't stand for it. Hopefully, the prince would come and collect the girl soon, and they'd finally be rid of her. Apparently, she'd even taken in some poor orphan girl who'd been skulking around the castle walls. Like they had the time and resources for that. He'd have to tell the servants to hide away the valuables.

Vivian and Jane had taken a step back, and Ban folded his arms.

"Do you believe you're helping with that attitude? None of us have been through war. You're just annoyed that you're being ordered around by someone you hate."

Anton opened and closed his mouth. Hate was somehow a strong word. He shook his head. "We're not children anymore. You don't have the right to speak to your lord like that."

Ban's face softened, almost disappointed. "You're right, I don't. But right now, you don't deserve my respect, either. You're the last person I expected to pull rank." Then, his mouth widened back into a grin. "Ah, that's it. You're still bitter about losing our archery competition."

Anton clenched his jaw. No, that wasn't it at all. But before he could respond, a voice called out. A soldier was running through the castle, gathering as many people as he could find in the servant's kitchens. Princess' orders, of course. Anton sighed as everyone else moved immediately. It didn't seem like he had a choice, but it couldn't get much worse than this.

The servant's kitchens had never looked this bad. Mountains of filthy dishes were stacked precariously on every surface, and the slightest breath could send the whole thing toppling. Grease seemed to creep over the walls, and bits of leftover food littered the floors. Anton wrinkled his nose. It smelled like sweat. That girl stood in the doorway, keeping her distance from the crockery. Now that she was dressed nicely, manual labor was clearly beneath her.

"We're having a banquet tonight, and this is the aftermath of the preparations. You two," she pointed at Anton and Ban, "get to work. I want this done before sundown." She walked off, leaving them to stare at each other. This was one of the few times when he would admit that he was wrong—it *could* get worse.

Ban flung his arm around Anton's shoulder. "This'll be fun, won't it?"

"You have a rather warped definition of fun." He could practically feel Ban's eyes glittering. Not again.

"You take that side, and I'll take this side. Whoever's done first wins."

"That's—"

"Afraid of losing?"

Anton clenched his fist. This was all her fault. He turned to Vivian, ignoring Ban. "Let's get this over with."

She nodded, not looking the least bit fazed by the amount of work before them. Vivian called over a few of her maids, instructing them to start toting and boiling water. Soon, they were buried arms-deep in soapy water, with Ban and Vivian delegating with ease.

Anton edged back and forth, unsure of what to do. Every time he moved to help, another pair of hands was already filling the gap, while Ban worked seamlessly with the others, calling out instructions exactly when needed. An efficient, productive line. Anton sighed, backing away. He'd never washed a dish in his life, and he clearly wasn't cut out for this.

Ban glanced up at him, tilting his head. "Giving up so soon? Guess it's my win."

"I'm not—"

"You haven't even tried."

Anton paused. This was none of his business, but Ban never left him alone. That was it. He headed straight for the back door. It didn't matter what that girl said; he wasn't listening any longer.

"What they say about you is only true if you believe it, too," Ban called out.

Anton stepped out onto the castle grounds, shutting the door and all of the noise with it. The Celestine Forest hugged the edge of the grounds like a silent, living wall. Ban had no concept of what was happening, and he never would. It was one thing for his sister to play around with arrows. But the second-born lord emptying chamber pots and ironing delicates? It was humiliating.

With the number of people who saw him doing menial tasks today, it was certainly a topic of conversation. The servants talked loud enough for him to hear, as if it hardly mattered if they were caught gossiping about the second born. And it didn't matter, he was simply the spare. Alexander was the only one not being subjected to this, and he was off doing dragon knows what with that girl and her friends.

Anton found himself wandering deep into the forest, traversing a trickling stream. The trees stretched their long shadows across the ground as the sun began to set, and he spied a foxen dashing through the bushes, its white bushy tail and almost clear, curved horns blending in with the surroundings. It was gone in an instant, the trail of pawprints lightly pressed into the snow the only evidence that it was even there to begin with. There were a couple of wild crowcodiles peering down at him from a tree, their beady eyes as unnerving as their many teeth. It was no wonder their presence was bad luck, but that didn't stop some of their men from taming them.

His head hurt, and he rubbed his temples, massaging them as he closed his eyes. What would happen if he kept walking and never returned? His brother would probably want to organize a search party, but his councilors would argue that they couldn't spare the manpower. Anton's duties weren't essential, and neither was his presence. He could just disappear.

He opened his eyes and stopped dead in his tracks. The

babbling stream, the rustling leaves, the chirping birds—it had all stopped. It was deathly silent. Anton whirled around, looking for the little colored lights that were usually around when something odd happened. But there was nothing. He hadn't left Anadrieth, but he was no longer there, either. It was as if nothing living had ever existed here at all—exactly as it had been in the arena. His heart was pounding. The emptiness was suffocating. He had to get out of here.

Anton backed up, tripping over his feet. He fell into something warm, and a hand closed around his arm. A calm voice cut through the silence.

"Are you all right?"

Anton shook the hand away, scrambling through the snow. The world throbbed back into focus, and slowly, the other sounds returned. His head tilted back, and a pair of stunning turquoise eyes gazed down at him. Like pools of still water, they drew him in, almost as if he were in a trance. Blonde locks fell over the man's forehead, gently cascading around his neck. A cloak was pinned around his shoulders, a waistcoat fitted around his lithe figure. That wasn't Anadese clothing.

Anton swallowed, standing up straight. The stranger was almost three heads taller than him.

"Are you all right?" the man repeated, enunciating his words. His lips were a pale red, his skin tan.

"I'm... fine." Anton didn't know where to look.

The man suddenly reached for his hand, peering at the wound that was now scabbed over. Anton blinked. His large hands were surprisingly soft.

The man frowned slightly. "Severe burn."

Anton was yanked sideways as the man strode toward the stream in one step, dragging him along. He firmly dipped their hands into the freezing water, and Anton yelped, his knees hitting the ground.

"What do you think you're—"

The man paid him no heed, staring intently into the stream. Anton's hand began to tingle, and he thought that he saw the little blue lights again, but they were gone almost immediately. As he lifted his hand from the water, Anton's mouth fell open. The skin had completely smoothed over, and not a trace of a wound remained. It was the same healing magic that Elaine could do, only far, far better.

The man stared at him, then brushed Anton's hair away from his eye, his fingertips briefly touching the scar.

Anton scrambled backward. "Don't touch me."

The man shook his head. "It's too old." Anton thought that he saw a twinge of regret pass over his face, but the man stood, offering him his hand as though the situation were completely normal.

Anton ignored the outstretched hand and reached for his sword, but it wasn't on his belt. It shouldn't have taken him this long to notice its absence, but his thoughts were more jumbled than usual.

"Who are you?"

The man seemed to study him for a moment. "Cynric."

Anton frowned. That was a strange name. "You're not from here, are you?"

"Calvera."

That explained the height. Anton's muscles suddenly tensed. Had they already been invaded? He scanned the forest, but there was no movement. Perhaps the man was just a scout, though the stocky horse behind him didn't appear to be the type for espionage. Then again, an enemy wouldn't heal him. His mind raced over the possibilities.

Cynric's expression didn't change. "I'm looking for Princess Mina."

The statement hit Anton squarely in the chest. Was everyone after that girl? She was nothing special. There was a good chance that Cynric wasn't part of the war, then, but Anton wasn't about to let his guard down. He pointed feebly toward the castle. If Cynric had hostile intentions, he was sure that his brother could handle one man, even if he did appear to be a half-giant.

Cynric nodded.

Suddenly, hands circled Anton's waist, and he found that his feet no longer touched the ground. The next instant, he was atop the massive horse.

"Wait a minute—"

Cynric mounted behind him, nudging the horse to a canter. His chest was pressed into Anton's back, and thick arms wrapped around either side of him as Cynric held the reins. Anton was frozen, trying to hold back a sneeze. He couldn't.

Cynric's voice was close to his ear. "Horses?"

Anton nodded. His mind wasn't functioning properly. It seemed like an eternity until they arrived back at the castle. Upon their arrival, the guards had finally caught onto the situation, and they surrounded them with their weapons drawn. Cynric remained composed, once again offering his hand after he dismounted, but Anton quickly flung himself off of the other side.

People were staring. The guards didn't even bother to ask Anton if the stranger was a guest or if he had been taken hostage. They bombarded Cynric with questions, though it wasn't long before the girl emerged.

"Cynric!"

Cynric's mouth curved upward as she embraced him, and he put his arm around her shoulder.

Anton stared at his feet, twisting his boot into the ground. Maybe he should leave.

Cynric began unwrapping her bandages, reaching for the gourd on his belt and pouring water onto his hands. Like he had done for Anton, her shoulder was as good as new. He was a truly talented healer; he didn't even look tired. The girl rotated her shoulder, grinning, and pulled Cynric inside.

"You're just in time for the banquet."

As if nothing had happened, the guards returned to their duties, and a servant took the horse to the stables. Anton trudged after them, keeping his distance. It wasn't like he cared what the girl did. She did seem to be excessively tactile with her friends, but it wasn't his business.

As he stepped into the banquet hall, his eyes widened. Within hours, it had been transformed into a room fit for imperial royalty, the entire hall immersed in white and gold. Where they had gotten all of it, he couldn't be sure. Dancers and musicians entertained from either side of the room, and rows of long tables had been placed in the center, piled high with smoked meats and other delicacies. Apparently, this was the type of occasion on which to waste a massive portion of their food stores.

Anton couldn't even tell the tables apart. Councilor Dallan sat beside Elaine, Master Raoul beside Jane. Men were with women, soldiers with servants, just as it had been all day. The girl stood at the front table with Alexander and Adelia, and

Anton took his place next to them. He sucked in a breath as Cynric stood to his right. He hadn't realized just how tall the man was.

"Welcome friends..." the girl began.

Anton tapped his fingers on the chair, tuning out the girl's voice, no doubt spewing some formal niceties. He scanned the crowd's attentive faces, each of them hooked to the girl's every word. What a difference birthright and a title made. Were people really that subservient that they would go along with whatever she said?

"—as we congratulate Ban. We are appointing him as your newest general."

Anton whipped his head to face her, then Ban, who slowly approached them. He looked just as shocked as Anton felt. His father, General Barret, was still with the others, staring down at the table.

"I don't understand," said Ban.

Alexander reached out his hand, shaking his. "The decision was mine. After watching you over the past few days, I can't think of a better man to lead my army. You have the respect of not only the soldiers but also the rest of the household, and I know they would fight to the death for you. I look forward to riding out to battle with you."

Anton turned away. Of course, he should have expected that the girl would pull out something like that. He couldn't disagree with the decision, however. Ban had a certain charisma that his father just never possessed. But if they were choosing a new general, why hadn't he been considered, as well? He could have done the job just as well.

He glanced at Ban and the crowd surrounding him, offering hesitant but warm congratulations. Anton let out a breath. No, he was only fooling himself. They wouldn't have reacted that way for him. He wasn't a leader—or their friend.

Everyone was seated a few minutes later, and the celebrations began once more. Anton resigned himself to putting some food on his plate. Oddly enough, the banquet hall didn't feel as awkward as he thought it would. People were passing plates around, chattering and laughing, just like they would do during the Celestial Dragon Festival. The only people who seemed irked were the councilors, but since they weren't sitting together, they were eventually pulled into conversation like everyone else. It was sort of nice.

Beside him, Alexander leaned closer to the girl, his hand running along the back of his neck. "About the other night," he began. Anton's ears pricked up. This should be good. "Circumstances have changed drastically, but I would like to... express my interest."

Anton stole a glance at the girl. Her expression was blank, well-practiced.

"The imperial household has, indeed, taken many consorts. There's nothing unusual about that. But I'm afraid I must decline, for your sake." She was quickly pulled into conversation with Kakeru, who was downing mugs of ale like water.

His brother looked perplexed. She was clearly the first woman to outright reject him. Anton almost considered that a point in her favor. Not many would have the dignity to reject a handsome lord like him.

Anton stifled a smirk. "Tough luck."

Alexander narrowed his eyes. "Shut up."

Anton twirled his fork between his fingers, listening to his sister at the other side of the table talking with the Lysanthian woman, who was waving her arms around and regaling some grand tale about fantastical machines. Whatever that was. He could tell that Adelia wasn't fond of their guests, but her curiosity had gotten the better of her.

That little orphan girl, Scarlet, was sitting on Adelia's lap, heavily engrossed in the food in front of her. Why she was sitting at the head table, he had no idea. Oddly enough, Scarlet seemed a little familiar, but he couldn't put his finger on it. She had a slight orange glow around her that ebbed and flowed randomly. Anton concentrated on them for a little while, trying to ignore the man to his right. There were two empty chairs beside them, as well, as if those people had somewhere more important to be.

Cynric sipped his drink, and even that movement was graceful. He wasn't muscular like Ban or his other companion, Kakeru, but a fight with him surely wouldn't end well. His homeland, Calvera, was built within the stonewood canopies themselves; he had to be considerably strong, even if he was a healer. Cynric tilted his head toward him, and Anton realized that he'd been staring.

"Nice weather we're having," Anton mumbled, shoving a forkful of roasted foxen into his mouth.

Cynric raised an eyebrow. "We're inside."

Of course, they were. What a stupid thing to say. Anton took a long drink, fighting the reddening of his cheeks. He nodded to the two empty chairs.

"You know who else was meant to be here?"

Cynric nodded, taking a bite of the ice pear pie, but he didn't respond. Anton awkwardly changed the subject.

"Why were you so far away from the main gates? Your companions entered from the front."

"I'm Calveran."

"Oh."

He must have known about the upcoming war and wanted to avoid trouble, which was surprisingly considerate—and clever—though it had come across as suspicious when he first encountered the man. Anton squeezed his hand into a ball. It really didn't hurt anymore.

"So, why did you help me?"

Cynric blinked. "Why wouldn't I?"

"I could have been anyone for all you knew, an enemy or something."

"Exactly," said Cynric. His eyes were soft, as though they were trying to convey a deeper understanding.

Anton stared at his plate. Perhaps this man saw no difference between friend or foe, as long as they were people who needed help, but it was a naïve worldview.

"Who gave you that idea?"

"Princess Mina."

Of course. Anton closed his eyes for a moment. "If she's so important to all of you, why have you only shown up now?"

Cynric looked pointedly at Anton's hand. "We have jobs that must be done."

"And what if she never made such a scene with that commander? How would you have found her?"

"Our task is to help people and it hasn't changed. Princess Mina is, as she keeps telling us, just one of those people."

It didn't make any sense to him, but he wanted to stop talking about her. As he opened his mouth again, a loud bang caught everyone's attention. The hall doors had been flung open, and a strange man stood alone at the entrance. From his hood to his boots and even to his gloves, he was dressed entirely in black, as if a shadow were engulfing him. He pulled the cloth from over his mouth.

"Are you all having a feast without me?" he said.

Guards caught up to him from behind, and some of the soldiers at the tables had drawn their weapons. Anton shook his head. Ban had his work cut out for him. Their men had some of the slowest reaction times he'd ever seen. Not like he could talk, though. Who was this man? Neither Cynric nor the girl seemed alarmed, so perhaps he was one of the missing guests.

Kakeru stood, bumping the table. "Hey—where is she?" he half-slurred.

"Sit down," Sara hissed, yanking his mug from him.

The man's expression fell, and he sprinted up to their table. He glanced over all of them, the bags under his eyes evident.

"Lord Tamar took Hanabi."

❀ 17 ❀

CHAPTER SEVENTEEN

ALEXANDER

"You had *one* job," Kakeru shouted, knocking his mug off of the table. "Of all the incompetent fools. I suppose it's now *my* fault I paired Hanabi with Ryuko."

Alexander assumed that this Hanabi and Ryuko were more of Mina's friends, or more accurately, her imperial guard.

The man—Ryuko—removed his hood. Dark hair framed his face, tattered and scruffy, as though he hadn't maintained it in months. He slammed a letter on the table and stared at Mina, blatantly ignoring Kakeru.

"I also intercepted this as I was arriving."

Mina broke the seal of the winding sea serpent—the Elorian crest. Alexander swallowed, leaning closer to her as she tilted the paper toward him. It was an extremely short letter, and he suddenly felt faint. His words barely escaped his lips.

"Eloria is... dissolving the alliance agreement?"

"What?" said Anton.

"Let's take this elsewhere," said Sara, glancing around the room as worried murmurs began to rise from the crowd.

Mina nodded, and they all stood. The councilors followed after them, hurriedly excusing themselves from the table. Alexander put a hand on General Ban's shoulder. "Keep everyone as calm as you can, please."

Ban nodded, hanging back in the hall.

Alexander followed Mina and her imperial guard in a daze. This couldn't be happening. Maybe his brother was right. Maybe he had spent too much time gallivanting around the castle with Mina after all. He should have taken care of this mess while they still had the chance. He clenched his fists. There was nothing he could do about it now. He had failed his people.

They all filed into the cramped war room and took their seats, some opting to stand behind the chairs. Alexander leaned against the back wall. He didn't deserve to sit at the head of the table. Was he even fit to rule?

"Let's assess the situation," said Mina, laying the letter in front of them.

Alexander shook his head. "What's there to assess? Clearly, Lord Reinhardt wasn't pleased we were unable to make it there at the appointed time." He sighed. "We didn't fulfill our end of the agreement, and therefore, he has no obligation to, either. We're at their mercy, not the other way around."

"They can't just end it like that," spluttered Councilor Raoul. Then, he looked at Scarlet, who shrunk behind Adelia. "And why is there a child in here?"

"Don't worry about her," said Adelia, cradling her arms

around Scarlet. "I'll go and talk to Lord Reinhardt. I'm sure I can fix this."

"No, there's something else going on." Mina turned to Ryuko. "But first, I need you to explain. We need to have the whole picture. What happened to Hanabi?" The councilors looked upset at the change of subject, but Mina held out a hand to silence them.

Ryuko clasped his hands, the worn leather of his gloves rubbing together. It was an interesting clothing choice; only those in lower-class professions needed to wear gloves. They didn't match the rest of his outfit, either, as everything else seemed to be meticulously cleaned and new, except his gloves, which looked like they'd been carefully repaired over the years. Ryuko took a deep breath.

"Hanabi had been wanting us to go to Lanadrin for ages, but I... wanted to finish what we were doing in Calvera. She wouldn't let it go, and when she found some sort of lead, I finally agreed to take her. We ended up getting separated, and it wasn't long before they spotted her. Lord Tamar seemed to know exactly who and what she was. The first thing he checked was her right shoulder for her temple mark. Luckily, I'd reminded her earlier that Lord Tamar had a particular interest in the temple girls, so she gave me this before we entered the city."

Ryuko pulled out an ancient-looking, leather-bound book edged in gold. Adelia gasped, and Alexander furrowed his brows, leaning closer to the thick book to see what the fuss was about. The book cover was blank, the only adorning feature a strap holding the pages shut. It bore a strange mark that he'd never seen before—a single dragon, clutching a book.

Alexander racked his memory. He'd never seen an imperial dragon symbol *without* a pair of them. Then again, they weren't the Empire of the Dragon Gods for nothing, and people often forgot about the Dragon Goddess of Chaos. Still, curiosity got the better of him.

"What is that?"

Adelia was almost climbing over the table to get a better look. "It's the mark of the dragon temple!"

Mina nodded. "Hanabi is from the line of imperial priestesses."

"Oh." That stuff again. Alexander glanced at Mina. With the actual existence of the dragon gods, it made a little more sense why they still worshipped them in the capital. He'd never really understood it until he saw the evidence himself.

"And she's the key to ending Anadrieth's war," Mina's words rang out.

Alexander stared at Mina blankly, not wanting hope to take root in his heart. This wasn't one of his little sister's storybooks, and one person alone couldn't turn this situation around.

"The key?"

"She's a *priestess*," said Adelia, looking at him pointedly. "It figures that you don't understand how powerful they are, though. You've never listened to me before." She pulled out the book that she seemed to always carry with her.

Alexander paused. Now that the two books were side by side, they looked quite similar, only Adelia's was much more worn. Perhaps he should have paid a little more attention to his sister's ramblings. He looked at the faded emblem, then down at the pin on his cloak. Did this have something to do with why Anadrieth's regional crest was a priestess temple?

Ryuko stiffened at the sight of Adelia's book. "Where did you get that?"

"I've always had it." Adelia shrugged. "But that's not important—"

"It means you're a priestess, too," Ryuko said in a low voice. "A woman with the ungodly power to manipulate the human spirit itself, like a puppet on a string."

"What? No, it's not *mine*. I've just always owned it."

"Stand down, Ryuko," said Mina.

Adelia fell silent, and Alexander began pacing. This was too much to process.

Kakeru rubbed his temples and clutched a jug of water, which sloshed onto Councilor Dallan's lap. "And you let them just take her?" he slurred, ignoring Dallan's protests. "I think *you're* the dreadful consequence. Why'd you go in the first place, if you *knew* that Lanadrin guy would take her?"

"Because of the sudden war declaration," he paused, sucking in his lips. "And she said she found traces of the Mistress." Ryuko's voice rose. "So, of course, we went immediately. Hanabi said there was something suspicious about the whole thing."

Alexander stopped pacing, and the room fell silent. Even Mina looked surprised. It couldn't be *that* woman. Not now. Not with everything else going on. He gripped his sword. The Mistress had almost single-handedly toppled the entire empire, including Anadrieth, then disappeared without a trace.

"Mistress Marionette?" the former General Barrett whispered.

"The one and only," said Ryuko grimly.

"Impossible," said Sara.

"She's dead," Councilor Raoul scoffed, flicking the leftover crumbs from his belly. "Those Celestial Assassins took care of her, for sure. She's been gone for, what, a decade?"

Ryuko glanced at Kakeru, who glanced at Sara and Cynric. After a moment, they collectively pulled out black dragon masks with a sliver of gold glinting around the edges.

"We didn't take care of her. She just vanished."

His councilors were taken aback. Councilor Dallan leaned as far back in his seat as he could. He had been strangely silent throughout the entire conversation. Maybe it'd been too much for him to take in, even Alexander's head was spinning.

Mina's imperial guard were the Celestial Assassins? That was the only thing that made logical sense. But everything else—that a single priestess was the key to ending the war, and that the Mistress was alive, having a hand in said war —did not.

Find the cause, Mina's voice echoed in his mind. Alexander rubbed his chin, the stubble pricking his fingertips. Maybe it *did* make sense. If the Mistress were behind the war itself, maybe it would explain Lord Tamar's erratic behavior.

"We've all lost to her before. How can we win now?" he muttered.

Mina stood, tightening her sword belt, and everyone turned expectantly. She had to have a plan.

"I'm going to see Lord Reinhardt. Alone. There's something I need to confirm." Her voice rang out loud and clear, though each syllable felt like ice. She took Lord Reinhardt's letter, slipping it into her pocket. "I'm afraid that your last mission as my Celestial Assassins will have to be taken without me."

Alexander blinked. "You're... leaving?" He searched her face. That couldn't be her plan. There was far too much at stake here.

"Last mission?" asked Kakeru, who seemed to have sobered up in an instant. "But we just got here." Her imperial guard seemed just as bewildered as everyone else.

Anton stepped in front of the princess, clenching his fists, though Alexander could tell that it wasn't quite in anger.

"You come and disrupt everything, and now you're deserting us?"

Scarlet jumped up, running over to cling onto Mina. "I'm coming with you."

Mina shook her head, giving the girl a gentle pat. "It's not time yet, my little phoenix. Stay with them. You'll know when to join me."

"But you can't leave us now," said Adelia, the pain in her voice unmistakable.

Mina's eyes swept over all of them, her expression unreadable. Like a beautiful statue, she felt so distant from them in that moment.

"Do you all doubt me?"

Alexander could practically hear the silence. "I..." he faltered. The words were lodged in his throat. Her question was directed at no one in particular, but he'd spoken too quickly. He wanted to say no, but the timing was undeniably suspicious. She wasn't just leaving; she was running as fast as she could. With practically the whole empire bearing down upon them—and the fact that their only hope a girl who was already in the enemy's clutches—he didn't blame Mina for wanting to leave. He wanted to believe her, wanted to believe *in* her. But the words wouldn't come.

Mina's eyes softened, and she gave them all a small smile, as though she knew things they didn't. Her gaze came to rest on Anton.

"Remember, I'm your friend." Then, she looked at Kakeru. "Tell Hanabi one last thing: remember your oath."

As Mina moved to leave, Kakeru stood, pulling out a small ceremonial dagger adorned with a tassel on one end.

"If... this is truly what you wish, I can't stop you. But before you go, I have one request. After all these years, we'd like to renew our oath of loyalty to you." He glanced at Ryuko. "All of us." Kakeru pressed the tip of his finger into the dagger, drawing a drop of blood.

Mina paused, then nodded. She drew her sword, holding it out in front of her. Kakeru held his finger over her sword, letting the droplet fall. It gave a slight hiss before the blood was absorbed into the blade. He then held out the dagger to Ryuko, who took it after a long pause. One by one, her imperial guard did the same.

Alexander felt a shiver go through him. He wasn't familiar with any of this, but even he could sense the binding power behind a gesture like that. Even his councilors were unusually silent.

Mina went to sheathe her sword when a voice called out.

"Wait. I want to take the oath, as well."

Alexander turned to see his sister holding out her hand expectantly. He shook his head.

"But—"

"It's not your decision," Adelia snapped. She took the blade and slid it along her index finger, meeting Mina's eyes. "I swear, I will always follow you no matter what happens.

Not because you're the princess, but because you're my best friend. You'll *always* be my best friend."

Mina smiled as the droplet sank into her sword with a slight hiss.

Adelia turned the hilt of the dagger to face Alexander. Her gaze was almost a challenge. She'd noticed his hesitation before and wanted to see if he'd do it, too. But he couldn't move.

Mina slid her sword back in its sheath, and the moment was lost. "These are my final orders to you all", she said to her guard. "Protect them all with your lives."

Her imperial guard put one hand across their chests and the other behind their backs. Mina mirrored their salute. Then, after one last look, she left without a backward glance.

Alexander ran his fingers through his hair. His hands were shaking, and his legs were numb. She was gone. A whirlwind that had barreled into his life and stirred everything up, only to leave the way she had come. Were they really on their own now? He gripped his Golden Dawn for comfort.

He had to snap out of it. He was the Lord of Anadrieth; it didn't matter if he didn't want the responsibility. His people had laid their lives in his hands. Whether they had the princess with them or not, he had to do something. He couldn't count on her to return; it didn't sound like she was going to, anyway. He steeled himself, mustering his courage. If he sounded confident, he could fool himself into being confident. It had always worked before, and it was going to work now.

"Councilmen, I want you to prepare Anadrieth for war under the direction of Lord Anton and General Ban. Get as many people behind the castle walls as you can. Adelia, work with the servants to prepare the supplies and get people settled." His siblings looked surprised, but he had no choice to lean on them this one time. They all had to step up now.

Alexander glanced at Mina's imperial guards. "As Princess Mina said, Hanabi is the key to ending the war, though I don't know how. If we go to Lanadrin, we may be able to find out more about the Mistress, and perhaps I could finally get an audience with Lord Tamar himself. Will you help me rescue the priestess?"

Alexander held his breath. To rescue a hostage in the heart of enemy territory with half-a-dozen people and no plan was insane. Not to mention, it would take at least three days to ride far enough north to cross the river, and the Plains of Scoria would only slow them down further. There was even a chance that Lanadrin was marching already. If that were the case, they'd run into them, unprepared.

"Of course," scoffed Kakeru. "We were already going to do that. But you follow our lead, got it?"

Alexander nodded, his mind focusing. Mina had set the stage; he was sure of that much. Now, it was up to the rest of them to finish it.

"All right. It's time for the rest of you to go back out there now. General Ban can only stall the people for so long."

For once, no one protested, and his siblings and councilors headed back out to the banquet. Alexander took a seat. There was a little more breathing room now.

"Does anyone have a plan to get into Lanadrin?"

This was one area in which he knew he couldn't take the lead. He'd never been to Lanadrin, and there was a well-known rumor that if you hadn't been there before, you couldn't enter, just like how their Celestine Forest and the

Plains of Scoria could be treacherous if one didn't know how to navigate them.

He had no idea how Mina's guard operated, though it would be somewhat of an honor to work with the legendary Celestial Assassins themselves.

Kakeru took a swig of water. "Sara, how long do you need to force everyone from the castle?"

Sara bit her lip, counting on her fingers. "A few hours to make more explosives, and probably half a day to infiltrate and plant them."

Alexander blinked. She could *make* explosives? They were incredibly rare.

"And the range?"

"If you can get close to the castle wall, I'll be able to control the ignition from there, and you can light it."

"Good. Cynric, you're in charge of getting her out."

Sara shook her head. "But I'll probably need Scarlet, and that's assuming I know where to plant them in the first place."

"Me?" Scarlet squeaked.

Alexander glanced at the girl. He didn't quite understand what Mina had told him—something about phoenixes—but the orphan girl was clearly important. She looked nervous, anxiously twirling her red hair around her fingers. There was something about her that was very familiar, but he couldn't put his finger on it.

"Right, Alexander, you'll be responsible for her," said Kakeru. Then, he stared at Ryuko.

Ryuko was drawing on a piece of parchment, his hand flying over the page. He held it out to Sara.

"Here. It's rough, and things might have changed, but it's basically what Lanadrin's castle looks like. The walls are tough, but there are several points of stress that will cause more commotion than harm."

Everyone stared at him.

"Of course, you'd know," said Kakeru as he rolled his eyes. "Once a traitor, always a traitor."

"Listen here, old man—"

"Boys." Sara snapped her fingers. "We need to get in there somehow, and Ryuko is the only one who knows how. Time is of the essence, and there's no point bringing up old wounds. This map will do. We should prepare to move out now."

Kakeru narrowed his eyes. "Fine."

Alexander blinked. "Wait, that's it?"

"I'll explain on the way," said Kakeru, sighing. "Let's move out."

A FEW HOURS LATER, the small band was riding out of the castle and into the Celestine Forest. Alexander was silent for most of the journey, concentrating on the dangerous ride in the darkness, while the little orphan girl clung to his mare's feathers in front of him. He didn't approve of taking her with them, nor did he approve of the fact that he was saddled with her, but Kakeru hadn't left any room for protests.

They headed north, as expected, until the other riders began to veer away from the path, leading them west. Alexander frowned. That couldn't be right. The Moonstone River was at its most treacherous there, with no way to cross. It certainly helped to lessen the number of soldiers needed for border patrols and forced anyone heading toward them to take the long way around, but that necessity went both ways.

They stopped at the banks—near the spot where they'd found Mina two years ago—and dismounted, approaching the water's edge. The deep rapids were almost black, the swirling void the cause of many a death.

Alexander scratched the back of his neck. "Is this part of the plan?"

Ryuko eyed him. "If you're going to follow the Celestial Assassins, you're going to travel like a Celestial Assassin."

Cynric cocked his head. "I could slow the rapids."

"I might be able to hover over it," said Sara.

Kakeru sighed. "Be reasonable." He pushed up his sleeves, kneeling down to dig his fingers under the snow. The ground began to rumble.

Alexander stumbled backward, shielding Scarlet as the earth flew out from beneath him. Pieces of the bank ripped themselves apart, crashing together and forming a makeshift bridge across the river that ended far off in the distance.

Cynric raised his hands, and the river gently rose to soak the earth, the clay binding the bridge together.

"Hurry up," Kakeru grunted.

Sara struck a piece of flint, sending a shower of sparks through the air as she knelt near the bridge. "I am, but you could have given me some warning."

She blew on the tinder until a tiny flame appeared. Alexander shuddered as a warm breeze suddenly swept past him. With her other hand over the flame, it grew, and Sara held her hand close to the bridge as the fire spread quickly across the clay. Alexander held an arm in front of his face, the heat too intense for his skin.

Ryuko flung his arms out, and a silvery liquid spilled out of his sleeves. It snaked its way across the bridge, hardening and lining it with some foreign metal.

Kakeru smacked his hands together, shaking off the dirt. "Now, that's how you get something done effectively."

Alexander couldn't stop gaping. It was just like Mina had done that night in the forest, only so much more. They didn't even break a sweat. If this worked, it would cut days off of their journey.

"Amazing," said Scarlet, her eyes glistening with excitement.

"Are you coming?" shouted Kakeru.

The rest of them were already making their way across the bridge without hesitation. Shaking himself from his thoughts, Alexander ushered Scarlet ahead of him and grabbed his horse's reins, leading it across. He placed one foot on the narrow bridge, then the rest of his weight. It felt as real and as stable as if it had been built from years of hard labor. The water rushed underneath them, close enough to touch and he couldn't help but bend down to brush his fingers in it. The water was ice cold of course, but it didn't bother him.

As soon as they were safely across, Kakeru snapped his fingers. The bridge broke apart, the earth returning to its original place, and the liquid metal slithered back into Ryuko's sleeve.

"Hey," snapped Ryuko. "At least wait until I get it back."

"Then, you better keep up," Kakeru said with a shrug.

"We can't read your mind!"

Alexander couldn't understand how they could possibly work together with so much squabbling. Any dissent amongst his men was squashed immediately. A unit could only function if there was one clear leader in charge. These two, however, were at each other's throats every time the other opened his mouth. As Sara stepped between them once again, he sighed. How were they ever going to infiltrate Lanadrin at this rate?

"They don't mean it," said Scarlet.

"What?" Alexander was surprised. She'd barely spoken since they'd left.

"Those two, they're like my old friends—always bickering, but they love each other all the same."

"I highly doubt that."

"Then, you're not looking hard enough."

Alexander frowned. The nerve of this girl. "Excuse me? You could stand to be a little more polite to the one who's sheltering you instead of throwing you back out into the streets."

Scarlet flicked her hair over her shoulder. "You might be the Lord of Anadrieth, but my only sovereign is the princess. Besides, I was just making a comment." She stared at him, her brilliant emerald eyes mirroring his. "It's not smart to get defensive that quickly. You never know who will take advantage of your weaknesses."

She was smarter than she looked. Alexander let out a breath. Why was he always in the wrong these days?

The others were on the move again, and they mounted his horse. Alexander couldn't help but look over his shoulder every other minute. If they were seen by a patrol, they would be done for, especially him.

The landscape around them was almost as bare as the Plains of Scoria, except there were more signs of life here. Deerabits bounded across the dry earth in packs, their antlers barely squeezing into the underground holes. It was his first time seeing them in the wild, and he marveled at how graceful they were. They could see a long way around them in all directions, but besides the small animals, he couldn't spot any other signs of life; more importantly, he couldn't spot any Lanadese.

Scarlet yawned, shifting in the saddle for what had to be the tenth time.

"You ever ridden a horse before?" he asked.

"Nope. And I don't really want to again," she added.

Alexander couldn't help but feel sorry for her. His first time riding a horse felt so long ago, but he would never forget how uncomfortable it was.

"So, you lived in... the Last Chance Orphanage, was it?" A dilapidated building that was. They could barely call themselves an orphanage. Her accent was undeniably from the streets, much like Elaine's, though a little more refined.

Scarlet nodded. "Had to fend for ourselves."

"Then, how did you end up at my castle?"

Scarlet shrugged. "Heard the rumors about the princess, so I thought there'd be something worth my freedom around."

Of course; she was a little thief. It was strange, though. She had come to steal from the princess, yet now she proudly pronounced her loyalty.

"I know what you must be thinking," said Scarlet. "And I can't explain it. As soon as I saw her, I was inexplicably drawn to her, like she was the only one in the world that mattered." She turned to face him. "Truthfully, I don't even want to be here. It's like everything inside of me wants to follow her—wherever she goes. She called me her phoenix. I know who I am, and I get flashes of our long history together. But..." Scarlet sighed. "I don't want to be this spirit guardian of fire or anything like that. I just want to find my friends." She pulled a trinket out from under her shirt, rubbing the surface with her fingertips, the silver glinting in the moonlight.

Alexander peered over her shoulder. His eyes instantly narrowed. "Can I see that?" Either she was a foolish thief, or his eyes were playing tricks on him.

Scarlet immediately tucked it back into her shirt. "No."

"I really need to see it."

She glared at him, her eyes like glowing embers. Her skin became hot to the touch, and even his horse was starting to get uncomfortable.

Alexander backed off, holding up one hand. As far as he could tell, this girl possessed the spirit arts, just like the rest of Mina's guard, and he certainly didn't want to catch on fire.

Scarlet took a deep breath, shaking her head vigorously, and the heat subsided. "Sorry. I didn't mean to do that. I don't... ever want to do that again."

At that moment, Alexander understood her tone. "You got someone hurt, didn't you?"

Scarlet paused, then nodded.

"You and me both," he said. "It makes you feel helpless. Like you have no control, even though you should."

Scarlet glanced at him, surprised. Then, she curled up as tight as she could against the horse.

"It was a man. He was screaming at his wife," she whispered. "I'd...broken into their house, thinking they wouldn't be home for hours. But they'd come home early from the festival, and I was trapped. Then, he killed her, and I lost control." Her voice was shaking and barely audible. "I killed him. The whole house went up in an instant, and I walked out unscathed. But I can't stop seeing his face."

Alexander pulled her into a gentle embrace, stroking her hair with one hand. She was trying to quiet her sobs in his chest. He couldn't help but think of his brother, curled up with his knees to his chest in the bath, clearly haunted by his first kill. The memory of that night at the festival surfaced. It had to have been her. The house was nothing more than ash, and the bodies had been reduced to shards of scorched bone. He hugged her tighter.

"It's always been my responsibility to take care of my little brother and sister," he said. Scarlet's sobs began to abate as she looked up at him. "Our father only loved Adelia, his little girl, and he saw value in me, the firstborn. Our mother only had eyes for me, and she despised Adelia. Anton had no one except Doll, his nursemaid. I had to be the one to protect them both."

His mare paused to nibble at one of the bushes, and Alexander gently nudged her onward. Dawn was beginning to show across the horizon, and they had a ways to go yet. Lanadrin's city was barely visible in the distance.

"Then, the Mistress got involved," he continued. "There was no proof, as usual, but there was no one else it could have been. My sister and I were right outside the room when it happened." Alexander gripped the reins. "Just a door away. A simple wooden door. I can't imagine what horrors my little brother faced inside that room, but he lost the only mother figure he had, along with our parents. He's never been the same since."

"That's not your fault," murmured Scarlet.

"It's not the only time I've failed to protect them," he said, shaking his head. "He was just a single door away."

"What happened?"

"Over here!" called Ryuko, pointing to a mound of large rocks under the shelter of some trees. "We're going to rest here for a bit."

Alexander nodded, grateful for the break. He wasn't sure what it was about Scarlet, but he felt like he could talk to her without judgment, even though she was just a child. She vaguely reminded him of his siblings, with Anton's stubborn but caring heart and Adelia's clever wit and wisdom beyond her years. And that locket. Even though he had only caught a glimpse, he was sure that it had belonged to his father.

As the sun began to rise, the dry earth readily lapped up the scorching heat. Alexander awoke from his light sleep, feeling the warmth seeping into his skin and the sweat soaking his clothes. He unhooked his cloak and stuffed it in his saddlebags, slowly shedding the layers of heavy cloth. It wasn't helping. Somehow, he was even hotter than before, and his exposed porcelain skin was turning bright red. No one else seemed to be as bothered as he was, except for Scarlet, who was fanning herself with the bottom of her shirt. Maybe if he took off his boots, that would help.

Scarlet pulled a face at him, half-covering her eyes. "What... what are you doing?"

Alexander glanced down. He didn't have much else to shed. Just when he thought that his cheeks couldn't burn any redder, they did.

Kakeru sighed, tossing him a small jar. "This will help with your skin." Then, a shirt hit him in the face. "And that'll make you look like you have clothes on. It's far more breathable."

Alexander hesitantly rubbed the cool cream into his skin. It was indeed soothing. "Thanks." He couldn't figure out if that man wanted to fight him or help him. He glanced around. The cracked earth seemed endless, but there was very little movement besides the couple of deerabits approaching him with curiosity.

"Why haven't we seen any patrols yet?" he asked.

"Do you want to?" muttered Kakeru.

"Because there aren't any." Ryuko dusted himself off. How he wasn't melting in all of that black leather was astounding. "We should get moving now."

Alexander frowned. "What do you mean, there aren't any?"

"They don't need any." Ryuko pointed north, at the Lanadese fortress in the distance. "You see that there? That's a mirage. The Nacre Wastelands have that kind of effect on people, especially after the sun rises. Any intruders just end up wandering across the wastelands until they succumb to it." He pointed to the west. "That's where Lanadrin's city actually is. Only people who have been taught the signs of what to look for know how to get there without losing their way, and only the residents have been taught."

Alexander peered across the wastelands. The mirage certainly looked convincing, and there was absolutely nothing but a hazy horizon in the direction Ryuko was pointing. He hoped this man was trustworthy; they could easily be following him into a trap. But Mina clearly trusted him, and though Kakeru had expressed issue with him before, he was silent now. There was just one question.

"Are you Lanadese?" He didn't exactly look it, but how could he know about the mirage if he wasn't?

"No." Ryuko mounted his horse. "Enough talk. We need to go."

Alexander nodded, though he wasn't exactly satisfied with the answer. Kakeru had called him a traitor. But traitor to what? Or to whom? He wasn't going to let his guard down around any of them, that was for sure.

They traveled in the direction Ryuko had pointed. There weren't any distinct landmarks, but he continuously stopped to check his surroundings. Every once in a while, he led them in odd directions and turns, instructing them to follow his exact path. Even the shape of his figure didn't seem entirely real. The sun steadily rose high above them and then began to sink once more, and Ryuko finally stopped.

Alexander's mouth opened when he realized that the light of the sun had been blocked by a massive wall with giant tusk-like spikes protruding from the top. He couldn't see the mirage from this angle anymore. They dismounted, leaving their horses behind the shade of some large rocks and trees.

Kakeru picked up a handful of the earthy dirt, dropping it directly into Alexander's hands.

"Rub this into your hands, face and clothes. You, too, Scarlet."

"Excuse me?" Alexander couldn't help but make a face. Scarlet didn't seem phased at all.

"You want to stand out even more? No one here has skin as pale as yours, Lord Winter. And cover up with these." He pulled out a couple of plain cloaks from his saddlebags.

Alexander reluctantly rubbed the dirt into his face. It was surprisingly soft. As much as he hated to admit it, it was better that he looked like a dirty commoner than a noble. The Lord of Anadrieth rolling in dirt—it was laughable. No one would suspect a thing. He wrapped a piece of cloth around his head and the bottom of his face for good measure.

Ryuko seemed more alert now, leading them quickly toward the wall. He felt around for a bit, running his hands over the surface.

"Here."

There was a small indent, and he pushed on it. A door opened straight into a crowded marketplace, and they slipped inside. Alexander held his breath. It couldn't be this easy. He half-expected guards to be upon them in an instant. But as they moved through the crowds, no one came to drag them off into the dungeons. In fact, the atmosphere of the city felt... relaxed.

Where Anadrieth was blanketed in shades of white and gray, Lanadrin was a rich, earthy palette of browns and reds. Everywhere he looked, the streets proudly displayed the Lanadese crest—two crossed axes atop a design he suspected meant 'family'. The entire city seemed to be in the middle of a festival, though at the same time, it was just an ordinary day. He frowned. From his experience, the Lanadese were supposed to be large, fierce warriors—barbarians, even. But the people around them came in all shapes and sizes.

Alexander tucked a lock of his hair under the cloth, keeping his eyes to the ground and his hand firmly clasped around Scarlet's as Ryuko led them through the alleys. It was tough to keep up, and if he took his eyes off of them for even a moment, they would be lost. And if he were recognized, it would mean certain death—for all of them. His heart was racing, thumping hard in his chest.

Everyone they passed greeted them, but he only managed a nod in return. This wasn't his best idea. He should have stayed behind. Everything about him would stick out. A smell suddenly hit him, like rotting meat and salted fish, and he gagged. This was either the part of the markets where they kept the food or the garbage.

They paused, gathering in a group. Sara would infiltrate the castle as planned, and the rest of them would split off so that they weren't traveling together. They would meet up again near the castle's inner walls at the rendezvous point at sundown. Ryuko, Cynric and Kakeru immediately disappeared in separate directions, leaving Scarlet with Alexander.

Scarlet clutched her stomach. "Can we get some food? It smells good."

"Are you sure?" said Alexander, holding his nose.

Scarlet dragged him up to the nearest stall, where a burly merchant gave her a toothy grin. The merchant was shorter than Alexander, and his lack of clothing exposed his sturdy body, covered in dark, inked patterns. The man could easily wield an axe, but his elegant skill with a butcher's knife made his profession clear.

Alexander adverted his eyes, nudging away another one of those furry deerabits nibbling at his boot. They were even more abundant inside the city.

"Two, please!" said Scarlet.

The merchant eyed them, then grabbed two large sticks of blueish meat from over a small stove. "Haven't seen you two round before. You new to this part of town?"

Alexander nodded, not making eye contact.

The merchant's face burst into an even bigger grin. It was unexpectedly genuine. "On the house, then. I love meeting new people."

Scarlet chatted with him for a few minutes, and then the merchant held out the two sticks. Alexander took one, sniffing it cautiously.

"You're really new, aren't you? I promise you'll love it."

"What is it?" he asked the merchant, taking a tentative bite. Salty, but it had been cooked long enough to fall apart in his mouth. It was certainly no animal he'd ever tasted before, but it wasn't as bad as it smelled, so he ate the rest.

The merchant pointed at the creature next to his foot. "It's deerabit. Quite the common food here."

Alexander stared at the deerabit, its large brown eyes looking up at him, then back at the empty stick in his hand. His stomach felt queasy.

Two small hands scooped up the furry creature, and a little girl grinned up at him. "Sorry, mister!" Then, she cocked her head. "Is there something wrong with your face?"

Alexander froze. Were even the children aware of their enemy's identity?

The merchant called her over, giving her a stern look.

"Sorry, sir, my daughter can be a bit loose with her tongue, but she's a good girl."

Alexander shook his head, daring to glance up at them, and the merchant smiled before turning to serve another customer. He let out a breath, allowing the tension to fall from his shoulders. There was nothing particularly barbaric about either of them. An ordinary man with an ordinary daughter.

Alexander turned, scanning the rest of the people. Now

that he stopped to think about it, they all seemed ordinary. Just common people, going about their business, laughing and playing with their children.

This couldn't be right. Every Lanadese he'd ever seen was massive, almost animalistic in their fighting style and black and white in their morals and actions. They weren't really people, not when they were on the other end of his sword. He suddenly felt a bit ill, but it was probably just the meat.

A middle-aged woman stumbled into view, screeching unintelligible words as she bumped into those around her. She was undeniably sick, her charcoal-gray skin dry and flaking. A boy with tears in his eyes ran after her, clutching a stuffed doll.

Alexander took a step back as the woman came closer. An undesirable. Had the disease spread here, too? He took Scarlet's hand. They should leave at once. The commotion could escalate, and he didn't want to be caught in the midst of it. Someone grabbed the woman by the arm, feeling her forehead. A man offered her water while another picked up her child, caressing his head.

Alexander paused. It was strange. They crowded around her, but it didn't seem to be in disgust. The whole atmosphere surrounding her was different than in Anadrieth. No one was screaming, throwing rocks or calling the guards; they were taking care of her. He relaxed his grip on Scarlet.

"Different, isn't it?" she said.

Alexander slowly nodded. "Different, indeed..."

They spent the rest of the afternoon wandering through the streets, making their way toward the castle. It was the same everywhere—friendly smiles and loving families. They weren't preparing for war at all. Was it ignorance? Arrogance? Complacency?

He clenched his jaw, tucking the hilt of his Golden Dawn farther under his cloak. His people had lived the last few years in fear and were now uprooting their entire lives in the hopes of escaping their fate. This wasn't fair. If only he could give Lord Tamar a piece of his mind. But it wasn't the people of Lanadrin's fault.

As the sun fully set, the crowds began to thin, and the night guards emerged to patrol the city. They looked more like the barbarians to which he was accustomed. Alexander shivered as the temperature dropped rapidly to a more comfortable level. The rendezvous point was in sight, and they ducked through the streets to get closer.

"Psst," a voice hissed.

Alexander looked around, then up. Kakeru was on the roof above him.

"Get up here."

Alexander frowned, looking for a way up. It was very high, and it made him queasy just looking at it. The walls were flat, with no ladder or stairs in sight. Scarlet rubbed her palms together, then took a running leap at the wall. She used her momentum to scale the side of the house, and Kakeru pulled her onto the roof. Clearly, she'd done this before. Alexander stood on the ground, peering at the wall. Maybe he wasn't cut out for this.

"Maybe he should have stayed with the horses..." Kakeru clicked his tongue. "Get a run-up and use that ledge to hoist yourself up to the next part."

Alexander gritted his teeth. He was Lord of Anadrieth, for dragon's sake. He wasn't going to be left behind. Taking a deep breath, he took a running leap at the wall, his fingers fumbling at the tiny ledge. There was barely enough purchase to launch himself farther up the wall. As he reached for the edge of the roof, his foot slipped. But before he could fall, a hand caught his wrist, yanking him over the side.

"You'll get used to it," said Kakeru, leaving him to pull himself up the rest of the way.

Scaling walls wasn't in their training regime, and he was not planning on adding it any time soon. The ground was quite comfortable as it was. Even at this height, he was a little light-headed. There was a reason he wasn't one to climb trees—unlike his siblings. They passed through the city above the eyes of the guards. At least leaping between the rooftops was much easier than climbing walls.

Eventually, they stopped on a building that appeared to be abandoned, even though it was clearly in a strategic location close to the castle. Alexander glimpsed the remnants of large structures within it that resembled a forge.

Across from them, the walls were high, and the defense seemed impregnable. The entire gates were made from blackscale, with iridescent threads running like rivers through the black metal. Lord Tamar's castle was similar in stature to his, but it spread over the land instead of stacking the stories on top of each other, and the guards were stationed at every visible point. His army would never have made it this far.

Kakeru pushed something into his and Scarlet's hands—a black dragon mask.

"It'll be easier to fight in than that scarf. Let's get into position."

Alexander removed his hood, unwrapping the cloth and fitting the mask to his face. It was an odd sensation, and his range of vision was a little narrower than normal. He pulled his sword out, tilting his head side to side as he looked at his reflection. Not bad. He shook off the soot that his boots had picked up.

"What is this place?"

"An iron foundry," said Kakeru.

"Wouldn't Lord Tamar be using it to prepare for war? It looks like it's been long abandoned."

He shrugged. "People say it's possessed."

"Possessed?"

"Human statues were found encased in solid iron. When they broke them open, they realized it was the workers, suffocated by metal. A witness called the culprit, 'the iron slayer,' and then, rumors went out of control."

"Foolish reason to desert a valuable resource," said Alexander. A spark caught his eye as Kakeru began to light a small fire on the ground. "Wait, what are you—"

"Shh. This is going to partially rely on you because I can't see air spirits."

"What?" Alexander hissed.

"The only reason I agreed to let you come was so you could help pull this off. This isn't exactly a stealth mission. That's why we're going to do this the quickest way possible. Lord Tamar won't have let Hanabi out of his sight, and this way, everyone will be forced outside." Kakeru stared at both of them. "Sara is going to control the gas in a concentrated stream toward us, and you're going to light it."

He pointed at the fire and removed the bow from his back. Dousing the arrow in a sticky liquid, he handed it to him. "Then, Scarlet is going to help Sara use the explosion to protect us and, of course, take out some of his army while we're here."

Alexander saw Scarlet pale out of the corner of his eye. "Absolutely not. She's just a child."

Kakeru shrugged. "So were we. It's not a time of peace, and if you have the power to take action, you should."

"By forcing a child to kill people? She doesn't even have the control you think she does."

"What would you know?" Kakeru put his hands on his hips. "Scarlet is the embodiment of the spirit of fire itself, one of the four original elements. She needs practice, sure, but not the decades of training we did. You don't even realize you possess the spirit arts yourself, do you?"

Alexander paused in his retort. "What?"

"Mina told me, but she didn't need to. If you're truly of the Winter bloodline, you have an equal affinity for air and water, meaning you can manipulate ice, just like your father and his father before that." He waved a hand. "Which means, right now, you're the only one of us that can see Sara's signal."

Alexander clutched the bow, almost snapping the arrow in his grip. Now that he mentioned it, he *had* noticed something of the sort before. A little bit of strange frost here and there, things becoming colder when he touched them, how he never felt the cold like others did.

Kakeru sighed. "I know it's a lot to take in, but we need you both right now if we're going to rescue Hanabi. Otherwise, this journey will have been for naught, and more than one of us is likely to get captured. And if that happens, the war is as good as lost."

"I'll shield us if I can," said Scarlet in a small voice. "But I don't want to hurt anyone."

Alexander relaxed his fingers. They didn't have much of a choice, and the longer they stood there, the more likely they were going to get caught.

"All right, fine. What do I have to do?"

"You need to concentrate on seeing, but not with your eyes. Feel everything around you. You want to tap into your spirit sight, the part of you that's connected to the spirit realm. It's the first thing we learn to do."

Alexander held his breath and squinted, scrunching his face. This was the kind of talk he would have expected to come out of Adelia's mouth, not a legendary member of the Celestial Assassins. He glanced around and frowned. Nothing.

"Is something supposed to happen?"

Kakeru slapped his forehead. "The point isn't to look like you're constipated, but to tune in to the world around you. Listen to the wind. See if you can hear its voice. Feel the air beckoning you."

Alexander closed his eyes, taking a few deep breaths. He forced his mind to slow and his body to calm. A slight breeze drifted over him, and his cloak lifted behind him. There was a sour, unnatural tang to the air. He slowly opened his eyes. Tiny silver lights danced around him, as though they were waiting for his command. He reached out to touch one, but it drifted away immediately. There was a concentrated line of them snaking through the sky, shimmering their way over to him from a distant point. They definitely weren't stars.

"I think I see it."

"Then, aim for it."

Alexander dipped the arrow in the small fire, drawing back the bow. Upon its release, it arced across the sky. As soon as the flame touched the silver lights, the sky ignited, and explosions rippled in a devastating chain reaction. The castle erupted into flame, slinging debris in every direction. The guards ran toward the commotion as the occupants inside the stone walls began pouring out.

"Let's go!" cried Kakeru.

They sprinted across the roof and over the wall, landing in the castle grounds. As if on cue, Cynric and Sara galloped toward them from the stables. Ryuko dropped down beside them, as well, matching their pace. His face was almost completely obscured, the mask over the top half of his face and a cloth over the bottom half.

"What took you so long?" he growled.

"You could have helped," said Kakeru.

Alexander ignored them as they regrouped, advancing in a line through the smoke. Amongst the fleeing servants and screams, a mighty figure strode from the castle, dragging a girl in one hand and dangling a massive axe from the other. His hair was tied back, and a braided beard covered his chin. Alexander stiffened. This had to be Lord Tamar; from his demeanor and the way he carried himself, it could be no one else.

The girl in his grasp struggled, her wrists bound in front of her. She was clothed in a sheer white nightgown, adorned with gaudy jewels that didn't quite suit her. She must be Hanabi. The barbarians surrounded them within a few moments, and Alexander found himself backing into a tight circular formation with his cohorts.

Lord Tamar grinned, revealing the yellow stains on his teeth. "I don't suppose you thought you could beat me with that little stunt." He released his hold on Hanabi, lifting the axe with both hands. It was a formidable weapon with a blade of blackscale and a handle of white stonewood. "At least engage me in a real challenge before I return with this one." He ran his tongue over his lips.

Kakeru silently notched an arrow, taking aim.

Lord Tamar laughed, snapping his fingers, and his men pointed hundreds of arrows at them from the battlements.

"Do you think you'll actually hit me before you're all filled with arrows? Come now. Surrender, and I'll let you battle me one on one before I execute you all."

Kakeru smirked. "Who said it was for you?"

Hanabi threw her hands up, and the arrow was released. Ryuko threw her the tome, and Sara flung out her hands. The heavy book seemed as light as air as it sailed straight toward the priestess. Just as the arrow pierced the rope and her hands came free, Hanabi caught her tome and launched herself away from Lord Tamar in one fluid motion.

"Fire!" spluttered Lord Tamar, lunging at her. A volley was released, and the arrows arced toward them from all sides.

Hanabi slammed a hand on the tome, sending out a blinding light and covering the book in strange symbols. Alexander tensed his muscles, but the impact of the arrows never came. All of the barbarians were frozen mid-charge. Some fell over, others were stuck with their mouths open, mid-battle cry. It was as if time had stopped altogether. He glanced at himself, then the others. None of them seemed to be affected. What was going on?

The flames from the castle were drawn unnaturally around them in an instant ring of fire, and the incoming arrows crumbled to ash. Scarlet's eyes were glowing as she directed the fire in a protective circle. But instead of remaining around them, the flames burst outward, scorching the men in the battlements. Kakeru thrust his hands to the ground, and the earth split apart, swallowing the barbarians to their left.

Alexander stood there, dumbfounded. His sword suddenly seemed very inadequate. A moment later, the remaining barbarians began to move again, as though nothing had stopped them in the first place. With their formation ruined and their men dying left and right, the barbarians backed off, glancing at each other nervously.

Hanabi staggered away from Lord Tamar, who clumsily dug his hands into the earth. The ground shook, enough for her to trip, and her movements seemed slow and painful.

Cynric dashed to grab her, hoisting her onto his back. Kakeru pulled up a large piece of earth, kicking it toward Lord Tamar at high speed. The fearsome man was knocked back as the earth crashed into him, and the large mass flew over him and into several other men.

"Let's go!" shouted Kakeru. He looked like he was gasping for air.

Alexander hesitated. If there was ever a time to finish off Lord Tamar, it was now. But more men began pouring out onto the grounds, and their escape route was shrinking by the second. He turned, sprinting after the rest of them.

Kakeru pushed the earth on which they stood, and it rose into a pillar, launching them back over the wall and crumbling the second they jumped off. A voice roared out after them, but Alexander didn't pause to look.

There was no further resistance as they fled the city.

CHAPTER EIGHTEEN

REINHARDT

L ORD REINHARDT CROSSED one leg over the other, leaning against his armrest. His deep blue cloak, pinned at his right shoulder with the Elorian emblem, caught in the sea breeze and billowed in his councilor's face. He casually tucked it behind him, trapping it between his back and the chair. Luckily, his councilor remained silent. That was embarrassing.

Before him, two of his best fighters faced off in the arena for the final round of the tournament for which he never asked. When one of his personal guards had injured his leg, his soldiers went wild over the available position. One thing led to another, and here they were, at an unscheduled event that everyone seemed to know about in advance except for him.

At least it would let some of them work off the excitement they'd built up, now that they weren't marching into battle against Lanadrin. Reinhardt shifted his sword belt again, the decorative sheath in pristine condition. The fighters were signaled to begin. This was a nightmare.

The two opponents went at each other with unbridled ferocity. Reinhardt adverted his eyes slightly, biting the inside of his lip with every clash of the sword. They could have at least used practice weapons. But no, everyone had insisted on steel—for the purpose of displaying their merit, of course. One let out a cry as a line of blood blossomed across his arm. Reinhardt tugged at his collar, swallowing. If they had used wooden swords, that wouldn't have happened.

"A glass of wine, my lord?" That silky voice again. With beautiful brown eyes and a dress that accentuated her already voluptuous chest, this noble girl wouldn't leave him alone.

He smiled at her. "No, thank you, Alyssa."

She slid in beside him, perching atop his other armrest. Ever since the women caught wind that the wedding was canceled, they seemed to be making even more of an effort to catch his attention.

"I'm sure you must be thrilled that my father's fishing endeavors have brought you much gold. Lysanthir is rather difficult to interact with, much less close a successful trading deal."

Reinhardt internally rolled his eyes. Someone had put those words into her mouth in an effort to make her sound more worldly and impressive, no doubt, but he could see right through it. The way she presented herself irritated him.

"It was indeed fortuitous."

Alyssa leaned in closer. "He thinks he found a way to cross the reef."

He blanched, staring at her. "Nonsense. There is nothing outside of our empire, and that reef itself is cursed. Anyone who approaches it dies in a violent storm. I forbid him to try."

Her hand flew to her chest. "My father is only trying to do what's best for me. If only I were married, he wouldn't have to worry about my wellbeing and find new ventures to take care of me."

Reinhardt relaxed his muscles. Good. It was just a silly ploy to get closer to him. The Sea of Dunite was treacherous if one went too far, and many of his best men had died trying to venture farther out. It was a well-known fact that no one could cross the reef. She began to press him further, but his eyes were drawn back to the duel. In a flurry of attacks, one man stopped just short of the other's neck.

Reinhardt stifled a gasp. The crowd erupted into cheers, and the winner was declared. Thank dragons that it was finally over and no one was seriously injured. Then, the announcer turned toward him in a grand gesture.

"And now, as one final test, the legendary Lord Reinhardt himself will duel the winner!"

Reinhardt only just stopped his jaw from dropping. The crowd's cheers intensified, and his eyes darted around. Perhaps one of his councilors would step in for him, give him some kind of emergency situation to which he must attend. But his councilors all nodded enthusiastically. Maybe he could feign an illness.

"The man who can slice a single hair down the middle... who can move as quick as lightning... who single-handedly defeated more than one hundred opponents in a single round," the announcer continued rambling.

The crowd started chanting his name. Reinhardt slowly

stood, brushing his cloak out in a grand gesture, like he was about to enter the arena.

Alyssa batted her eyelashes. "Good luck, my lord."

He gave her a tight smile, taking a step forward as he spied his personal attendant sprinting toward him.

"My lord," Jonathan hissed in his ear. "The princess herself is reported to be riding toward our castle at this very moment."

Reinhardt let out a breath. A fantastic excuse—no, a legitimate reason. That's what it was.

"Go on, tell them at once."

Jonathan bowed and rushed to inform the announcer, who immediately began shouting again.

"In an unexpected turn of events, our long-awaited imperial highness, Princess Mina, is gracing Eloria with her presence! We will commence immediate preparations!"

Lord Reinhardt began delegating. They didn't have much time to receive her as properly as he would have liked, but he was determined to make everything as perfect as possible. He strode from the arena, crossing the gardens to the front of his castle. His guards were lined up on either side of the path, standing at attention, their Elorian blue and white uniforms immaculate—as they should be. He glanced behind him.

Eloria's castle was one of the most elegant structures in the entire empire, second only to the imperial palace. The smooth white walls covered the spiraling, sky-high towers and expertly crafted archways and bridges. The floor-to-ceiling windows were crystal clear, with the two at the entrance depicting the great sea serpent, their mighty emblem. Waves crashed against the rocks at the base of the cliff beneath the castle, completing the picturesque scene. He was certain this would be a welcome change from Anadrieth's drab city; Princess Mina would have no choice but to be impressed.

The crisp, salty air filled his lungs as he took a deep breath. It was peculiar—and rather dangerous—that she would come alone. The entire empire had heard of her return, yet she was coming here first. He was certain that this was about the alliance, but the timing was off. She wasn't an ordinary young woman, but there's no way she could make that journey in a day. Even his messenger wouldn't have delivered the news to Anadrieth too long ago. In fact, he hadn't returned yet.

But Reinhardt was no fool, and he knew full well that the legends behind the imperial family were more than just stories. He and the princess had only met once before as a child, but even then, she'd moved with the grace of a warrior, her mind as sharp as the blades she carried.

As the princess eventually galloped into view, he could clearly see that she was as beautiful as he remembered, but he wouldn't be taken in like the others. His people gathered before the castle, dropping to one knee on either side of the path.

Reinhardt bowed deeply from his waist.

"Your Highness," he said. "Would you like a hand?" He knew that she didn't need one.

Mina dismounted with ease. "I'm fine, thank you." Her horse didn't seem the least bit exhausted, and neither did she. She carried no baggage, no supplies for the long journey. Peculiar, indeed, almost as if there was something otherworldly going on.

"I only wish we could have had more time to prepare for your arrival," he said.

"No need. I won't be staying long. We both know why I'm here."

"Of course. Please, join me inside." Reinhardt gestured toward the castle.

She placed a hand on his outstretched elbow, and he led her inside. The windows caught the afternoon sunlight at just the right angle to reflect the stunning colors across the marble floor. The entrance hall was just as beautiful as the exterior, but it was no place to discuss matters of grave importance. He led her to a smaller room, where a table displayed their finest selection of sweets and baked goods.

Reinhardt pulled out a chair for her. "My chefs are preparing a special meal for us as we speak, but please, help yourself."

Mina picked up a sweet, a pale yellow one in the shape of a shell, and popped it in her mouth.

"Just as good as I remembered."

Reinhardt smiled. He waited for several minutes as she sampled more of their treats.

She looked at him expectantly. "Well?"

He paused. "Please, elaborate."

Mina wiped the sugar from her hands with a napkin. "I'm waiting for an explanation." She laid a letter on the table, the wax seal broken. So, she *did* receive it. She couldn't have been traveling for much more than a day or two.

"I don't regard Anadrieth as an enemy by any means," he said carefully. "But I'm afraid that since they didn't deliver on their terms, I cannot offer them my assistance." She was watching his every movement, and he wondered whether she could tell that it was a lie.

Mina crossed her legs, leaning back in her chair. "I was

asking why you offered them an alliance in the first place. Eloria lacks nothing."

Reinhardt raised his eyebrows. He wasn't expecting that. "You're right, there's not much that Anadrieth can give us right now. Lord Alexander is a talented leader, but he also lacks the judgment to put the right people in the right positions. He projects his self-absorbed, heroic image onto those that don't deserve it and shelters those who would blossom under adversity."

Mina smirked. "A perceptive assessment, as usual."

"I have my sources. But I understand the considerable tension they face with Lanadrin, and I wish to avoid bloodshed. I felt I'd be more... inclined to assist if I cared for someone who had strong ties with her homeland."

"I didn't think you were the type to pursue marriage that way."

Reinhardt shook his head. "I'm twenty-eight. Lord Alexander isn't the only one under pressure to provide an heir." He waved a hand. "Of course, I never planned to marry her if she didn't desire me. I have no use for an unhappy ornament, beautiful as she may be."

"And if she'd refused, would you still have supported them in war?"

"I'd honor my agreement, and I'd hoped that the alliance would dissuade Lord Tamar from proceeding with the war entirely." He sighed. "I never actually promised to support them in the battle itself. If both Lanadrin and Calvera march, the battle is already lost, whether Eloria joins or not." He didn't really want to leave his region, anyway. "And Prince Yukiya has officially supported the war."

Mina stiffened, her fingertips brushing along her swords.

Reinhardt reached inside his breast pocket, pulling out a letter, this one marked with the imperial seal.

"Eloria will not, under any circumstances, aid Anadrieth in the coming war. The penalty for high treason is death, by order of Prince Yukiya."

Mina snatched the letter. "Yuno…" she muttered. She cast it aside, meeting his eyes. "And if I ordered you to?" she articulated. The air around her changed, and he could feel a storm brewing.

Reinhardt fought to remain expressionless. "It is not my death he is referring to," he said quietly. Though he would probably die, too, he understood the meaning of the threat, loud and clear.

Mina's face softened, and the tension evaporated. "May I see her?"

He narrowed his eyes slightly. So, Mina knew about her, as well. Nothing got past the imperial couple, it would seem. It was a heavily guarded secret, and only his most trusted people had knowledge of her existence. It dawned on him that this might have been what the princess had come for, but he couldn't pinpoint a possible reason.

Leverage, perhaps? It had to be more than sheer curiosity. There was no point in refusing since she already knew. Reinhardt nodded silently and led the way.

The east tower was guarded at all times. No one was allowed to see her unless he was with them. The two guards immediately bowed in unison upon their approach and stepped aside. Reinhardt unlocked the door with his key, pushing it open. As they ascended the white staircase, Mina spoke.

"One would assume a prisoner resided within these walls."

He grimaced—she wasn't wrong—and changed the subject. "How did you know about her?"

"I have my sources, too."

How cryptic. Reinhardt unlocked the door at the top of the tower with a second key. The spacious interior appeared anything but a jail. The room's central feature was an enormous four-poster bed, complete with dainty curtains and sheets made of the best white spidion silk. matching silk curtains and sheets. They would tear under the slightest bodily weight.

Matching curtains wafted in the light breeze from the large open window, which was far too high for anyone to climb from the outside—or inside—but he had guards patrolling below regardless.

A long chair on which one could lay was positioned near the window, in perfect view of the sea. It was made of stonewood, making it impossible to break or move closer to the window. The closets, cabinets and drawers were overflowing in enough feminine finery to last a lifetime.

A smaller, plainer nook with only a bed was attached to the side of the room for the maid, with no doors separating the two spaces. Tabitha, a servant girl, was currently preparing tea inside. Lord Reinhardt's most trusted maids would only leave when another came to take their place.

Everything had smooth, rounded edges.

It was a beautiful cage, but a cage, nonetheless.

"Brother," a voice murmured from the bed, carefully tucked amongst the pillows. Her voice was a mere whisper of what it should have been, but Reinhardt's ears were trained to hear even her slightest sound.

He took her hand and sat by her side. "I've brought

someone to see you." He turned to Mina. "This is my little sister, Lady Rosalie."

She smiled. "My name is Mina."

Rosalie turned her head with some effort. Her skin clung to her bones, and the dark circles around her eyes heavily contrasted with her abnormally pale skin. Her hair was withered and frayed as it sprawled across the pillows. Her hazy eyes lit up at the sight of her new guest.

"Is that... Princess Mina? Forgive my... impertinence... I cannot..."

"It's quite all right. I came to talk to your brother and thought I should pay you a visit."

"I am... honored," Rosalie wheezed, managing a weak smile.

Tabitha came over with the tea. "Pardon me, Your Highness. It's time for my lady's medicine."

Mina nodded, and the maid placed the tray on a side table. She produced a tiny vial of dark red liquid, which seemed to stick to itself as it sloshed around inside. She gently tipped back Rosalie's head, opening her mouth. A single drop of liquid thicker than water slid down her throat, and the vial was carefully stoppered and placed back in a secure box.

Reinhardt held his breath. His sister closed her eyes for a moment, then sat up. A slight color was returning to her cheeks, and the dark circles were becoming less prominent. He smiled. This was his favorite part of the day.

"Would you like to be near the window today?"

"Yes, please. I have a feeling it will be a lovely day today. I want to take advantage of the cool breeze," said Rosalie, with more volume in her voice. She was like a flower frozen in winter that had come alive once more.

He carefully scooped her tiny frame into his arms and carried her to the chair, positioning her until she was comfortable. Reinhardt glanced over her. Her limbs were thin and bony, with an uneven coloring from the lack of sun. It was a significant improvement, but today was no different from any other day.

The medicine wasn't a cure; it just prolonged the inevitable.

"Princess," she said, a little livelier, "may I be so bold as to make a request?"

"Go ahead."

"Will you tell me something of the outside world?"

Mina nodded, taking a seat beside her.

Reinhardt stepped away, letting the two of them talk in private. He approached Tabitha, opening the box and peering at the vial.

"How long?" he asked her in a low voice.

"A week, at most, my lord. Will another vial be arriving soon? It was rather small this time."

He nodded noncommittally. It was intentional—and cunning—on the prince's part, meant to keep him on a tight leash. The medicine was unique, unlike any potion, toxin, or remedy that they had ever seen. His best medics and alchemists couldn't recreate it at all, but without it, Rosalie would die within days.

In his youth, he had stolen a drop of it himself, the metallic taste instantly confirming his suspicions. Energy had surged through his veins, and he had dashed around the castle, sparring everyone in sight in order to work off the energy. The rumors of his combat prowess hadn't stopped following him around since.

Reinhardt closed the box once more. If that was what an ordinary person felt like after taking the medicine, how close was *she* to death every day?

She'd contracted the mysterious illness when she was four, and that was when Rosalie died to the outside world. She was far too frail to venture outside, and if anyone else knew, she'd be a sitting target. It was no way to live one's life, and that knowledge was a stake in his heart, twisting ever deeper.

No one seemed to have any answers to her illness, so when an imperial messenger first arrived with the vial, he was undeniably suspicious. He'd held his breath for the day when it would be used against them. Nineteen years had been far too long to use it as leverage, but the favor couldn't simply be out of benevolence. Perhaps the previous emperor had been kind, but Prince Yukiya, too? Impossible. He had no choice but to obey whatever the prince asked of him.

After a while, Mina stood, bidding his sister farewell.

Reinhardt pressed a gentle kiss to Rosalie's forehead. "I'll come see you soon."

"I look forward to it," said Rosalie, smiling.

When the door was safely shut and locked behind them, he searched Mina's eyes. "You know what's wrong with her, don't you?"

"I do."

Hope surged through his chest, and he fell to his knees. "Please," he whispered. "If you can help her, I would gladly follow you. Into battle, if that's what you wish. Anything. I don't know what else to do." He held his breath.

Mina slowly shook her head. "War has many casualties, Lord Reinhardt, and not all of them are on the battlefield."

He clutched the hem of her dress, pushing his forehead to the floor. "Please! Any information would—"

"I cannot help you."

Reinhardt leaned back on his heels, his mouth dry.

"I can tell you this. It's not an illness. You've got the wrong people looking at her. But *I* cannot give you what you seek." Mina looked away. "I must leave. Time is imperative." She dashed down the stairs, two at a time, without looking back.

For a moment, he couldn't move. Perhaps he had misjudged her. Why wouldn't she tell him more? His fist hit the floor. His face was burning up, and his eyes were wet. Did she have no compassion? Or was she as double-sided as the rest of the imperial family? In that case, she was on her own.

He chose his family, and he always would.

✸ 19 ✸

CHAPTER NINETEEN

ADELIA

"HOW MANY DOES THAT MAKE?" asked Adelia, her hand poised over a piece of parchment. She was currently stationed in the great hall, overseeing the preparations with Anton. He hadn't taken quite as active a role as she had, as his voice cracked every time he spoke and he couldn't look people in the eye. He'd ended up disappearing outside with the soldiers, but she couldn't afford to worry about how he was faring.

Vivian gave a little bow. "All the nobles have been moved inside the castle, and all the villagers from the western sector have settled into the far side of the castle grounds." The head matron waved her hand toward the city. "The eastern sector is still filing in as we speak, but it will be a very tight fit. We won't have enough shelter for them."

Adelia tapped her finger to her lip. "We received a delivery of tarps a while ago, didn't we? That should help. Otherwise, distribute all the blankets and straw we have available."

"Yes, Milady." Vivian nodded and hurried off.

"Lady Adelia," said Jane, gasping a little. "Reporting from the infirmary."

Adelia smiled. Little Jane had really found her place there after Elaine had taken her under her wing. But upon seeing her, she frowned. Jane's skin was quite pale, with more color seemingly draining away every second. Her eyes had dark bags under them, and she looked like she was about to collapse. Then, she felt it. Adelia's eyes widened. It was the same sickness as her brother, James, had had, though not nearly as advanced. Was she becoming an *undesirable?*

"Sit down, Jane," Adelia instructed. "What happened?"

Jane wiped her brow, falling into the nearest seat. "Not sure, Milady. Don't feel all that well. But I should be right with a little rest. About my report, we've prepared the field medical supplies... with those who will be traveling. The rest are staying here with... Elaine," she huffed. "We're toting a lot of water for her, too."

"No, I mean when did you start to feel ill? I'll get someone else on all that. You just rest." Adelia pressed the back of her hand to the girl's forehead. She was ice cold to the touch, and bits of her skin had begun to flake off.

"This morning, I think. Didn't do anything different, I swear."

"You're not in trouble," said Adelia. "I'm just worried about you. Go back and see Elaine, and take it easy for the day. We don't need anyone collapsing on us now." She helped Jane stand as she escorted her to the doorway.

Councilor Raoul almost ran into them, and he leaned against the doorframe, sweat pouring down his face. He was panting, but it seemed to be more from the stress of his body having to walk up and down the halls.

"Uh, Lady Adelia," he said. "The... delivery is here."

Adelia frowned. "What delivery?"

"The princess asked for weapons to be carved out of silverlight." He handed her a slightly sticky note. "There's a cart outside."

Silverlight weapons? Adelia thought. They had plenty of weapons for the soldiers already, and this new delivery wouldn't be useful on the battlefield. She glanced outside. Groups of their people were practicing out on the grounds, the soldiers still paired up with their servants. She'd had them rotate in shifts between what Mina had told them to do and what Alexander wanted them to do. Mina must have meant for everyone, including the servants to be armed, as well.

"Distribute them amongst the most capable of the household, then," she said. "Have they returned from the border yet?"

Councilor Raoul was breathing hard through his mouth. "Yes, General... Ban is giving out the Lanadese axes... we collected as we speak. The bodies have also been brought back for burial."

"Excellent." Adelia nodded. When he wasn't around the other councilors, he took orders quite well; he just needed to lose a few pounds. Former General Barrett was still sulking after his demotion, and Councilor Dallan hadn't reported back to them in a while. "Please continue overseeing the equal distribution of rations in the meantime."

"Right away, my lady."

Adelia let out a breath. Now that things were starting to come together, maybe she could squeeze in a little practice with the rest of them. Everything was going quite well, considering the circumstances. It took a little bit of reorganizing to get people moving, but once they did, it seemed to go far smoother than before. She wandered outside.

A group of maids and soldiers were squabbling excitedly, one of the maids having actually hit the target with her bow. Another group of them were teaching the soldiers the proper way to use a needle and thread, and still, others seemed to be showing them how to tie bandages properly. There was a certain sense of comradery that had emerged over the past few days, and she could tell that even in the midst of war preparations, friendships were forming. This must have been what Mina had been hoping for.

Adelia approached one of the groups who were repairing some leather armor. Maybe she could talk with people, too.

"Can I help?"

Their laughter died out, and they looked at her with wide eyes, like she was a talking foxen. Maybe she shouldn't have interrupted them. The silence was awkward, and their uneasiness was growing by the second. They glanced at each other before a servant spoke up.

"It's... quite all right, Milady. You needn't trouble yourself with things like this."

Adelia plastered on a pleasant smile. "Of course."

She tried a few more groups, all to a similar response. What had she been thinking? No matter what she did, she would always be Lady Adelia, the pretty maiden who should have been happily married by now. Admired like a beautiful flower, but trapped in a glass cage. Her chest was tight, and she bit her lip. Even though their people were becoming more comfortable with each other, the difference between her and them was still too great. No one would understand what she was going through.

Adelia sighed, wandering off to a more secluded corner of the grounds. At least on this side, it wasn't filled with people just yet.

She felt a presence approach her and couldn't help but frown when she realized who it was—Anton. She braced herself, hugging her arms tighter. She was sure that he was about to lecture her or make some snide comment. But to her surprise, he stood next to her in silence, watching a lyrecrane take off from an ice pear tree.

"Do you remember when our... when Lady Adalynn made you attend finishing school?"

She stared at him. That was unexpected.

"How could I forget?" replied Adelia. "I spent the night crying in your room after the first day." And then, he'd spent the next two weeks helping her cause enough mischief to force their mother to get her a private tutor instead. Those nasty girls just hadn't left her alone.

He nodded. "It hasn't changed."

"What hasn't?"

"People will always treat us differently," Anton murmured. "We'll always be a lord and lady, even though we aren't like our brother. Some are jealous of what we have, others resentful. They'll fear us, ridicule us or use us and leave. No matter what their reaction to whatever we do," he glanced at her, "no one will ever just... be with us."

Adelia didn't know what to say. This was the most he'd spoken to her in a long time.

"What brought this on?" she asked carefully.

Anton shrugged. "Watching you get your hopes up with those servants. There's no point exposing your heart when you know it's going to get crushed."

Oh, Anton. Was this how he saw it? There was a silent sadness behind his words, even though his voice held no emotion. Time hadn't been kind to the little boy who once wore his heart on his sleeve.

"But if I hadn't," she said, "I wouldn't have met someone like Mina."

This time, Anton met her eyes. He was just a little bit shorter than she was now that they'd nearly grown up, though she'd never gotten the chance to tease him about it. His scar hadn't changed, though; the same pink line that she remembered crossed over his eye. He'd never told them how it'd happened or even who did it.

"Do you really still believe in her?" asked Anton. It was a strangely earnest question, almost childlike.

Adelia steeled herself. "Of course. I'm sure she had important imperial duties to attend to. If she needed to leave, she needed to leave."

Even to her, it sounded like false words. Her only friend, the only person who truly understood her, had left, and it didn't look like she was going to return. She almost wished that Mina had never regained her memories. The way things had been when she was just Mina the Servant had been comfortable. She'd made life bearable. But now, everything was back to the way it was before.

Anton didn't miss a beat. "But is that how you feel about it?"

No. It wasn't fair that she'd left, just like that, and it didn't make sense. Adelia crossed her arms, brushing the little scab on her index finger. Why had she made that silly vow? It wasn't for Mina. It was to spite Alexander. He'd hesitated to trust Mina, and she felt it. But the truth was, so had she. It was nothing more than a flamboyant gesture that didn't even serve to convince herself.

"Mina shouldn't have left us," Adelia muttered. "It was selfish and unnecessary."

There. She'd finally said it. She stomped her foot hard in the snow, but it didn't release the tension in her body. She didn't care whether Mina had duties or whether she was being irrational about it. Mina had abandoned them—abandoned her—plain and simple.

"You were always good at acting strong in front of others, just like our brother," said Anton. "But you've never been good at lying to yourself."

"And what would you even care?" Adelia's hand came to rest on her hip. She had no idea what he was trying to do, but the fact that she *didn't* feel like he was hiding some ulterior motive made her even more annoyed. He couldn't just waltz up to her and start speaking as if they'd never stopped, not after all these years.

"Because right now, you're doing what I can't, and every time you pretend it's okay, you fall apart inside." Anton waved a hand at their people. "They're relying on *you* right now, not me." His jaw tightened. "I—just forget it. Forget I said anything." He shuffled away before she could blink, his head tucked into his chest and his arms wrapped tightly around himself.

Adelia let out a frustrated sigh. Even if that was his awkward way of showing compassion for her, it was too little, too late. Eleven years later, they weren't the same people they once were, and they never would be. Too much had happened. She could reminisce and hope all she wanted, but her brother was long gone. He left her alone *first*. They all had to move forward from their past, and she wasn't planning on getting hurt anymore.

Adelia returned to the great hall, throwing herself into her work. There were preparations to be made, people to move and a region to save. She didn't have time for anyone's attitude. Even Barrett seemed to keep his distance from her. She knew that Alexander would want Councilor Dallan to be taking charge, but if he wasn't going to show his face, she didn't need him. Good riddance to that awful man.

It was afternoon by the time she finally sat down for a moment. Her heart was racing, and she'd never felt more energy pumping through her body. It felt good to be on the move.

"Milady," called Vivian as she stopped in the doorway. "They're back."

Adelia looked up. "Right. See to it that they're looked after, and tell my brother I'm in here." She rested her head against the table. Although she was glad for their safety, she wasn't in the mood to rush off to welcome them home. No doubt that her brother would take over just as she'd finally found a rhythm, but that was his right, and she couldn't really complain. It was a big enough deal that he'd asked them to get involved in the first place. Though perhaps, just maybe, Alexander would see that they could handle things without him.

She mulled over her thoughts for a bit, calming her annoyance. She should really get back to translating her book, if only she could find a spare moment.

"—everything is moving along at a steady pace, my lord. We should be fully prepared to march into battle in about a week," said Councilor Dallan, walking through the door with

Alexander. He glanced at her. "Oh, and Lady Adelia was a fine help."

Alexander nodded. "Thank you for taking care of things as always, Dallan. I appreciate everything you've done."

Adelia stared at them, her mouth slightly open. The anger bubbled up again in an instant. *A fine help?* That bastard. She could feel his internal grin, as though he was simply doing this to spite her. Her brother would never believe her over his most trusted councilor. Dragons to both of them. They could get lost.

Alexander gave her a tired wave. "Sister, we're home."

Adelia picked up her skirts and stormed right past them. She blocked her ears to her brother's shouts as she hurried down the hall. She didn't give a dragon's claw what either of them wanted to say. If there were one death she wouldn't miss on the battlefield, it would be that of that damn councilor.

Adelia clenched her fists. People were staring at her as she passed, but for once, she didn't care. In her oblivious rage, she crashed straight into someone, and they fell over in a heap.

"Sorry," Adelia mumbled, almost growling. Then, she glanced at the girl. She looked to be a few years younger than herself. Her ebony hair was brushed against her shoulders, and her eyes carried an innocent warmth, their rich green matched by her jade hairpin and earrings. If someone had said that she was Mina's little sister, she would have believed them.

Adelia held out a hand, and the girl took it. She had such a frail grip, and it was almost no effort at all to pull her to her feet. She had the frame of a little girl and couldn't have been much more than five feet tall.

The girl didn't seem the least bit annoyed to have been knocked down. "My, my. I sensed a violent storm rushing my way, but I didn't think it'd be another priestess." She dusted herself off. Her robes were perfectly draped around her figure, the red pleated skirt tied around her petite waist with a bow, the hem barely brushing the floor. She had a tome that mirrored Adelia's own tucked away in a pouch on her hip.

Adelia frowned. "Huh?" Maybe she hit her head a little harder than she'd thought.

"My name is Hanabi, the Head Priestess of the Imperial Dragon Temple." Even her voice was gentle and melodic. So, this was the girl they'd all run off to save, the so-called key to ending the war. She clasped her hands together, the large white sleeves practically engulfing her slender arms. "It's been a long time since I've met another priestess. I hope we can be good friends."

Adelia opened her mouth, then closed it. "Hold on, what?"

"I hope we can be—"

"No, before that."

Hanabi blinked, her mouth slightly parting. "You didn't know?"

"Should I have?" Adelia fought to keep the exasperation from her tone. It wasn't like she was ever told anything. But a priestess? *Her?* It was the same thing that the Ryuko person had accused her of. Adelia patted the book on her side. "Oh. No, you see, I just carry this around." Now that the subject had been brought up, she could feel a vastly different energy coming from Hanabi. It was soft and gentle, but at the same time held a commanding presence.

Hanabi raised an eyebrow. "Come now, your mother must have been a priestess, as well. Didn't she tell you anything?"

Adelia shook her head. "I'm sorry, I don't have time for this." She moved past her. It was passed down through blood, and there was no way that Lady Adalynn was a priestess. Hanabi was making assumptions, and Adelia didn't want to deal with it.

Before she could get far, her legs suddenly seized up. Adelia was frozen to the floor as an invisible force made her limbs unbearably heavy. There was a strong urge deep within her mind, telling her that she didn't want to walk away, that she was being rash. She needed to calm down, turn around and listen. The thoughts came in her own voice, too, like she was really considering changing her mind.

Adelia clenched her jaw. She wasn't fooled. She could feel a strange power behind her. It was not unlike Mina's aura, though it had a different flavor. Hanabi was doing something, and she didn't like it.

Not on my watch.

She resisted.

She willed her legs to move.

She shouted in her mind, louder than the voice that wasn't hers.

Adelia's foot budged. As the hold on her dissipated, she spun around, grabbing Hanabi by the shoulder and shoving her against the wall.

"Never do that again," she said in a low voice. Her head spun, and a wave of dizziness washed over her. Suddenly, her body felt extraordinarily tired, as if she'd just gone for a mile-long sprint.

Hanabi gave her a knowing smile. "Impressive. Even without a conduit, your will alone is strong enough to resist mine. That's something no ordinary person can do." She held up her hands, the light fading from the tome by her side. "I won't do it again. But it was the quickest way to show you that I'm not playing around with you. They told me about you on the way here, Lady Adelia. And I believe we have a lot of work to do."

Adelia took a step back. Hanabi didn't appear to be lying, but she had a sinking suspicion that she might not be able to tell even if she was. The dizziness passed, and she shook her head.

"Fine, I'm listening."

"Let's go somewhere quiet."

Adelia let out a sigh and led Hanabi to her room, keeping her in her peripherals at all times. This woman was incredibly dangerous, and even if she was part of Mina's entourage, Adelia didn't trust her. When they entered her room, Hanabi's gaze wandered around, first at the tapestry, then at the papers strewn across her desk. She sat down, her breathing abnormally heavy for such a short walk.

"Are you sure you didn't know you were a priestess?" she asked.

Adelia gritted her teeth. "No one tells me anything. Are you planning on explaining, or do you just want to point out my ignorance some more?"

Hanabi didn't seem fazed. "Actually, you're far from ignorant. I thought I'd be dealing with a complete beginner." She picked up one of the papers. "Can you read dragon script?"

Adelia stopped, her interest immediately peaked. "Can you?"

"Yes. It's foundational knowledge for any priestess."

Her hostility dropped a level as Hanabi nodded. This is part of the reason why she wanted to visit the imperial temple in the first place, and this woman must know so much about all of this. Adelia grabbed her book, pushing it toward Hanabi.

"Please, I have to know what this says."

Hanabi took it, running her fingers over the cover. Her brows furrowed. "Where did you get this?"

"I guess you could say it's a family heirloom."

Hanabi handed it back. "This is a *syra*, or the object into which a piece of one's spirit is infused, and it's an incredibly powerful one, at that. I can still feel her presence even after so many years. Your mother was a priestess, too. It's bound to your family line, so I can't open it."

"Why do you keep saying that? Lady Adalynn was nothing of the sort," Adelia snapped.

"As old as this *syra* is, the power of the spirit arts is passed down without fail. It never skips a generation, even if she never used her powers. Did she seem to tune in with the emotions of those around her?"

Adelia snorted, then covered her mouth. "If she did, she didn't care."

"And you've hated me from the moment you saw me," said Hanabi. "I don't care if you do, but I must know your background before I tell you anything. We must be related somehow. The only line of priestesses still in existence is mine." Hanabi unsnapped the leather pouch on her hip, pulling out her tome and flipping it open to the first page. "Can you read this?"

Adelia pursed her lips but squinted at the symbols nevertheless. Most of them were still unreadable, but the first three words were clear.

"Do not... use?"

"Yes, it's a reminder I wrote to myself. 'Do not use unless

you are prepared to die.'" Hanabi shut her tome. "Do you know why I'm the head priestess, despite being such a young age?"

"Talent?"

Hanabi shook her head, giving her a wistful smile. "There are others at the temple, but I'm the last priestess left in the empire. At least, I was, until I met you. I watched my little sister die trying to help one of the *dysconae*. She was frailer than me from the beginning, though, so it was only a matter of time."

Adelia's expression softened. "She died? I'm sorry." After a pause, she asked, "What do you mean by *dysconae?*"

Hanabi's fingers dug into the cover of her book. "The spirit arts are incredibly dangerous, Adelia. That much you must understand now. It's less so for those who can manipulate the elemental spirits, but for those like us, who can manipulate the human spirit," she stared up at her, "we put our life at stake every single time. The *dysconae* are the disconnected. Those whom we are meant to shepherd the most."

Adelia swallowed. This was all more serious than she'd imagined. She started to feel a little foolish for trying to brush her off earlier. She'd been acting like Alexander. Any other day, she would have jumped at the chance to meet this woman.

"I don't know what came over me." She glanced at the floor.

"You were frustrated because you felt slighted and taken advantage of right before I ran into you and made it worse. Again, I apologize for that."

Adelia paused. "How did you know?"

"A priestess' duty is to take care of people's spirits. I could feel your emotions, no matter what your body was showing, and it didn't take more than a glance to put together the pieces."

"I'm sorry," Adelia said, sighing. "How about we start over?"

Hanabi nodded. "I'd like that."

"Hold on, do you mean that other people can't... feel emotions?"

Hanabi winked. "That's a pretty clear sign of a priestess. We are connected to the spirit realm like no one else, like a bridge between worlds. A person's emotions are undeniably tied to their spirits, and we often help them come to terms with those emotions. A friend to all, one who quite literally knows what they're going through."

"And control it," murmured Adelia. A thought popped into her mind. "Wait, the war. If I can learn some of these things in time, we could turn the tide—"

"*No.* We will not be getting involved in this battle."

Adelia frowned. "Why? Mina said you were the key to ending the war. She said to remember your vow. Doesn't that mean you're supposed to help us?"

Hanabi froze for a moment. "She said that?" she whispered. There was a momentary flash of panic before her calm demeanor resettled.

"That changes nothing," she said. "The cardinal rule of being a priestess is that our abilities must never be used to harm another person. Not only would it get out of hand, but if you are connected to that person, you will feel everything, including their death. Swear this to me right now, as a condition of teaching you." Hanabi's face was more serious than General Barrett's had ever been.

"You must promise to uphold the sacred laws of the dragon temple," she continued, "and to give your life in service to the empire. You must vow to uphold the cardinal rule above all other—to never bring harm to another living being as a priestess of the empire, on pain of death."

Adelia hesitated but put her arm across her chest all the same. "I promise." Hanabi had overreacted, but there was something else going on there, too.

Hanabi stared at her for a moment, as though she was searching for signs of deceit.

"Good. Now, let's start with the basics." She started drawing on a piece of paper.

"Everyone has an affinity for one of the four elements—earth, air, fire and water—and if it's strong enough, they can be awakened by a priestess, which means we help balance their spirit to be in alignment with the spirit realm. If they are not awakened, eventually, their spirit becomes disconnected. They become one of the *dysconae,* and they lose their minds." She tapped the desk. "Our numbers have been dwindling for hundreds of years, unfortunately. The only awakened spirit arts users I'm aware of belong to Mina's imperial guard, as well as a few others.

"Once a person's spirit is awakened, they become in tune with the spirit realm, and they gain their spirit sight, which is the ability to see their element in the spirit realm. The stronger the affinity, the more influence they have over that element."

"Influence?"

"This is important. The elemental spirits are not something that can be taken or used. If your affinity is weak, they will simply refuse to listen to your commands. Those truly in balance with their element are able to accomplish the most amazing feats. The only beings who can create an element from nothing are the four elements themselves—the spirit guardians."

"Like Scarlet," Adelia said.

Hanabi nodded. "It was an honor to meet her, though I would have expected a higher number of fire spirit arts users to be present with her around. The spirit guardians rotate, you see. Whichever one of them has manifested in our world, we tend to see imprints of their influence everywhere.

"Now, the first thing you'll need is your own *syra*. It has to be something important to you, so think long and hard about it. Once you have one, you'll be able to use the power of your own spirit to help the empire."

Adelia thought for a few long moments, her mind in overdrive. It was a lot to process, but what Hanabi was saying was slowly filling in the gaps of her knowledge. There was something she'd said, though, that sounded strangely familiar.

That's it!

She grabbed Hanabi's hand, pulling her to her feet in one quick motion.

"Come with me." It just had to be them. And she and Hanabi could help them, just like the boy in the markets.

Hanabi didn't protest as Adelia dragged her straight into the infirmary. She came to a stop before several patients—the undesirables. Their ashen eyes almost lit up as they struggled in their bonds, meaningless words rolling from their cracked lips. Jane was lying amongst them, looking far worse than she had that morning but not completely insane yet.

Adelia forced herself to make eye contact with each of them, letting the heavy atmosphere surround her. She wasn't going to ignore them this time, not if she could help them. Her chest tightened, and her heart beat rapidly as she concentrated on them. They were terrified. She could feel it now, the *off* feeling that surrounded them. It was like their spirits had no tether. They weren't *anchored* in this world. Her hands began to shake.

Hanabi dug her nails into Adelia's arm.

"Pull back, or you'll lose yourself. You aren't trained for this yet." Her soothing voice was enough to bring back Adelia's focus, and she shook her head vigorously, clearing the fog from her mind.

"These are the *dysconae,* right?"

Hanabi nodded, pulling out her tome and approaching the first patient, touching her hand to the woman's forehead. A soft white light emanated from her *syra*, the dragon script on the cover glowing.

"Anchiore."

Hanabi undid the woman's restraints as her strangled gasps eased to normal breaths. She blinked, gazing around the room, then clutched Hanabi's arm. "Thank you..." she whispered, her voice shaking and raw.

Hanabi smiled before moving on to Jane. Adelia felt the atmosphere lighten with each patient saved, as though a great weight had been lifted from her chest. It was incredible. She hurried to untie them and helped them drink some water as they slowly came back from insanity. After the final patient's spirit had been anchored, Hanabi stumbled into the nearest chair, doubling over and panting heavily.

Jane sat up, feeling her forehead. "Oh, Lady Adelia, I was so frightened. I thought I was losing my mind. It was so cold."

Adelia put a hand on her shoulder. "It'll be okay now."

A familiar voice called out. "What's going on around here?"

Adelia grinned, running up to fling her arms around Elaine, and nestled her cheek into her gray hair.

"They're okay. They're finally okay."

Behind her, the Calveran man named Cynric ducked under the doorway. She couldn't help but stare now that he was up close. His stature was intimidating, though he seemed quite refined.

Elaine shifted in her embrace. "All right, all right, child. Let go." She hobbled over to the patients, and her eyes went wide. "How is this possible?"

Adelia placed her hand on Hanabi's shoulder, puffing out her chest. "It was all her. Something that could never have been achieved with medicine."

Elaine checked her patients over, examining their bodies and asking questions. They still looked sick, but some of the color had returned to their cheeks. She nodded at Hanabi.

"I won't pry how, but I owe you one."

Hanabi gave her a weak smile. "Not at all. I see you're a spirit arts user yourself."

Adelia sucked in a breath. It was starting to make sense. "Is... is that where the healing comes from?"

Hanabi closed her eyes. "I need rest. Cynric, please."

Cynric motioned for all of them, including Jane, to follow him to the other side of the infirmary where the other nurses fussed over the wounded soldiers. They quickly backed away as he walked straight toward a man with a deep cut on his leg, the bone showing and the blood seeping into the bedsheets underneath him.

Cynric scooped a handful of water into his palms from the

bucket beside the bed and let it trickle through his fingers onto the wound.

"Water. Neutral element. Affinity for healing."

"Neutral?" asked Adelia.

"It isn't bonded to a dragon god like the other three."

The man hissed through his teeth, gripping the bed. When Cynric lifted his hands, the man's leg was completely healed. Adelia raised an eyebrow. The nurses were considerably more interested in Cynric than they were when Elaine did the same thing, but he didn't pay them any attention. He was looking at Jane.

"Were you watching?"

Jane gulped. "I have no idea what just happened, sir."

Elaine tapped Adelia on the arm. "Apparently, the lass has a talent like ours, according to the tall lad." She waved a hand at Jane. "Don't you worry. We'll teach you a thing or two."

Jane nodded, though she seemed pale as Cynric took her aside to show her his work.

It was starting to make sense. The disconnected were people who possessed the spirit arts, but they had never been awakened, which meant that a part of their spirit wasn't tethered to either realm, and it slowly drove them insane. And if the only people who could anchor their spirits to the spirit realm were priestesses who could manipulate the human spirit, but the only priestesses in existence were Hanabi and herself, there was no one to help them.

Adelia swallowed. She could have helped them this whole time, as well as the countless other people who had died because of it. Now that she knew, it was her responsibility to look after her people, one that she couldn't ignore. But this was not a responsibility just to her people. The whole empire must be full of suffering spirits, and it was partially her fault.

Elaine prodded Adelia's side. "You haven't come to see me in a while."

Adelia looked away. "I've been busy."

"Don't give me that, child. I know when there's something troubling you. Is it Anton again?"

Adelia shook her head. "It's just everything. I don't know what I'm doing anymore."

"Tried talking to anyone?"

"There's no one to talk to."

"I'm here."

Adelia smiled. "I know." She always had been. Where Lady Adalynn had never been her mother and Papa was always busy, Elaine was there for her. But some things just couldn't be put into words, and others seemed too silly to burden someone else with. Besides, with the upcoming war, there was no time to waste on heart-to-heart chats.

Adelia approached Hanabi, who was still half-slumped over a bed. There was a sense of exhaustion surrounding her that didn't seem to be because of a lack of fitness.

"Hanabi, please teach me everything you know."

Hanabi stretched, dragging herself upright. "Didn't Cynric explain anything?"

"Not really," said Adelia.

Hanabi rolled her eyes. "We'll take our leave, then. I'll just need your help to get back to your room."

"What happened?"

"Nothing can be done without sacrifice. In the case of the elemental spirits, they take some of your energy to perform what you're asking them to do. Obviously, the more complex the task or the higher the frequency, the more energy they're going to drain."

Adelia slipped Hanabi's arm over her shoulder. "And that's what happened to you?"

Hanabi shook her head. "Not quite. Being a priestess is far more dangerous. A spirit arts user can knock themselves out as easily as we can accidentally kill ourselves, but I'll explain when we're in private."

They left the infirmary, and Hanabi glanced left and right along the halls. When Ryuko rounded the corner, she waved him down.

"Just the man I've been wanting to see. Ryuko, will you help us for a minute?"

He stiffened, then sighed. "If I must."

Adelia tilted her head. His irritation had risen dramatically. It was odd, given that he seemed to be her partner and the one who led her rescue. She stole a glance at Hanabi. The priestess didn't show that she'd noticed Ryuko's demeanor, but Adelia was sure that she had.

"Wonderful. Can you demonstrate your spirit arts for us?" asked Hanabi. "And explain what you're doing, for Adelia's sake."

Ryuko gave her a thin smile and held out a gloved hand. A silvery metal snaked down his arm, pooling in his palm.

"First, I have to tap into my spirit sight, and then I'm able to do something like this."

It rippled and changed, shifting into the shape of an intricate flower, which he held out to Adelia. "If your affinity isn't high enough, it's going to backfire. The others use theirs sparingly. It takes a lot of practice to use it in constant combat like I do."

Adelia twirled the flower between her fingers, admiring it. The craftsmanship was beautiful. She wouldn't have believed that it was just liquid a few moments ago, but the solid weight in her hand was proof. Something nagged at her, though.

"Weren't there only four elements?"

Hanabi nodded. "In rare cases, a person can have dual affinity. In Ryuko's case, he has an equal affinity for earth and fire, which combine to form the secondary element, metal. Your brother, Alexander, is another one of these unique cases. His bloodline has long possessed the ability to manipulate ice."

"My brother?" Adelia almost laughed. Her brother, the one who didn't believe in any of this *nonsense,* was uniquely attuned to the spirit realm? How ironic.

Ryuko took the flower, and it melted under his sleeve once more. "But I can't use the base elements, earth or fire. Sara is the only person I know who can use two separate elements, though in her case, it didn't manifest into another."

"I still remember the day my mother told me about the boy she'd awakened with dual affinity. It was one for the history books," said Hanabi.

Ryuko slipped his hands in his pockets. "If you don't mind, I'm going now."

Hanabi glanced between them. "Adelia, you've probably learned more than enough today, right? Why don't you go on ahead and have a rest?"

Adelia blinked. There was a hint of desperation from the priestess that was quickly masked by cheerfulness.

"All right," she said, playing along. She lingered at the end of the corridor, holding her breath.

Hanabi followed Ryuko, grabbing his arm. "You disappeared on me," she hissed.

Ryuko whirled around. "I told you I didn't want to go to Lanadrin."

"You could have gotten me killed."

"I left to pursue a lead."

Hanabi crossed her arms. "That's not what you told them. You stole my tome. I'm a tolerant woman, but you're not being honest with me right now."

"No, I'm not."

"And?"

"You're supposed to be this almighty priestess." Ryuko gestured to himself. "Why don't you just *read* what you need?"

"You know it doesn't work like that. I can't read minds."

"And exactly what *can* you do? I'm not stupid. I've been watching you, and I know why Mina wanted to keep you close. It all seems awfully similar to that woman."

Hanabi took a step back. "If you're insinuating what I think you are, then let me ask you this. Why didn't you use your spirit arts in Lanadrin? You just stood there while everyone else fought, and that seems awfully similar to a traitor's behavior."

Ryuko towered over her, lowering his voice.

"And why were *you* so interested in going there in the first place?"

They stared each other down for a moment, then Hanabi sighed.

"Because we're partners, and we're meant to trust each other. I know when you're acting strange. The truth can be the difference between life and death."

"Yes, it can. So, tell me the truth. Or..." Ryuko held out his hand, and the metal extended to form a sharp blade. "I could just kill you now, and there won't be any doubt, Mistress."

Hanabi grabbed her tome, the light streaming out between her fingertips, and Ryuko stopped.

"I'm not the Mistress, nor do I have any relation to her. Now, if you don't tell me what your problem is…"

The metal in Ryuko's blade started to curve back toward himself, as though Hanabi was the one manipulating the elements. But Ryuko just chuckled.

"And break your own precious code? You'll toe the line, but this, my dear, is an empty threat. But rest assured, my so-called problem is entirely unrelated to what's happening now. Shouldn't you trust me on that, partner?"

Hanabi pursed her lips. "Fine. But the second it's relevant, I need to know."

The light faded, and Ryuko's blade receded.

"Besides… it's not good to keep things bottled up," she said, softening her tone.

Ryuko shook his head, walking away. "You won't need to know."

Adelia clutched her chest, sinking back against the wall. Underneath all of that hostility, she felt agony. She couldn't tell which one of them it came from, but what she felt only scratched the surface. She took several shuddering breaths as the pain began to subside. Clearly, physical distance from them helped to reduce the feeling's intensity.

Although they hadn't exactly been discreet, it wasn't lady-like to eavesdrop. But there was no way that she could ignore what she'd heard—and felt. Adelia clenched her fist. Maybe she could help them. She hurried back to her room.

When she arrived, her door was slightly ajar. She hesitated

but gave the door a massive push. There didn't seem to be anyone in her room. There was, however, something on her desk.

She tentatively stepped in, scanning the room for any obvious danger before approaching her desk. There was a small bundle of parchment that had clearly been ripped from their source and rebound, and a note stuck out of the side of the bundle. Adelia paled. She knew exactly what this was. The parchment had the distinct dragon script all over it. She pulled out her tome, opening it to the missing pages. That had to be it. Adelia picked up the note, which was written in common tongue, and her blood went cold.

It's time you knew the truth. Don't show Hanabi. —M.

❧ 20 ❧

CHAPTER TWENTY

ANTON

ANTON LEANED over the edge of the balcony, watching the people go about their business. His sister was doing a pretty good job, not that he expected anything less. Him, on the other hand—not so much. The pressure just scrambled his mind and made his heart race, and there were far too many people looking at him at once, so he fled. He could see now why Alexander hadn't wanted to put him in charge of anything; he knew that he couldn't handle it.

He wasn't even fit to be the spare. If his brother died, there was no way that he could take his place. Perhaps he was simply fated to be useless—Lord Anton, the one that historians wouldn't bother to include in the books. He sighed, letting his fingers run along the stone. He didn't care so much about being remembered, but it was embarrassing, all the same. He couldn't fight like Alexander, lead like Adelia or even clean like a servant. There wasn't a single thing he could do to help, except stay out of everyone's way.

He was just as hopeless as that servant girl—no, princess. Anton clenched his fist. That princess, who had turned out to be as unreliable as anyone else. She'd raised their hopes and then left. Not that he was hopeful or anything; he'd just expected that a princess with the power of a god would have been more helpful. Anton slapped his forehead, and little bits of wet frost dripped down his face.

He couldn't understand why he was so upset about her leaving. Adelia had every right to be, as did Alexander. But he had wanted her gone more than anything. For their own safety, of course.

No, that wasn't it.

Anton sank his head into his hand. The princess had been irritating, yes, but she had also saved his little sister's life when he couldn't—in more ways than one. And there was nothing in the world that could repay that debt. The longer he searched his mind, the more he failed to come up with any wrong she'd done to him. But he could never forget those piercing eyes that stared deep into his spirit.

Remember, I'm your friend.

Why had she said that? It wasn't like they were friends in the slightest. And for some reason, there was a burning urge to find out the answer.

Out of the corner of his eye, a girl rushed down the hall. Anton jerked his head back. Was that her? She was wearing white and red robes with a large bow tied at the back and looked like she was about to punch a wall. No, it wasn't her; this girl was too short. There was a book, just like Adelia's, situated in a pouch on her hip. He let out a breath. It must be that girl—Hanabi—his brother had gone off to rescue, which meant that they'd returned.

Hanabi stopped dead in her tracks and slowly turned toward him. Her face was scrunched up in a mixture of confusion and disbelief.

Anton self-consciously glanced down at himself. Nope, everything seemed to be in order.

"You..." Hanabi approached him in the same way a foxen would when it was deciding if you were friendly or not. "You're like Adelia."

He frowned. "She's my sister."

Hanabi shook her head, her curious gaze sharpening to suspicion. "No, Alexander is her brother, but not in the same way you claim to be." She began to circle him. "Impossible."

Anton scoffed. "I'm not claiming anything. It's a fact. Alexander is my brother, and Adelia is my sister."

"Are you sure you were born a man?"

This woman was insane. "Excuse me?"

With lightning speed, Hanabi grabbed between his legs. Anton recoiled, shoving her away, and she lost her footing, tripping backward onto the ground.

"Don't touch me," he hissed. His arms wrapped reflexively around his body, and his heart was flailing inside his chest. He couldn't stand being touched, much less where she'd just grabbed him.

Hanabi got up, dusting herself off. "Sorry, I had to make sure. The truth is, you shouldn't exist."

"Explain," he snapped. He didn't need another person confirming that his birth was a mistake, but he was going to get an explanation from her, whether she liked it or not.

She took a deep breath. "I'm Hanabi, the Head Priestess of the Imperial Dragon Temple. I knew about Lord Alexander's gifts, as they are of his bloodline, and I assumed Lady

Adelia was born of another means and adopted. But you two have the same energy."

Anton shook his head. "Explain *better*."

"Your sister is a priestess, like me. That much is a fact. The other fact is that priestess blood can only be passed on from another priestess. Therefore, her mother had to have been a priestess. And because I thought I was the only one left, I thought Adelia and I must be related somehow."

"That has nothing to do with me."

"It has everything to do with you," said Hanabi. "The third, irrefutable fact is that a priestess can only bear female children. If you were Alexander's brother, it would make sense, but your aura is like nothing I've ever seen before." She stared at him with wide eyes. "Yet, you're the son of a priestess, and her blood flows through your veins."

Anton threw up his hands. "I don't know what kind of nonsense you're spitting out, but just stay away from me. And from Adelia, too." He walked past her.

"You can see the lights, can't you?"

Anton stopped in his tracks, gritting his teeth. He didn't want to turn around, but he couldn't bring himself to walk away. She obviously knew something.

"I'll be blunt, since you clearly don't want the long version," said Hanabi. "They're spirits. You're looking at elemental spirits with your spirit sight, and if my intuition is correct, you can see *all* of them. As far as I'm aware, you're the only one who can, besides the dragon gods, of course." She held up her hands. "But I know when I'm not wanted. I'll give you a tip, though, because I can tell that the spirits bother you. Talk to Sara. She's out on the far end of the western grounds with Scarlet. She can help you."

Certain that she wasn't going to say any more, Anton stormed away. He couldn't believe that he'd almost mistaken Hanabi for the princess, who would have never done something like that. Hanabi acted like a spoiled brat who got everything she ever wanted, which was probably the case if she was the only priestess in the temple. He exhaled. Not only that, but what in dragons name had she just dropped on him?

His sister being a priestess was, more or less, not that surprising, though he didn't really know what the big deal was. And his brother had always been talented, so what was an extra talent to him? But the fact that she'd insinuated that the three of them weren't siblings because of some stupid rule that he shouldn't exist? Ridiculous. As if he needed another reason not to exist, anyway. All of this bloodline nonsense was going right over his head. He wanted answers, but not from her.

Anton headed to the western grounds, stomping his feet in the thick snow as he went. When he finally looked up, he paused. In the distance, there was the little girl, Scarlet, dancing near Doll's grave. Fire trailed from her hands like a dancer's ribbon, twirling and twisting in gentle shapes. It glowed bright orange, and the little lights glided through the fire. Sara stood nearby, watching her and tending to a small fire. The flames were getting dangerously close to Doll's tree.

"Hey!" he shouted, breaking into a sprint.

They glanced at him, and a piece of the girl's flaming ribbons seemed to break away. It caught on the uppermost branches, and the silverlight wood began to burn.

Anton ran, his lungs bursting. "No!" He pointed wildly behind them.

The girls turned toward the tree in surprise. With incredible speed, Sara threw something at the branches, and the top of the tree broke off. An unnatural breeze blew the branches to the ground, and the fire died in a matter of seconds after it hit the snow. Anton finally reached them, panting, his hands resting against his knees.

"I'm sorry," cried Scarlet. She backed away from the tree into the open grounds.

Anton paced around Doll's grave, his eyes darting over the tree and her little stone. He let out a sigh of relief. Other than the burnt branches, everything seemed to be unharmed.

"I apologize," said Sara. "I didn't realize this was something important. We were trying to get distance from all the people."

Anton shook his head. He was annoyed, but something else nagged at him. He pointed to the charred wood; the once translucent beauty was now blackened with ash.

"How did you do that?"

Sara unhooked a circular object from one of the pouches by her waist. "I used my chakram. It's made from silverlight, so it's virtually invisible in the air—one of my father's brilliant ideas."

He took a closer look. It was indeed made from silverlight, and the outside edge was razor-sharp, while the inside concealed a sturdy handle. As he studied it, he realized that it was the same object pictured on the outside of the Lysanthian emblem—a throwing weapon that could be deadly in the right hands.

Anton looked over Sara more closely. She was taller than him, and her lithe figure was covered in strange leather clothing. Her skin well-touched by the sun, her hair was pulled back and she wore glasses on her pointed nose, which was uncommon since glass that fine was more of a luxury. She carried an array of objects with her, but he could only see one chakram amongst the pouches. He frowned.

"Aren't you meant to have more of those?" It was like having only one arrow; unless you wanted to get close to the action, you couldn't get it back very easily.

Sara turned to face a different part of the forest and threw it at another tree ahead of her. It whizzed off, then disappeared. The little silver lights appeared in his vision, carrying her chakram in an entirely different direction. A branch snapped to her left, falling to the ground, and the chakram flew back into her hand. It was a clean cut.

"Normally, yes. But I'm manipulating the air currents to affect the direction I want it to go."

Anton raised his brows. That was the first time he'd ever seen the little lights move like that—or *spirits,* as that annoying priestess called them.

"I think I saw," he murmured. Although he didn't like Hanabi, there was a certain peace that came with the knowledge that he wasn't going insane. The lights he'd seen all of his life *meant something.*

"You saw?" asked Sara, rubbing her chin. "Oh, Hanabi must have sent you. You have an air affinity, correct?"

Anton shrugged. "She dumped a barrage of information on me. I'm just here to find out what all these lights are." He kicked the snow. "And to get away from her," he muttered. "There was also something about being a non-existent priestess' son and how I'm unrelated to my siblings and have good sight or something."

Sara grimaced. "Ah. Yes, she can be a little... abrasive. Unfortunately, her talents as a priestess are unmatched.

Anyway, I'm trying to teach Scarlet how to control her fire. We're starting from the basics. Do you want to join us?" She took a few steps toward Scarlet, who was keeping her distance from the forest.

Anton let out a breath that turned to mist in the air. It would take his mind off of things, at least, and he had nothing better to do.

He trained with them for a while, listening to Sara's teachings. The spirit arts were less about *bending* an element to your will and more about connecting with the element itself. When a spirits arts user was practicing, what they were really doing was *asking*, not commanding, and they always gave something in return, most often energy. It was a natural give and take, the original state of this world. Balance was key, like the unchanging cycles of day and night, dark and light. People were always meant to be one with nature, and nature one with them.

Scarlet was a natural at all this of course since she was a spirit herself, albeit she was a little afraid. Spirit sight, as he learned, allowed him to see into the spirit realm and manipulate the elements. That is, theoretically; he just had to get it to work.

Anton closed his eyes, trying to calm his nerves. Still, nothing. This was ridiculous. The one time he actually tried to see those damn lights on purpose, they wouldn't appear. He was literally surrounded by the elements but blind as an oyfish, which had no eyes at all.

"Why can't I do it?" he said, stomping his foot in the snow.

"Sometimes, even the first step is a difficult one," said Sara gently. "Where have you been when you've seen the spirits before?"

"Alone," Anton snapped. "More often than not."

"Perhaps you need to get some space for a bit, then. Being frustrated isn't going to help you at all."

"This *is* where I get space."

Sara adjusted her glasses. "Take a walk, Anton. You'll feel better."

"Fine." Anton began to walk, then he paused. "Can I ask you something? Both of you." They nodded. "Why are you still here? You know a war is coming, and there's still time to leave."

"Because our princess asked us to stay," said Sara.

Scarlet shrugged. "And she said for me to stay with them."

"And you just do what she says, even after she left you all here with a slim chance of surviving the war?"

Sara nodded. "Mina never does anything without a reason, and I trust her with my life."

"My spirit says to trust her," said Scarlet, glancing down. Her red hair fell over her face, reminiscent of his own familiar movement. "But I don't know."

Anton waited for them to say more, but they didn't. "I see." Their answers didn't satisfy him or help clear up the doubt in his mind, but he was sure that that was all they would give him. "All right, I'll take my leave now." They nodded, and he wandered back toward the castle.

What a day this was turning out to be. The other areas of the grounds were packed with Anadese people, and the castle was stuffed to the brim with nobles and the like. The only place he could think to go that was quiet, other than his room, was the library. While it might not be the best place to practice his spirit sight, perhaps he could find a book on the subject.

The library was darker than he'd imagined and smelled a little like mold. The maids evidently didn't visit this room as much as they should, though he was rarely in here himself. The ceilings were as high as the great hall and packed tight with books, the rows only a few feet apart. He could imagine his little sister climbing up and down the ladders all day long to retrieve the tomes at the very top of the shelves, and of course, she'd be one to put them back exactly as she found them. If she returned them, that was.

He, on the other hand, had no idea where to start, and there was no one around to help. He browsed one row after another, but the books didn't seem to be organized in any logical manner—not by name, title or subject. The books near the entrance were all concerned with Anadrieth, followed by the empire, the other regions and combat, but the rest was a complete mess, and he didn't see anything on the spirit arts at all. Whoever arranged them must have had their priorities confused. Maybe if there were a few more windows in here, it would be easier to find something.

A soft beam of light illuminated the row to his left, and he turned down it, following the light. As he reached the end of the row, his breath caught in his throat. Sitting at a table amongst several open volumes was Cynric, busily pouring over a notebook. The thin frames of his glasses sat delicately on the bridge of his nose, his gaze keenly focused on his work. His hand danced across the page, the neat sloping handwriting accompanying several complicated diagrams. Anton edged closer until he was practically hovering over his shoulder.

Chapter Six — Managing internal wounds in the field.

Anton absent-mindedly touched his palm. So, he was a medic. No wonder he knew how to heal his burn. The content seemed far more advanced than what he'd done, though, and didn't mention anything about using water for miraculous healing. On the contrary, it appeared rather technical and mundane.

"Yes?"

Anton jerked back and found Cynric's turquoise eyes staring at him. He fought the color rising in his cheeks and turned his nose up. He felt like he'd seen those eyes before, but he brushed it off.

"I was just looking for a book and thought I'd ask if you knew where anything was."

"It's my first time here."

Anton swallowed. "Right. I knew that." He cleared his throat. "You're interested in medicine, I see."

"I am."

"It's just that men aren't brought up to be in that... profession."

Cynric blinked. "Do I have to follow what everyone else does?"

Anton paused. It certainly wasn't traditional, and traditions were there to follow. If you didn't, you'd be an outcast. He didn't look like an outcast. Cynric didn't seem to want to talk about it so he decided not to press the subject. "Are you writing a book?"

"For injuries on the battlefield."

"Ah." He had little interest in medicine himself, but Cynric's dedication was admirable. Perhaps he was writing it for the war, as there would be a good chance that Calvera would ride into battle alongside Lanadrin. Then, a thought occurred to him.

"Are... are you going to be all right? If you're joining the war, I mean."

"I'm not on the frontlines."

"But your people..."

Cynric placed his quill down, turning his whole body to face Anton. "I cut ties with them long ago."

Anton didn't know how to respond. He'd never left Anadrieth himself, so he couldn't possibly know what it was like to leave home. Something must have happened—people rarely left their home region for no reason—but he didn't want to pry. Perhaps he was an outcast, after all.

"What book were you looking for?" asked Cynric.

Anton rubbed his arm, glancing around. "It doesn't really matter. I wanted to know more about this whole spirit sight thing. It only works when I don't want it to, it seems."

Cynric's lips curved downward slightly. "Ask the girls." He pointed farther back into the library. "I can help later, but if you'll excuse me for now." He turned back to his work.

Anton opened his mouth, but the man had already started writing again. His work was probably important, and he didn't want to disturb him any more than he already had. Anton headed in the direction he'd been pointed, and two voices came into earshot. He peered through one of the bookshelves to find his sister... and that damn priestess girl, Hanabi. Anton gripped the shelf, staying out of sight. If that girl tried anything with his sister, she would answer to his sword.

Adelia was staring down at something in her palm. It looked like the lyrecrane pendant she never took off. Of all the gold and jewels she owned, that little thing made of cheap moonstone, worth a meager silver coin, was her favorite. The craftsmanship was decent but far from that of Anadrieth's finest jeweler. It wasn't unique or ornate in any way. Just a trinket from the marketplace. However, it had been a gift from the princess, and that made it priceless in his sister's eyes.

"Have you thought of something yet?" asked Hanabi.

Adelia showed her the necklace. "This has to be it."

"That? If it breaks, you'll die. You could lose it, or someone could steal it. Your *syra* must be something you can protect, and you can't change your mind."

"You said the more important it was, the better. Plus, I heard Ryuko took *your* spirit tome."

"He was just... holding onto it for me. Fine, if you insist, we'll use that." Hanabi sighed. "Now, what we're going to do can be extremely dangerous, but without your *syra*, you can't use your spirit arts. Unlike the dragon gods, our human spirits simply aren't powerful enough on their own." She pulled out her tome, setting it on her lap.

"But as priestesses," she continued, "we can take a piece of our own spirits and imbue it within an object, then use it to channel our power. However, this comes at a cost. With even a fraction of a piece missing, our physical bodies become weak. There will be days when you won't even be able to get out of bed, and that's why we toe the line of death." Hanabi didn't break eye contact. "This process is dangerous. There's a possibility of you splitting too much of your spirit apart, and if your spirit leaves your body entirely, you'll die. Do you understand?"

Adelia nodded, but Anton was shaking his head. There was no way she would do something so risky. The books he was leaning against tumbled to the floor. The girls glanced in his direction as he hurriedly put them back. He hardly cared that he was caught eavesdropping, and his anger bubbled up.

"Adelia," he said, "this is madness. That girl isn't safe."

"Anton—"

"Don't eavesdrop," said Hanabi.

Anton felt the tips of his ears going red as he stalked toward them. "Don't kill my sister."

Hanabi gripped her hand on her tome, and intricate symbols appeared on the cover with a blinding light.

Anton stumbled, falling onto the ground. He couldn't do anything—couldn't move or speak, as if his will had completely evaporated. He could sense the priestess taking over, invading his senses, and he couldn't do anything about it.

The barrier he'd wrapped around himself came crashing down, and a great sense of calm enveloped him. He saw his little sister's smile as they ran through the forest, his father's hand on his shoulder, a woman gently stroking his head. Warmth flooded his chest, pushing back the cobwebs of his heart. Then, the moment passed, and he was pulled back to reality, his fingers digging into the stone floor.

Anton clutched at his chest, his breathing ragged. He stood, his knees shaking a little, and he kept his distance. Hanabi's presence and the light were gone, but something inside of him felt raw and painful. As he checked himself over, he realized that he wasn't hurt, but he felt something that he hadn't experienced in a long time—vulnerability. He was unsteady on his feet, still not feeling quite himself.

Adelia stood over Hanabi. "I told you not to do that again."

Hanabi glanced at her. "This time, I was doing my job and

calming him down, amongst other things. It was more inva-sive than usual, but he'll thank me later." She gestured to him. "Now that you're here, we could use your help for a few minutes. Adelia will be safer if someone else is here."

Anton's senses were coming back to him, but he felt strange. It was like the wall he'd built around and within himself had crumbled to dust. More than anything, he was dazed.

"Anton, I know this is a big ask," said Adelia, not taking her eyes away from Hanabi. "But she's the only one who can teach me these things. I *have* to do this. No matter the cost."

Anton stared at her for a moment. When she had that look on her face, there was no changing her mind. And if Hanabi was telling the truth, she would be safer if he stayed.

"Fine."

"Good," said Hanabi. "Stand here and place your hand on her shoulder. You and I will be the *anchiores*, or anchors, that will keep Adelia from losing herself in the spirit realm while she makes her *syra*. All you need to do is tune into your spirit sight and keep in contact with her at all times." She ran a hand through her hair. "I'll admit I... actually haven't done this before. But not to worry. As long as you concentrate, I'll take care of the rest."

Anton frowned. "That's not comforting. Besides, I can't tune into my spirit sight yet."

Hanabi sighed. "The contact itself will help, but still try. Are you ready?"

Adelia nodded, and Anton let out a breath through his teeth, placing a stiff hand on his sister's shoulder. His heart was still racing, and he could barely concentrate, but he had to try.

"Just breathe," said Hanabi.

Cynric stood by a bookshelf, holding his glasses in one hand. He gave Anton a nod, and the boy quickly glanced at the floor. Eyes like water, beautiful, calm and still. A deep voice, quiet and strong. A man of few words. He remembered his large, warm hand enveloping his, plunging it into the freezing water. Anton caught himself. That was simply a bizarre incident that had no meaning at all, and he shouldn't be thinking about it, especially not now.

But Cynric had a calming presence, all the same.

When Anton opened his eyes, he could see. Tiny colored lights—no, spirits—floated all around him. They seemed playful and alive, though not in the same way that he was alive. Everything was slightly duller, almost hazy, yet he'd never seen the world as bright as it was at that moment.

Anton relaxed the tension in his arms as a silvery air spirit flitted by his hand. Then, violet auras appeared around him, far more defined than the air spirit and most certainly human-shaped. Each of their auras were distinct, undeniably an imprint of their individual spirits, but they were all beautiful in a way. He could even see his own, but unlike the previous times he'd seen it, he knew what was going on.

Hanabi gripped her tome, which held the same aura as her, yet duller, and he could see her spirit nestled inside the tome, just as he had seen the princess' incredibly bright spirit within her swords. Her spirit took his sister's hand, guiding it outward. As soon as Adelia's spirit began to leave her body, he felt an enormous energy fill the air, and the pull to the pendant was incredibly strong. It was pulling him in, and Anton gasped. He let go.

And everything disappeared.

An absolute emptiness filled him to the brim, and the others were no longer in sight. He vaguely felt himself collapse to his knees, sweat dripping down his temple, his heart about to beat out of his chest. He was still in the library, but at the same time, he wasn't. He was entirely alone. It was the same as it was in the arena—a lonely, melancholy world where no one existed.

Anton's cheek stung, and he hit the floor, the impact making his ears ring. When his eyes finally focused, everything around him was normal once again, like he had never left.

Hanabi stared at him, the obvious panic streaking across her face. Adelia lay still on the floor, and Cynric hovered over her, checking her pulse.

Anton scrambled over, his knees dragging on the stone floor. "What happened?"

Hanabi was in a daze, and her eyes refused to leave him. "You... you crossed over. To the spirit realm. You completely disappeared."

Anton blinked, ignoring her. His little sister was as pale as snow, her limbs still and lifeless. He searched her up and down for signs of life, his chest tightening. He remembered her lying in the ravine, the branch jutting through her leg, her pretty dress stained with the blood of his mistake. It was all his fault.

"She's alive." Cynric's tone was calm and even, silencing the vivid memory. He scooped her into his arms with ease, her limp frame appearing even smaller against his body. "Come," he said. In several large strides, he was out of sight.

Anton's legs were trembling, and he couldn't stand. The ground was blurry, and tiny black spots dotted his vision. He clutched his head, doubling over until his forehead touched the floor. It was all his fault. His breaths came in gasps, getting shorter by the second.

It's all my fault.

A hand tentatively rested on his back, and he flinched, but he didn't have the energy to brush it away. Anton turned slightly.

Hanabi's tear-stained face was close to his shoulder, her eyes raw, her expression unsettling. Why was she so upset?

This is her fault, too.

The woman's voice returned, her shadow by his side. But he didn't need her encouragement. Anton tackled Hanabi to the floor, his hands gripping her shoulders, his eyes boring into hers.

"If my sister dies... I will kill you."

Anton let go and followed after Cynric. His mind was nothing more than a rumbling storm, his thoughts a dark blur. He barely registered the people staring at him as he swept through the halls, his body moving automatically. He could hear Hanabi running after him, but he paid her no mind. When he arrived at the infirmary, Elaine was already checking Adelia over.

"She's as white as death, she is. What happened?" She looked as calm as Cynric, but he could hear the quiver in her words.

"We... had an accident," said Hanabi, hanging by the door.

Elaine glared at her. "I'm gonna need more than that, missy."

Hanabi crept over, wringing her hands. "There's nothing any of you can do. If her spirit is strong enough to pull her through, she will."

Anton stood by his sister. He could see her aura, a muted, dull violet emanating from her body; her light was almost out. But against her chest, shining brighter than ever, was her lyre-crane pendant. He snapped out of it and turned to Hanabi, speaking in a low voice.

"What happened exactly?"

She gripped the edge of the bed. "I tried to... I couldn't stop her. You crossed over."

"Be. More. Specific."

"If I hadn't pulled you back, you would have been lost in the spirit realm, forever." Hanabi took a shuddering breath. "By then, it was too late. But I had to make a choice."

"Her spirit is almost gone," Anton said. He straightened, clenching his fists. "You chose wrong."

"You... you can see that?" asked Hanabi. "How?"

He pushed past her. She disgusted him, and he refused to continue the conversation.

"Wait—"

Anton ignored her, storming out of the infirmary. He had to get out of there. He sprinted through the castle, not caring who saw him. Picking up the first sword he saw as he passed through the armory, he threw the sheath to the ground and swung at the nearest wooden practice figure. First, Hanabi had practically attacked him; then, she nearly got his sister killed in some ridiculous ritual.

Damn her.

He made a deep cut in the figure's neck, his arms shaking from the strike. He didn't know how long he'd been there, but the head of the figure was nearly completely off. As he yanked the sword back to swing again, another sword blocked it.

CHAPTER TWENTY-ONE

ALEXANDER

ALEXANDER SAW his brother sprinting straight past him. He called out, but Anton didn't seem to hear. Why did his siblings always seem to be running out on him? He'd been able to slip away from his councilors for a bit, hoping for some much-needed peace and quiet, but clearly, Anton needed someone now. He ran after him.

Alexander found him hacking away at a training dummy, with spectators slowly backing away. This was the most out of control he had ever seen his brother, and he couldn't just let him continue to embarrass himself. He drew his Golden Dawn, intercepting Anton's next strike.

"If you wanted someone to spar with, you need only have asked."

Anton didn't reply, only aimed his next blow at him—and the next, and the one after that. They landed haphazardly, and Alexander remained on the defensive, only moving enough to parry his attacks. He knew what his brother was feeling all too well, as he had often taken out his frustrations with a sword. But for Anton, this was far from normal. He didn't seem to be having an episode, but Alexander wasn't sure what else could have provoked such a reaction. Finally, he expertly disarmed the young lord, flinging his sword away.

Anton leaned against his knees, panting.

"Brother, I know you can do better than that," said Alexander. "Tell me what's wrong. I've been trying to find you all day."

Anton shook his head. "I... made a mistake," he whispered.

Alexander nodded. "I understand. We all make mistakes—"

"No!" Anton stepped within an inch of him, raising his chin. "Shut up. You wouldn't understand, not one bit. You've always been perfect Lord Alexander, the fearless leader everyone looks up to, while I've nearly killed my sister—twice, now. Don't you dare say you understand what it's like to be me, the spare, the second born that's only needed if his perfect older brother dies in heroic combat." Anton's cheeks were flushed, and his eyes were bloodshot. "You don't make *mistakes*. That's something reserved only for me, the disgrace of the family."

Alexander stared at him for a moment, taken aback. His little brother never raised his voice like that, and he had no idea where this was coming from all of a sudden. He'd done nothing to warrant this barrage, especially not in front of other people. But Anton's anger was infectious, and he wasn't going to let such disrespect slide.

"And I suppose you'd know all about running a nation on the brink of war?" Alexander's voice was lower than it ever had been, his tone edged in frost. "I don't make mistakes because I *can't* make mistakes. Every eye in Anadrieth looks to me to be their unwavering leader. I don't have the freedom to make a mistake. If I did, the consequences would affect everyone. So, stop trying to be me. The only one forcing you to stay in my shadow is yourself." Alexander took a deep breath, unclenching his fists.

"You know what, Anton?" he continued, unable to keep the anger at bay. "I have made mistakes, especially with you. You don't understand how much I wanted to be in that room, taking your place instead of waiting helplessly outside. It was my fault that I didn't see it coming. I could have spared you from that. And maybe if I had, you wouldn't have turned out like this." He gestured up and down at his brother, and his tone thawed. "Instead, I gave you the freedom I could never have had, to do whatever you wanted without the weight of Anadrieth bearing down on your every move. But you've convinced yourself you can't do any better than people's expectations, so you never will. And that's not my fault."

"I didn't ask for your *freedom*. And neither did Adelia." Anton's fists were trembling. "Your freedom caged us."

Alexander shook his head in disbelief. "And you want to be caught up in the bloodshed, the manipulation, the suffocating pressure? I did this because I care about you both."

"You care? That's news to me," scoffed Anton, looking away from Alexander. "It didn't matter what kind of life it was. We were meant to do this together, like you promised."

Alexander almost lost it, and his heart pounded in his ears. "Like *I* promised?" he hissed. "No. You're the one who shut us out, Anton. You're the one who broke us apart. We gave you as much time as you needed, but you still left us." He enunciated each word with venom. His brother was being nothing but selfish, and he wasn't having any of it. Alexander turned on his heel and stalked off.

"And *you're* still standing outside the door," said Anton.

Alexander pursed his lips, looking back over his shoulder. "What?"

Anton gave him a look that he'd never seen before—a dark sorrow, caged by a raging wildfire.

"You weren't there for her. Again."

Alexander frowned, but his brother's expression brought dread seeping through the cracks.

Adelia.

He sprinted toward the castle, his footsteps falling heavy as he swung his head left to right, scanning for his sister. She didn't seem to be in the great hall. Nor the library. Nor her room. Servants and soldiers alike stumbled out of his way as he barreled through the castle. He had an inkling of where she might be, but it was the last place he wanted to check. In the end, he didn't have a choice. Alexander tore open the door to the infirmary.

There she was, lying on the bed. She was pale, and a sickly shade of yellow marred her complexion. He took a few steps forward. When he saw her chest rise and fall ever so slightly, he let out a sigh of relief. If she had died, he would have never forgiven himself.

Hanabi sat next to her, holding her hand and flipping through pages in her tome. Cynric was sitting on her other side, monitoring her pulse and making notes in his book. Elaine hobbled over to him, patting him on the arm.

"She'll be right now. Still breathing, at least. The lass is taking good care of her."

"What happened?" he asked through clenched teeth.

"Ask her."

Alexander approached the edge of her bed, gripping the wood. Whatever happened must have driven Anton's fragile psyche over the edge, as even the two normally stoic figures of Hanabi and Cynric seemed tense, though they weren't in a panic like his brother. Hanabi was murmuring to herself, running her finger back and forth over the slightly glowing symbols in her book. When he opened his mouth, she held up a hand to stop him. Alexander narrowed his eyes. He had the right to know what was going on, and he was going to get answers.

A wave of clarity suddenly settled into his mind like a soft, warm blanket. He was being irrational and impulsive, and he needed to calm down. He took a few deep breaths and began pacing in a circle. He was just stressed because his brother was angry. He felt everything melt away, and for a moment, he was calmer than he had been in months. At last, he could think clearly again, thank dragons.

Hanabi turned to him. As her hand left her book, the glow faded from the symbols.

"There's been a bit of an incident. However, this was necessary for Adelia's growth as a priestess, and she was fully aware of the consequences."

Alexander frowned. "She's a priestess?"

"Yes. This is a complex and confidential matter, though, and I'll only be able to determine the full extent of the damage if she wakes up."

He blanched, the worry beginning to creep back in. "If?"

Hanabi nodded, her short hair bobbing back and forth. "I'm not going to make light of the situation." She briefly explained the workings of a priestess' spirit arts and why they needed to go through such a dangerous procedure, but he was only half-following the situation. He cursed himself for not paying a little more attention to all those years of Adelia's ramblings.

"She's got a strong heart, so I believe she'll pull through. But," Hanabi clutched her book, "only a fraction of her spirit remains in her physical body. The effects won't be good." She stood. "I'm going to eat something, call me if her situation changes."

Alexander slumped into a chair beside Cynric. His brother was right. He *was* standing outside the door again—unable to prevent it from happening, unable to fix it. He rested his head in his heads. This situation was completely out of his territory. If they were to be attacked right now, Adelia would be a sitting target.

Your freedom caged us.

Was Anton right? If he hadn't pulled away from his siblings, would they have even been in this situation? He kept telling himself that it was for their own benefit, but maybe they never saw it that way. He closed his eyes, and a memory flashed through his mind. They were back in his room, giggling inside the mini-castle they'd made from blankets and pillows. Adelia was telling them a story about a brave king, while he was acting out the parts, much to Anton's delight. Alexander shook his head, brushing away their childish laughter. It was too late to turn back the clock now. The three of them had been broken into far too many pieces to mend.

"Ever let down your family, your region and everyone who depends on you at the same time?" he asked despondently.

"Yes," replied Cynric, without looking up.

Alexander glanced at him. He hadn't been expecting an answer, let alone one so straightforward.

"Well, I guess you'd know how it feels." He sighed. "My brother was wrong. He's not the disgrace of the family; I am."

"So?" asked Cynric.

"So, what?"

Cynric stopped writing, removing his glasses to look at him. "What will you do?"

Alexander threw up his hands. "I don't know! My siblings hate me and probably wouldn't let me help them, even if there was anything I could do. My councilors haven't stopped piling complaints and worries on me since I got back. And I haven't had a wink of rest in dragon knows how long." He clicked his tongue. "The only viable option is to surrender and try to bargain for my people's lives. Maybe there's someplace they can evacuate. I just don't know. I can't send my men out there, knowing they're all going to die. There's nothing else I can do."

Cynric shook his head, returning to his writing. "You could stop feeling sorry for yourself."

"Excuse me?"

"No problem is solved by giving up."

Alexander didn't have a response. He wasn't giving up, was he? There just came a point when your options became so narrowed that you only had one choice.

"There you are, my lord," called Councilor Dallan. He stood, panting in the doorway, his beard frazzled. "Where have you been? There's still much to discuss—"

"Can't you see I'm busy?" Alexander didn't spare him another look. There were only so many meetings he could take, and right now, attending to more complaints wouldn't do anyone any good.

Councilor Dallan waltzed in, glancing at Adelia. "I hoped you would've had the sense to get your priorities straight. Thousands of people need you right now. You can't just hide in here. I thought I taught you better than this."

Alexander gritted his teeth. "It's my little sister."

"And the needs of one outweigh the needs of many?" Councilor Dallan's brows furrowed. "Without the alliance, she's of no real use to us anymore—"

Alexander's fist connected with the man's face.

The councilman staggered back, clutching his cheek. He spat a mouthful of blood into his palm, looking back at him in shock.

"Get out," hissed Alexander. It took everything he had not to pummel him to the ground then and there. Councilor Dallan didn't respond. With narrowed eyes and a ramrod-straight back, he stalked from the room, slamming the door behind him.

"... What's all the racket?"

Alexander whirled around to see Adelia groggily trying to sit up. She suddenly covered her mouth and slumped over the bed, vomiting into the bucket Cynric held out.

Cynric nodded at them. "I'll get Hanabi."

She wiped her mouth, then turned away, groaning and clutching her head.

Alexander moved around the bed, squatting down beside her. "I'm so glad you're awake. How are you feeling?"

"Like I died." Adelia coughed violently and spat on the floor. Her breaths were labored, her eyes unfocused.

He waited for her to lie back down before handing her some water. "Here."

She tried to take the cup, but her hands were trembling too much. He put a hand behind her head and helped her take careful sips. When she seemed to calm down, he took a seat. He wasn't sure what to say.

"Are you feeling any better?"

Adelia managed a slight shake of her head. Hanabi and Cynric returned and were by her side at once.

"Can you sit up?" asked Hanabi. "Wiggle your fingers and toes?"

Adelia scrunched her face in concentration, trying to use her elbows to prop herself up. When she couldn't, she settled for moving her toes, though even that seemed strenuous.

Hanabi checked her over for a few more minutes, but her face was set in a grim mask.

"You should be less nauseous once your body adjusts and you get some rest. But I'm afraid..." She glanced at the floor. "The damage is permanent. Because most of your spirit resides outside your body, you will probably find even basic movements difficult. And... I don't believe you will ever walk again."

Adelia's speechless expression mirrored Alexander's.

"I'm truly sorry," said Hanabi. "I didn't expect things to get so out of hand. But on a positive note, if you can manage the risks, you're probably the most powerful priestess that has ever existed."

"Can we... reverse it?" asked Adelia.

"I'm afraid not. Once a spirit has left the body, that's it. It can never be returned. It is only by our priestess blood that we are able to sustain a piece of our spirit externally. Anyone else would die."

"Why wasn't I informed that you were even attempting this?" Alexander asked. He didn't know if he'd have been able to stop it, but he might have been able to do something. Truthfully, the whole situation was just making him feel even more helpless.

"I knew... the risks," Adelia panted, sinking back into the pillows.

Alexander shook his head. "You would dance with death for the sake of no one but yourself? You would trade your ability to walk for some unknown power?"

Adelia shot him a look that chilled him to the core. "You have no idea what you're talking about."

"No, I don't. Because I'm not told anything," he huffed.

She let out a humorless laugh. "And when have you ever listened? Don't bother, Alexander. Save your worries for someone you actually care about."

Alexander was speechless. It seemed that he didn't know how to communicate with his siblings anymore. Maybe he never had. He could feel the others in the infirmary averting their eyes and pretending to go about their business. It was all too much. He gave her one last look, but she was already ignoring him and talking to the others.

He left the room silently. He just wanted to be alone for a bit.

Normally, he would have called Mina over to talk things out, but she wasn't here anymore. What would Mina have said to him? Probably something similar to what Cynric had said. He didn't even want to think about it. She'd been his confidant, just as much as Councilor Dallan. Now, both of them were gone. And he wasn't even sure if he wanted them back. Mina was their princess; she was meant to do something about all of this. And Councilor Dallan was meant to support him, not tear down his family. There seemed to be fewer people on his side every time he turned around.

Alexander weaved his way through the castle, avoiding eye contact with everyone he passed, a feat that was proving quite difficult with how crowded it was. The grounds were full of his people, hiding behind the castle walls, cowering in fear. He could feel their judgment—their disappointment. His pace quickened. He wasn't entirely sure where he was going; he just wanted to get away from everyone.

A small hand grabbed his arm.

"Psst..." It was Scarlet. "This way."

There was nothing stopping him from following her, so he did. She led him to the eastern tower, trudging up the stairs. How did she know where she was going? Even he didn't know this section of the castle as well as she appeared to, though he didn't usually come over to this wing. At the top of the tower, Scarlet began to climb the ladder that led to the roof.

"Hang on a minute," said Alexander.

"Come on!"

She scaled the ladder in mere seconds, pushing open the door and hoisting herself up. He hesitated. He hadn't even realized that there was a rooftop entrance, and he wondered if the ladder would hold his weight. The view from the small windows was already high enough. Wouldn't they fall off when they got to the top?

As he stood there, weighing his options, Scarlet leaned through the open roof hatch.

"Are you coming?"

Alexander sighed, taking one step, then another, until he reached the top of the ladder. He poked his head through the open hole in the roof and almost immediately recoiled from the strong breeze.

"It's not that bad," said Scarlet, sticking out her hand to help him up.

Alexander gritted his teeth, carefully maneuvering himself out onto the roof while trying to stay as far from the edge as possible; it was a long way down, should he fall. After several minutes of shifting, he finally sat next to her, his left hand tightly clutching the open hatch.

"So, why are we here?"

Scarlet smiled, gazing off into the distance. "I always find a way to get up high, no matter where I am. It means I can be alone. I thought you'd appreciate that. Plus, you can almost see the whole region from here. It's pretty."

Alexander took his eyes away from his knees for a moment. She was right. His people were like small, frantic dots down below, and their deserted city lay beyond the castle walls—a city he'd already failed to protect. Anadrieth was lost.

It didn't matter how prepared they were; they were completely surrounded. Behind them lay the dark Jade Mountains, it's gloomy presence a constant reminder that no refuge lay that way. And to the east sat Eloria and the Sea of Dunite, blocking off any hope of escape.

"It's far from pretty. All I see is a region that's backed against a wall, full of abandoned houses and frightened people," murmured Alexander.

They sat in silence for a long time, watching the people down below. It was indeed peaceful up here, but it only let his own voice of despair take a stronger hold. What would happen if he jumped off the edge? It wouldn't be fair to anyone, even if he were to spare himself the pain. The sun crawled across the sky, sinking lower and lower. He shook his head. No matter what, he wouldn't take the coward's way out. But that didn't change their circumstances.

"You're wrong." Scarlet's small voice cut through his thoughts. "Let me tell you what I see." She stood up, holding her arms out, and Alexander instinctively wrapped a hand around her ankle. "I see a region that's still standing. I see people that haven't given up on their leader. Anadrieth may have many dark places, but dawn always rises." Her crimson hair whipped around her face, and her voice held an astounding amount of conviction for someone her age. He couldn't help but admire her for it.

Alexander gave her a little smile. "How'd you get so wise?"

"The streets aren't a kind place," said Scarlet. "But I never stopped moving forward. You learn to do things quickly, whether it's accepting a hard truth or appreciating the little things." She put her hands on her hips. "You know, you're supposed to take care of people like us, the ones that have nothing, that come from nothing. You made Anadrieth an awful place to live, and I won't forgive you for that."

It hurt to hear. Alexander gripped the roof. It was yet another reason to be ashamed.

She looked back at him, and there was a subtle warmth in her eyes. "Even so, this is my home, and I want to protect it. Don't you think others feel the same way?"

Alexander slowly shook his head. "But there's no hope left."

"Only if that's what you believe." Scarlet squatted, staring directly at him. "But do you think you can decide that for other people? If you can't fight for your own hope, fight for theirs." She pointed toward his people down below. "That's what a great leader would do." She grinned, a spark lighting up her eyes. "And I believe you can be a great leader."

Alexander ran a hand through his hair, and he couldn't help but let a real smile grow on his face. She was right, as was Cynric. He might have felt like giving up, but there were many people down there who hadn't. His people believed that there was hope, and if he could believe in *their* hope, they might have a chance. It was time to stop feeling sorry for himself and keep moving forward, no matter the outcome. He ruffled her hair.

"Thanks, Scarlet. Let's go get everyone and decide what to do."

As he stood, his foot slipped, and he hurriedly crouched to grab hold of the hatch. He'd almost forgotten that they were so high up. He planted his feet back on solid ground as soon as he could, and together, they ran through the castle. They split up, gathering everyone of importance in the great hall for what could be the final meeting of Anadrieth—no, he had to have faith—the meeting to decide the *future* of Anadrieth.

Everyone slowly assembled in the great hall. Alexander stood at the head of the table, with the princess' imperial guard sitting on one side and his councilors on the other. Cynric had carried Adelia down from the infirmary and carefully placed her in a chair next to himself, while Scarlet had dragged Anton into the hall, who was now standing awkwardly at the other end of the table. Neither of his siblings made eye contact with him, but at least they were here. He scanned the room. There was one person missing.

"Where's Councilor Dallan?"

Everyone looked at each other and shrugged. No one had seen him recently, and he wasn't in his room. Their meeting would have to proceed without him. Alexander stood before them. He hadn't bothered changing into his lordly robes. It wasn't necessary; he was just Alexander, asking his people for a favor.

"I know I haven't been the best leader," he looked at his councilors, "or ally," he looked at the princess' imperial guard, "or brother," his gaze fell on his siblings, "and for that, I'm sorry." Alexander took a deep breath. "It's true that I'd stopped fighting because I thought that everyone else had, too. But I was wrong. If there's just one person that believes we have hope, then I want to protect that hope, even if our chances are slim." He nodded at Scarlet, who gave him a thumbs up. "I'd like to hear from all of you. What do you think we should do now?"

There was a moment of silence.

"The choice remains the same, fight or surrender," said Barrett. "Although my son has some... unorthodox leadership tactics, he will be able to lead his men into battle alongside you. I, for one, refuse to lie down and give Lanadrin a single inch."

"*We'll* be able to lead them," said General Ban. "I can't do this without you, Father."

"That's the spirit," cried Councilor Raoul. "We haven't exhausted our resources for nothing."

Ryuko nodded. "Lord Tamar likes to hold grudges. After our little visit, there's only one choice."

"Nor is there any guarantee your people would be safe under his rule," said Sara. "Father would say it's better to die fighting."

"I agree," said Kakeru. "Though I don't plan on dying." Cynric nodded in agreement.

Alexander looked to his siblings. Adelia seemed deep in thought, and Anton was leaning with his arms crossed against the table. Neither seemed like they were going to offer their opinion.

The doors to the hall were suddenly pushed open, and a man ran toward them at great speed—at least, for him. Dale stumbled forward, leaning on his knees and gasping for air. His hair was receding in a circular shape on top, while the remaining strands attempted to cover his balding head.

Alexander closed his eyes. "Oh, no," he muttered. As Councilor Dallan's eldest son, Alexander had been forced to give the bumbling idiot a job that seemed important, without actually being too important.

"Milord!" Dale cried a little too loud, and Alexander wiped a fleck of spit from his face.

Dale wiped his brow and flicked his damp fringe to the side, taking a dramatic pause. "You wouldn't believe the things I've seen! When I left my house in the morning four days ago, right after the rooster crowed—you know, that brown one with a slight limp—I forgot to bring my lunch of roast beef pie and berry pudding for dessert that Mother made me— she's a fantastic cook, I must bring you her food someday— anyway, I was gallantly scouting the area, as is my humbly bestowed duty, and lo and behold—it must have been fate—I found a bush with some delicious-looking red berries on it!"

He spoke so fast that Alexander could barely get a word in.

"Dale—"

"I was so looking forward to the berry pudding, but I

thought these would have to do, instead, so I picked a dozen —or maybe it was only half a dozen and some smaller, unripe ones—anyway, I ate them all, and they tasted nothing like pudding, but the red juice stained my new leather pouch, which Mother had just sewn for me, and, oh, I couldn't bring it home looking like that. So, I went to the river and washed it, but to make matters worse, the berries made me sick!"

"Dale—"

"I cannot stress enough not to eat those berries, especially the red ones, for though they may look like the ones you put in pudding, they are most certainly nothing of the sort, and I spent at least half an hour squatting in the bushes doing—"

"Dale!" Alexander shook him by the shoulders. "Get to the point!"

Dale blinked in surprise. "Of course, Milord. I was getting to that, but then, I remembered that Mother always packs some stomach medicine in my pouch for emergencies, and I thought this was truly an emergency of extreme proportions, and luckily, I was already near the river, so I could wash it down with something. While I was there, I courageously snuck close to enemy territory to spy on those despicable Lanadese—Mother always says it isn't the soldiers who are the bravest but the scouts—you know, I risked my neck for you, all by myself, to get this valuable information. Where would you be without me, I do say..."

"Closer to solving our problems," Alexander muttered, counting to ten. It was no wonder no one would partner with him. The general even sent him on the farthest missions available, probably hoping he'd get heroically killed, no doubt. Councilor's son or not, Alexander was about ready to throw him out.

"And so, an army of Lanadese will reach our northern border by dawn!"

Alexander spluttered. "What?"

"That concludes my report, Milord. I'll be off now. Mother made her famous stew for dinner, and I think there's pudding." Dale bowed and trotted off even quicker than he'd arrived.

Alexander's mouth was dry. They were marching already, even after the blow they'd dealt them when they rescued Hanabi? His mind raced over the logistics. They were already crossing around the river to the northern border, so they'd have to come through the pass and along the Plains of Scoria, then through the Celestine Forest, before getting to the city. That would give them more time to prepare, but Anadrieth wasn't a fortress.

"We can't fight near the city," said Councilor Raoul, like he'd read his mind. "Our assets would be under threat, and there are too many civilians. We'd have an advantage in the Celestine Forest."

"Not against Calverans," said Cynric.

Sara shrugged. "Who knows if they'll even show up."

"It's likely, given the alliance," said Kakeru. "If I were them, sending an overwhelming number of men would decrease their casualties and secure their victory."

"What about the Plains of Scoria?" said Adelia. Her voice was surprisingly strong, given how weak she looked. "Ride out to meet them there."

"No one goes there," said Barrett, shaking his head. "Don't be ridiculous."

"There's only one entrance, so they have to come through

the pass, and we'd be certain to catch any ambushes," she said adamantly.

Alexander frowned. "It's a death trap..." Even though it was part of his territory, it was a barren wasteland, dotted with pits of inescapable black tar and geysers that erupted in boiling steam. It was difficult enough for a small party to navigate the terrain, much less an entire army, but it was the only way to travel north.

Councilor Raoul scratched his chins. "They should be forced to cross it before reaching us. It would give us more time."

"But then, they'd have enough time to be careful, and we'd have our backs to the wall," insisted Adelia. "If we fight here, they have even more of an advantage on us. Out there, they have a disadvantage. We're used to fighting in the snow, where the ground is unstable, just like the plains. Although it's hot out there, I feel that the Lanadese would find the terrain difficult. Same with the Calverans, since the plains are flat. It's the only position where we might be able to stand a chance."

"If we're ready for them, it might work," said Ryuko. "We could even set some traps."

Kakeru rubbed his temple thoughtfully. "It's not a bad idea."

Sara nodded. "We don't have a lot of options."

Alexander rested his hand on his sword. There hadn't been a war in over two thousand years, but no one was more knowledgeable on such a topic than his sister. He met her gaze, nodding. It was time to put an end to this.

"Then, it's settled. Prepare every able-bodied man in Anadrieth to march to the plains at sundown. At dawn, we fight."

22

CHAPTER TWENTY-TWO

ADELIA

ADELIA STARED down at her body, trying to force it to move through sheer willpower. Unsurprisingly, it didn't work. The room was spinning, and she was unable to keep her eyes fully open. Her pendant was almost humming against her skin, and she didn't have to use her spirit sight to feel it. There were too many people in the room, and their emotions were wrapping around her in confusing waves. She could barely manage to grip the armrests to stay upright in her chair, but she wasn't about to fall over—not now. She had to keep it together, as any proper lady would.

"I've been training the men in a technique to counter the Calveran's spears with the assistance of Cynric," said General Ban. "And I've given our most elite the handful of Lanadese axes we retrieved. There are quite a few men now who have picked up additional skills from the servants, like rudimentary field first aid, and I've already reorganized the squadrons to spread them out. They've even worked together to identify the best natural poison we have, and we've coated silverlight caltrops with it." He put his hands up. "As far as our information goes, we've done all we can, training-wise."

"Plus," said Councilor Raoul, sticking up a hefty finger, "the large delivery of silverlight we received from our woodworkers was also distributed. We gave the swords to the household, as Lady Adelia suggested, but we are also fully stocked on small projectiles. The Lanadese won't know what hit them."

"The crowcodile trainers are ready for combat, too," said Barrett. "We can station them in the back of the western squad closest to the Celestine Forest to assist the cavalry. Between them, we should be able to break their frontlines. The main problem will be that our infantry is significantly weaker than theirs."

Adelia found a moment of clarity in her nausea. "Magnalite," she managed. "And oil. There's a tactic we can use to control the battlefield, especially on the plains." Now, she had everyone's attention. "The plains are structurally unstable, the tar pits are hot and the geysers spout boiling steam. But it's also highly flammable. Lanadrin doesn't have a high focus of archers, as they prefer the honor of hand-to-hand combat—but we do."

"We took out a significant portion of his archers on our mission, as well," said Alexander.

Adelia nodded. "So, if we coordinate it right, we can use flaming arrows wrapped with oil-soaked fibers to light up the battlefield and create barriers from fire."

Barrett gave her a look, and she could feel his spark of respect, which came as a surprise to both of them.

"Not a bad strategy. I think we can handle that. We'll be

able to split up their lines and cut off portions of their troops. But what did you want to do with magnalite? We had a delivery come in from the Jade Mountain miners, though it's in storage."

"Magnalite reacts with fire to create a blinding light, and if the molten metal touches your skin, it's impossible to get off," said Adelia. "I thought we could somehow use it as a projectile."

"I'm impressed that you know your alchemy, Adelia," said Sara. She pulled out a few vials of shimmering metal from her bag. "But magnalite is volatile to the user, as well. It's an instant reaction. I only use it as a last resort because I can control the flames and where it lands."

"Perhaps this is a last resort," Adelia replied. "It could be thrown in a sling or something, and there'll be plenty of fire around. No matter how tough the Lanadese are, if you get molten magnalite burning on your face, you're as good as dead."

General Ban jotted something down on a piece of parchment. "I'll include it in the preparations. You're right, my lady. If we have it, we should use it."

Alexander nodded at Sara. "Speaking of alchemy, can you make more of those things we used in Lanadrin?"

Sara rubbed her lip. "I already used up the last of the explosives. It will take time to make more, and I don't have the resources."

"What do you need?" asked Councilor Raoul.

"Liquid nitren."

Councilor Raoul tapped the table. "We've got perhaps a few flasks worth, but it will be impossible to get more on such short notice."

"We wouldn't need a lot," said Adelia. "If we can get someone to scout ahead and strategically plant them in some of the bigger tar pits, we could have a large-scale attack at our fingertips."

"The fire would cause devastation at that point," said Barrett. "This would have to be one of our first moves so that we aren't caught in the explosions."

Kakeru scratched his head. "You do all understand how unstable the plains will become with all of this firepower? We'll probably end up with unplanned explosions all over the place."

"It's better that everyone is disadvantaged than to just wait to be slaughtered," said Adelia, turning to face him.

"You have... earth spirit arts, right?" asked Alexander. "Can you stabilize our side and destabilize theirs?"

"I can, to a degree. However," Kakeru gave each of them a hard stare in turn. "This is a battle of attrition. We cannot use our spirit arts recklessly, or we'll end up unable to fight at all. Remember, we don't know when Calvera will be joining the battle, but we can assume they'll want to strike when we are worn out. So, save your strength for when you have no other choice. And don't even think about using yours." He nodded at Alexander. "There simply isn't enough time to train you. If you fall, the chain of command collapses."

The table fell silent. It made sense, especially given her current state. But if they couldn't use their spirit arts, what else were they supposed to do? Adelia racked her brain for ideas, but none came. They could employ as many tactics as they could manage, but in the end, they would only be delaying the inevitable. There were simply too many of them. But there was one thing they had yet to address.

"Hanabi," she said. "What's your role in this? Mina said that you were the key to ending the war."

Hanabi sighed. "I'll be on the battlefield, but there's little I can do. I'm honestly not sure what Mina meant. There's a very specific circumstance in which I could act, but it would be nothing short of a catastrophe." Her gaze pierced Adelia for a moment. "And remember, a priestess' vow is to never bring harm to another living being."

Adelia shot a glance at Ryuko, who rolled his eyes. Her definition of harm seemed somewhat gray. Hanabi hid her emotions well, but Adelia could tell that she was nervous. There was something she wasn't telling them.

"We'll do whatever we can, then." Alexander gave the imperial salute. "I thank you all, on behalf of Anadrieth, for your service. Let's get moving."

Everyone except for her stood, returning the salute. They all scattered in different directions to carry out the orders, leaving Adelia to sit awkwardly at the table. She felt what was left of her strength drain away with them. She may have helped during the meeting, but she would be useless to help any further. It wasn't as though she couldn't feel her body or move her legs; it was more like her body was made of stonewood—heavy and useless. No matter how hard she tried, she could only muster so much strength.

Alexander approached her, his hand around Scarlet's shoulder. There was a closeness between them that she suddenly resented. She'd spent more time with Scarlet than he had, yet she could feel a bond between the pair that she simply didn't have—with either of them.

"I'd like Scarlet to remain with you, Adelia. No matter

how useful her abilities might be, no child needs to see the horrors of war."

Adelia eyed them. "And is that her choice or yours?"

"Mine," said Scarlet, a slight tremble in her tone.

Adelia's expression softened. "All right." She didn't need her spirit arts to know that the girl was afraid.

Her brother turned, then looked back at her for a moment. "And Adelia?" He paused, and she could see him wrestling with everything he wanted to say, could feel his heart quicken. "Thank you. For everything." He shuffled off quickly, leaving Scarlet by her side.

It wasn't much, but it was something. But if it would ever be like it was before, they would all have to start over. And given the stubbornness of all three of them, that probably wasn't going to happen.

Adelia grimaced. She wasn't going to be able to get up, let alone leave the room. She bit her tongue and glanced at Cynric, who was the only one left at the table, scribbling away in his notebook.

"Cynric, could you..."

He didn't respond for a moment. As he jotted down the last word, he slipped his notebook and glasses in his pouch and nodded at her, reaching down to scoop her up. Scarlet trotted along beside them.

Adelia clenched her teeth. She didn't even have the strength to loop her arms around his neck. She was the epitome of helplessness, and she hated it. The most she could do was tuck in her skirts so that they wouldn't accidentally show her legs. People stared at her, and she could feel their apprehension and pity. The scenery passed by them, and she tried to take a good look, since she would probably be confined to her room for the rest of her miserable life. When he brought her back to the infirmary, however, she frowned.

"This isn't my room." She didn't relish the thought of anyone seeing her in such a pathetic state.

"You should be around people. And you can see outside," Cynric said, opening the window for her and propping up her pillows.

Adelia laid back, somewhat uncomfortably. The sickening smell of herbs and ointments filled her nose, and she could detect an underlying hint of blood in the air. She was surrounded by the groans of the wounded, the grave whispers of the nurses and the tossing and turning of those unable to find sleep.

Perhaps this is how the *dysconae* felt—trapped in a bed, a prisoner in their own skin. No brave prince was coming to rescue her now. And even if he did, he wouldn't want what he saw. She closed her eyes. Even thinking was exhausting. But she couldn't just fall asleep while everyone around her was working.

Adelia pulled herself into a more upright position and looked outside. Soldiers and servants scurried around, while others shouted orders. It looked hopelessly unorganized. The more she stared at them, the more her heart rate picked up. Her pendant glowed ever so slightly as the adrenaline flooded through her, and she felt like she was alongside them. They were terrified, as they should be, and she had to pull back. She imagined herself wrapped in a warm cocoon that drowned out everything else.

Breathe. Focus.

Slowly, she was able to calm her nerves and center her

mind. Everything was so much more vivid now, and it was difficult to focus on herself.

"Adelia?"

She glanced up. Scarlet was perched on the edge of her bed, and she could feel the girl's heart fluttering. She was just as nervous and uncertain as the rest of them. Scarlet reminded her of her brothers—earnest and brave like Anton, yet headstrong and mature beyond her years like Alexander. Perhaps the two girls could help each other take their minds off of everything.

"Why don't you run along to my room and grab some books? We can spend a little girl time together."

Scarlet hesitated for a moment before nodding and running off.

She returned a little while later with an armful of books that almost covered her face. When she splayed them out on the bed, Adelia frowned. It was a rather strange array she'd picked. There was *The Lonely Princess*, one of her favorite children's stories, but there was also *Elorian Cuisine: The Sweet Secrets*, as well as *Alchemic Discoveries of the New Ages* by Master Sabir—the greatest inventor to have ever lived. There was even one of her notebooks in which she practiced dragon script, among other irrelevant texts. Then, it dawned on her. It was the same awkwardness that she had felt from Jane.

"Scarlet, can you read?"

Scarlet shook her head, her cheeks slightly flushed. "The matron thought to teach us how to do chores, instead."

Adelia smiled. "Then, I guess that's step one." She began writing a list of repeated symbols in the common tongue. At least she could handle writing if she concentrated. "This is the common alphabet..."

They continued for a while, drowning out the stress of the war preparations. The more she concentrated on teaching Scarlet, the less other people's anxiety affected her. Scarlet seemed to relax around her, too, though she wasn't exactly a fast learner, and Adelia could feel the girl's frustration mounting. Eventually, she threw up her hands.

"I can't do it anymore," Scarlet huffed. "There's just no point."

"Reading and writing is a vital skill—"

"I know that, but I won't be around long enough for it to matter."

Adelia gave her a strange look. "You're only young, Scarlet. There's plenty of time to learn. Take it slow."

She shook her head. "You don't understand. I'm not a normal kid, and I never have been. People who are different don't have a lot of time, just like Ivory." Scarlet sighed.

Adelia put a hand on hers. "Ivory?"

"She and Blue were my best friends. Ivory suffered from something... something no one could fix. They left two years ago to search for a cure and never returned. She didn't have a lot of time left."

Adelia sensed the sorrow buried in Scarlet's heart. Scarlet had been alone for a long time, just like herself. And it certainly hadn't done *her* any good. If she could help it, she wouldn't let Scarlet grow up to be like her.

"Everyone's different, you know." Adelia glanced at her still legs. "Sometimes, we mistake that to mean that we aren't capable, worthy or important. What happened to your friend is unfortunate, but there's no guarantee it's going to happen to you." She smiled. "The important thing is, you're here now, and you have the choice to act. You might get nowhere, but if you don't try, there'll be no chance."

Scarlet looked up at her, her hands clasped in her lap. "I'm the spirit of fire... and that's not a fate I can escape. There are things I don't have a choice about."

Adelia knew that she was right. She slipped into her spirit sight, taking a mere moment to concentrate; it was as natural as breathing now. Scarlet's spirit was a burning orange, almost impossible to look at directly. It was almost as though it lay dormant—a brightness that had far from reached its full potential. Adelia glanced at the others within the infirmary. Including herself, their spirits were all an ethereal violet—the mark of a human. There was no hint of humanity within Scarlet at all.

Wait.

There was a tiny flicker within her, deeply intertwined with the fire spirit. Just the barest of hints—enough for Scarlet to be Scarlet.

"You might not be able to choose the hand you've been dealt or even the things that happen," said Adelia. "But you can choose what you do about it."

Scarlet gave a tired smile. "Maybe."

Adelia took a breath, pulling her close and nestling with her amongst the books. "Come on, tell me all about your friends. Where did you all get such funny names?"

Scarlet leaned on her shoulder. "Well, actually, if you didn't have a name, the other kids kind of gave you one, but not in a nice way. I was Red, of course." She twirled her hair. "They bullied Ivory about her white hair, so that's what she was called." She propped her head on her arm. "But Blue saw something more."

"So, Blue gave you both new names?"

Scarlet nodded. "Blue said we deserved names that made us feel beautiful." She sighed, gazing off into the distance. Then, a smile crossed her face as a memory came to the surface. "And then, there was that time we all played a joke on Penelope..."

They talked and giggled for what seemed like hours. It was only as Scarlet began to drift off in her arms that Adelia realized that she hadn't even thought about their situation for a while.

"You'll always have a home here," she whispered.

Adelia sighed, staring at her legs. They didn't move, despite her earnest concentration. At least she was less nauseous and could move her arms more freely now, but they could hardly support her entire body weight. Before all of this, she could have at least been helping Cynric and the others gather supplies. But now, there was nothing she could do.

What use was she? Frustrated tears pricked at her eyes. It wasn't fair. Hanabi could still walk, could still do her job. All she had wanted was to help people, but the cost had been too dear. Her brother would surely be more protective now. Dragons, if she couldn't even relieve herself alone anymore. At that thought, Adelia repressed the urge. It was humiliating. She was weak, defenseless and pathetic—just like everyone had always wanted a Lady of Anadrieth to be. Even worse, she would never again have the chance to see the ocean.

You're stronger than you know.

Mina's words echoed in her mind, and she brushed them off immediately. The princess couldn't possibly know what she was going through right now, and she clearly didn't care. She regretted making that blood oath. There had been real power behind it, and she didn't know what had come over her. She didn't blame her brother for not following suit. It was foolish and impulsive, and Mina had deserted them at the last moment. What could be more important than this?

Adelia squeezed her eyes shut, then snapped them open, forcing those thoughts from her mind. Despite everything, Mina had still been her closest friend. There must have been a good reason behind her actions, even if she didn't understand it.

You're stronger than you know.

Adelia gritted her teeth. She wasn't strong, not physically. But there was one thing she *could* do. Adelia struggled to pull her book out from her pouch and somehow managed to heave it onto her lap. Tucked inside was the little *gift* that had been left on her table. She assumed Mina had sent the letter, but she couldn't understand why she'd only written her initial, but right now, it didn't matter. The information inside was far more important.

Adelia scanned her notes, flipping to the page where the section was torn out. She still couldn't decipher much more, only that it was under the heading *forbidden*. There was a symbol that referred to self, then the one next to it meant an action or feeling involving oneself.

She clicked her tongue. There had to be something she could do to figure out what the rest of it said. All her other notes were back in her room, so she'd have to rely on her memory.

Surprisingly, it wasn't as difficult as she'd thought it would be to remember what she'd already translated. There seemed to be a slight connection between her and the words now, as though they made a little more sense. But there were no clues in the new pages she'd been gifted. It was entirely in dragon script, and if anything, the handwriting was more scribbled than it had been before. As though it had been written frantically... or in anger.

Adelia let out a frustrated sigh. If Mina had wanted her to read it, she should have left a note about *how*.

Scarlet stirred, yawning. "What's wrong?" she murmured.

"It's nothing," said Adelia. It looked like whatever was in her book would be trapped behind years of research that they didn't have. She would have to get to the capital and get her hands on the imperial temple's library, but of course, that would be impossible now.

"What..." Scarlet blinked at the book on her lap. She scrambled upright, leaning closer and flipping through the pages.

"Be careful," snapped Adelia, pulling it from her grip. "This isn't something you can practice reading."

"No, wait." Scarlet grabbed another book, thumbing through it and looking at the common language. "Definitely not. Let me see that again," she said earnestly.

Adelia hesitated, but there was a curious desperation coming from the girl. She opened the front cover.

Scarlet stared at it for a while, squinting.

"Property... of Marie Bellemore—for Bellemore eyes only," she said slowly.

Adelia stared at her. Even she hadn't been able to read that part, and she'd been trying for dragon knows how long. Could it be?

"Try this sentence." She flipped forward to a place where she knew she had the translation right.

"Priestesses are the... steward of all living beings." Scarlet frowned. "What's a steward?"

Adelia couldn't believe it. Her heart beat loudly, her hands trembling with excitement.

"How is this possible?"

Scarlet shook her head. "It's like, I've never seen those symbols before. They're unfamiliar, just like the other books, but the meaning is imprinted in my mind. This has to be the same language Mina spoke to me... the language of the spirits."

Adelia's mind was reeling. Of course, it made sense. The dragon gods' original purpose was to control the balance of nature, after all, and since Scarlet was a part of that nature, her spirit must be able to innately recognize her original language. She quickly placed the extra pages in front of her.

"Please... it's so important that I know what this, what *all* of this, says."

Scarlet paused and nodded. "I'll give it my best shot." She squinted at the words. "Winter, Year 1970 of the Fey Dynasty. That's almost four hundred years ago, right?"

"Yes." She was too eager to know more, but she forced herself to calm down. "Please, continue."

Scarlet sounded out the words, reading so slowly that it was almost painful, and Adelia scribbled down the translation as she went. After a few minutes, she had finally begun to unlock the secrets that had eluded her for so long.

I write this to preserve the records of our existence and knowledge, for it will soon disappear from the people's memories. As the only daughter of Celia Bellemore, the Head Priestess of Anadrieth, it is my solemn duty. My name is Marie Bellemore, and I am the last priestess standing.

CHAPTER TWENTY-THREE

ANTON

ANTON TIGHTENED the straps of his leather armor, shifted the sword on his waist and wrapped his cloak around his shoulders, fastening the pin. They would be riding out shortly, and he would be at the front with his brother. He caught a glance of himself in his mirror and paused. He wore the clothes of his status, but he looked nothing like a lord or even a soldier. His face held a heavy exhaustion, and he felt hollow.

His brother had wanted him to cut his hair a little so that he wouldn't be hindered on the battlefield, but it wouldn't have mattered if he did. His fingers brushed over the scar that was covered by his hair. His left eye was marred by a faint milky white that clouded the piercing blue. He'd gotten used to it over time, so much so that it didn't bother him anymore, but he'd never truly get his full sight back in that eye. Elaine kept her mouth shut, though, as he'd asked.

He shook his head. He couldn't linger here any longer. He'd already said goodbye to Doll, but there was still one more thing he needed to do before he rode out. Anton closed his door, setting a brisk pace. He didn't know if he'd be welcome, but there was a very good chance that he'd never return to Anadrieth again.

His chest felt heavy and fluttery at the same time. Ever since that awful Hanabi had used her powers on him, everything was coming in more *vividly*. He was acutely aware of his inner thoughts and the subtle shift in his chest as his heart beat a little faster. And he knew that this might be their last chance to talk; he would regret it if he didn't take it. Anton took a deep breath and opened the infirmary door.

"Adelia."

His little sister glanced up at the sound of his voice. With the late afternoon light streaming across her bed, she looked as radiant as ever, if not more so. The little redhead was curled up with her, and they were both engrossed in a book. He almost didn't want to disturb them, but he approached anyway.

"It's almost time," he said.

"Oh." Adelia glanced behind him, her eyes searching the doorway.

Anton shook his head. "It's just me. He's... not coming." Adelia looked at the sheets, and Anton cleared his throat. "I'll be at the front. His orders."

"I see," she said. She was attempting to hide her dejection, but he could see it as plain as day. They gazed at each other for a long moment. There was nothing to say, not after all this time.

"I..." he faltered. "Keep each other safe."

Adelia gave him a small smile. "Good luck."

Anton's fingertips tentatively touched her hand. "It'll be

all right," he whispered. He pulled away quickly and left the room, their touch leaving a burning imprint on his skin. He paused outside the infirmary and swallowed, taking a deep breath. He would hold his head high, at the very least.

The soldiers were stood in rows outside, ready to march. Their people crowded the grounds and spilled out into the streets, making a path for them. Anton joined his brother at the front and mounted his horse. When Alexander gave the order to move out, they began their slow trek from the castle grounds.

All was silent, save for the sound of the horse's hooves echoing on the stone. They'd be forced to travel in the dark in order to meet the Lanadese on the battlefield in time, and that could lead to casualties by itself. The villagers held out flowers and handkerchiefs, wishing them luck, but the solemn atmosphere was suffocating. A child wailed in the distance before being hushed by their mother. It was as if everyone seemed to know that this would be their final march. Anton gripped the reins and averted his eyes. He couldn't handle watching everyone else's sorrow, too.

"For Anadrieth!"

A voice cried out at the top of her lungs, and Anton whirled around, along with everyone else. Adelia was leaning out of the window, whistling and cheering. The corners of his mouth tugged up slightly. It was just like her to make a scene. Her cries resonated throughout the streets, and soon, the villagers joined in, their cheers escalating.

"For Lord Alexander!"

"You can do it!"

"We'll be victorious!"

"Protect our home!"

"Anadrieth's finest heroes!"

"Dinner will be waiting!"

The soldiers returned their cheers, raising their fists in the air. Anton stole a glance at Alexander. Neither of them joined in, but he could tell that his brother was secretly comforted by the show of support. As Alexander raised his sword in the air, the crowd cheered louder. The soldiers spurred their horses forward, picking up the pace as they cut through the city streets. Their people's cries slowly faded off into the distance, and they headed into the Celestine Forest.

Anton gripped the reins, doing his best to breathe through his mouth. His horse's feathery mane almost seemed to envelop the horse itself, but their rushed exit left no time to tend to something so insignificant. Still, he had to conserve his energy, and it was better than walking, like some of the other soldiers had to do.

He sneezed twice. They weren't the delicate kind of sneezes, either. A few people turned to stare at him, and Anton kept his chin held high and his back as straight as a board. Luckily, by this time, it was already getting dark. He almost thought that he was using his spirit sight again, until he realized that the hundreds of little lights that floated in the air were actual lanterns, trailing behind them in a long line. Anton turned his head slightly, watching the men whisper out of the corner of his eye.

"This is real war, ain't it?"

"I wish it weren't. You ever killed anyone?"

"What do you think? I can barely use my wife's kitchen knife."

They were right to be scared, even the ones that had been in battle before. He didn't have much confidence himself, either. He swallowed with difficulty, his throat dry. A man yelped in front of him, and Anton's horse stumbled, sliding a little in the snow before regaining its balance.

He clutched his chest, breathing out. There was a little slope behind them with a few invisible roots sticking out of the ground. Maybe he should have been paying more attention instead of focusing on his nerves.

"My ankle..." the other man moaned.

Another soldier supported him, calling for aid. Anton sighed. This was ridiculous. Most of the preparations had been taken care of, but they were still left with a dangerous trek through the dark forest. Another cry called out in the distance. At this rate, they were going to lose half of their army before they'd even gotten there.

His mind began to wander, and he wondered where the princess was now. Was she reclining in her palace? Perhaps she was with the prince. Did she even know that they were marching to their death?

Remember, I'm your friend.

He still couldn't figure out what she had meant by that. If there was anyone who didn't have a single friend, it was him.

"Thinking?" said a voice beside him. He didn't have to look to know that it was Cynric. He sat so much taller in the saddle compared to him.

Anton met his eyes. If even the young lord felt betrayed by the princess' abandonment, he couldn't imagine what her imperial guard must have been feeling.

"Why are you still here?" he asked.

Cynric gestured at the man who tripped. "Injury."

"I meant, why haven't you all just left? This isn't your fight."

"Orders are orders."

Anton's horse drifted closer to his. "You can't be serious. She even said they were her final orders."

"She knows something we don't."

Anton shook his head. "But if she's not coming back for you, why do you feel the need to obey her?"

Cynric stared at him for a long moment, and Anton shivered, tearing his gaze away from his eyes and looking at his chin instead.

"I don't think you understand what loyalty means."

Anton jerked the reins, and his horse shook its head, making him sneeze. Of course, he knew what loyalty meant; he was riding to his death for the sake of his brother and his people. If that wasn't loyalty, what was?

"Says the man who rides against his own people," he snapped. Cynric was Calveran, and there was a high chance that they would be there, fighting alongside the Lanadese.

"Loyalty is different to obligation," said Cynric gently.

Anton was silent. There wasn't that much of a difference, if you asked him. If he weren't loyal to his people, he couldn't fulfill his obligations, and if he didn't have obligations, he couldn't show his loyalty. He was about to retort when another voice joined in.

"He's right. We're loyal because we choose to be."

Anton peered in the darkness, then blanched.

Oh, dragons, not her.

Hanabi nodded at him from Cynric's other side, and Anton pushed his horse a little faster so that he didn't have to look at her. He couldn't believe her. She acted like nothing was wrong, that she didn't just ruin his sister's life. And now, she was lecturing him, too. He nudged his horse forward, widening their gap even more. No, he wasn't going to listen to that at all. The farther he was from her, the safer he'd be.

It was a few hours before they arrived at the plains, though they were only the first of many groups. The soldiers began setting up a few tents and organizing their equipment per his brother's orders, and several small squads ran ahead to prepare their traps. Anton rubbed his arms, wrapping his cloak tightly around him. He closed his eyes for a moment. It would be at least a few more hours until dawn, and Alexander was going to have a tough time raising morale in this state.

A heavy blanket landed in his arms.

"Here. Get some sleep if you can." Cynric pointed to the medical tent into which some of the nurses were carting supplies.

"Right," he said. Alexander was off finalizing their strategy with General Ban, Barrett and the others, so he wouldn't be needed for at least a little while. Anton settled himself into the back corner of the medical tent, curling into the blanket. It was warm and inviting, with a hint of Cynric's scent. His eyes closed.

Then, hands were on his shoulders, shaking him awake.

"Brother, wake up. I've been looking all over for you."

Anton blinked slowly. He'd barely fallen asleep, and the green eyes were far too close to his face. He drew back, sinking further into the blanket.

His brother shook his head, pulling the blanket off of him. "Come on, it's almost dawn."

Alexander dragged him to his feet and out of the tent, and Anton yanked his hand back. He didn't need to be led around like a child. Fixing his clothes and smoothing his hair, he followed his brother through the sea of faces as they made their way to the front.

Light spilled over the plains, and shades of brown and gray stretched forward endlessly, the cracks in the ground forming unique patterns. The barren earth seemed hazy as hot steam crawled across the ground. He could smell it from here—the faint scent of something rotting. It was thicker in some places than others, and he knew that that was where the dreaded tar pits were.

Steam erupted into the sky from a nearby geyser, then again from another. Even the Moonstone River—as magnificent as the waterfall over the distant cliffs appeared—was dull and gray here, as though life itself had been sucked out of the land. The Scoria Plains—it was a peculiar name. Perhaps they should have renamed it the Scoria Wastelands.

The soldiers fidgeted behind them, but no one spoke. All eyes were fixed upon the rocky pass, the only entryway to the southern regions for miles. But their army was entirely alone.

As Anton watched his brother pace back and forth, he felt his own anxiousness rise. "Should we have, perhaps, verified that that buffoon Dale was giving us accurate information?" he hissed.

Alexander paused for a second. "He's an idiot, but he's not a liar."

Of course, he would trust Dale at face value. Someone could have bought him off or planted false information. For all they knew, the army he saw could have been trees. Maybe those berries had caused more damage than he thought.

"There!" cried General Ban, along with several others.

Or not.

Anton gulped. Figures spilled from the pass like water,

slowly covering the other side of the plains beneath the cliffs. Decorated in red, the Lanadese filed out into organized regiments, their army growing larger with every step. Their bodies could have been a solid wall.

Their men paled, shuffling nervously. They were already outnumbered, and this was just the Lanadese. Anton shielded his eyes as the sun pierced the horizon.

Dawn had broken.

A small squad of Lanadese began riding out, their red cloaks trailing after them.

Alexander nodded to him and the others.

"Let's go."

CHAPTER TWENTY-FOUR

ALEXANDER

ALEXANDER STEELED HIMSELF. His heart pounded, and it was harder than ever to keep a calm demeanor. It looked like Lord Tamar himself was weaving his way across the plains on one of the handful of horses on their side. This might be their last chance to negotiate, but he didn't hold out much hope. He spurred his horse on, with his brother, Kakeru, Sara and General Ban in tow. Every hoofbeat resonated in his chest. He didn't want to admit that he was intimidated by Lord Tamar, but the little taste of his presence earlier hadn't done him much good.

Both sides stopped in the center of the plains, the riders remaining on horseback. Alexander kept his head held high, but Lord Tamar sat taller than him on his hefty horse. He was at least in his late forties, probably older, with a broad grin that was as unsettling as a crowcodile. His chest was more defined than any soldier in their army, with only a deep red cloak covering the dark patterns and images that were inked onto his skin. Alexander wasn't quite close enough to tell exactly what those symbols were, but he knew the Lanadese tradition was to permanently mark their greatest victories and treasures onto their skin. He shuddered. He couldn't imagine having his own skin look like that.

Lord Tamar's signature axes were strapped to his back, and Alexander wasn't sure how his horse was handling all of the weight. The axes didn't look as though they were heavy, with their long, spiraling handles and thin blades, but he knew that stonewood and blackscale weren't things to be taken lightly—literally.

They stared at each other, and he suspected that Lord Tamar was waiting for him to speak first, perhaps to beg for surrender. He certainly wasn't waiting out of kindness.

Alexander cleared his throat. "Lord Tamar, I'm going to request once more that you withdraw your army. Anadrieth has no qualms with Lanadrin. No one has to die today."

Lord Tamar stroked the braids of his beard, a glint in his eye. "Oh, but they do."

It was as he feared. He wasn't going to be rational enough to negotiate.

Find the cause.

Alexander grimaced. It was far too late for that to matter, but maybe he could get some information out of him now that they were finally face to face. He studied Lord Tamar for a moment. Everything about his demeanor radiated confidence, and his expression was designed to provoke him.

Yet Lord Tamar had never demanded that they surrender. He knew he could win, but was he really willing to risk the casualties? Even for these barbarians, who enjoyed fighting, forcing an all-out war to satisfy that itch was difficult to comprehend. No one willingly walked into a battle without reason.

"You're quite confident there, Lord Tamar. Though perhaps that's just a front," said Alexander, tilting his head to the side. "Surely, a well-trained and supplied army such as yours wouldn't require an alliance with Calvera and the support of our prince to defeat our meager soldiers," he paused for effect, "unless there's something else going on."

The grin on Lord Tamar's face widened. "Playing ignorant, I see. How... dishonorable."

Alexander gripped the reins tighter but kept his face neutral.

"So it seems," he said. "Then, by all means, enlighten me."

The smile faded from Lord Tamar's lips. He looked down at his chest, pointing at the symbols on his skin.

"This is my wife, Lady Tahlia." He moved his hand slightly. "And this is my little girl, Tia."

Alexander wasn't sure where this was going. "And this is my brother, Lord Anton." He waved a hand to his right.

Lord Tamar's expression darkened. "I thought you'd like to know that they had names." He narrowed his eyes, and suddenly Alexander could sense the weight of a quiet rage behind that gaze.

Had?

"I *commend* you on how well you've remained inconspicuous until now, but there's no point in acting innocent just because the princess' lackeys are with you." Lord Tamar nodded at Alexander's companions, pure disgust now dripping from his gaze. "It's not like she gives a dragon's claw about it."

Alexander had had enough. "Lord Tamar, I give you my word that I have no idea what you're talking about."

Lord Tamar spat on the ground, and it instantly evaporated from the dry earth.

"Like the word of someone like you means a damn thing."

Alexander shook his head. "Then, don't you at least care about the peace the imperial family has fought so hard to protect?"

"Peace?" Lord Tamar snorted. "Don't tell me you're that stupid. The imperial family is nothing but a convenient front to cover the cracks in this empire."

Alexander exhaled through his teeth. "We can be the first step to mending it."

Lord Tamar shook his head, the rage creeping into his eyes once more. "You've had more than enough time to *mend* it. Instead, you chose to come pay me a little visit. I'd have challenged you to a duel instead of this, but you've only made me even more sure that slaughtering every last one of you is the only option." His muscles were visibly tensing. "I'll take from you what you took from me tenfold."

"This is absurd," said Alexander, unable to keep the distress out of his voice. "On my honor, we've done nothing to warrant this. Spare my people and take me, if that's what you're after."

Lord Tamar didn't miss a beat. "You've had your opportunity to come clean. If you believed you had a chance against us, fear not. The prince himself is in favor of your complete annihilation." He turned his nose up, looking down on him. "You sealed your fate long ago, Alexander."

Alexander stiffened. This man was insane. It wasn't about land, wealth or power. He clearly had some misguided grudge that was severely clouding his rational judgment. This was personal. Was this all part of the Mistress' plan? Alexander gritted his teeth. It didn't matter. He wasn't going to stand for this any longer.

"So be it, then. Anadrieth *will* fight."

He signaled to the others, turning his horse and galloping back to their people. This was it. He was leading his people into war against a deranged tyrant. There was no turning back now. As they neared their camp, Kakeru pulled him aside, forcing their horses to slow down. He gave him a look full of contempt.

"Understand that this is suicide. But we have been ordered to protect you with our lives. Otherwise, we would not stay."

Alexander nodded curtly. "I'd expect nothing less, and I appreciate your help. All of you."

"Lord Tamar knows we can't replicate what we did at Lanadrin. Their sheer numbers would overwhelm us, and we'd be out of action in minutes." Kakeru narrowed his eyes. "But do anything stupid, and I'll kill you myself."

Alexander smirked. "Then, I'm afraid you'll be out of luck."

He took a deep breath, drawing his sword and riding up to address his soldiers. He thrust his sword into the air, and his soldiers did the same, their weapons rising up in waves, from the frontline to the rear guard. He had one last moment to rally their troops.

"Friends!" he cried. "We stand here today to protect our people, our land and our home! We will not bow to their steel. However mighty they may seem, all men are mortal. To fall here will be the greatest glory a man can receive, and I am honored to stand with you!"

Cries rose from their men, vaguely echoing their enemy's cries across the battlefield. Alexander faced their foes, his eyes ablaze. The battlefield would soon bleed death into the river, and everyone knew whose blood it would be. Yet his people followed him, anyway. He *would* fight for their hope. He paused as Lanadrin's army began to rush toward them. Then, Alexander looked to Sara, who nodded at him.

"Fire!" His cry was echoed by General Ban.

The first volley sailed across the battlefield, their flaming arrows soaked in oil. With Sara's volatile brew spread across the tar pits, there was no escape. As the Lanadese ran past, the air around them ignited. Burning tar exploded around them, throwing blackened, sticky lumps in every direction. The pits turned to fire, with the flames sitting on top of the tar. Screams filled the air as the blaze landed on their bare skin. Some of them fell into the tar pits, and once the tar had grasped hold of them, it didn't let go. It was over.

As they tried to move forward, their lines broke further as they stumbled around the battlefield. The layer of poison-coated caltrops was slowing them down, and even though their feet were tough, they were still pierced by the silverlight. The clear wood would break off into their skin like splinters, allowing the poison inside. It was a double-edged sword, though; the silverlight was almost impossible to see, and it was likely that the Anadese would suffer the same fate when they entered the fray.

Alexander tried to ignore the screams, keeping his eyes focused on the battlefield. Timing was critical. He signaled to General Ban again, and volley after volley shot past the Lanadese, this time, aiming for the ground behind them. Fire filled the air once more, taking the earth with it. A wall of flames began to form around the barbarians, the roaring fire fueled by the oil. It split their army in two, with those who charged first now with their backs to the flames.

"For Anadrieth!" Alexander shouted. The responding cries filled the air, and he led the charge across the plains. The Lanadese regrouped quickly, bracing themselves for impact. The first wave of their army raced across the battlefield, a sea of gray crashing against a sea of red. Despite everything, the Lanadese held strong, and their axes cleaved a path through their men.

Large black creatures flew past Alexander's vision, and their razor-sharp claws tore into the barbarians' flesh. Their pointed beaks held several rows of sturdy teeth, immediately ripping into their eyes and faces. The crowcodile trainers whistled and called the scaly beasts to pick off their targets, one by one. The Lanadese flailed and swung at them but met only air, their flying speed outmatching even the swiftest of men. He'd never truly seen them in action before, but they were just as terrifying as he'd imagined.

Alexander's men used the opportunity to break the barbarians' frontline, splitting their forces even further. He kept an eye out, but it didn't seem like Lord Tamar had led this charge. Amidst the turmoil, men from both sides continued to fall prey to the black tar, with hooves and hands alike clawing at the air as the still-raging fires consumed them. Some of the Lanadese had begun to stagger around as the poison from the caltrops kicked in. Alexander struck down their men with his trusty Golden Dawn, steering the reins with his other hand.

The ground beneath them rumbled, and the fissures in the cracked earth widened. Suddenly, everyone was scrambling for footing as parts of the earth began to cave in, leaving the grounds littered with deep holes. Boiling steam rushed up through the cracks, and the nearby geysers burst around them.

Alexander narrowly swerved his horse out of the way of a direct blast, but many men on both sides had been caught in the steam. Howls came from all around him as the soldiers clutched their melting skin and armor. A screaming man ran into his horse and fell backward, his face peeling and bubbling in a horrific mess.

Alexander fought through the crowd. Both sides had completely broken down in the turmoil. For a moment, they were all just people, scared and struggling to cling to life. The damp heat began to creep into his skin from a combination of steam and sunlight. Moisture and sweat mingled on his brow, dripping into his eyes. He could taste the salt, as well as something foul. The smell alone was almost as bad as the taste.

He quickly wiped his face, shouting at his remaining men to retreat and reform the line. The Lanadese had begun fighting their way through the fire, and a second wave was coming. Another wave of arrows soared over them, fueling the fires. They would be out of prepared arrows soon, and then their own second wave would be able to join them. Alexander panted as he rounded up his men.

The plains were already covered in bodies, but there were just as many Lanadese as there were his own men, and more of theirs were left standing, it seemed. Alexander took a few deep breaths. Maybe they did have a chance. As the second wave came to meet them, his expression tensed.

This time, Lord Tamar was at the front.

CHAPTER TWENTY-FIVE
ADELIA

ADELIA WAS RUNNING through the snow. The wind whipped through her hair, and a grin was plastered on her face. Anton would never find her here. It was the perfect hiding place! Suddenly, the snow caved in from underneath her, and she was falling through the air, a searing pain shooting through her leg.

A strange woman, pointing a silver staff at her. The smell of rotting flesh. A face she could never forget.

Adelia twitched in her sleep, her eyes still closed. Her brother shouldn't have blamed himself. It wasn't his fault. She tossed and turned into the pillow. The scar on her leg burned, and the tingling sensation shook her out of her dream.

It was dark, but there was someone standing over her. It wasn't Scarlet; she had gone back to her own room. As she stared, she realized there were two of them, one aura female, the other male. Strange—the men should have all gone to war.

Adelia groggily rubbed her eyes. It seemed like it was harder to wake up than usual, too.

"Step aside," growled the man.

"What do you want with her?"

"None of your business, old hag."

Adelia frowned, slowly crawling through the fog of sleep. Her eyes began to adjust. One of the figures was Elaine, standing with her back against her bed. She seemed smaller than usual, but perhaps it was just a trick of the dark.

"What's wrong?" Adelia murmured.

"Wake up, child," Elaine hissed, an unmistakable tone of urgency in her voice.

Adelia forced her eyes to open fully, and she peered at the other figure. Was that Councilor Dallan?

"Where've you been?" she asked him, focusing on the muscles in her arms to prop herself up on one elbow. She didn't see him smile, but she could feel it. Her blood instantly ran cold.

"My lady," he drawled. "How nice of you to join us. I require your person at once."

"What for? You should be with my brothers."

He took a step forward, and a sliver of light crossed his face. It was definitely the councilor. "For the sake of Anadri-eth, I'm delivering you to Lord Tamar."

"Traitor," spat Elaine. "Always knew you were a vile human being—"

Councilor Dallan rolled his eyes and closed the distance between them. There was a sickening sound of steel meeting flesh, and Elaine slumped to the floor, pulling the sheets with her as she fell.

"Good riddance, you decrepit fool."

Adelia grasped the edge of the bed, staring at Elaine's writing form.

"Mama..."

She couldn't get up, couldn't go to her, even though she was right there.

Elaine let out a gurgling moan, her hands clasping at the wound in her belly. There was no water nearby to heal herself. Councilor Dallan bent down, pulling the dagger from her stomach in one motion, and Elaine screamed. Adelia screamed with her, clawing at the bed. She could barely drag herself to the edge; her body was entirely uncooperative, immovable.

"Long have I been loyal to Anadrieth, faithfully serving Lord Alexander and Lord Alastair, before him," said Councilor Dallan. "And long have I watched them continue to make mistakes, especially concerning women." He kicked Elaine to the side, stepping over her.

Adelia dug her nails into the bed, but she couldn't even pull herself to the floor.

"You filthy bastard!" she cried, hot tears pooling in her eyes. Elaine stayed home. She didn't go to the battlefield. She was supposed to be safe.

Councilor Dallan tilted his head, tut-tutting her. "This is why Alexander should have married you off long ago. Frankly, your rebellious and rude attitude has never befitted a proper lady. Or perhaps it just wasn't beaten out of you enough. I suppose that's not your fault. Your parents were murdered before they could instill proper manners for your superiors." He towered over her.

"And what do you possibly get out of this?" she hissed

through clenched teeth. His aura looked like it was dripping in poison; it sickened her.

He raised an eyebrow, locking his grip around her chin. "It's not wrong of me to protect my own neck. I simply chose the winning side. A group of Lanadese is at my disposal, taking over the castle as we speak. Lord Tamar is putting me in charge."

She jerked her face away from him. "How long have you been planning this?"

Councilor Dallan chuckled. "Alexander sealed his fate when he began listening to that stupid servant princess. I gave him many chances, but it's far too late now." He appraised her slowly, lifting a piece of her golden hair with the bloody dagger. He brought her hair to his nose, inhaling deeply.

"I can see why they desire you. I'm sure Lord Tamar won't mind..." He placed his hand on the other side of her, bringing one knee onto the bed. "And when the time comes, I'll take delight in your agonizing death," he whispered in her car.

Adelia froze, the words lodged in her throat. She glanced at the doorway, but there was no knight coming to rescue her. Her brothers were gone. Councilor Dallan reached for her chest.

You're stronger than you know.

There was no way this piece of filth was getting away with this. A blinding white light radiated from her, and he stopped, shielding his eyes. She was suddenly calm, her path clear. She could see his corrupted spirit before her, the violet light trembling. It was in her grasp, easily manipulated.

The light pulsated and grew brighter as dragon script spilled from her pendant, covering her chest and spreading down her arms. Her hair drifted around her, carried by an invisible wind, and a smile crept across her face as confusion crept across his.

"What in dragon's name is this?" he shouted.

She felt a flicker of fear, but it wasn't her own. "Get off me."

Councilor Dallan obeyed immediately, his eyes darting around wildly. She didn't want to hear another word from him, so she stole his will to speak. He clutched at his throat, and she reached further, smothering his spirit with hers. She could feel him struggling to breathe as the pain resonated in her own throat. But it didn't matter. He was all hers now.

Elaine's blood pooled around his boots. There was only one way this was going to end.

Slowly, his hand was raised in front of him, the dagger pointing toward his body. His fear intensified, and sweat rolled down his temple. She could feel him struggling to cry out, to beg for mercy. But she had none. She was far too strong for him; it was like molding snow in her palm. His arm moved in and out, in and out, sending flecks of blood onto her white sheets.

She knew it was excruciating, but her own pain was a distant memory, as the barrier between their emotions had slammed down like stonewood. His eyes went glassy, and the light of his spirit left him. Adelia let his body collapse to the ground, the stains of his death fouling the floor. The light from her pendant began to fade, but an idea struck her. They hadn't read that page yet, but somehow, she knew what it contained.

"A forbidden action involving oneself," Adelia muttered. She turned her focus inward, toward the spark of what little bit of her spirit was left in her body. It was warm and fluttering, like the frail heartbeat of a dying lyrecrane.

Move.

Her limbs were suddenly filled with energy, the heaviness momentarily lifted. Adelia threw off the covers, tentatively stepping onto the floor. She could feel the soles of her feet connecting with the stone. It was working. She could manipulate her own spirit.

Her energy levels were higher than they'd ever been, and she controlled its flow, lowering it to the bare minimum. Her pendant only gave off a slight glow now, the light almost invisible. It was dangerous, and she could feel it. The balance not only had to be perfect—it had to be maintained. She was filled with energy now, but she wouldn't be able to keep it up for long.

Adelia knelt next to Elaine, the edges of her dress dipping in the councilor's remains. Although she was still alive, her breaths came in heaving shudders, her spirit nothing more than a faint light. It was too late for her. Adelia cradled her head on her lap. There were a thousand things she wanted to say.

"I'm sorry," she whispered.

Elaine shook her head with the slightest of movements. She lifted a trembling hand to Adelia's face.

"You... look just like your mother." Her voice was strained, the whisper barely audible. "She would've been so proud..." Her mouth went slack, her chest still.

Adelia watched the last of her spirit leave her, the light fading into the darkness. She gently closed the lifeless eyes, resting her head against Elaine's.

"You fool... I look nothing like my mother," she whispered. "It was always you." The tears had dried on her face, and a great emptiness took their place.

Screams echoed in the distance. It had to be the Lanadese that the bastard had brought in. Adelia stood, clenching her fists. There would be time for grief later. She took a shaky step forward, then another, and another, until she broke into a run. Using her spirit arts like this was taxing, and she wouldn't be able to maintain it for much longer. But her people were in danger, and this time, she would be the knight.

Her bare feet hit the floor, each step echoing the pounding of her heart. The screams grew louder, fear practically feasting upon them. Adelia gripped her pendant, blocking the wave of their emotions out. Their terror still shook her to the core, but she managed to stay upright.

A stream of villagers barreled toward her, tripping over each other like a stampede of frightened deerabits. Adelia dove to the side, struggling to push through the crowd. Children wailed, stragglers abandoned in the fray. Her heart tugged toward a little boy lying still on the ground, but she didn't have time to save him. Hundreds more were rushing through the halls toward her. If she tried to calm them all now, she would risk collapsing before she got to the Lanadese.

"Make way!" she screamed, pushing her will outward. It rippled throughout the crowd, her strong suggestion parting the villagers in waves as she ran through them. She could feel their confusion, but as she passed, they soon resumed fleeing into the castle. Adelia finally emerged into the courtyard, panting for air. Her legs were starting to shake.

Half a dozen Lanadese barbarians were advancing through the castle grounds, toying with her people. Some of the servants stood their ground, gripping their silverlight swords, while others fled. But the swords shattered, one by one, as the Lanadese swung, mere twigs against their mighty axes.

Adelia stared on in horror. Their training had been for naught. An arrow struck a barbarian in his meaty arm, and he roared. He sprinted straight for Vivian as she tried to notch another arrow, but she was too late. He wrapped a large hand around her neck and lifted her off the ground. She spat in his face.

Adelia doubled over, reaching out to the captured girl through blurring vision. "No!"

The barbarian snapped Vivian's neck in one movement, then threw her to the side. His cruelty wasn't alone, as none of the small army hesitated to cut down the women before them, cleaving a pathway with their axes.

Adelia collapsed to her knees, gasping for air, unable to stand any longer. She had to act now. The men slowed their pace as they approached, towering over her.

"What do have we here?" The voice was rich with an unexpected accent rolling off the tongue.

Another barbarian grinned. "This one's pretty."

"Doesn't she match the description?" One of them bent down, peering at her face.

"Even if it's not the Lady of Anadrieth, I'm sure we can find other uses for her."

"Later. We're taking over the castle first," said the biggest one. "But she can come with us." He reached for her arm.

Adelia threw out her hand, the light exploding from her pendant and the dragon script covering her skin once more. She gave them her rage—filled them with it. She forced out their rationality, letting her rage consume them. The barbarians paused, then took up arms against each other.

Adelia concentrated on maintaining the wall between them, blocking out their agony. It still felt like she was dying, but she could dull the pain enough to stay conscious. One after the other, they hit the ground, until the last one took his own life. A trickle of blood dripped from her nose and rolled over her lip. She could feel it dripping from her ears, too.

The remaining villagers had stopped running, and she turned to meet their terrified eyes. This time, their fear was directed toward her. Summoning the last of her strength, she projected her voice in the most commanding tone she had.

"Citizens of Anadrieth, what you've just witnessed is the true might of our people!" Silence fell over them. "I am Lady Adelia, a priestess of the empire, sister to Lord Alexander and friend of Princess Mina. At this moment, our soldiers march to the battlefield to protect your lives!" Some of them gathered closer, and whispers filtered through the crowd. She clutched her chest. It was getting harder to breathe.

"I ask that you have faith in us, and we will show you that it is Lanadrin who should be afraid! Those who were lost today are heroines among us." She gestured at the fallen figures around her. "Their deeds shall not be forgotten. Comfort each other in this time and trust that our people will return home. We won't disappoint them by allowing our home to fall!" she cried.

The villagers glanced at each other, the uncertainty plain on their faces.

Adelia leaned on her arms, which collapsed underneath her. The stone floor was cool against her cheek, and her legs had folded in an awkward position, but she had no strength to move them. It was hopeless. Her chest seized up with an uncomfortable pressure that clutched her heart. A cold sweat formed over her brow, her arms felt like stonewood and her jaw was unbearably tight. She lay there, panting, unable to do anything.

It hurts.

No one was going to listen to her in this state. The weight of what she'd done began to creep up on her, and she didn't have the energy to resist. She'd protected her people, but at what cost? She just killed half a dozen men. She gritted her teeth. There had to be at least a hundred more dead, littered around the grounds. She hadn't come soon enough, but if she hadn't come at all, the entire kingdom would have died.

Scarlet pushed her way through the crowd, heading straight for her.

"Adelia! What happened?"

Several servants began to surround her, and Jane scooped her head off the ground, leaning her body against hers.

"Milady, are you hurt?"

"What do we do now?" asked another.

Adelia wiped the blood from her face as they looked at her expectantly. There wasn't time to feel sorry for herself. Her job wasn't over yet. She took a shuddering breath and mustered her strength.

"Round up all the able-bodied women and barricade the gates with anything you can find. Gather the injured and the children in the great hall and treat any wounds as best we can. Then, set up the hall as an infirmary for when the others return home. Leave the dead, for now."

The women nodded.

"Yes, Milady."

Adelia clenched her fist as much as she could. She might

need help to do the simplest things from now on, but that wasn't going to stop her from doing nothing—not anymore.

"*No one* is going to get past us again," she said to them.

No matter what, she was Lady Adelia, the last priestess of Anadrieth, and she had a job to do.

26

CHAPTER TWENTY-SIX

ANTON

ANTON SQUEEZED his thighs around his horse, his muscles tensing. General Ban and his father would be leading the main charge any second. The archers had run out of flame arrows, and when the volleys of regular arrows ceased, they would all be joining the battlefield. From a distance, it looked as though they'd won the first exchange, but there were more enemies pouring through the fire that raged across the battlefield. They'd certainly done their job, but it wasn't going to win them the war.

The men beside him were cheering. The first little glimmer of hope seemed to have boosted their morale, but he was anything but excited. He couldn't stop trembling. He forced himself to take deep breaths. The battlefield was a wreck, and they weren't going to be able to pull out any more tricks. They'd have to fight head-on. And it was terrifying.

General Ban rode out in front of them, calling out his final orders. There was no more time to prepare himself.

Their army rushed forward.

Anton spurred his horse as fast as it would go; the last thing he wanted was to get trampled by his own men. His heart was practically in his ears, but he kept his eyes open. He couldn't afford to flinch, couldn't afford to hesitate. He drew his sword. There was no backing out now. They quickly regrouped with the remaining men, and he spotted his brother at the front. Good. At least he was still alive.

And here they come.

The next wave of Lanadese was already upon them. Anton swung his sword at the first barbarian, dragging a deep slice across his chest, and a soldier behind him finished him off. He gritted his teeth and kept going. It was all the same.

Don't think.

There were bodies all around them. Mangled. Blood-stained.

Don't think.

A comrade's terrified scream rang out as he flailed in the tar.

Don't think.

His sword connected with flesh and blackscale again and again, but he didn't have the luxury of dwelling on the consequences. His survival instinct had taken over. Faces became blurred. He could only see gray and red. He couldn't remember the faces of those he fought, nor those beside whom he fought. It was all the same.

A tar pit exploded off to his right, flinging the burning tar high in the air.

"Shield formation!"

The nearby soldiers rushed together, creating a barrier with their shields above them. The Lanadese howled, covering their faces, but they were unable to escape the tar that clung to their skin. Their soldiers lowered their shields, and they seemed mostly unscathed. They took advantage of the opportunity to take down the injured Lanadese.

Anton continued on, remaining wary of anything that might come from above. He didn't know how long it had been since they rushed in. It felt like hours. The fires were still burning, and parts of the plains continued to collapse. Their enemies seemed endless. He blocked an axe swing, and a crowcodile swooped in, its claws tearing into the man's face. He screamed, clutching the strips of skin that had peeled off. Anton ended his life with another swing. It was all the same.

Slowly but surely, the battlefield had become more jumbled. There were no lines, no sides. The chain of command for both armies seemed scattered, and there were fewer soldiers now. Anton took a moment to breathe and checked his surroundings. His eyes widened. He'd pushed too far ahead. Amidst the steam, he couldn't see a single gray cloak.

Several Lanadese came at him from different directions.

He tugged sharply on the reins in panic, his horse rearing. Anton clung to its mane, accidentally inhaling a handful of horse feathers and immediately launching into another sneezing attack.

Not now, he thought. He'd managed to keep it relatively under control, but now, his eyes were watering like rivers. He swung his sword aimlessly at the first barbarian. It didn't connect, but the barbarian fell all the same. Something sped through the air, taking down his attackers in one swoop.

Anton steadied his mount, searching behind him. A hand

suddenly grabbed his, and a figure pulled itself onto his horse. He whirled his head around, coming face to face with Sara.

"What the—"

She was panting, and a trickle of blood ran down her forehead. She reached out to catch her chakram with one hand and looped her other around his waist.

Anton froze.

Sara kicked the horse's flanks, and it took off. He scrambled to grasp the reins again, turning back toward their comrades, but the extra weight was throwing him off balance. He tried to shuffle forward, and Sara held onto him tighter.

"We must reform—" she shouted, her lips just touching his ear. He jerked backwards at her contact, surprised, his head smashing into her nose.

"*Really?*" Sara exclaimed, clutching her nose.

Anton winced, rubbing his head. "Can't you ride with anyone else?" He was tempted just to give her the horse so that he could escape the situation.

Sara's grip tightened. "Well, pardon me for saving your life."

"I can handle this," he growled. Why was she clinging on so tightly? She was tolerable from a distance, sure, but right now, she was far too close.

"Clearly. Your horsemanship is appalling." She yanked the reins from his hands, looping her other arm around him as she guided them back across the battlefield.

"That's your fault," he spluttered. He had to admit, though, that she was getting them out of danger.

Sara exhaled, her warm breath tickling the back of his neck. "You're such a hard-head, both inside and out."

Anton rolled his eyes. "At least my hard head isn't as pointy as your nose."

"Great, that's just what this empire needs... another true gentleman."

Anton gritted his teeth, then pointed at another rider. "There's a horse. Go get on it."

Sara flicked her hair over her shoulder, her nose upturned. Her retort was drowned out by a loud horn, the deep pitch cutting across the battlefield. Everyone turned toward the sound.

"Calverans," Anton whispered.

The Lanadese untangled themselves from the battle, reforming their line. They cheered and stomped the ground, parting their ranks down the center as the Calverans marched onto the battlefield.

Anton guided the horse back toward their soldiers, joining the hasty regrouping. His nervousness had returned full-force.

The half-giants marched in perfect rows toward them. They had to be a least ten feet tall. Like trees themselves, their bodies were built for a life in the high canopies. Emerald green cloaks were draped around their shoulders, and they wore little else. Each carried a white stonewood spear taller than themselves and a long-pointed shield strapped to their arms, bearing the Calveran crest—a great stonewood tree.

Standing next to Cynric hadn't been nearly as intimidating as this. The simple Anadese steel swords would be no match for these opponents. They may have been hanging on by a thread until now, but it was plain to see that this would be the beginning of their demise. Even Sara hadn't said anything.

Their own men shuffled backward into each other, but there was nowhere to go. Alexander was shouting from a distance, and Ban was pushing his way to the front of the right flank. Anton steeled himself as a moment of silence bound them, each soldier waiting for the other's first move.

The horn sounded again. This time, the Calverans and the Lanadese advanced.

❦ 27 ❦

CHAPTER TWENTY-SEVEN

ALEXANDER

ALEXANDER SPURRED HIS HORSE, leading the rest of his exhausted men with a cry. Things were going from bad to worse. He hadn't heard word from his brother or his general yet, their troops were scattered and, now, the Calverans were advancing. Throughout the battle, Lord Tamar had held back, staying within sight but always out of reach, as though he were taunting them—or simply biding his time. Now, Alexander knew why. He gripped his Golden Dawn, taking out a barbarian with one swoop.

A Calveran charged at him, and he ducked, the spear narrowly passing over his head. He rammed his blade through his opponent's abdomen, and the half-giant collapsed on top of him, knocking him off his horse. Alexander kicked at the body, straining to push the Calveran off, but he felt as heavy as two men. With another heave, he rolled out from underneath the corpse, withdrawing his sword with a grunt.

The battlefield was in utter turmoil. His men were falling

with little resistance now, their weapons splintering against the stonewood. He pushed away from the ground, launching himself at another barbarian.

It's not over yet.

His sword was a blur, an extension of his arm. He didn't pause, didn't stop. There was no time for calculations, no time for strategizing. Only survival. His clothes clung to his sweaty body, and the steam radiating from the plains was almost unbearable. The Lanadese had the advantage now; they were used to this kind of heat. But for Alexander, it only amplified the smell of death, as the bodies had already begun to rot in the midday sun. Even his toes could feel the heat through his boots.

He blocked an incoming strike, pushing back against the axe. He saw another swinging at him out of the corner of his eye, and he knew he didn't have time to block it.

Then, an iron glaive came into view, knocking the axe off course. The figure spun, striking both enemies with the blades on either end of his polearm, though it didn't seem to be with the sharp side of the blades.

Alexander stumbled back, peering at the figure. He wore his dragon mask, but his black leathery attire was easily recognizable.

"Ryuko?"

Ryuko nodded, targeting another Calveran and wielding his weapon with ease. Alexander fought alongside him, their attacks falling into an easy rhythm. Ryuko's sword had power, and his glaive had reach, shifting with every strike, changing and morphing at will. Alexander stole a glance at him every so often. He must have been sweltering in all of that black, but he didn't have time to question it. If he wanted to pass out in the middle of the battle, that was his choice.

As they fought, he realized that Ryuko seemed to be avoiding the Lanadese entirely. In fact, he hadn't seen him this entire battle, not even at the beginning, when they met with Lord Tamar. Alexander sidestepped a barbarian deliberately, and Ryuko took him down with a blow to the side of the head—a non-lethal blow. So, he wasn't mistaken. Ryuko hadn't killed anyone when they went to Lanadrin, either, yet he had no qualms with killing the Calverans. There was definitely something strange going on.

A second sword joined alongside them—another familiar figure he hadn't seen for a while.

"Why are you wearing that mask, you fool?" Kakeru shouted over the noise.

"None of your business," Ryuko replied. Two Lanadese came at him at once. Ryuko dropped to the floor at the last moment, sliding beneath their swings. His glaive curled backward and struck the back of their knees. Again, non-lethal. Alexander narrowed his eyes. He'd definitely seen it that time. That was hesitation. If Ryuko didn't want to kill the Lanadese, why was he even fighting with them? It didn't make any sense.

"If you could see properly, you wouldn't be having so much trouble," said Kakeru, finishing them off.

A spear narrowly grazed Alexander's arm, drawing a thin line of blood. Kakeru used the earth to propel him, launching himself skyward and driving his sword into a half-giant's stomach.

"Pay attention! I knew I'd have to keep you out of trouble at some point," he grumbled.

Alexander ignored him, catching his breath and glancing around. They were getting pushed farther and farther back as an endless stream of enemies poured forward. They needed to retreat and regroup. Kakeru backed into him, and they were suddenly surrounded. The three of them stood back to back as the Lanadese encircled them. It was too late to retreat. Several barbarians jeered, waving their weapons at them.

"It's not over yet," Alexander said under his breath. It couldn't be over. Mina's smile echoed in his memory, then his siblings, laughing as they ran through the forest. He had to see them smile again. He tightened his grip.

No matter what it takes.

The barbarians paused, staring at their weapons. The metal itself began to shift, bending and twisting. In an instant, the blackscale axes turned to strike their wielders. Alexander blinked, his mouth slightly open. With his hand by his side, Ryuko's fingers closed into a fist, and their enemies fell in a heap around them. Something rolled out from underneath his mask, dripping onto his boot. Alexander couldn't tell if it was tears or sweat.

The few remaining Lanadese shuffled backward with looks of horror crossing their faces, their eyes flickering between the three of them.

"That's the..."

"Which one?"

"It can't be."

"It's the iron slayer."

Murmurs rippled through the Lanadese, and Ryuko took a step back. His other hand covered his face, pressing tightly on the mask.

Kakeru nudged Ryuko in the ribs. "What's going on?"

Alexander stared at Ryuko, thinking back to what Kakeru had told him at the iron foundry in Lanadrin.

Human statues were found encased in solid iron.

It could only have been Ryuko, the man with the power to shape metal. But it didn't add up. The Lanadese were practically cowering in his presence now. Such fear could have worked out in their favor, but he chose not to reveal it. And if Ryuko *had* struck such fear into them in the past, it didn't explain his behavior now.

The enemy soldiers began to part, making way for an entourage of both Lanadese and Calverans, and two lordly figures strode through the crowd. Lord Tamar's eyes were murderous as he approached, his clothes soaked in blood. Alexander readied his sword.

"Where is he?" Lord Tamar shouted. He ran straight for them, swinging a mighty axe in each hand.

Alexander dove to the right, rolling on one shoulder to a crouch. It would be dangerous to try to block a handle made of stonewood. The earth suddenly split, and a deep chasm snaked its way between them, blocking Lord Tamar from his target. Alexander managed a nod at Kakeru. The gap wasn't so wide as to be unable to leap over it, but it was wide enough to make someone think twice.

Lord Tamar spat into the gorge, narrowing his eyes.

"Calm yourself, Lord Tamar," said the Calveran beside him, holding out his arm to stop his comrade. He must be Lord Cypress. Blonde hair swept past his neck, and emerald green and white attire draped around his slender frame. His entire person was completely spotless, as though he hadn't just crossed a battlefield. There was an intimidating aura about him, and Alexander could tell that he was the kind of man who would stab his closest friend in the back without a second thought to get what he wanted.

Together, they were a frightening pair.

"Where is he?" Lord Tamar asked again, this time in a more menacing tone.

Alexander and Kakeru exchanged glances. Ryuko was nowhere in sight.

"Bastard," growled Kakeru. "How did he even..."

Alexander didn't blame him. Obviously, he had seen his opportunity and took it. They should have done the same. Visibility was poor across the plains, and the battlefield had thinned considerably. It looked like Kakeru was the only ally around. Maybe they could stall for reinforcements. Alexander straightened his back, clearing his throat.

"Who are you looking for?"

Lord Tamar's face was scarlet, a vein bulging from his forehead. "The iron slayer." Spit escaped his mouth.

"Why?" asked Alexander. Perhaps the so-called iron slayer was part of Tamar's misguided revenge.

Lord Tamar's eyes narrowed, and he grasped his axe, bringing it to rest on the floor with a threatening thud.

"Are you protecting them? Or perhaps it's been you all along." He took a step forward, his foot on the edge of the little cliff.

"This isn't looking good," hissed Kakeru.

Alexander kept his face blank. "I don't know who you're talking about." Whether or not Ryuko was guilty, it felt wrong to point and run in the other direction, even though he had deserted them.

Lord Tamar bunched his muscles, readying his axe. "Liar!"

Lord Cypress held up a hand. "Our orders were to keep

Lord Alexander alive, if at all possible, so please, don't lose your temper. This battle is already won. There's no need to exert excessive force to pick off the survivors."

Alexander stared him down. What an arrogant sort. But whose orders were they following?

"I understand you have an individual by the name of Cynric with you," continued Lord Cypress.

"What do you want with him?" said Kakeru, digging his fingers into the ground. Alexander wanted to nudge him to be a little less aggressive, but he refrained.

"I'm simply—" Lord Cypress paused, making a show of choosing his words, "—concerned with his wellbeing. Where may I find him?"

Kakeru's grinding teeth were practically audible. "Not here."

"Pity. Hasn't left his ways, I see." Lord Cypress tilted his head, a small sigh leaving his lips.

"And who is he to you?"

"Interesting," Lord Cypress enunciated with a growing smile. "He hasn't told you who he is."

Kakeru stiffened, and Alexander had to kick him in the side. He might be an excellent fighter, but his words only ever seemed to escalate conflicts. Kakeru grunted, but the kick didn't stop him from speaking up.

"Cynric is my comrade. The princess trusts him, and so do I. That's all I need to know."

Both lords began to chuckle.

"You're more of a fool than I thought," said Lord Tamar. "I was considering offering you a position in my upper ranks. A man of your skill doesn't need to be around people like these. Turns out you're just like the rest of them."

"A fool, indeed," said Lord Cypress, staring down his long nose. "How much do you really know them, these people you bet your life on? Do you even understand who the princess truly is? She's a monster. A beast in human form."

Alexander figured he'd have to stop Kakeru from lunging at them, but the man was still, and his eyes dropped to the floor. It was clear that Tamar and Cypress were intentionally trying to sow doubt into their minds. Alexander didn't know much about this imperial guard, but he did know Mina. The real Mina—without obligations, responsibilities or a title. She was clever, headstrong and loyal, the kind of person who stood up against injustice while everyone else was silent. The servant who had never stopped being a leader.

Alexander shook his head. He may have never truly had a chance with Mina, but she *was* his friend. She had her reasons for leaving, but he was sure that she hadn't abandoned them. She wasn't the kind of person to do that.

"Don't listen to him—"

"I'm not," Kakeru said quietly. It didn't sound entirely convincing.

"I tire of this," said Lord Cypress, dusting off his robes, even though they were already immaculate. "Our imperial guests should be here soon, and we don't want to miss them." He turned his back on them, and his guards formed a tight circle around him.

Lord Tamar turned up his nose as he heaved one axe over his shoulder.

"You're lucky I can't kill you just yet. Stay alive long enough for the finale."

Their men retreated, leaving Alexander and Kakeru staring at each other. Alexander couldn't help but be a little relieved. For some reason, they wanted him alive. For now, at least. A large number of their combined army was still stationed against the cliffs, just watching the battle, or rather, the slaughter. It was as Lord Cypress had said; they didn't need to exert unnecessary force.

Alexander turned in circles. The battlefield seemed quieter now. He saw his men, but they were mostly splattered across the plains in pieces. The fires had begun to die down in some areas, revealing blackened corpses in their wake. Emptiness began to consume him again. Was it even worth fighting anymore?

"What do we do now?" he whispered. He glanced at Kakeru and paused. The man hadn't shaken that look off his face. It must have mirrored his own. Helpless. Lost. Afraid. Alexander gripped his sword.

No. It's not over yet.

He was Lord Alexander of Anadrieth, and his people were still out there, fighting. He couldn't afford to think like this. He grabbed Kakeru's shoulder, shaking him to his senses.

"You aren't taking what they said seriously, are you?"

Kakeru yanked his shoulder away. "I know who Mina is. Don't you dare try and lecture me."

Alexander stared at him for a moment. "Fine. Then pull it together."

A familiar shout caught his attention. Alexander turned, but he couldn't see from where it had come. He scanned the battlefield, and... There! He spied a crimson head in the distance and began sprinting toward it.

Anton, I'm coming.

❦ 28 ❦

CHAPTER TWENTY-EIGHT
ANTON

ANTON SUCKED in a breath as Sara tightened her arm around his stomach in a death grip. He almost wanted to throw her off the horse altogether, but they had the Calverans on their tail, and they were advancing fast.

"Put your sword away and get us out of here," hissed Sara. "I'll take them down."

He slid his sword back in its sheath with emphasis, spurring their horse into action. She was right, though. Swords were shattering left and right against the Calveran's stonewood, and their men were falling in waves. A man sailed through the air in front of them, narrowly missing their horse.

Anton leaned forward, concentrating on keeping them out of harm's way. They weren't wearing much armor; even if they could get past the stonewood, they were still flesh and blood. Four Calverans fell to the ground, then another, and another, a deep slit carved into their throats. Sara's silverlight chakram whizzed past his ear and returned to her hand, soaked in blood.

Anton gulped. "I thought you weren't meant to use your spirit arts!"

Another Calveran swung his spear at them. They ducked, and Sara threw her chakram again, bypassing the man's shield at an unnatural angle and going straight for his throat.

"Desperate times," she said. "Look out—!"

A spear grazed Anton's leg, piercing their horse's flank. Its legs gave out, and they hit the ground hard, tumbling for several feet. He coughed violently, spitting out dirt. His arm stung, and his leg was bleeding, but a quick once-over told him that it wasn't too bad. Still, the world was throbbing in and out, and he struggled to roll to his hands and knees. The massive spear had completely impaled their horse, the stonewood tip piercing its shoulder and coming out the other side. Sara kicked and pushed at the horse, one leg partially trapped underneath it.

"Happy now?" she shouted as Anton staggered over.

"That wasn't my fault," he shouted back. They *were* off the horse, just like he wanted, but this was much worse, he realized. The Calveran soldier was gaining on them now. Anton wiped his mouth. "Weren't you meant to stop his spear with your air nonsense?"

"It was aimed at you!" Sara pushed at the ground. "I barely had time to change its trajectory as it was."

Anton put his hands on the horse's rump and pushed with all his might, but Sara was still stuck. The Calveran caught up to them and swung the sharp edge of his shield at Anton's neck. The boy ducked and rolled over Sara, accidentally kicking her in the face but still managing to draw his sword. He stayed low, launching off the balls of his feet to slice at the Calveran's leg.

The Calveran leaped out of the way, grabbing his spear and yanking it out of the horse, pulling the beast with it. Sara dragged her leg out as the horse's body was momentarily lifted, and she immediately threw her chakram at the half-giant, her blade quickly ending his life. She leaned over her knees, panting heavily.

Anton glanced away as she shook her head, brushing the dirt off her legs.

"Thanks," he muttered.

"What was that?"

"Nothing."

As he paused to catch his breath, he scanned their surroundings. The steam was getting thicker, making it difficult to see, but the noise had quietened. The battlefield had thinned out now, and there were more dead than alive. Their enemies were holding back, and they still had the upper hand. Was it time to retreat? Or were they doomed to die? Anton clutched his sword. He had told Adelia that it was going to be all right. It *had* to be all right.

Sara spat on her glasses, rubbing them on her sleeve before pushing them back onto her nose.

"We have to keep moving."

Anton took a few steps back as more figures began to materialize from the steam. He and Sara ran, but they weren't fast enough. Another Calveran emerged, his long legs gaining ground. He swung his spear at Anton as though it were a staff, and the young lord dived out of the way, landing in a crouch. They'd have to face them.

Sara turned and grabbed the spear, using the momentum of their foe's swing to propel herself upward and deliver a powerful kick to the Calveran's temple. Anton lunged forward, seizing the opportunity to drive his sword into the soldier's meaty thigh. The half-giant cried out, toppling backward, and as he fell, Anton went for the killing blow. Blood spattered on his hands, and he quickly looked away from his enemy's agonized face.

Sara ducked behind a rocky pillar, and Anton followed her. As his hand touched the rock, he jerked it back, feeling an enormous heat radiating from it—a geyser.

Sara poked her head around the side. "There are at least a dozen of them coming."

Anton glanced around the other side. "We're about to be surrounded. They're too close to outrun."

Sara put her hands on the rock, squinting at it. "I have an idea. But you're going to have to get their attention away from me for a few moments and make sure they're all headed straight for you."

"Are you insane?"

"Father says brilliance is often mistaken for insanity."

Anton stared at her, hoping she was joking. She wasn't. He sighed. "Fine. But don't say I've never done anything for you."

Sara grinned. "Great. Over by that tar pit should be fine. When I yell, drop to the ground."

Anton waved a hand. "I got it, I got it." He hoped she wasn't using him to make a run for it.

He sprinted for the nearby tar pit. It wasn't one that had been on fire, and it was only covered in dry leaves and ash, but the soldiers were being more careful of where they ran— probably because the majority of the pits had at least one poor soul trapped in it. Their screams were hard not to notice.

Anton readied his sword, thrusting it in the air. "Hey! Come and get me, you fools!" he yelled lamely. He couldn't think of anything more intimidating to say, but it seemed to have done the trick. There were at least seven Lanadese and four Calverans who now turned their attention toward him. They glanced at each other, chuckling, and one of them began to walk around the pit in exaggerated steps.

"I know you're desperate, but this is just sad," said the barbarian. The small group didn't bother to charge at him.

Anton fought the urge to look at Sara. He could feel his cheeks turning bright red. These may very well have been his last moments, and he didn't want to spend them acting like a fool. She'd better have a plan.

"Hey," said one barbarian. "He's got red hair. You think he's Lord Alexander?"

"Could be," replied another. The two of them shot him a grin, and all of them advanced closer.

Anton shifted back and forth, his impulse to bolt excruciatingly powerful. Now, they were all bunched together.

"Anton!" Sara yelled.

He dropped to the floor. A massive jet of steam exploded from the geyser, but not upward. It shot over Anton's head in a split second. He yelped, rolling out of the way as he brushed off a few droplets that fell onto his arm. It was scorching hot. Screams echoed around him as their enemies clutched at their faces. Their skin was bubbling, raw and exposed, and they blindly staggered into each other, with two of them tripping into the pit.

Anton tore his eyes away from the scene and ran back to Sara, who was lying on the ground, her legs crumpled underneath her. He sucked in a breath, and his heart stopped. He rushed to her side, checking her over. Was he too late again? Adelia flashed into his mind, her tiny body lying at an awkward angle in the ravine.

"Did we... get them?" Sara asked, blinking slowly. She looked like she was about to pass out again.

Anton looped his arm around her, supporting her weight on his shoulder. Thank dragons, she was alive.

"You did good, Sis," he murmured. He half-dragged her across the battlefield, but he could only see the forest, and the ravine. Her legs were struggling to support her. She was practically dead weight in his arms, and it took all of his strength to keep moving.

Sara tugged his collar. "I need to... I can't..."

Anton stopped, bending his knees and readjusting his hands. "Get on. We don't have time."

She hooked her arms around his neck, and he hoisted her onto his back. He ran. They had to get out of there. It didn't matter where they went; anywhere was better than there. His heart pounded in his ears. If they stopped running now, they were going to die.

Just keep moving.

A cloaked figure stood in his path. It was obscured by the steam, but something silvery glittered in its hand. Anton stopped dead in his tracks.

"What are you doing?" cried Sara.

"That... woman." His head was throbbing, and he could barely hear the noises around them.

"What woman?"

"There!" He almost let go of her to point straight ahead.

Sara craned her head over his shoulder. "The only woman here is me."

He shook his head violently. "I saw her, Adelia!"

There was a moment of silence. Anton grimaced, sucking in his lip. The woman was gone, like she had never been there in the first place. It had been so real. The way Sara was lying had been exactly how he'd found his sister in the ravine all those years ago. The heat must have been making him see things, and it couldn't have been a worse time to have another episode.

He jogged at a steady pace, refusing to comment on his visions. Sara seemed a lot heavier now, but he was grateful that she didn't comment on his outburst. He ran past a few of their soldiers locked in combat. They were forced to work in pairs to counter even one Calveran, which made their numbers even smaller, but he couldn't stop to help them. Another explosion shook the ground in the distance, and a small, fiery plume erupted to his right.

Anton stepped around the dead, their bodies almost forming a maze of their own. Broken swords littered the ground, their steel useless against stonewood. Their enemies had clearly taken significant casualties, but their own army was scattered and broken. It was simply a matter of picking off the survivors.

Out of the corner of his eye, a couple of Calverans were advancing on two more of their men. They stood back to back, swords drawn. Anton almost kept running, until he caught sight of their faces.

"Ban!"

General Ban and former general Barrett turned at his cry. One of the Calverans rushed forward, thrusting his spear at them. They dodged just in time. Another Calveran swung his shield at them. They were forced on the defensive, unable to do anything else.

Anton let Sara slide off his back. "Keep going! I have to help them," he said.

"Wait—"

Drawing his sword, he took off, sprinting across the battlefield.

Ban sidestepped a spear, slamming his foot down on the tip to drive it into the ground. His father closed the distance from behind, leaping up to throw his cloak around the Calveran's head. Barrett pulled his cloak tight, locking his arms and legs around the Calveran and bringing them both to the ground. Ban lunged at them, but another Calveran intercepted, thrusting his spear toward the young general.

Anton swung at the second Calveran with a cry, but his opponent turned, landing a solid kick to his abdomen. Anton was knocked to the ground, gasping for air that wouldn't come. The Calveran readjusted his grip on his spear, aiming for him.

Ban sped forward, using both hands to bring down the Lanadese axe he wielded. The stonewood spear cracked under the blackscale, and one half of the spear flew in one direction while the other half was still clutched in the Calveran's hand. The half-giant glared at Ban, and with lightning speed, he sliced at him with the shield on his arm.

Ban fell backward.

Anton's eyes widened. His body moved on its own, closing the distance. He feinted, creating an opening, and moving low, he slid beneath the half-giant's legs, dragging his sword upward as he went. The Calveran shrieked and stumbled, and Anton whirled around, thrusting his sword through his opponent's back. The man went limp, falling to the ground.

There was another gurgling cry as Barrett managed to slash at the second Calveran's throat. He unlocked his legs from around his chest, shuffling back to untangle himself from the body.

Anton ran over to Ban. He lay on his back, a deep cut across his stomach and blood covering his face. Anton dropped to his knees, grabbing Ban's face.

You can't leave me, too!

"Just like old times, hey," said Ban, coughing. "Another... win for me."

Anton let go of him, scoffing at the grin on his friend's face. It seemed he would recover, after all. "Don't scare me like that."

Ban rested his head back on the ground. "Give me... a few minutes." He closed his eyes, his hands clutching at his stomach. Thank dragons, it wasn't a fatal wound, but he needed to get to the medical tent immediately before he died from blood loss.

Anton suddenly tasted dirt as he was flung to the ground. A fist hit his face—once, twice, three times.

"Father, stop!" Ban cried.

Anton could barely bring his arms up to protect his face. Barrett was on top of him, pinning him to the ground.

"You almost got my boy killed with your incompetence," Barrett growled. His eyes were hollow and bloodshot, his face twisted in rage. He grabbed Anton by the tunic, landing another blow to his jaw. Anton's ears were ringing, and black spots began to form in his vision.

"I won't lose my only son because of the *spare*," Barrett hissed in his ear. He let go of him and stood up. His hair was a ragged mess, with bits and pieces escaping the once neat ponytail. His uniform was disheveled and caked in dried blood.

Anton gritted his teeth and dug his nails into his palm to ground himself. They were being slaughtered by their enemies, and *he* was the one on which Barrett was taking out his anger? His fists trembled. It wasn't his fault that he was born after his brother, and it wasn't his fault that Ban got hurt. He dug his knuckles into the rocky earth, heaving himself to his knees, then his feet. He grabbed his sword, wiping blood from his mouth.

"I've had enough." He trudged forward, slowly pointing his sword at Barrett. "I am *Lord* Anton, and by dragons, if you're going to turn on your fellow soldier in battle, then I have no choice but to label you as a traitor to Anadrieth."

Barrett turned his head, a dark smirk on his face. "You don't know who you're dealing with, boy..."

Anton narrowed his eyes, trying not to let his momentary courage dissipate. "Even if you survive this day, you'll be tried for treason, and I'll duel you after this is all over."

Barrett shook his head. "Pity. I'm ready now."

Barrett lunged toward him, and Anton blocked, pushing his back leg into the ground. He countered with a strike of his own, aiming for Barrett's leg. He shouldn't have lost his temper. What had he gotten himself into? Barrett was better than him. He always had been, and they both knew it. They exchanged several strikes, but Anton was quickly pushed onto the defensive.

"You should have stayed quiet," Barrett growled, knocking Anton to the ground. He raised his blade over his head.

Anton stared at it. His brother would have beaten the former general with ease. No, Alexander wouldn't have gotten himself into this situation in the first place. He would have talked him down. The princess would have let her swords do the talking. Even his sister would have studied her opponent's movements and come out the victor. But he couldn't do any of that.

Stop trying to be me.

Anton rolled out of the way just as Barrett's sword hit the ground where he'd been.

The only one forcing you to stay in my shadow is yourself.

He swept his leg around, connecting with Barrett's leg, bringing the man down on the ground beside him.

You've convinced yourself you can't do better than everyone's expectations, so you never will.

His brother was wrong. Their expectations were simply the truth. He was utterly incapable, and perhaps it was a mistake for him to have been born.

Anton leaped on top of Barrett, landing an uppercut to the jaw. Barrett grinned, spitting blood on the ground. He grabbed Anton's shoulders, flipping them over and wrapping his hands around his throat.

"You've got some guts, boy, I'll give you that," Barrett said, pressing his thumbs into his windpipe. "But you'll never be like your brother."

Black spots dotted Anton's vision once more, and he clawed at Barrett's hands. They wouldn't budge. He could vaguely hear Ban shouting at them. Maybe he really couldn't do any better, even if others thought he could. Anton struggled to push him off, but he was too heavy. Maybe he should just accept his death. He was a nobody, after all—just the spare.

Anton the Brave.

The woman whispered in his ear, coaxing him back into the darkness. It wouldn't be so bad. They could be together again. She was the only one who ever believed in him, anyway. Her lips touched his forehead, and he closed his eyes.

Do I have to follow what everyone else does?

Cynric's turquoise eyes gazed at him in his mind's eye, his calm voice enveloping his senses and cutting through the darkness. Anton blinked. Cynric had forged a life of his own, away from his homeland, his family and whatever his duties once might have been. He followed his own path and never looked back. That was true bravery. Anton let his words fill him, warm him to the very core. The woman faded away with the darkness.

But even if he could follow his own path, what more could he do?

His eyes snapped open. The spirits were in full color, dancing around him and illuminating his vision. In a single instant, he felt calm and more in tune with the world than he ever had before. Everything was vibrant and teeming with life. This was something he had that his brother didn't. He could *see.*

Barrett's spirit was a storm of violet, emitting the energy of a savage beast. The glow was fainter on his left side, and he had an idea. Anton slammed his knee upward, and he heard a rib crack. Barrett's hands released his neck, and Anton coughed violently, gulping in as much air as he could. Barrett howled in pain, clutching his side, and Anton staggered to his feet. He pressed his sword against Barrett's throat, looking down upon him.

"Anton, don't!" cried Ban. He clawed at the ground, trying to get up.

But Anton wasn't listening. He was observing. Barrett's spirit was full of rage, but there was a softness there, hidden deep inside. For a moment, Anton saw an innocent child, blindly following the rules he'd been taught, only to grow into a man so ingrained in his ways that it would take death itself to undo.

"I pity you," said Anton, his voice barely escaping him. Someone like this would never let go of a grudge.

"Kill me if you want," said Barrett through clenched teeth. "But I refuse to ever acknowledge you."

Anton lowered his sword, offering him his hand. "It doesn't matter. My brother and all of Anadrieth need you right now."

Barrett ignored his hand as he stood, letting out a hiss of pain.

Ban smiled. "There's the Anton I remember."

Anton rolled his eyes, helping Ban stand.

"What the dragons was all that about?" cried Sara, stumbling as she made her way over. She still looked like she wasn't holding up too well, but at least she could stand. "We don't have time to be fighting amongst ourselves." She pointed in the distance. "Look!"

Atop the cliffs that separated the capital from Anadrieth marched a tiny row of figures. They were dressed in a stark white and gold, bearing flags with the golden symbol. It was the imperial army in all their glory. A massive cheer went up as their enemies regrouped behind them.

Anton paled. There was no one in sight from their side—at least, no one alive. If they weren't in trouble before, they were in big trouble now. "We have to go—"

A spear flew out of nowhere, and Ban was shoved aside, falling to the ground. The weapon cracked the ground beside them; it was a direct hit.

"Father!"

Blood burbled from Barrett's lips, the spear impaling his back. Ban scrambled to his feet, yanking at the spear, but it wasn't going to budge. Anton grabbed his arm, pulling him away. Barrett was already dead—as they were about to be if they didn't move. Their enemies' cries grew louder as they renewed their advance. But Ban refused to let go of the spear.

"It was aimed at me... it should have been..."

Anton slapped him across the face. "He wouldn't want you to throw your life away so soon after he just saved it!"

He dragged his grieving friend from the body, and the three of them ran. More spears came flying, the stonewood puncturing the earth with ease. Anton's heart was in his throat, his legs were burning and his breathing was shallow, his lungs working overtime. They were all injured, and it was unlikely they were going to make it.

He whipped his head around. The army was gaining on them. Dots began to cloud his vision. His foot caught, and gravel scraped his face while dust filled his mouth.

"Anton!" cried Ban. He and Sara turned back, pulling him to his feet. A barbarian leaped at them, swinging his axe. Ban parried, and Sara struck him with her chakram. They had no choice but to fight.

Anton drew his sword, dodging a spear and nicking a Calveran's arm with the edge of his blade. He whirled around to face his opponent, but the Calveran's shield was quicker.

It smashed into the side of his head, and the world went black.

CHAPTER TWENTY-NINE
ALEXANDER

ALEXANDER SPRINTED, his legs flying across the ground. He hardly noticed his lungs screaming for air. It didn't matter that the imperial army was on his doorstep, and it didn't matter that his army was scattered and useless. The steam had cleared enough for him to see a direct path. His little brother lay on the ground, a Calveran poised to strike above him, while Ban and Sara were struggling to fend off the incoming wave. Adelia's scream resonated in his mind. He wasn't going to make it. And this time, Mina wasn't there to help them.

A boulder sped past him, crashing into the Calveran's skull and knocking him back. Kakeru kept pace beside Alexander, ripping up pieces of the earth, some of it still on fire, and hurling it toward their enemies as they ran. Alexander managed a quick nod at him but felt the resentment bubbling up. Once again, he couldn't save his own family.

He drew his Golden Dawn, leaping over his brother and bringing his blade down upon a barbarian, forcing the man to the ground. His blood was boiling, the adrenaline surging through his veins. He drove his sword in again, just to make sure his foe was down.

A Calveran thrust his spear toward them, but Alexander dodged, ducking low to strike his legs. He spun around for a second strike, and as he dragged his blade across his opponent's chest, the half-giant stumbled, doubling over.

Alexander positioned himself in front of his brother, willing him to get up. He didn't. Blood trickled across the young lord's face, and it was all he could do not to think the worst.

More boulders flew past them, but this time, the Calverans were prepared. As soon as the rock hit stonewood, it broke into harmless pieces of gravel and dust.

The wounded Calveran eyed Anton before running straight at them, shield-first, swinging his stonewood downward. Alexander blanched. If he dodged, his brother would die. But he didn't have time to push Anton out of the way. There was only one choice. He raised his sword to block. The metal shattered—bone snapped. A stabbing pain shot through his arm, and he fell to his back.

Kakeru barreled into the Calveran, knocking him to the ground.

Alexander clutched his arm, biting down on the inside of his lip and tasting blood. The jagged shard of bone split his skin, and his arm bent at a stomach-churning angle. He turned his gaze away, breathing hard through his teeth. His brother's chest moved minutely. Thank dragons, he was still alive.

Kakeru rushed over, pulling him to his feet. He grabbed

the ends of Alexander's cloak and quickly wrapped it into a makeshift sling.

"Can you walk?" he shouted.

Alexander nodded, unable to manage the words.

Don't think. Don't think.

If he didn't look, he couldn't feel it. His other hand picked up his sword hilt, its broken edge glaring back at him. It had truly served him well all these years. He slipped it back into his belt. There wasn't time to reminiscence; more enemies were approaching.

His remaining soldiers began to gather around them, working together to hold their enemies off. They used everything they had left, throwing silverlight knives and lighting the magnalite in their slings. Blinding flashes began going off in front of them, and cries echoed across the battlefield, with some of the magnalite hitting their enemies and others exploding in their own soldier's hands.

Alexander could barely think straight, and he'd only be able to push through the pain for so long. General Ban was clutching his stomach, Sara was barely standing, Kakeru looked exhausted and his brother was passed out behind him. He couldn't carry him with one arm and protect them all at once. His soldiers were buying them time, but to what end?

They weren't going to escape. Even if they could survive this wave, there were more enemies coming, and there were no more reinforcements. The people they left at home depended on them. He couldn't run, couldn't fight. He clenched a fist. It couldn't end like this.

The steam pricked at his skin, and for a moment, he saw a tiny droplet sticking to the hair on his arm. He closed his eyes.

He could feel it—the roar of the Moonstone River in the distance, the steam that swirled across the battlefield, the air that beckoned him. The spirits were there, by his side, like old friends who had never left. Every inch of his body was alive and tingling. He was born to do this. This was his birthright, his bloodline.

Please. Help us.

Alexander drew the spirits toward him, condensing them, molding them to his will, and they complied with childlike eagerness. He could sense the sheer amount of energy they claimed from him in return. He opened his eyes. The battle in front of them almost hung in stasis, and everyone glanced at what was going on around them. The temperature dropped as the wind picked up. The moisture in the air was crystalizing, and the steam began to dissipate, forming thousands upon thousands of razor-like shards hanging mid-air.

Ice.

They waited for his command. Alexander thrust his arm out with a cry, and the shards whizzed through the air, impaling each and every one of the barbarians and half-giants before them. They snaked around the stonewood, flying in every direction, searching for their targets. Alexander gritted his teeth. This was for taking away the lives of his men. This was for forcing his people to fight.

This was for Anadrieth.

Their enemies fell in waves, and for a moment, the battlefield was all but quiet. Alexander fell to his knees, clutching his chest. The energy had left his limbs, and he could suddenly feel every inch of the exposed bone and flesh of his arm. He bit down on his tongue hard, drawing blood.

He could vaguely hear his soldiers cheering around them. But he knew it wasn't enough. The Lanadese and Calverans still had their primary forces on standby, and all the while, the imperial army loomed over them. If anything, it was just a simple diversion—a moment to breathe. But it wasn't enough.

A powerful wave of energy suddenly passed through him, filling every part of his senses and suffocating him in terror. It was unnatural, immeasurable, yet there was a hint of familiarity. Every instinct told him to run and never look back. But his legs were rooted to the spot. He turned toward the source. The others could sense it, too.

All eyes on the battlefield looked to the east, where a lone horse and rider sat on the horizon.

"Mina," Alexander murmured. Relief flooded through him. They were saved. He searched the landscape behind her. She must have brought reinforcements. Did Eloria come? He kept his eyes trained on the horizon as Mina sped down into the plains. They would come over the hill. Any second now. She galloped toward them, her command ringing out across the battlefield.

"Fall back!"

Kakeru and Sara moved immediately, grabbing Anton between them. They didn't hesitate in the slightest. His men glanced at each other, then at him.

Alexander's mouth parted. No one else was coming. Not a single person. Was she asking them to surrender? He didn't understand.

General Ban grabbed him by the arm. "My lord?" His eyes searched him, pleaded with him.

His men looked desperate, clinging to any hope they might have left. They wanted a reason to escape the battlefield, to flee on her command. But they all looked to him. He could see it in their faces. In the end, they would follow him to their deaths if he asked.

Fight and die an honorable death, or flee and trust that Mina had a plan, though she brought no one but herself.

Remember, I'm your friend.

Alexander punched the ground, then leaned on Ban to stand. He had to make a choice.

"Fall back!" he yelled, waving his arm in the air. "Fall back!"

His men didn't need any more encouragement. They retreated in droves. His feet moved of their own accord, passing over his fallen men, their bodies blanketing the battlefield. His muscles quivered as heat flushed through him. His face was red, and frustration pricked at his heart. Alexander pushed himself harder, his footsteps falling heavier. His ears pounded, and mercifully, the sensation in his arm was muted.

They were running with their tail between their legs, and Lord Tamar was probably laughing at their backs. They had all been right; if he couldn't protect his region, he didn't deserve to rule. He was a failure as a lord.

His men flooded into their camp, collapsing on every available surface. The medical tent was suddenly swarmed with people, and the nurses were overwhelmed in an instant. Alexander spied Anton through the crowd and gritted his teeth, shoving people out of his way.

"Move!"

Soldiers dodged left and right as he followed his brother, his crimson hair a beacon to his gaze. This was the least he could do. He rushed into the tent. Kakeru and Sara were panting at the entrance, his brother slung over their shoulders.

Alexander went straight for Cynric, grabbing his arm and dragging him over. Cynric pried his hand off with surprising strength and bent down to examine Anton. He checked his pulse, searching for any other wounds.

"Put him there." He pointed to a spot in the corner.

Alexander blinked as Cynric moved onto the next patient without a second glance. He couldn't just abandon his little brother. He jumped in front of Cynric's path, glaring up at him.

"What are you doing? Help him!"

Cynric opened Alexander's makeshift sling. After a moment, he grabbed him by the collar and dragged him out of the tent. His eyes were furious, but his voice remained level.

"I don't care who you are. This is my domain. He will wake up on his own." He let go of him. "There are far more pressing injuries to deal with, not including yours. If you're going to act like a hysteric, you're banned from this tent." Cynric turned abruptly, ducking back into the tent.

Alexander stumbled back, stunned. Cynric was scarier than Elaine, though it looked like he was barely holding things together. His next patient howled when he approached, and the nurses had to hold the screaming man down.

"Murderer!" the man cried, spitting at Cynric's direction. "Bastard!" He screamed obscenities and hurled insults, but Cynric didn't bat an eye. Alexander was struck with pity. Cynric was doing more than enough for them, but his men seemed to be traumatized by the sight of another half-giant in their midst.

Alexander shook his head, trying to let his muscles relax.

Elaine was going to have her hands full when they got back. *If* they got back. At least his brother would be okay.

Alexander looked out over the battlefield as the last of his men returned. It was odd; their enemies hadn't pursued them. He hissed out a breath, cradling his arm as the pain began to set in once more. A bead of sweat rolled over his lip, and his cloak was soaked in blood. He had to focus on something else. Anything else.

Mina appeared at the entrance to the camp. As she leaped from her horse, it immediately laid down, as though it had only now realized just how exhausted it was. Her body was shimmering, as if the outline of her form couldn't quite decide what it wanted to be. Her gaze met his, and her eyes were a deep violet, the pupils no longer human. His men gave her a wide berth. Then, she looked past him.

"Remember your duty," she said. It was her voice, but it wasn't. Her words rippled over his skin, the tone slightly richer than he remembered. He turned to see Hanabi and the others, standing beside him. The priestess was visibly trembling, her fear almost tangible.

Mina pivoted her stance. The earth crumbled under the pressure, as though a great force pushed down upon it. Her presence settled over him again, only far stronger.

Everyone fell to their knees.

Alexander was frozen on the ground. Her presence suffocated him with a terrifying but enchanting aura that spanned out, blanketing everyone in sight. The entire battlefield had gone deathly silent, as though every being in the empire had been forced to acknowledge her powerful presence—captives under her spell.

With almost imperceptible movement, she pushed off the

ground, launching forward. Within seconds, she appeared again in the center of the plains.

Alexander swallowed. He couldn't pretend any longer that she was simply an extraordinary human. He had to acknowledge her for what she was.

Mina stood alone in the face of three armies, but none moved. She drew her swords, the dragon script glowing intensely at her touch. They floated for a moment before spinning to slice her palms. She grasped the hilts, the blood flowing freely down the blades.

Her swords suddenly changed form, and her arms became encased with an ethereal substance—in the shape of dragon's forelimbs, growing larger by the second. The men didn't have a moment to blink as they were swept away by one of her massive claws. Her other arm followed suit, striking their enemies without mercy.

Panic ensued. The Lanadese and Calverans scrambled in different directions, some fleeing the scene, while others foolishly attempted to attack her. But their weapons had no effect. They passed through her as if she weren't there.

Mina threw her head back, letting out a deafening roar that shook the battlefield as though the very ground beneath them was alive. Alexander clutched his ears, the shockwave hitting him like a ton of stones. Screams filled the air.

Her ethereal shape expanded, completely encompassing her. It grew and grew until the shape of a dragon began to take form around her—an enormous head with two curved horns, murderous jaws that housed teeth as large as men, wings that stretched across the entire plains, a tail as long as the river. Drifting in the middle of its chest was Mina, her tiny body covered in blood. All the tapestries in the empire couldn't have done her justice, the artists unable to envision such a creature.

She was frighteningly magnificent.

She raised her arms, the dragon spirit mimicking her movement. With a single flap of her wings, the steam was blown from the battlefield entirely, and the fires were extinguished. Then, she brought her claw down into the earth, sending debris flying as the earth split and groaned.

Their enemies tried to flee, but there was nowhere to run. The cliffs were at their backs, the pass too narrow for all of them at once. The imperial army remained stationed along the cliffs, not one of them retreating.

The dragon lowered its head. The Calverans raised their shields, while the Lanadese dropped to the floor. She inhaled. More screams rang out as tiny, ethereal forms of violet were ripped from the soldiers' flesh, becoming absorbed into her dragon's form. There was no escape from such an attack.

"*Syravia,*" Hanabi whispered beside him.

Alexander grabbed her shoulder. "What's going on?"

"It means spirit reaper..." She seemed to be in a horrified trance. The men fell in waves, their bodies like empty husks. None of them tried to attack the dragon now.

Hanabi suddenly snapped into action, flipping open her tome to a page with one line written on it. She let go of the tome as it glowed, floating in mid-air. Cupping her hands, a tiny sphere of ethereal light appeared. Her entire body was shaking. She took one glance at Mina, and the light disappeared. Hanabi cursed, trying again, but to no avail. With every attempt, the light flickered out.

Alexander put his hand on hers. "Stop. Whatever you're doing, you have to calm down."

She jerked her hands away, her breathing rapid and shallow.

"I don't have time! Can't you see?" Hanabi nodded at their fleeing enemies. "She's done what she needed to do to save you all, but I'm the only one that can stop her before she goes too far. Only a spirit can harm another spirit." The light flickered again, then disappeared entirely. Hanabi stamped her foot. "She's pulling the dragon into the human realm, and if that happens, it's over—for everyone. She has to be stopped."

Alexander stiffened. "You're going to kill her?"

"If that's what it takes." Hanabi's face was two shades whiter than usual, her skin clammy. "It's my duty."

A massive crack caught their attention, and the dragon roared again, Mina's agonizing scream echoing with it. She slumped over, her body seeming a little less tangible, and her blood flowed through the dragon's veins in crimson rivers, circulating throughout the spirit. White bone materialized, cracking as the pieces snapped into place, forming the beginnings of the spinal cord.

Hanabi's hands fell to her sides. "It's too late, it's too late..." she whispered.

"What can I do?" cried Alexander.

"I'm here," said Kakeru.

"You don't have to do this alone," said Sara. They gathered around her, waiting for her instruction.

Hanabi shook her head violently. "There's nothing you can do!" She clutched her head in her hands. "I'm not strong enough."

The dragon's spine stretched down to its tail, the ribcage beginning to emerge.

Sara grasped Hanabi's other arm, looking directly at her. "What do you need?"

Hanabi's eyes were wet. "Spirit energy."

Sara placed her hands on the priestess, and Kakeru followed. "Take it."

Alexander did the same. The next moment, his knees collapsed to the ground. Darkness throbbed in his vision, and he cried out, catching his fall and cradling his arm in agony. He tried to stand, but he couldn't. The pain gave him a lifeline to barely stay conscious. The others were all but passed out on the ground beside him.

The sphere of spirit light in Hanabi's hands was blinding now; she was practically glowing herself. She moved her hands, crafting the ethereal light and stretching it into the shape of a bow as tall as herself, notched with a single arrow.

Bones grew along the dragon's wings, and she gave them an experimental beat, the motion ripping distant trees from their roots and blowing their enemies away. It flattened a whole section of the Celestine Forest. Then, the dragon froze, her wings perfectly still.

Another spirit light echoed Hanabi's, piercing the horizon along the cliffs.

Alexander shuddered as the light's sheer power surged through his body, the its quiet presence mirroring Mina's and spilling over the battlefield. It engulfed his spirit and filled him with a different kind of energy, though one that was equally as terrifying. That kind of power could only be another dragon god.

Alexander squinted, shielding his eyes. He could no longer see the cliffs. The blinding light was incredibly powerful, far more so than Hanabi's meagre attempts.

The dragon's lips curled into a snarl, malice dripping from her sharp teeth. She beat her wings once more, launching herself into the sky, disappearing into the clouds as she gained height.

Hanabi drew her spirit bow. Its form wavered in her unsteady hands, bending out of shape.

"Come on," she muttered. The bow glowed brightly for a moment, then sputtered, dropping on either end, the arrow fading into nothingness and the spirit energy lost. She opened her mouth as the weapon slipped through her fingers.

"No..." She collapsed to her knees, the spirit light completely gone. "This was her plan all along, wasn't it?" she murmured to herself. "The Mistress has bested us again."

Alexander narrowed his eyes, but his attention was drawn back to the sky as the dragon dived toward the cliffs. The light in the distance suddenly changed, concentrating into a shape—a glowing figure, holding a massive bow. The arrow arced across the battlefield, the brilliant light cutting through the sky. Alexander held his breath.

The bolt impaled the dragon, piercing straight through the spirit and Mina's tiny form with one blow. The dragon howled, but it was much weaker than before. Its body immediately began to fade, and its blood and bones blackened, disintegrating to ashes that scattered into the wind.

Then, Mina fell.

Alexander clutched his chest, his heart pounding. He could do nothing as he stood there, helplessly watching her fall through the sky. Then, a figure leaped from the cliffs, and ethereal, feathery wings carried him across the battlefield. It had to be Prince Yukiya. He caught her mid-air, circling toward the north, back toward the capital.

As soon as they were out of sight, the white cloaks along the cliffs began to retreat, and the imperial army left the battlefield.

Alexander's mouth twisted into a scowl. Evidently, they never intended to get their hands dirty in the first place, not when they had others to do it for them. The rest of their enemies had all but fled, and the remainder were in no state to pursue another battle. He let out a shuddering breath. The tension left his body, and the dragon's presence was gone. She *had* come back for them, but now... He had no idea what would happen to her now.

"At least we're safe," murmured Hanabi.

Alexander couldn't believe his ears. "Excuse me?"

She turned to look back at him. "It's the truth, even though it's not the best outcome."

Alexander blinked. "You are the last person who should be saying that..." She couldn't be this dense. He clenched his fist, grinding it into the dirt. "First, my sister, and now, this? Is Mina even alive?" She didn't stop Mina; the prince did. She hadn't done a single useful thing during the battle that claimed thousands of lives. And now, she had the gall to claim that they were safe.

Hanabi tucked her book to her chest. "I..." Her voice was barely audible.

Alexander shook his head. "This is your fault. She trusted you, the only one who could do this, and you failed. Just like my sister trusted you with her life, and now, she'll never walk again." His voice trembled. "You have information about the Mistress that could have stopped all of this. I know you do. So, don't you dare say we're safe, as if you had *any* part in keeping us so."

Kakeru shuffled between them with a grunt. "Stop fighting. This isn't the time."

Alexander spluttered. "Are you serious?" This man caused nothing but fights. He wasn't in any state to try to reign in Alexander's anger. "Every time you open your mouth, you rub someone the wrong way. I can't believe Mina had someone like you by her side."

Kakeru lunged over Hanabi to tackle him, his fist landing on Alexander's face. "How dare you..."

Alexander tasted blood. He yanked on Kakeru's shirt, ramming his head into the bridge of his nose. His own vision blurred, and his ears rang, but it was worth it. Kakeru fell back, clutching his head for a moment. They were both exhausted, their movements haphazard and slow.

As they moved for each other again, Sara held her chakram between them, the blade facing both of their throats.

"Boys!" Her eyes signaled behind them. A crowd of onlookers surrounded them, his men watching silently. She withdrew her blade, then pointed at the battlefield. "We have a visitor."

Alexander gave Kakeru a hard look, then pushed himself to his knees. She was right. They couldn't do this here, couldn't fall apart in front of his already broken men. But the damage had already been done. He cursed under his breath, then inhaled deeply, turning toward Sara's outstretched arm.

A single rider made their way across the plains through the corpses, a white cloak trailing behind them. Alexander steeled himself. This couldn't be good. He struggled to get to his feet. As much as he wanted to just lie down, he couldn't appear weak in front of an imperial messenger. Did they just want to taunt him? He didn't know anymore. As the rider moved closer, he realized that it was a woman.

The messenger dismounted her horse, making her way straight for him. She was pretty, with chestnut brown hair neatly tied back and a soft gaze, like a foxen's. Her clothes were plain, but she was clearly from the imperial palace—not the kind of girl you'd normally send into enemy territory.

Alexander hailed her cautiously with his free arm. "Greetings."

She bowed, bringing her hand across her chest. It was a well-practiced movement.

"Be at ease. This battle is over, and I congratulate those of you who've kept your lives." Her voice was silky, warm and inviting, but it carried a threatening undertone.

Alexander gritted his teeth. The empire had this whole thing planned from the beginning. Her tone left no room for error.

"I am Supreme Commander Yuno's personal servant, Lyra." She held out a letter. "I come bearing an invitation."

When she failed to move forward to hand him the letter, Alexander was forced to close the distance. He didn't miss this subtle show of power. He broke the imperial seal, holding his breath. It was handwritten in beautiful cursive.

To Lord Alexander and all associated parties,
You are hereby invited to celebrate the imperial wedding of Prince
Yukiya and Princess Mina.
We look forward to seeing you participate in the traditional imperial
tournament.

Lyra was no messenger; she was their escort. They already

knew they'd get Mina back by the end of this. Was the whole war simply a front? Or were there more players than he'd originally thought? Mina was right. This was far from over, and he needed to be more cunning if he planned to come out on the other side alive. Whoever held the most information held the most power in this dangerous dance.

Lyra tilted her head expectantly. Alexander steeled himself. *Invitation* was simply a polite word for summons, and he had no choice but to play the game in which he was likely a mere pawn.

He neatly folded up the letter with one hand, meeting Lyra's gaze with his own expression of confidence. If he had anything to do with it, he wasn't going to stay a pawn for long.

"I accept."

❦ 30 ❦

CHAPTER THIRTY

YUKIYA

FAR BEYOND THE BATTLEFIELD, Prince Yukiya's spirit wings carried them across the lands. He cradled his princess, nestling her close to his chest. Her blood attempted to seep into his clothes and skin, but it had no effect on him; the droplets simply turned into steam upon contact.

Yukiya smiled. It had been a good idea after all to use that petty war to get his princess back. She wouldn't have done that for people she didn't care about. He may even have that *Lord Alexander* to thank for that, though his brief respite would be followed by a painful death. But for now, none of it mattered. She was back in his arms.

He passed over his army, flying across the empire until he landed on their balcony. The imperial chambers would at long last be occupied once more. He touched down softly, careful not to make a sound. Holding her for what felt like an eternity, he gazed at her unconscious form. It was the closest he'd been to her without an attempt on his life since they were children. It seemed almost comical that his beloved had to be unconscious for the curse to be at ease.

Yukiya leaned his forehead against hers briefly, his heart fluttering like a child's, feeling almost giddy. Gently placing her on the bed, he encouraged her wounds to knit themselves together, and the blood on her skin absorbed back into her body. It would be painful, but it had to be done. A dragon's blood couldn't be wasted.

He didn't leave her side for even a moment, and he ordered the guards at the door not to let anyone disturb them. The wedding preparations would be well taken care of in his absence. For now, he would stay. Yukiya's fingers touched the golden bracelets in his robes, and he glanced back at his princess. His faithful patience had been rewarded with this fleeting moment of peace, but he would remain vigil until she awoke.

Welcome home, my beloved.

A LETTER FROM ALEXANDER

Winter, Year 2161 of the Fey Dynasty

Dear reader,

Words cannot express what I'm feeling...

We haven't yet tallied the dead and Lyra is already urging us to leave. We have three days until we must travel to the capital for the imperial wedding, and of course, the coronation. I don't understand why Mina did what she did, all I know is that I have a bad feeling about the coronation.

We're down many good men and those who are alive did not come out unscathed. I was told a few of us collapsed for a time, but the only person who hasn't woken up yet is my brother.

Tensions are high amongst us and I can only hope we can hold everything together long enough.

I need someone I can rely on wholeheartedly.

And that's why I must ask a favor of you, dear reader.

Please leave a review so that others may know of our story and are prepared for what is to come.

I will do my best to make sure everyone stays alive.

Lord Alexander Winter

ELEMENTAL SPIRITS

Dragon God of Destruction: Unknown
Dragon God of Rebirth: Unknown
Dragon God of Chaos: Unknown

Elemental Spirit Guardian of Earth (The Golem):
Unknown

Elemental Spirit Guardian of Air (The Pegasus):
Unknown

Elemental Spirit Guardian of Fire (The Phoenix):
Scarlet (Aged 11), raised in The Last Chance Orphanage —
'Her aura was like an inferno, simmering under the surface,'
according to Adelia

Elemental Spirit Guardian of Water (The Sea Serpent): Unknown

THE CAPITAL

Princess Mina Fey *[me-nah]:* (Aged 18), known to be one of the legendary dragon gods — *'The servant who had never stopped being a leader',* according to Alexander

Prince Yukiya Fey *[yu-kee-ah]:* (Aged 20), known to be one of the legendary dragon gods — *'He is the curse upon this world, one I will end',* according to Mina

Supreme Commander Lord Yuno Fey *[yu-no]:* (Aged 22), leader of the imperial army — *'He was always the confident one, sometimes overconfident',* according to Yukiya

Lyra: (Aged 22), personal servant to Lord Yuno — *'Lyra was no messenger, she was their escort',* according to Alexander

Lucan: (Aged 33), Prince Yukiya's servant — *'Lucan always seemed to know exactly where he was, then again, that was his job',* according to Yukiya

Ryuko *[ree-yu-koh]:* (Aged 32), Celestial Assassin, metal spirit arts user — *'This is the man you wanted, the traitor?',* according to Kakeru

Kakeru *[ka-care-roo]:* (Aged 37), Celestial Assassin, earth spirit arts user, the emperor's former servant — *'This man caused nothing but fights',* according to Alexander

Hanabi *[ha-nah-bee]:* (Aged 24), Celestial Assassin, Head Priestess of the Imperial Dragon Temple — *'A spoilt brat who got everything she ever wanted'*, according to Anton

Demetri: (Aged 9), lives beneath the imperial palace — *'It wouldn't be fair to give him a glimpse of the outside world, only to confine him once more'*, according to Yukiya

Late Empress Minako Fey *[me-nah-ko]:* (Deceased, aged 18) — *'My Minako wasn't strong enough'*, according to the former emperor

Late Emperor Masaru Fey *[ma-sah-rue]:* (Deceased, aged 25) — *'How could I possibly forget someone as stubborn and ridiculous as you?'*, according to Kakeru

Commander Ido *[eye-doe]:* (Deceased, aged 54), commander of the imperial army — *'He wasn't foolish enough to offend a powerful man'*, according to Alexander

Mistress Marionette: *'Mistress Marionette the called her, the one who pulled the strings'*, according to Mina

Lucille: *'Lucille would have wanted you to finish this'*, Mina to Ryuko

ANADRIETH
[ah-nah-drey-ith]

Lord Alexander Winter: (Aged 27), ice spirit arts user —

'Confident, overprotective and dismissive of others, but he means well', according to Kakeru

Lord Anton Winter: (Aged 21), unknown type of spirit arts user — *'You're the one who broke us apart, we gave you as much time as you needed, but you still left us',* according to Alexander

Lady Adelia Winter: (Aged 19), priestess of Anadrieth — *'Because right now you're doing what I can't, and every time you pretend it's okay you fall apart inside',* according to Anton

General Ban: (Aged 24), General Barrett's son — *'He looked every bit his father's son, but acted nothing like the general',* according to Anton

Councillor Raoul: (Aged 45), in charge of all the merchants and trading routes — *'Rumor had it his unfortunate seamstresses struggled to keep up with his ever expanding girth',* according to Alexander

Dale: (Aged 35), Councillor Dallan's son — *'The bumbling idiot',* according to Alexander

Jane: (Aged 15), water spirits arts user — *'A perfectly presentable maid, several years younger than herself and never so much as a word out of place',* according to Adelia

James: (Aged 16) Jane's brother, the blacksmith's apprentice — *'The undesirable had a stagnant aura, one that made her want to turn away',* according to Adelia

Henry: (Aged 56) — owner of *'The best bakery in the city'*, according to Mina

Marianne: (Aged 42), Henry's wife — *'Her face held remnants of a woman who was clearly beautiful in youth'*, according to Adelia

Penelope: (Aged 8), adopted daughter of Henry and Marianne — *'Sweet little Penelope, with a tongue as nasty as a crocodile'*, according to Scarlet

Blue: (Aged 16), *'Blue said we deserved names that made us feel beautiful'*, according to Scarlet

Ivory: (Aged 16), *'She didn't have a lot of time left'*, according to Scarlet

Late Lord Alastair Winter: (Deceased, aged 34) — *'A true Lord of Anadrieth should be willing to go to whatever end to protect his people'*, quoted by Alastair

Late Lady Adalynn Winter: (Deceased, aged 32) — *'She shouldn't give a dragon's claw about what the late Lady Adalynn— her mother—had thought'*, according to Adelia

Councillor Dallan: (Deceased, aged 57), Head Councillor of Anadrieth — *'He'd been his greatest confidant and mentor through his own transition to leadership'*, according to Alexander

General Barrett: (Deceased, aged 51), Anadrieth's former general — *'He was overconfident to a fault and would often taunt his opponents into making a mistake'*, according to Adelia

Elaine: (Deceased, aged 73), head medic and water spirit arts user — *'I look nothing like my mother... it was always you'*, according to Adelia

Vivian: (Deceased, aged 39), matron of Anadrieth's household — *'The matron's life of hard work seemed to be paying off in a very unexpected way'*, according to Adelia

Doll: (Deceased, aged 26) — *'Here lies Lady Doll the Kind-Hearted, year 2150'*, according to her gravestone

Marie Bellemore: *'The last priestess standing'*, according to Adelia's priestess tome

LANADRIN
[lan-nah-drin]

Lord Tamar: (Aged 42) — *'Everything about his demeanour radiated confidence and his expression was designed to provoke him'*, according to Alexander

Lady Tahlia: Unknown

Lady Tia: Unknown

ELORIA
[el-lore-e-ya]

Lord Reinhardt: (Aged 28) — *'Lord Reinhardt and I barely know each other',* according to Alexander

Lady Rosalie: (Aged 23), bedridden to a mysterious illness — *'She was far too frail to venture outside and if anyone else knew, she'd be a sitting target',* according to Reinhardt

Alyssa: *'The noble girl that wouldn't leave him alone',* according to Reinhardt

Jonathan: Lord Reinhardt's attendant

Tabitha: Lady Rosalie's attendant

CALVERA
[cal-vere-a]

Lord Cypress: (Aged 40) — *'The kind of man who would stab his closest friend in the back without a second thought',* according to Alexander

Cynric: (Aged 27), Celestial Assassin, water spirit arts user, competent medic — *'Cynric's dedication was admirable',* according to Anton

LYSANTHIR
[lis-an-th-ear]

Lord Bahram: Unknown

Sara: (Aged 31), Celestial Assassin, air and fire spirits arts user, competent alchemist — *'She was tolerable from a distance, sure, but right now she was far too close,'* according to Anton

Master Sabir: *'Only the greatest inventor to have ever lived'*, according to Adelia

KNOWN INFORMATION CONCERNING THE EMPIRE

Bearion — a massive creature with a tough hide and claws like blackscale, found in Anadrieth

Deerabit — rabbit with branching deer antlers, seen in packs, a pest in Lanadrin

Crowcodile — a large black scaly bird with a sharp teeth, a fierce companion when trained and a symbol of bad luck, commonly found in Anadrieth

Foxen — a small four-legged creature with translucent fur, two curled horns and a bushy tail, found in Anadrieth

Lyrecrane — a white bird with a magnificent tail, a symbol of good luck, found all over the empire

Oyfish — a small shelled marine creature with fins, a common delicacy in Eloria

Spidion — a small creature with eight furry legs and a venomous stinger, found in Lysanthir's deserts

Ice pear — velvety pink-skinned fruit, grows all year around in Anadrieth

Frostberry — sparkling red, semi-clear berry, found in Anadrieth

Vythorn — black thorny ivy which drops seeds contain a fatal poison, found rarely in Lysanthir

Nettlefern — spiny green shrubbery with medicinal value, found in Calvera

Blackscale — heavy black rock with shimmering rainbow threads, when melted into a weapon it becomes the strongest weapon in the empire, only mined in Lanadrin

Silverlight — light but durable glasslike wood, found in Anadrieth's Celestine Forest

Stonewood — densest and heaviest wood in the empire only breakable by blackscale, found in Calvera

Magnalite — a light metal that has a dangerous reaction with fire, mined only in Anadrieth

Nitren — a rare substance for making explosives, mined only in Anadrieth

Celestine Forest — the snowy forest containing silverlight trees, protecting Anadrieth

Jade Mountains — the mountains behind Anadrieth and Lanadrin containing many rare metals

Moonstone River — the massive river that runs through every region in the empire

Nacre Wastelands — arid land which surrounds Lanadrin and causes one to see strong mirages

Plains of Scoria — Anadrieth's dead land with hot tar pits and boiling steam geysers

Sea of Dunite — the sea which surrounds the empire with the dangerous reef, only accessible from Eloria

KNOWN DRAGON SCRIPT

Anchiore — anchor

Awyviene — awaken

Dysconae — disconnected, or those who possess the spirit arts but haven't yet been awakened

Mysoviere — my sovereign

Phaenyx — phoenix

Syravia — spirit reaper, the name given to Mina's swords

Syra — spirit aura, or a priestess' conduit for her power

Syra artse — spirit arts

FOUND A TYPO?

While every effort goes into ensuring that this book is flaw-less, it's inevitable that a mistake or two will slip through the cracks. Hey, I ain't perfect.

If you find an error of any kind in this book, please let me know by emailing me at:

paris@originpublications.com

I appreciate you taking the time to notify me. This ensures that future readers never have to experience that awful typo.

You are making the world a better place.

The Empire of the Dragon Gods Trilogy

The Last Stand (Prequel)

The Dragon Princess

The Dragon Empress

The Dragon Goddess

Chaos, Destruction and Rebirth... the three legendary dragon gods who rescued their people from certain death and brought peace to all for two thousand years.

Or so the legends say.

If you love strong female leads, intricate magic, complex fantasy plots and of course, dragons — join the journey and stay tuned for the Empire of the Dragon Gods Trilogy!

https://parishansch.com/jointhejourney

YOUR NAME MIGHT BE HERE

I know this is the 'boring' section no one reads, so I'll make it quick!

I couldn't have done this without the support of people closest to me; my amazing parents, my quirky D&D group, Amelia, and of course, Jamie. Love you all.

To my first fan and amazing beta reader Michelle, who had to endure all my shitty drafts, thank you. You helped make this book so much better, and were the inspiration behind the mysterious Mistress Marionette.

A big thank you to my awesome editors Josiah and Alice, my mentors Jonathan and RE Vance, and everyone over at YWW for their support.

I'd also love to thank my amazing tribe for their support, with a special shout out to Gaby, Jeff, Marty, Carol and Beaulah!

And of course, YOU. Thank you for taking a chance and

picking up my book, I truly appreciate it and I hope you enjoy all the books to come.

ABOUT THE AUTHOR

Paris Hansch (*Homo sapiens*) is a fantasy fanatic, biologist and avid reader, native to Australia. Common behaviour includes living in her own nerdy world of sword and sorcery, playing D&D and writing kickass women in fiction.

Armed with her motto of, 'No More Damsels In Distress', she battles to see a world where everyone can stand as equals, have the freedom to be exactly who they are and portray real female characters we can show our daughters and say, 'be like her'.

Will you join her on this journey?

Join The Journey!

https://parishansch.com/jointhejourney

facebook.com/parishanschauthor
instagram.com/paris.hansch
bookbub.com/authors/paris-hansch
goodreads.com/parishansch